Only Darkness Every Day

A Novel

Doug McCall

Rose,
Thanks for reading "O.D.E.D."
Doug M
9/29/10

ISBN: 978-0-578-10463-8

Published by Desk Lamp Publishing

1-601-898-3459

For Charles and Mike, brothers and friends

ACKNOWLEDGMENTS

I would like to thank the following people for their advice, support, and encouragement in regard to my writing: Anna Furr, Terry Dexter, Cherry Prather, Nora and David Donald, Lemma and Marvin Vernon, Mike Garner, Ruth Broome-Hackman, Ron and Shirley Martin, Virginia Wilson Mounger, Bee Donley, Cynthia Gandy, and Karen Reed. Also, my Missouri sister, Marilyn Michael and her husband Bill, and last but not least, cousins Linda Poe, Kathy Batson, and Emily Jones, who, fortunately for me, enjoy reading. Also my sincere thanks to Emily's Starkville, Mississippi, book club.

Thanks again to Sandra Goff for her outstanding work on cover design, and to Neil Carter, who guided me through many technical minefields in completing this book.

Also by Doug McCall:

BY PROXY: A FINAL GOOD DEED

BLIND TRUST

BENEATH FORBIDDEN GROUND

INDIANA DEATHS: QUESTIONS OF GREED

ONLY DARKNESS EVERY DAY

Chapter 1

All-in-all, it was a pleasant night for a torture, if only the victim would cooperate.

Ghost-like thin clouds streaked their way slowly across the star-dotted ebony sky, presenting the only interruptions standing in the way of viewing the pale yellow face of a full moon, and then for only seconds at a time. In all respects it was a beautiful night in the Mexican state of Sinaloa, with warm breezes whipping through the canyon walls paralleling the path of the Fuerte River. The gently flowing river meanders in a southwest direction nearly two hundred miles, formed by the junction of the Verde and Urique rivers in the Sierra Madre Occidental Mountain Range, before emptying into the Gulf of California. Water from the Fuerte is used primarily to irrigate the numerous mango plantations sandwiched-in among the craggy hills.

Sweet scents of the popular fruit carried along by the winds struck the nostrils of the man standing at the crest of one of the hills. He breathed in the aroma, while wishing he was in the arms of one of the lovely senoritas he had spotted in the nearby town of El Fuerte over the past few days. Better yet, he wished he had one with him... here... in this seemingly romantic spot, viewing the spectacular evening with him. When the business at hand was finished, he would seek one out. The people in the town knew of him —

knew of his reputation, which meant he could have any woman he desired. But until he had taken things as far as he could with the task before him, his libido must be contained. However, his patience was wearing thin, being eroded away by the festering anger of delayed vengeance; retribution that had been too long in coming.

He winced only slightly at another ear-splitting menacing growl of what he was certain was a puma. The mountain cats were rarely seen in Mexico any longer, having been hunted into oblivion by native as well as American hunters entering his country, seeking trophies. But they did still exist, especially farther to the south, in the territory of his youth. Since the cries of the animal echoed through and off the darkened hills, its distance was hard to determine, as was its direction. He felt no threat from the existence of the puma; he was well armed. The three men who worked for him were near at hand, fortified as well. His involuntary reaction came only from the spine-cringing, primordial sound of the screeching predator, who would no doubt be equally leery of the human if they reached close quarters.

The piercing howls were now joined by another sound, that of a man screaming, the blood-curdling yells blending with those of the night prowler, until it was hard to distinguish between the two. The pointless emanations from the man strapped to the metal table in the building at the foot of the hill below seemed to ignite more frequent responses from the cat, as if in a form of communication — a challenge.

Luis Torres stood with his brown, hard-crusted fingers hooked inside his leather belt, which was adorned with silver and turquoise medallions, his posture slouched while inhaling the warm night air. His eyes were covered by ever-present dark glasses, even in the dead of night. Thick, silver hair was combed back firmly into place, a sign of vanity he no longer made any attempt to hide. Success in the drug trade in Central and South America brought with it tremendous power, and his level of success meant he could do as he pleased, without fear of contradiction or criticism. He was of medium height and build, age approximately fifty-five, but appearing much older, with dark eyes behind the shades that seemed to cast suspicious glances on anyone he encountered. He was constantly on the alert for younger men he knew were out there, some with ambitions similar to his at an earlier age, who might be tempted to wrest power from him. Quick and brutal punishment was the only answer.

Torres knew the screams of the man wouldn't last much longer. No one could withstand the torture he was enduring for long. He would either talk or perish, as had the man's brother, the first to face Torres' wrath.

Sudden footsteps behind him caused him to turn to face the man approaching. A huge, solidly built man with dark brooding features was making his way up the slope of the hill, his body bent forward against the rocks to ease his climb. He carried something in his hands, something wrapped in brown paper showing grease stains.

"Sènor Torres," the man said when arriving within a few yards, after regaining his breath. "Juan has prepared garnachas. I have brought you one."

Torres eyed the man carefully. He cared more about the progress of the interrogation down below, but willingly accepted the spicy native preparation. Without thanking the man, he peeled back the wrapping, revealing the mase cake, similar to a tortilla, piled high with black beans, thinly-sliced skirt steak, and a dark, habanero chili-peppered sauce that would bring tears of pain to normal men. Devouring the treat in three large bites, each accompanied by the continued screams of man and cat, he then accepted the water bottle Angel Xminez handed him. Wiping his mouth with the back of a hand, Torres nodded in the direction of the shed.

"What do you have to report to me?" he demanded, spittle cascading down his chest. Xminez shook his large head, glancing back down the hill. "He either knows nothing, or perhaps is the most foolish man I have ever seen. His stomach is now covered with burn marks, and the acid we have placed between his legs has almost eaten down to bone." Pausing, Xminez shrugged his thick, broad shoulders. "I think it is the former, Sènor Torres. And I don't believe he can hold out much longer. What are your instructions for the man?"

Torres looked away from Xminez, thinking long and hard before answering while gazing into the valley below. It had taken over six months to get to this point, a period of time so extended he had begun to think he might never get to confront those responsible for such a huge loss. The $16 million he had expected to share with the family of the man being tortured had vanished along with the massive shipment of cocaine smuggled into Texas, then transported cross-country to the city of Atlanta in August of the previous year. The new year had come and gone. It was now early March, but his anger and suspicions had not diminished.

The transaction that had turned so violently sour had been arranged by the son of the man strapped to the table below, a son who had perished in the bloody rampage along with the others gathered for the large drug buy. Carlos Medina, the son, had been the man in charge of delivering the white powder to the American drug dealers, and the one who had argued so convincingly in favor of the deal. Torres and the rest of *his* family had resisted, saying it was too risky to expose such a large shipment to the wary eyes of U. S. drug agents. But explaining the economics of sending one large delivery as opposed to several smaller ones over many months, Medina had finally won his argument. Plus, even though there *was* danger in one large shipment, there was even more chance of detection if many trips into the lucrative American market were made during the course of a year's time.

The Torres and Medina families each provided half of the precious cargo, and were to split the $16 million, minus Carlos's travel expenses, which were nothing compared to the total. The cocaine had no doubt been seized and destroyed immediately by agents of the U. S. Drug Enforcement Administration following the sabotage. But the money was still unaccounted for. It was clear the man who had orchestrated the murders had taken the money from the bloody scene, fleeing to the beaches of Florida to make his escape. When he was gunned-down by assassins belonging to one of the American dealers, the trail of the millions had become cloudy.

Ordinarily, it would be hard to imagine Carlos being a sacrificial lamb for his own family if they had assisted in the double-cross, joining with the ruthless murderer. But in the violent, mercenary world of drug trafficking, nothing — and nobody — was beyond suspicion. There was simply too much money involved to rule out any possibility. And it was impossible to forget how adamant the younger Medina had been in promoting the transaction.

Pablo Medina, Carlos' father, and Jesus, Pablo's brother, the patriarchs of the Medina family, must have been aware of how things would be viewed by their dangerous business partner; they had gone into hiding as soon as news of the ambush made its way to Mexico. Familiar with Torres' hyper-paranoid, brutal nature, they sought refuge deep in the Sierra Madre Oriental mountains to the east, a range near the coast, bordering the Gulf of Mexico.

A team of trackers hired by Torres finally located the two men, their faces now disguised with heavy beards, and their weight reduced by starvation diets. After massacring the villagers who had shielded them, leaving several be-headed, the bounty hunters strapped the two men to the backs of burros to begin the journey out of the mountains. Once out, the Medina brothers were placed in the trunks of separate vehicles for the cross-country delivery to Torres, where he could begin his own methods of interrogation.

Jesus, the elder, hadn't lasted long. Being the first tied to the table in the shed below, he was secured tightly with barbed wire. He began to sweat profusely as the first branding iron was being applied to his chest, then fell limp from a heart attack. His body was removed, and the belligerent but terrified Pablo was brought in. He professed the innocence of himself, and the two men who meant the most to him — his slain son, and his now deceased brother. Pablo was stronger than anticipated, bearing up under tremendous pain and torture. So much so that Torres was beginning to agree with Xminez's assessment that the man knew nothing.

Regardless of whether the Medina family had indeed shared in the plot, he felt it was none-the-less important to carry out the punishment. It would serve to let the other families in the wide-spread drug community know he wouldn't tolerate any hint of double-cross. Fear in the violent drug trafficking world was a necessary tool.

"So, you think he is near death?" Torres finally asked matter-of-factly, without looking at the other man. A sudden erratic moonbeam struck a gold tooth in his mouth, reflecting briefly in the pungent night air.

"Sì, Sènor Torres. It is only his will that is keeping him alive," Xminez said. He patiently waited for a pronouncement from the man. He knew it might be dangerous to offer his own advice. Shuffling his feet, he pulled a stick of gum from a shirt pocket. Unwrapping it, he stuck the cinnamon-flavored gum into his mouth, quickly working it with his teeth until the juices flowed. Carefully folding the wrapper, he put it into the same pocket, as he always did.

Angel Xminez, or Angel X, as he was known by many, was an enormous, intelligent, meticulous man of many contradictions. A ruthless enforcer for Torres, willing to kill without hesitation, he enjoyed surfing the internet during whatever free time he had and when a computer was handy, searching for information that might be useful. Cyberspace intrigued him. It was his way of viewing the outside world, an escape from his otherwise dark existence in the shadows of Torres' family. On one web site, he had learned that cinnamon was seen as a deterrent to factors involved in diabetes, the disease that had taken his father, shortly after having both legs amputated. He didn't completely understand the relationship between the spice and the blood-rotting illness, but a constant supply of the flavored gum seemed worth an attempt to ward off genetic traits.

"Then end it," Torres finally said, his decision made. "We are wasting valuable time. There is a more important task for you to attend to, one you must begin right away."

Xminez's spirits immediately lifted. He knew the way his boss' mind worked, and if he anticipated correctly, it was an assignment he would enjoy. "Sì, Sènor Torres. I will see to it at once." He turned to retrace his steps to the scene of laying waste to the body below. Torres suddenly stopped him.

"Wait, Angel. I have another thought. Do not kill Pablo. Find a local doctor to dress his wounds, so that he will live. Then release him to his family."

"But, Sènor. Is that wise?" The words escaped Xminez's mouth before he could think. He knew better than to question the man. Thankfully, whatever was in the older man's eyes was hidden by the dark glasses, but surely it was a look of warning.

"I will send him back to his family as a constant reminder of my response when I feel someone has stolen from me. His appearance will be a never-ending memory of how I deal with my suspicions."

"Sì, Sènor. That *is* very wise. I will search for a doctor we can trust." Xminez again started to move down the hillside. This time, he stopped himself. He decided to risk a question. "The assignment you mentioned?"

Torres turned to stare at the gently flowing waters below, waters he could hear more than see. He paused a moment before speaking. When he did, his voice was firm and steady. "If the Medinas know nothing about the money, then it must still be somewhere in America. I want you to find it, Angel. Follow whatever trail you must."

Angel Xminez's dark heart leaped. It was as he had wished. He enjoyed making trips to the country to the north, as he had on several occasions. Even traveling incognito, which was usually required, there was a freedom of movement in the vast country that was never felt by him in Mexico. Modern conveniences were everywhere; a quality of life that encouraged others to make their way into the country, either legally or otherwise. He especially enjoyed California, but was fairly sure this particular search would not lead him there.

"You will take Cesar with you. His skills will be useful."

Xminez's excitement was immediately dampened by this added news. He couldn't keep the displeasure from masking his face, but covered it up quickly, again not wanting the powerful man to think his command was being questioned.

He chanced another question. "Where should we begin our journey, Sènor?"

Torres turned now to stare intently at the man standing several feet below him. "I am certain Frapiana had the money with him when he returned to Florida. It would be easy to say the men who killed him took the money, but they were killed also. And they were alone, as far as I know. Frapiana's wife was known to be in Florida with him, but she disappeared as quickly as the money. Perhaps... with the money."

"The Frapianas lived in the city of Atlanta, as I understand."

"Sì, Angel. But you may not find her there. The other American dealers who were also cheated by the man may be looking for her, so she could be in hiding." Torres paused once more. "There is something else to consider."

"Sì?"

"From reports given by the American authorities that we have been able to see, there was the possibility another individual was involved in the killing of Frapiana. But nothing has been revealed about who he or she was, or what became of them."

"I will find out, Sènor," Xminez said confidently.

"Yes, I am counting on that, Angel. However, I do not wish to hear of the usual trail of blood that normally follows in your path. You must keep a low profile. I do not wish to have attention given to your search, by either the authorities or our American customers. If you heat the pot too rapidly, it will boil over, and they will come from the woodwork. Use whatever means you can to avoid violence, unless it is needed as a final resort. Is that understood?"

"Sì, Sènor. I understand."

"Good. Now, finish up with Pablo, then you and Cesar report to me. I will give you more instructions, then send you on your journey."

Torres again faced the river, then gave Xminez a final preview of his coming assignment, speaking in a detached manner, as if addressing the dark hills stretched out before him, instead of his enormous bounty hunter standing patiently below.

"You should start with the woman."

Chapter 2

She sat alone...more alone than she ever thought possible...but there was no option.

The third balmy, sunny day in a row possessed just enough wind current to put the low-hanging Spanish moss into motion, shimmering silently in the warm, gentle breezes. Clinging to the bottom branches of majestic live oaks, the movement was practically hypnotic. The noon-day crowd spread among park benches, or reclining on grassy areas of Crawford Square near downtown Savannah, seemed anxious to take advantage of the lull between late-winter doldrums and the heat and humidity lurking; they were purposely oblivious to what lay ahead. Spring was waiting in the wings to punish southeast Georgia.

The park was one of several small and medium-sized oases scattered in and near the historic city's business district, most named for a key event or person from its rich past. The square was a perfect example. Native son

William H. Crawford had been a Secretary of the Treasury for one of the country's early presidents — no one could recall exactly which one. The people gathered in the park on this lazy day could care less about this history, instead choosing to enjoy the present. The citizens scattered here and there were generally buoyant, basking in the respite.

The woman sat solo on a cement and wood-slatted bench, unable to absorb the glow of the early tease of spring. Most days were cloudy for her; no light was allowed to shine in, sunlight or otherwise. Her life — or after-life — as she chose to consider it, when she allowed herself to be pulled into the bottomless pit of despair that now consumed her, was one frightening, desolate day following the one before, one varying shade of grey after another.

It had been several months now, over half a year, since the events that had brought her back to the city of her youth had occurred. When the few well-meaning people who actually knew what had happened, what she had endured, tried to assure her none of it was her fault and she needed to get on with her life, she would politely nod and agree, then return to her private hell.

Most people she encountered on any given day *did not* know the whole story...the true story, choosing to fill in the gaps themselves with whatever details suited their thirst for salacious gossip. Even some she had known since grade school didn't bother with uncovering the facts, which by their very nature, were certainly hard to determine. After all, she had been gone from Savannah for almost fifteen years; she had become a virtual stranger to them. They were aware she had moved to Atlanta, married a man who turned out to be a murderous drug dealer, who himself was gunned down somewhere in Florida. A lot of what they knew came from sketchy news reports that surfaced soon after she returned.

And she would never volunteer her history herself; it was simply too horrifying, too chillingly twisted to relate to anyone. Her parents knew the truth, but beyond that, she internalized her recent past. Those who didn't know created their own stories, spiked by curiosity, boredom, and in some cases, jealousy.

Michelle Frapiana, occasionally contemplating becoming Michelle Lovejoy again, taking back her maiden name, remained a striking woman. Aged only slightly by the horrific turn her life had taken, she maintained a grace and natural beauty that was easy to cause envy. Her honey-blonde hair, today pulled back into a ponytail, was a hairdresser's dream, full and lustrous. Rays of sunlight filtering through the majestic oaks made her hair appear golden — not that she cared. Perfect high cheekbones and a graceful chin structure only made things worse. The only lingering hint of her ordeal was around her blue-green eyes; lines were starting to appear, the results of sleepless nights occupied by jumbled thoughts of reliving the past and worrying about the future. The other effects, the ones more lasting, remained hidden deep inside her.

She completely understood the suspicions and doubts of others; she may have felt the same if roles were somehow reversed. Was she part of the drug business? Had she tried to help her brutal husband escape? Did she know he was going to kill all those people? And what had happened to the money the news items had mentioned? No one, least of all her, knew for sure how much. These were the unspoken questions she knew were on their minds. She could read the questions in their faces.

Scanning her surroundings, an image interrupted her dark thoughts, an image from one of her favorite movies, *Forrest Gump*. She had seen the film a decade earlier, with her then-future husband, Richard Frapiana, a.k.a., Dickie Frapiana, at a time when they still resembled a normal, relatively happy pair a year before their marriage, on one of their many dates. It was the beginning scene in the movie, with the main character sitting on a park bench, ironically set in this same Georgia city, only blocks from where *she* now sat. A white feather floated aimlessly around the man as he talked to a woman sitting next to him, telling her his life story. It was the feather she remembered most. It was no doubt meant to illustrate Gump's own path through life, but it paralleled too closely her own, and what it had been, and continued to be. Her existence had been predicated by others; she was nothing more than an observer, while others controlled her drift through time. And it had nearly destroyed her. It would be easy to say it actually had.

A Frisbee rolled to a stop at her feet, interrupting her dark reverie. Bending and reaching to pick it up, she saw two young girls running to retrieve it. They were seven or so, a couple of years older than her own daughter. She wondered why they weren't in school. Surely they were of age? Then she remembered — spring break.

"Sorry, ma'am," one of them said with a sheepish grin.

Michelle forced a smile. "That's okay, honey. Here you go." She flipped it to the one closest, missing badly. Nosediving, it hit the ground and rolled away. "Oops. I was never good at Frisbee tossing."

"Neither are we, I guess," the shy girl said. Before turning away, she looked for a second at the woman, seeming to stare into her haunted eyes, as if gazing into a bottomless pit of despair, which in fact, she was.

The girl quickly turned, and she and her friend ran laughing back to where others were waiting. They raced across the hairy grass. It was still too early in the spring to give it its first cut, but late enough that dandelions and other weed-like sprouts gave the park a slightly overgrown, unkempt appearance.

Watching the girls leave, Michelle thought about Allison, her only child. She was just five, but whether she was fully aware of it or not, she had already experienced things most people never have to at *any* stage of life. A bright, beautiful, innocent girl, she had actually been the one anchor her troubled mother could cling to over the past months. Michelle's only true moments of happiness were when the two were together. But even then, her thoughts would involuntarily drift back to their former life — a sorry excuse for a family life, especially in the final years.

Allison had adjusted as well as could be expected to life in Savannah. A sympathetic pre-school teacher had made things as easy as possible, encouraging the other children to welcome the newcomer. Even under the best of circumstances, moving to new surroundings, encountering only strangers, could be devastating for a child. And these were the *worst* of circumstances. Kids at this age didn't have agendas, unless their developing minds were poisoned by remarks made by their parents. Michelle saw no evidence of that yet, and for that she was thankful. Hopcfully, by thc timc Allison's classmates were old enough to understand things, and know enough to ask questions and share rumors, her father's deeds would be a faded memory.

And having the girl's grandparents close at hand was a godsend. They had been the reason Michelle and her daughter had come back to the city, delivered from the sure danger of her husband by a selfless, sympathetic Tennessee couple, appearing almost as angels on the beaches of Destin,

Florida. The pair had been recruited by someone else, a man she thought of often, always with sadness, given his fate.

Brushing crumbs from the lap of her faded designer jeans, she crumpled the paper bag that had held her sandwich, then stood, tossing it and her empty water bottle into a trash can. Taking a furtive glance around the park, then one last look at the girls continuing to chase the errant plastic disc, she put an end to her lunch break, then began the short walk back to the book store where she now worked, keeping an eye peeled at all times. It was a habit she had been forced to adopt.

Liberty Lady Book Store was an inviting throwback to what community booksellers once resembled, before big-box stores, and then internet booksellers came into existence, when personal service was still important. A relatively small store-front shop, nestled in between a florist and a brick building housing law offices, appropriately facing East Liberty Street, it still managed to attract a steady stream of loyal readers. A warm interior was crowded wall-to-wall with book shelves and tables, causing shoppers to sidestep their way through narrow aisles.

The bell hanging over the door announced Michelle's re-entry into the shop, drawing the attention of the other two employees in the store. One was Sandi Booth, the owner-proprietor of the store, and one of Michelle's closest friends from junior and senior high. Other than her own parents, Sandi had been the first to welcome Michelle and her daughter home, willing to sit and listen, offering a hand to hold or a shoulder to cry on, without asking questions that might be hurtful. When Michelle had finally reached some form of equilibrium, Sandi had talked her into coming to work for her, with one word of caution.

"The big stores are making it tough on independents like me," she had admitted. "Not sure how long I'll be able to hang on, but as long as I do, you've got a job."

Michelle was grateful for the chance to stay busy, keeping her mind occupied. Plus, the modest paycheck was sorely needed. Sandi, in turn, was propped up financially by her father, a successful civil attorney who occupied half of the building next door. She was divorced, with two sons whose ages were sandwiched around that of Michelle's daughter. Tall and slender, with auburn hair always cut short, she had a sometimes feisty demeanor that added fire to her green eyes. And she was as true a friend as anyone could ask for.

"How was lunch?" Sandi asked, giving her friend a measured smile.

"Fine. It's nice out." Michelle wasted no time getting back into the swing of work, busying herself with straightening a stack on a nearby table. "You know, sometimes I forget just how beautiful Savannah is. I'm beginning to realize how much I missed it. And friends like you." She tried to smile, but it was hard these days, with emotions constantly bubbling just below the surface.

Sandi knew to keep a close eye trained on her friend, looking for signs that she might start to completely fall apart. She had suggested, on more than one occasion, that she consider counseling — something similar to grief counseling, although what she was experiencing wasn't the usual form of grief, in her opinion. If she was in fact grieving, Sandi was convinced it was directed more toward the people her husband had destroyed rather than the man himself. Michelle had agreed it might be a good idea, but hadn't sought help yet, as least as far as her friend and boss knew.

Something else Sandi had suggested, only a little more cautiously, was for

Michelle to start dating, or at least double-dating with her and the new man in her life. It would be an easy way to dip her toes back into a semblance of normal life. It was a harder sale, met with firm resistance.

"I'm just not ready, Sandi," Michelle had replied during those conversations. "And who in their right mind would want to accept the baggage that comes with me?"

"More than you might think, honey. Several guys have asked about you."

"And they know? They know everything?" Michelle would ask, knowing her friend was prone to overstatements.

"Some do... some don't. But once they get to know you, it won't make a smidgen of difference."

"I don't know, Sandi. I just don't think it's time," was the way those talks had always concluded.

Now, watching her beautiful, tortured friend, Sandi decided it was time to try again. Maybe she would catch her in a weak moment. Pitching in at the stacking job, she began slowly.

"Listen, sweetie. Jeff and I are heading down to an open-air concert in the brick street area Friday night, near the Hyatt. We're just going to walk around for a while, listen to the bands, maybe have a few drinks. Why don't you join us?"

"It'll just the two of you?" Michelle asked, shooting a knowing glance at the other woman, while continuing to work the books into order.

"Yeah. Well, a friend of Jeff's might be meeting up with us somewhere down there. You know. It's not certain, but he may show up."

Michelle leveled an accusatory, yet friendly smile. "I see. It's not certain, huh? So maybe he won't show up?"

"Well, probably."

"Then I'd be cramping Jeff's style with you, or maybe your's with him, if he didn't. Three's a crowd, you know."

Sandi hadn't been prepared to fall into a trap, so she gave up on the charade. "Oh, come on, Michelle. He's a nice guy. A dentist. And he really wants to meet you, or I should say, get reacquainted with you. He went to high school with us. You remember Royce Glynn."

Michelle furrowed her brow, trying to recall, but not trying too hard. "Oh, yeah. I think so. Played basketball, didn't he?"

"Right. Went to Georgia, then to dental school up in Augusta. He's got one of the busiest practices in town now, and like I said, he's really a good guy. Jeff says he asks about you every time they talk. And they've talked a little about...well, you know... you and Dickie. He doesn't care. He really wants to get to know you. I promise you'll like him."

"I bear witness to that," the third employee spoke from behind a book shelf.

Fred Huth stepped from between the rows of books, carrying an armload of new arrivals. He was a junior in a local college, earning money to pay his way. He was one of the two part time employees who helped out in the store. His job was to do most of the heavy lifting, plus keep the coffee urn in a nook toward the rear of the store filled. On the slim side, with long, stringy, unkempt sandy brown hair and a metal stud in one ear, he never hesitated to speak his mind.

"I was here the other day when you were out, Michelle, when Jeff came by. He's not going to leave our boss alone until she's able to hook you up with Dr. Glynn. And I agree, he *is* a nice man. He's my family's dentist —

has been for a few years. And he has the most gentle hands." Making a squeezing motion with his hands, Fred directed a teasing grin toward Michelle along with the last comment.

Michelle blushed bright red. Sandi couldn't resist a high-pitched, cackling laugh.

"So there. How can you say no?" Sandi said, leaning across the books on the table, moving in for the kill.

Michelle looked down at the stack in front of her, then through one of the two front windows, scanning the outside world for signs of trouble. It was a glance she made several times during the course of a day — another forced habit.

"I'll think about it," was the only ground she would give, before leaning back into her work.

Chapter 3

The setting sun caused Michelle to tighten her squint through the windshield. The drive to her small apartment on the western edges of Savannah took her directly toward the day star hanging low on the horizon. The visor was down, but gave only minimal relief. As always, since her escape to her home city from the threats surrounding her husband, she kept a wary eye on the rearview mirror. The warnings left behind by the DEA agents that had sought her out after Dickie's crimes and subsequent murder had made paranoia a necessary part of her daily life. Each car that seemed to be trailing her path was suspicious; each person spending more time loitering outside the book store than she thought necessary was cause for concern. As a precaution, caller I. D. had been her first investment when moving to her apartment.

"*They might come...looking for their money,*" one of the agents had said. Church was his name — she couldn't recall the other's name. She had trusted what the agents had said, but they had also scared her.

"But I don't know anything about any money," she had argued.

"*They don't know that. And they may assume you do.*"

The words still echoed in her mind over six months later. She began to wonder if she would ever feel safe.

Glancing down at Allison, engrossed in reading a children's book her teacher had loaned her the week before, Michelle tried to engage her daughter.

"Did you have a good time with Granma and Granpa today, honey?"

"It was fine," the girl answered softly without looking up.

Allison was staying with Michelle's parents for the week, while the pre-school she attended fell in line with the other schools during spring break. The older couple had lobbied to keep her on a daily basis when their daughter had started working, but Michelle decided the girl needed to make connections with other kids, which seemed to be going well so far. But having her folks on permanent standby was a gift impossible to measure.

"What did the three of you do today?"

Allison leaned her head back on the seat, appearing a little impatient with the questions. "Granma let me watch some Disney movies she rented. And then Granpa took me to get ice cream when he got home." She quickly returned to the book.

"Sounds like a good day."

The girl nodded slightly, but didn't reply, engrossed in the story.

"What are you hungry for tonight?"

Allison shrugged. "I'm really not very hungry right now. The ice cream made me full."

"But you will be later. Think about it, then let me know."

Following a few seconds of silence, the small voice said, "Maybe pizza."

"We've had that twice this week, honey. Anything else sound good?"

Another shrug of the tiny shoulders. "Anything's okay."

A gradual turn to the north finally gave relief from the sun. Darting quick looks at her daughter, trying to judge her reticent mood while maintaining an eye on the road, as well as the mirror, Michelle wondered how much she still thought about her dad. He had disappeared from her life so suddenly, she must have some unresolved issues over the drastic changes in her young life. She had stopped asking questions about him after a few months, but there was no way to tell what was in her small head. It might be just as well, since the entire story may be too much for her to deal with at such an age. The time would come soon enough to discuss it more fully.

The well-meant suggestions by Sandi to explore counseling might be better suited for the girl than herself. She would give it some thought.

Allison had not attended the services for her father on the outskirts of Chicago. His parents had requested, and Michelle quickly agreed, to have his body shipped north for burial in his home town. She was sure it was his mother's idea, since Dickie and his father had never been close. The grave-side service was the last time she had seen or spoken to the Frapianas, and the last time she hoped or expected to. Not having a relationship with their granddaughter was their loss, but it was how things had to be.

She let her thoughts drift to the efforts of Sandi to jump start her social life. There were several reasons she was reluctant to take the plunge. First, as she continued to argue, it simply *felt* too soon. Restructuring a life from scratch took time to adjust to, creating confusion as to which direction was the correct one, especially when there was a child involved. At her current stage, she wasn't actually sure what her options might be, but dating seemed a strange concept. Then there was the scare-factor. The fear of dating was common among those who found themselves alone after marriage. Apparently, the longer the first union, the more frightening it loomed. Her marriage had lasted almost a decade, and ended in a manner that would be awkward to discuss during small talk. Which led to another factor; no matter how understanding prospective suitors might appear to be, however much they may say her past wouldn't matter, when it got down to it, when a closeness developed that called for the entire story, would the details be too much to handle? Or would they hang in there? It was a lot to ask.

But the strongest reason she clung to, though it was entirely pointless, had to do with the man who had saved her from the clutches of her husband. She had known Brent Musso for less than four days, yet his insistence that she leave the Florida coast before her husband returned from his murderous rampage to collect her and their daughter, had left her with an aching memory she couldn't shake. He had made sure they were safely on their way to Savannah before returning to his home in Houston, while neglecting his own disease, which she later discovered was fatal. He was gone now, but each time she thought of him... while working... dressing in the morning for work... or getting Allison ready for school, she would find herself tearing up. His actions would remain with her always, which she had finally decided was the way it should be. So whoever was out there waiting to sweep her off her feet had a lot to overcome.

Pulling her four-year old Nissan Altima into its usual parking space immediately in front of her apartment on the bottom level of the two-story building, Michelle helped Allison grab her book and the notebooks she had taken to her grandparents' house, then fought to un-snap the girl's seatbelt, which always seemed to catch. The tiny apartment was in stark contrast to the pretentious luxury of the home she had left behind in Atlanta, and even to her parents' comfortable home where the two had lived for the first few months.

Exiting the car, Michelle said, "Let's check the mail before we go in."

Holding hands tightly, they walked the thirty or so feet to the grey-metal cluster of lock-boxes mounted head-high on a pedestal. Inserting the small key kept on her chain, Michelle extracted a fairly light stack of envelopes. Locking the box, she again took Allison by the hand, then began walking toward her front door, while flipping through the envelopes with her free hand. In the gathering darkness, she could make out the logos of the electric utility company and her cell phone carrier — two bills she had been expecting, plus a couple of junk mail items. The last envelope was letter-sized, plain white, with no return address. A postmark barely legible indicating it had been mailed from Texas was the only clue to its origin. The city's name was indistinct, but the state instantly conjured up Brent Musso's image. It was just as quickly dismissed. She looked at it curiously for only a second. Gripping the stack between her teeth to free-up her hands, she unlocked the cylinder lock and the dead bolt. Entering the apartment, she tossed the mail on the sofa. She would deal with it all later.

Chapter 4

The line of vehicles waiting to be checked, then either allowed to pass or ordered to pull to the side for further investigation, was long, moving at a snail's pace. The heavy-set off-duty Mexican border patrol officer shifted his bulk in his seat while he waited. He was growing impatient as he inched his boxy S U V toward the bridge spanning the Rio Grande River, connecting Ciudad Acuna, Mexico to Del Rio, Texas. He felt insulted to have to wait his turn like everyone else, as if he were trying to escape into the "land of the spoiled gringo brats", as he referred to it. He had no desire to join some of his family members and friends in trying to find a better life on the American side of the river. Besides, there were ways to make money by staying in his home country — if you knew the right way to go about it. The trick was, staying alive to enjoy it, a trick becoming harder by the day in the drug-infested territory in and around the border.

The traffic was always noticeably heavier in the direction he was traveling, with the only vehicles coming from the opposite side being either day tourists or small business owners in the Del Rio area trying to establish profitable markets across the border. NAFTA had opened things up, and a growing number were doing their best to take advantage. The reasons for crossing into the country to the north at this and other border crossings were sometimes business related, but not always. The patrol officer had his own motives.

Finally reaching the Mexican-controlled check point, his vehicle was given a cursory once-over by the officers on duty, all of whom he knew fairly well.

"Hola, Hector," one of the men in green khaki uniforms greeted as the driver lowered his window. "You are crossing over for a while?"

"Sì, but only for a little while. Someone on the other side of Del Rio called me. They have items stolen from one of my relatives. The thieves must have discarded them after they crossed over. I am to collect the things and bring them back to my family member."

The guard nodded. A thin smile under dark glasses indicated he didn't completely believe the story. "You are a good relative, Hector. But you will not be gone long, sì?"

"No, not long at all. I am on duty tonight, so I must return soon."

The guard smiled another knowing grin, nodded, then slapped the top of the S U V. "Adios, my friend."

Hector again fell in line with the traffic, enduring another wait until reaching the American check point fifteen minutes later. He was prepared for a more thorough examination by the U. S. Border Patrol officers, hoping to remain calm. Reaching into his shirt pocket, he extracted and unfolded a sheet of paper with the name, address, and phone number of the person he was crossing over to see. They may want to read it, possibly even place a call to the person to see if he was actually expecting the Mexican officer. It would pose no problem if they did so; the individual knew what to say.

The American officer took note of the insignia on the side of the vehicle, and the uniform of the man inside. Hector thought the man recognized him.

"Good day, sènor. What's your business on our side today?"

Hector told the same story, offering the sheet of paper to the officer, who wore a darker, olive-colored version of the border patrol garb, a sidearm strapped to the waist. He appeared to be in his late twenties. "You may call him if you wish."

"That won't be necessary," the young man said, waving the paper away with a bored expression. "But we will need to examine your vehicle."

"Of Course. I understand." Hector had expected a close inspection on this side of the river. The pressure was building on the Americans to stem the tide of the increasing numbers of illegal immigrates, as well as the flow of illicit drugs into their country. There were no exceptions to intense searches. He watched with a steadily growing amount of nervous concern as two armed officers circled the vehicle, one holding a rod with a mirror attached to the end, bent at an angle to allow a view of the underside of the vehicle. Opening the tailgate, the other bent to take a quick look inside. Hector tightened his grip on the steering wheel, watching through the rear view mirror. With the air conditioner losing momentum while idling, and his own fraying nerves, the beefy Mexican was beginning to perspire heavily. The officer soon closed the door, and he loosened his hold. Glancing over to the guard house, he saw the two German Shepherds on leashes that were usually on hand to help sniff out drugs. Hector knew if there were any doubts the men had, the dogs would be brought over to zero-in on contraband, and that would indeed be bad.

The American officer finally returned to the driver-side window. He looked again at the side of the dusty Chevy Suburban, it's official Mexican Border Patrol sign nearly covered with dirt. Taking one last glance inside, he said, "Have a good day, sènor. Welcome to the U. S. of A."

Exiting the check point area, the relieved Hector continued at a pace slower than he desired, with the vehicles ahead still jammed up, none seeming sure of their destination. Finally, he was able to break free of the pack, and made his way to State Loop 239, following it through Del Rio and onto U. S. Highway 90. Leaving the town on 90 heading east a few minutes later, he turned off the highway into a nondescript neighborhood of cement block homes, then drove for several blocks. The location where he came to a stop had been chosen for him by others. It was a vacant lot hidden behind a chainlink fence overgrown with weeds.

Stepping from the vehicle a minute later, he scanned the lot, looking for the man who was supposed to be waiting. He didn't see him at first. Through a gate hardly visible in the weeds at the rear of the lot, the man suddenly appeared, approaching the vehicle at a leisurely pace, eyes darting in all directions.

Hector then moved to the rear of the SUV, took a look around, then bent to open the tailgate. Pulling back velcroed strips in the corners of the carpeted flooring, he loosened two toggle bolts and removed them. Raising the false-flooring, he spoke into the tailgate. "We are here, amigos."

Two men were lying on their sides in fetal positions, facing each other, yet head-to-toe, like a pair of new shoes crammed into a box. It took a few minutes to untangle their bodies that had been stiffened into place during the three hour drive.

Hector offered no assistance in extracting the hidden passengers from their nest. In fact, he backed away from the vehicle, keeping his hand near his own holstered weapon. Aware that the men were unarmed, he was also aware of their well-earned reputations, especially the bigger one. It was unwise to take anything for granted when dealing with such men as these. He also kept a wary eye on the man drawing near to the vehicle.

"You're late," the newcomer growled. He was an American, bearded, with a pot-belly hanging over his tight jeans, applying stress to his shirt. The bottom buttons were left undone to provide room. Dirty boots kicked up dust from the bare ground.

Hector glared hard at the gringo. "You think it's easy timing a border crossing? It is getting harder each week." He spit a brown wad of something onto the ground. "If you are not happy, sènor, tell Torres to find someone else next time." As if anyone could tell the cartel ruler what to do. The mere thought that the drug lord might somehow get wind of his comment made him instantly regret it.

The man didn't answer, instead observing the men who had managed to crawl out, now stretching their legs. The journey had been much harder for Angel Xminez, since he was somewhat larger than Cesar Javier, and several years older. His body ached from his neck to his ankles; each part that had been twisted to fit the cramped hiding place stiffened in pain. Cesar, some ten years younger, trim, with unusually light features for a Mexican, moved easily, as if he had ridden in a passenger seat. As they straightened up, the bigger man quickly distanced himself from the other with a shove.

The American spoke to Hector. "Someone will contact you when it's time for our friends here to return." He handed a bag containing the items the officer had supposedly come to retrieve: useless credit cards banded together; a wrist watch, appearing to be an expensive one, while, in fact, a knock-off; and a handheld video camera, also of the cheap variety. They would be needed to prove the reason for the journey across. "I'll take over from here," he said.

As his passengers and their greeter turned to walk away, Hector stopped them. "Wait, sènor," he said to the larger man. "My money? The other five hundred?"

"Of course," Angel X replied. He pulled folded bills from his pocket and tossed them to the officer. "I almost forgot."

Hector glared and nodded, spending a prolonged second counting the money. He placed it in his pocket next to the first half of the payment given to him earlier, feeling around to make sure it was still there. He climbed back into his vehicle. The tires spun up dust as the filthy Suburban quickly exited the lot.

Watching the man drive away, the American motioned to the other two. "Follow me. My house is one block away. I have the car Sènor Torres requested, and the other things he asked for." He led them through the gate he had entered minutes earlier. As they walked, he gave a curious look back to his guests. "It's no skin off my nose, and ain't none of my business, but why the hell didn't you two cross the normal way? I don't reckon Torres would have any trouble gettin' proper credentials for you. Why the Houdini stuff?"

"You are correct, sènor, it's none of your business," Angel X answered calmly. "You would be wise to simply do as you're told."

The American took the hint, shrugged, then continued on.

Xminez silently admitted to himself the man's question made sense. He and Cesar probably could have found a more comfortable way across. But it was important their presence in the U. S. be kept from as many eyes as possible. While they would be able to travel at will in the interior of the country to the north, their faces were well known by officials on both sides of the border, and their images on cameras mounted on the guard houses would certainly ring alarm bells, especially for the larger man. The mission ahead required free movement during their search to the greatest extent possible.

His joints now beginning to loosen as he walked, he felt his spirits start to rise. Within the hour, he and Cesar Javier would be on the road to San Antonio, one of his favorite cities.

Chapter 5

Michelle clutched the letter in her trembling hands, shaking not so much from fear, but from the shock of the contents, although she couldn't deny the shock *did* bring a level of fear with it. She was trying to digest the words she had just read for the third time. They made no sense at all — there had to be some kind of unimaginable mistake. Flipping the envelope over once again, reading her name as addressee, then reading the letter heading, it definitely said Michelle Frapiana. She sat back in the hard wooden chair in her small kitchen, letting the page drop to the table. Her body had grown limp, but her heart was pumping at an alarming rate; her breath coming in short bursts. Leaning in, she picked up the paper again, and read it one more time.

Dear Mrs. Frapiana,

I am corresponding to inform you of something that will be coming your way in the next few days. By way of introduction, my name is Arthur George.

I am an attorney in Houston, Texas, but other than my name, there is no need for you to know any other information about myself.

An anonymous benefactor, who must remain so, has established a trust account in your name, with income payments beginning in the amount of six thousand and five hundred dollars ($6,500) per month, adjusted annually based on the performance of assets within the trust. In the event of your death, the payments will continue for the benefit of your daughter, Allison Elizabeth Frapiana, in a like manner, until her death, or the unlikely occurrence of trust assets being depleted, whichever event occurs first.

The trust assets are being managed by a financial institution, whose identity you will become aware of when your initial payment arrives. Accompanying your first payment will be a form to return to the payor if you desire a direct deposit be made each month to the financial institution of your choice. In any event, the payments should be treated as taxable, so you may want to consult your tax advisor.

I'm quite sure this letter comes as a shock to you, therefore I have simplified the matter as much as possible in my explanation. It is my hope, and that of your benefactor, that you will make the best use possible of this unexpected windfall.

In closing, let me stress that you should make no effort to contact me, since I can tell you no more than I have stated in this letter. It was also the wish of your benefactor that you make no attempt to discover their identity.

Wishing you the best of luck, and with my warmest regards,

Arthur George

Placing the page flat on the table, Michelle tried to calm herself, letting a barrage of thoughts enter her mind. The image of Brent Musso first appeared. He had lived in Houston. But that surely must be only a coincidence, since he was no longer living. And besides, she hadn't pictured him as being wealthy. Even if he was, he had a family. He had talked about them. It made no sense for him to neglect them in favor of her and Allison, two people he hardly knew.

Next, a troubling, sickening notion. She recalled once more the D E A agent's words involving the missing money. *"But they don't know that... and they may assume you do."* Could this be related to that? That would mean Brent had...

"No, That's impossible," she said out loud, interrupting her own thoughts.

"What, Mommy?" Allison, sitting on the living room floor, only a few yards away, looked up.

"Nothing, honey. Just talking to myself."

It was impossible, because Brent had left for Houston before her husband had arrived back on the beach — she was sure of that. And he had died over four months ago. The letter was dated... she ran her eyes back to the top of the page...three days ago. Dismissing the idea, the fact that more money than she ever thought possible was about to be dumped in her lap still made her nervous. If the people the DEA agents thought might come looking knew of this, or if the federal agency itself learned of this, her tenuous life could become more complicated — probably dangerously so.

It wasn't that she couldn't use the money, because it would save her financially. The $80,000 life insurance proceeds she had fought to receive from Dickie's policy were evaporating rapidly. The insurance company had refused to pay at first, claiming her husband had died in the commission of a crime, which was an exclusion under the terms of the policy. Sandi's father had gone to bat for her on a pro bono basis, corresponding with the company, arguing quite strenuously that Dickie Frapiana had never gone to trial, and therefore not convicted of any crimes, despite overwhelming evidence he was involved in several. Following months of delay, the company finally caved, paying the death benefit, plus a small amount of interest accumulated during their stalling tactics. Her parents had filled in the financial gaps until things were settled, but she didn't want to rely on their help any more than necessary.

The house in Atlanta that had once been her home, but more of a prison in the later years of her marriage, still had not been released to her by the federal law enforcement agencies involved, and it appeared it might never be hers to sell. Only a few personal items were allowed to be removed by her from the house, and then only as they watched her closely. So with a salary of less than $1,000 a month received from the book store, an amount she was sure strained Sandi's meager budget, this bolt from the blue, if it materialized, would be crucial. She would insist that Sandi reduce her salary. But could she explain why? The clear answer was no; she would have no choice but to hide her windfall from her best friend...her *only* friend.

She suddenly realized she was treating the new-found money as only a possibility — something that *might* happen. But it *was* going to happen, the letter seemed to leave little doubt. With realization slowly settling in, she knew she needed help — someone to talk to. That could only be one person — her dad. After all, he would be the tax advisor the attorney referred to in the letter, so she would be consulting him soon anyway. He was the one person she could trust above all others to make sense of it all.

A Certified Public Accountant, Silas Lovejoy was a partner in one of the oldest accounting firms in Savannah. But even more than his professional knowledge, his judgement in all things seemed right more often than not. If she had only accepted his gentle hints about Dickie Frapiana a decade earlier, and called off the wedding, her life wouldn't have turned so tragic. But then, there would be no Allison — two realities hard to reconcile.

She placed the call.

"Hi, Mom."

"Oh, hello, dear. Did you forget something when you picked Allison up?"

"No, nothing like that. I just need to speak with Dad for a second. Is he busy?"

"Don't think so," Mary Lovejoy said, starting to put the phone down. "Before I get him, why don't you two come over for dinner Friday night? Silas is grilling burgers."

It sounded tempting, and Michelle started to accept. She knew there was little chance she would change her mind and agree to what amounted to a blind date Sandi had proposed. But the letter had created a sudden, undeniable feeling of confidence about the future, so she decided to leave it open. "I may have plans Friday night. How about Saturday?"

"Oh, okay." There was a noticeable hint of optimism in her mother's tone. "Anything you want to tell me about? About Friday, I mean."

Michelle managed to form a rare smile, picturing her mother's hopeful expression. "Afraid not. It's not definite anyway, but I'll tell you more later."

"Well, just a minute. Let me get him."

Following a moment's pause, Silas Lovejoy was on the phone. "Don't know what you told your mother, but she's beaming from ear to ear."

"Oh, it's nothing really. I'll tell you more tomorrow."

"Tomorrow? Something happening tomorrow?"

"Yes, that's why I was calling. Do you think you can carve out a few minutes for me tomorrow? I have something to show you. Something I need your advice about."

"Oh? What's that?"

"Believe me, this is something you need to see before we discuss it. But it's very important."

The line was silent for a second as Silas Lovejoy considered his Thursday schedule. "How 'bout lunch? If you can come to the office, say, shortly before noon, I'll order in sandwiches for us, and we can talk."

"That sounds good. I'll check with Sandi in the morning to see if she has a problem with me sneaking out. Unless I call you, expect me."

"No clue what this is about?"

"If I told you, you probably wouldn't sleep tonight."

"Oh, really? Well I may not anyway, since you put it that way."

"Thanks, Dad. See you tomorrow."

Hanging up, Michelle Prepared to read the letter one more time, just to make sure. Before she did, she approached the relatively wide horizontal window looking out from the den, peering into the darkness, seeing nothing but her reflection. For some reason that she could only chalk up to a silly case of paranoia, she twisted the thin plastic rod to close the vertical blinds. She wanted complete privacy for what she promised herself would be the final read-through.

Chapter 6

Angel Xminez rode shotgun, with Cesar Javier taking his turn behind the wheel of the drab Chevrolet Impala the American had provided. The car was a three year old, dull grey, four-door sedan, purposely chosen to draw as little attention as possible. It provided a decently comfortable ride, which was all that was required for the two-and- a-half hour drive to San Antonio. Xminez did his best to enjoy the bland Texas scenery, while Javier chattered away, touching on trivial subjects holding little interest for the bigger man. The blond-haired man was a talker, who could switch easily from Spanish to fluid English within the same sentence, a skill important in assignments such as this. Contact with local citizens along the way would most likely be necessary at some point; it was one reason Torres had selected him to accompany Angel X, one of his most valuable assets, on this particular search. The other was that he could blend-in with Americans, his lighter appearance the result of the brief encounter of his mother with a California man. Neither of these advantages did anything to alter Xminez's uneasiness with the man. He made a point of ignoring Javier's attempts to draw him into his rambling monologue. He didn't like Javier to begin with — didn't like what he'd heard about the man's lifestyle. He had only heard rumors, but they were enough to produce a queasy feeling of unease. It was a feeling he had been reluctant to mention to Torres, afraid it might be seen as questioning his judgement. But it was the hyper-active dialogue of the man driving that was grating on him now. So much so, he wondered if Cesar had secreted a stash of the product their organization was notorious for somewhere in the small bag he had brought. That would be strictly contrary to the rules of engagement laid down by Luis Torres, and also contrary to Xminez's own questionable value system. Although he was willing to murder and maim anyone in support of Torres' cocaine empire, he would never allow the poison to enter his body in any fashion. He had witnessed what it could do.

The Chevrolet had just passed through the small town of Hondo, leaving roughly thirty miles to San Antonio, when Xminez made a decision. He interrupted Javier's one-way conversation. "Before we go to the airport, Cesar, there is a stop we need to make."

Javier cast a sideways look. "A stop? Where will we be stopping?"

Pausing a beat before answering, Xminez reached into the vehicle's console, grabbing the Samsung phone Torres had requested the American in Del Rio also have waiting, along with credit cards and fake drivers licenses. The phone had every feature modern technology could provide: email and internet capability; GPS availability; texting; mapping capability; and of course, phoning ability. He was amazed by the functions at his disposal, having spent the past hour exploring each, like a child with a new toy. It was his good fortune Torres had wanted to maintain contact with his hunters, while giving them every device possible to help find his money.

"I have a friend in San Antonio I must see," he said, while slowly working the gum in his mouth.

"I don't understand," Javier said nervously, taking another glance. "Sènor Torres said we were to go straight to Atlanta."

"Sì. But there is something I need to take care of first."

"Something to..." Javier stopped, his face developing into a frown. He had *his own* suspicions about the other man, knowing Angel X's reputation well.

Xminez spoke without looking at the smaller man. "Sènor Torres did not arrange weapons for us. He wishes for us to avoid violence, but we must protect ourselves. As he told us, there may be others seeking the money as well. If so, I do not wish to face them unarmed."

"You are going to purchase a gun?" Javier was truly concerned now.

"Sì. I have a contact in San Antonio who can help."

"But Torres will never agree to the purchase."

"I will spend my own money for the weapon. He will never know." Xmincz turned to look menacingly at the driver. "Unless you tell him, Cesar."

The look terrified Javier. He clutched the wheel and leaned toward the driver side door, as if the extra few inches would protect him. "Of course not. I won't say a word, big man." The car was silent for a moment before the blond man spoke again. "But, Angel, you can't carry a gun on the plane."

"Sì. I'm aware of that. But I'm sure my friend can contact an associate in Atlanta, who will have one waiting for us. He has friends everywhere."

"I don't know, Angel."

“You do not have to know, Cesar,” Xminez said casually. “Just drive, while I call my friend.”

The stick of cinnamon gum had been worked until its flavor was gone. Reaching into his shirt pocket, he grabbed the empty wrapper, spitting the useless remains into it, then folded it in a tight ball. Lowering his window, Xminez tossed it out, then cradled the phone and started punching-in the numbers of the man in San Antonio.

Chapter 7

The office building housing Lovejoy and Haskins, LLC, stood on the corner of Barnard and West Broughton, near the heart of downtown Savannah. Beginning to reflect its fifty-year old existence, the three-story brick and mortar structure was showing its age, as was the mix of professional organizations within. Its location was prime, in the midst of the rapidly transforming area experiencing increasing tourist traffic drawn to the genteel charms of the historic city. Many tenders had been made to purchase the building, raze it and rebuild, or at least bring it up-to-date. But Lovejoy and Haskins was part owner, and they had resisted all offers so far. They weren't purposely holding out for more money. The conservative group was simply resistant to change.

The accounting firm, which had never been large personnel-wise, now consisted of Silas Lovejoy — one of the founding partners, five associates, three of whom also possessed C. P. A. designations, and a clerical staff of seven. The other founder, Jarome Haskins, a few years the senior of Lovejoy, who himself had approached and passed seventy, had retired due to health concerns five years earlier, but still maintained stock in the business. It was not an ideal situation, since he now contributed nothing to the organization. But loyalty, plus a desire to do what was right by his friend, required the remaining founder to direct a share of the profits to the retiree. Silas felt strongly about it, since the senior man had established many of the well-paying clients the firm still serviced.

Entering the second-floor office shortly after 11:45 Thursday morning, Michelle was greeted as always by the round, smiling face of Shirley Kinnebrew, the receptionist, a twenty-five year employee. "Hi, honey. Your dad's waiting for you in the conference room."

Michelle's senses were immediately struck by an enticing aroma wafting from the direction of the private meeting room.

"Doesn't smell anything like sandwiches to me, Shirley," she said, frowning, though in a bemused manner. "What has he done?"

"You'll see," the woman said, pointing with a pen toward the room.

Silas Lovejoy sat at one end of the mahogany conference table, a guilty grin showing under his neatly trimmed salt-and-pepper moustache. He rose to hug his daughter in his usual firm embrace. Since the only child and grandchild of the Lovejoys' had miraculously been delivered to their doorstep six months earlier, they had showered them with affection, emerging from the feelings of despair that they might be shuttered out of their lives forever.

Stepping back from her father, Michelle admired his still trim build, kept in place by tennis matches when he found the time. This was his busy season, so chances were few and far between now. He was only a few inches taller than his daughter, with hair matching his moustache. A friendly face hid behind bifocals.

"I thought you said sandwiches, Dad," she said, eyeing the Styrofoam boxes labeled "Lady and Sons" on the table. The popular restaurant had become something of a local phenomenon, feasting on the notoriety and success of its founder, a star on a national cable food show.

He shrugged. "When I told your mother you were coming by for lunch, she wouldn't hear of it. The sandwiches, I mean. So I managed to sneak down to the restaurant before they opened, before the crowd started lining up."

"Well, you really shouldn't have. My lunches are usually light. This'll ruin me for the rest of the day."

"Got your favorite," he said hopefully. "Baked chicken, greens, sweet potatoes, and jalepeno corn bread. Iced tea too."

She couldn't suppress a smile. "And what about the smaller containers?"

Silas cleared his throat, once again looking embarrassed. "Oh, just a little peach cobbler."

Giving in to his trickery, she smiled and shook her head. "Okay. I surrender. And thanks."

Resuming his seat, he pointed to the chair next to him. "Come on, while it's warm." He then gave a questioning gaze. "Whatever it is you wanted to tell me about, or show me, let's have it." The accountant wasn't one for small talk, and he knew both he and his daughter could allow themselves only short lunch breaks.

Taking her seat quickly, Michelle eased the strap of her bag from her shoulder, then unsnapped the clasp. Removing the folded-up letter, she hesitated slightly, as if reluctant to share the news, uncertain of the affect it would have on his psyche, then slid it across the table.

While his daughter started to eat, Silas adjusted his glasses, then ignored his own advice about the food growing cold as he began to read. Between bites, she watched his reactions closely. There was no expression when he scanned the page once, but his brow began to furrow when he read more carefully the second time through, just as she had. Still holding the paper, he stared across the table with his mouth hanging slightly open, a look she had seldom seen on his usually placid face.

"This is quite incredible," he said. He turned the page over, then back again. "Is this all that came with it?"

"Yes. That's it."

"What about the envelope?"

"Plain, and it had no return address. But it has a postmark from somewhere in Texas. Houston, I assume, since that's where the attorney said he's from."

Silas brushed his moustache absently with his fingers, clearly as dumbfounded as Michelle had been. He read once more, this time pointing to each line with a finger. "Any ideas about the benefactor?...the person who set it up?"

"Not really." She had decided not to mention her initial thoughts about Musso, since they now seemed absurd.

"What about this attorney?" He pointed at the name. "You sure he's not someone you've met? Maybe your paths crossed in Atlanta, then he moved to Texas."

That possibility hadn't occurred to her. She thought for a second, then said, "No. I'm sure I would've remembered. And I don't know anyone in Houston, or anywhere else in Texas." *Not anymore, at least.*

The C.P.A. finally took a small bite, then put his fork down. "Wait a minute, honey. Didn't you tell us the man who helped you and Allison was from Houston? Could it possibly be him? What was his name? Musso, wasn't it?"

She took a deep breath. For reasons she hadn't entirely understood at the time, she had chosen not to mention Brent Musso's death to her parents. It had been a private phone call to Brent's son that had revealed his fate to her, and it had remained a private matter with her. She hadn't told anyone. But now she felt she had no choice.

She looked down at her food, avoiding eye contact, feeling somewhat guilty for harboring a secret she now had to tell. "I don't think that's possible, Dad. You see, a couple of months after I came home, I tried to track Brent down in Houston, just to see how he was doing. He had appeared ill when he left Destin. When I found his phone had been disconnected, I couldn't recall the name of the firm he worked for, so I tried every Musso in Houston information, until I found his son. That's when I found out he had died not long after returning home."

Seeing her dad's questioning gaze, she added, "Pancreatic cancer." Recalling the conversation with Brock Musso, she felt her emotions rising to the surface once more.

Silas continued to stare at his daughter, evidently having trouble deciding how to deal with this news. "I see." Pausing briefly, he asked, "Michelle, not that it matters, but why didn't you mention this to us?"

She shook her head slowly, pushing the remains of her meal away. She had lost her appetite. "I'm not sure, Dad. I guess I just didn't want to talk about it. You know how important he was to Allison and me. I'm convinced he saved our lives. The Tennessee couple helped too, of course, but he was the one who figured everything out. Maybe I was just trying to keep him alive in my memory."

They were both silent for a moment. Silas, after thinking through what she had just told him for a few seconds, then looked at the page once more, squinting at something in particular. "But, honey, did you notice this line?" He leaned to show her. "It's the last line. It says 'it *was* the wish of your benefactor',which could certainly mean whoever it is is no longer living."

Looking at the line in question through slightly moist eyes, she had to agree that did make sense. "I don't know, Dad. I'm sure Brent... Mr. Musso... didn't have this kind of money. I certainly didn't get that impression."

"But since he's since passed away, perhaps there was insurance. It could've funded this trust."

"Yes, Dad, but he had two kids he seemed to care about more than anything in the world. He indicated they were the main reason he was heading home. I'm sure any proceeds would've gone to them."

The room was silent again for a minute. Silas took another bite, then pushed his food into the center of the table to join hers. He crossed his fingers across his chest, then shook his head. A deep frown shadowed his face.

"I don't want to give that monster any credit he's not due, but do you think there's any possible way Dickie might have set this up before...?"

Michelle stopped him abruptly before he had a chance to finish the thought. "Absolutely not, Dad. He never thought about anyone but himself. Least of all, Allison and me. It was amazing he had any insurance at all. What little there was, he purchased right after we married. I think that was just for show, to make me think he was a loving husband."

"I'm sure you're right, dear. Just trying to cover all bases."

"I'm sorry, Dad. You always do. Didn't mean to snap." She managed an embarrassed smile.

The room remained still for a few more seconds, this stretch of time seeming much longer. Father and daughter looked away from each other, then their eyes locked, sharing a thought neither wanted to entertain. Silas finally spoke, knowing it had to be said.

"Could it possibly be... that Musso...?" His voice trailed off.

Michelle took a deep breath. "No, Dad. That's impossible," she said, probably more forcefully than intended. "It just can't be."

He nodded slowly, then said, "I'm sure you're right, honey." He started to grab the neglected boxes. "Don't suppose you want your cobbler?"

"No thanks. Don't think it would go down well now." She glanced at her watch. "I'll need to be getting back soon anyway."

"Well, there is *one* positive side to this news," he said. "I'm sure you can use the money."

"Obviously, I can. And it'll relieve some of the burden I've caused you and Mom."

Silas furrowed his brow once more, shaking his head. "That's no burden to us, honey. You should know that."

Tossing the boxes into a corner trash can, he paused to stare at his daughter. "Would you like to know how much is in the trust?"

She stared blankly. "You can determine that?"

"Within a small margin of error, I think so."

"Would it take long?"

"Not at all. Follow me to my office."

They made the short march down the hall, and entered his comfortably appointed office, which was cluttered with evidence of a busy tax season. Closing the door, pushing a foot-high stack of files to the corner of his desk, Silas motioned for Michelle to pull her chair next to his behind the desk. Clicking-on to an icon on his computer screen so quickly she couldn't read what it had read, then another click, a work sheet of sorts instantly appeared. "Now," he began, "I think what you have is a form of a unit trust."

"A what?"

"A unit trust. Meaning the investments in the trust your benefactor has set up are combined with those of many other trusts, managed by a trustee somewhere. The overall gain, or loss, of the investments are spread among all individual trusts participating on a pro-rata basis."

Seeing her confusion, he quickly continued, "Don't worry about all that. The most important thing for you to remember is that your income will fluctuate depending on the results of those investments. That's what the attorney meant by your payments being adjusted each year. Your income is a percentage of your trust assets — probably around five percent. That percentage, or one near it, is set assuming trust assets will grow at that same rate each year, so that it never depletes itself. In other words, your income will always be five percent of the current value of trust assets, whatever that amount is."

The explanation and figures were passing right through Michelle's brain; numbers were not her thing. "If you say so," she said, playing along.

"Now," he continued, while hitting keys on the keyboard,"if we plug in a rate of five percent, and your beginning yearly income of $78,000, which is $6500 times twelve, we come up with a beginning amount of about $1,560,000. Probably it's a little more, since there are management fees involved."

The obscene amount stunned her. The question remained: *where did it come from?* She didn't respond to his calculations right away, trying to digest the numbers. Glancing at her father, she noticed a look of concern building on his face. "This is bothering you, isn't it?" she asked.

Pursing his lips, he nodded. "It's just that, with Dickie's history and all, I can't shake the thought it's related to what happened to him, or rather, what *he* caused to happen. Sure hope I'm wrong."

"I do too, Dad." Unfortunately, she was aware of the fact his instincts were rarely wrong. Taking another quick look at her watch, she did her best to erase those troubling thoughts from her mind, while standing to leave. "I've got to go. I'm already late."

Michelle picked up the letter, which her father had been referring to for his computations, and which now seemed to carry a heavier weight, placing it back in her purse. She paused before heading for the door, wrestling with a decision on another matter. "Say, Dad. Do you think you and Mom could keep Allison for a while tomorrow night? Sandi's invited me to something."

The moustache creased into a smile. "Of course we can, honey. I think your mother will be pleased, if it's what she thinks it is."

Michelle couldn't keep a flash of red from her cheeks. She leaned and kissed his forehead."Might be. And thanks, Dad — for everything."

Chapter 8

Walter Church pulled the Velcro strap tighter on his Kevlar vest as he took his position next to the stone gate. A typically humid Atlanta March night on the eastern outskirts of the city was causing beads of sweat to form instantly around his neck and waist. Resenting the constricted feeling of the vest, Church accepted it as a hazard of his trade; personal comfort had to be overlooked in order to achieve personal safety, or as close to it as possible. As dicey as the next few minutes might be, he anticipated the air conditioning inside the massive house would hopefully bring relief. He exchanged a quick thumbs-up with his partner, Chris Steen, who stood close by, meaning they were good-to-go. Waving with the hand not holding his semi-automatic weapon, he motioned for the other team of DEA agents to ready themselves. He leaned in close to speak in subdued tones to the only person *not* wearing the black uniforms of the federal team, initials of their agency stenciled boldly on their backs. The man was a reluctant guest, who would rather be anywhere else than where he now stood. But he had no viable choice. He reacted slowly to the agent's command.

"Okay, Lincoln, let's see how good an actor you are." Church shoved the wiry little man in front of him, until he stood next to a speaker-box mounted in a carved-out cavity of the fieldstone and iron gate looming over the assembled group. The man started to push a call button with a sweaty, shaky hand, but was stopped by Church, who reached and pulled the hand back.

"Wait just a second. You sure there're no cameras here?" He ran his eyes around the edges of the gate, then toward the top of the fence.

"Damn right, I'm positive. I sure as hell wouldn't be standing here with you guys if I thought there was. Shands keeps talkin' 'bout puttin' them in, but never gets around to it." Lincoln raised his hand again to push, then hesitated, only this time without any help. "You gonna get me outta here soon as the gate opens, right?" He stared hopefully at Church, looking for reassurance.

"That's our deal, Lincoln. Do your thing, and you'll be on the sunny beaches of south Florida by noon tomorrow. Now, get us in." How long the snitch would be safe there was anybody's guess. People who ran in his circles had to know there were no easy-outs.

An impatient voice crackled over the intercom a few seconds after the button was activated. "Yeah? Who is it?"

"It's me, Shands. Linc."

A short pause, then, "Thought you said you weren't coming."

"My other deal got canceled. Lemme in, it's suffocating out here."

There followed a brief pause; the intercom clicked a couple of times, evidently being turned off and on. The man inside was cautious."You alone?"

"Fuck, yeah."

"Okay. Give me a second."

A buzzing could be heard, emanating from the locking mechanism of the lattice-steel gate, then it began to slowly swing open. As soon as he saw the motion of the gate, the man known as Lincoln double-timed it to a waiting black vehicle parked on the edge of the street, stumbling as he went. His betrayal completed, he wanted to get as far away as he could, as fast as he could.

As the team leader, Church quickly led the team in, jogging the fifty yards or so up the gentle incline of the circular drive to the front of the two-story house, an impressive Georgia limestone structure belonging to Kevin Shands, one of the most successful defense attorneys in the capital city. His clientele consisted of low-lifes like the now-departed Lincoln, who in fact had been a client in a drug related case that had been settled in his favor after the federal attorney prosecuting the case dropped the charges. A few weeks later, with Lincoln free to walk the streets, away from the daily monitoring of Shands, the feds approached him with a deal: help put Shands away, and the government would conveniently misplace the five other cases pending against the unfortunate small time dealer. Such dealings, counter to commonly accepted principles in the criminal justice system, were used often in the critical war against drugs, a war that would most likely never be won, with or without these backdoor deals. Church viewed it as being similar to fishing; toss the small ones back, then wait for a chance to hook the lunkers.

When the assault team neared the front door, two agents peeled off toward the left side of the house; two more did likewise on the right side. They would watch for possible escape attempts on each side, plus from the rear of the house. Church, Steen, and the remaining agents headed straight for the massive door. One carried a steel battering ram of sorts, with sturdy leather straps attached for ease of swinging. DEA agents were not restricted by usual police obligations to identify themselves before gaining entry; the element of surprise was critical in their operations. The battering ram was their means of entry — normally no more than two or three strokes were required.

Allowing just enough time for the flanking members to take positions, Church wiped a final bead of moisture from his eyebrows, then gave the order to the man with the steel device. "Do it."

Following two mighty swings, the expensive wood door was demolished, the lock assembly pushed away from the frame. They entered in slightly stooped stances, weapons held shoulder-high, swung back and forth in all directions.

"DEA! Everybody freeze right where you are!" Church yelled as the team spread across the marble-floored foyer, each heading for a different room on the bottom level. The layout of the house had been studied closely with the cooperation of the design architect, so they knew the critical points — the potential hiding places and escape possibilities.

"Shaw!" Church commanded to the lone female agent, a new recruit on her second field exercise. "You take position at the bottom of the stairwell in case someone tries to come down. We'll move up after we secure the bottom level."

She nodded, then chose her spot on one side of the bottom step.

Sounds of panic could now be heard from different directions inside the house. Voices yelling, mixed with the clatter of feet on marble floors created a cloud of confusion. A man and woman, the man wearing only his underwear... the woman nothing... ran from what was known to be the game room, heading down a hall emptying off the foyer. The woman was screaming as she tried to keep up with her companion.

Knowing they couldn't go far, Church ignored them, making his way into the game room. The couples' clothes were strewn on the floor. In the center of the room stood a pool table, and in the center of the felt-green surface of the table, a glass mirror, roughly three-feet square, lay where they had left it. Streaks of white powder on the mirror surrounded a thin glass tube perfect for inhaling the coke. Trails of the powder ran to the edge of the table, a sign of their hasty dismount from the surface. The pair had been busy using the table — but not for shooting pool. Keeping his gun trained, he surveyed the room, seeing no exit doors or closets. Other than beneath the pool table, there was nowhere else to hide. The room was empty.

Exiting the room, he removed a green marking pen from a pocket, putting a check mark on the door frame, the team's method of noting the room had been cleared. Glancing down the hallway, he saw another agent hovering over the couple who were on their knees.

The woman's screams had changed to pitiful sobs, while she covered herself with her trembling hands as much as possible. Church re-entered the game room, grabbed her flimsy dress, then marched down the hall, tossing it to her. Not bothering with putting it on, she draped it over her body.

"The study's clean, Walt," the agent standing guard said. "I marked it."

"Good enough. Read these two their rights, then put bracelets on him. Don't think you have to worry 'bout her going anywhere." Church nodded at the woman, then looked up and down the hall. "Where's Steen?"

The agent motioned with a nod of his head. “Checking out the guest bedroom on the rear of the house. He thinks he got a glimpse of Shands headin’ back there.”

Church started to walk in that direction, when another agent emerged from another room in the hall. It was known to be a small office the attorney used. “In here, Walt,” he motioned with his head.

Entering the room, Church discovered two men laying face-down on the carpeted floor, their hands secured behind their backs. One had jet-black hair, appearing to have dark features on a somewhat thin face. It was hard to tell from his vantage point, but the man looked to be of average height and build. The second, a black man, had the athletic looking body of a younger man. His face was turned away, so the agent circled to get a better look. Twisting his face in line with the man on the floor, before he quickly turned his head away, he thought he recognized a second round draft choice of the Falcons two years back. He hadn’t panned out as the team had hoped, which left the young man unemployed, but with a boat-load of signing bonus money. *This* was how he had chosen to spend it. Church shook his head in disgust. “What a waste,” he muttered.

In the corner of the office was a small brief case, opened to reveal plastic bags filled with white powder, no doubt the traveling inventory of the dark-featured man. Next to the case lay a pair of automatic weapons, well out of reach of the prone men.

“How’d you take’em without fire?” Church asked, admiring the agent’s work.

“They were trying to bust through the window there,” he pointed with his weapon. “They didn’t know there were bars on the outside. Didn’t give ‘em much time to turn on me."

"Solid work, Jordan," Church said, impressed. "Looks like you get the gold star tonight." He nodded toward the dark-haired man. "I'm thinking that's our dealer." He turned to leave. "Hold your position here. I'm going to check on Steen."

Agent Chris Steen was busy at the moment, easing his way into the well-appointed guest bedroom. He always viewed these rooms with trepidation, especially those with beds having side material hanging to the floor — skirts, he thought they were called. They provided easy cover for his prey; more than a few fellow agents had been left with shattered ankles by rounds fired from beneath beds such as the one he now approached. He high-stepped his way, as if he was walking across hot coals, giving the smallest target possible if they were aiming at his legs. He knew he looked weird, even comical, but didn't care; no one was most likely watching, and surely, no one that mattered.

He had to know. Girding himself, he bent low, lifting up the corner of the skirt with the barrel of his gun, keeping it pointed just in case. He peered under the four-poster bed. Nothing. Moving to the closet, he stood to the side of the double-doors, then threw them open while holding his automatic at the ready. Noticing a light switch on the wall next to the door, he flipped it on. No feet could be seen beneath or behind the hanging clothes. Satisfied it too was clear, he turned toward the other door in the room, the one leading to a bathroom.

Halfway to the door, Steen stopped; sounds could be detected behind the door. There were scrapping noises, soon joined by whimpering sounds. Continuing on, he put his free hand on the doorknob, ready to face whatever or whoever was inside. The door opened inward, so he stood to the side away from the knob. Turning the knob, he shoved the door halfway open with his foot, leveling his gun toward the end of the room he could see. There was a glass-walled walk-in shower at the far end, with a bench just outside, a stack of towels resting on it. Scanning the rest of the room as it came into view, he saw twin marble-topped vanities, loaded with appliances and cosmetic containers of various shapes and sizes.

"DEA!" he announced. "Toss your weapons on the floor! I'm coming in!"

The whimpering grew louder. It was coming from his right, in the end of the room he still couldn't see. Lunging quickly through the doorway, he pointed his weapon at a door on the far end, no doubt leading to a privacy toilet. He approached the door. Leaning against a sidewall, he twisted the brass knob, and threw the door open, revealing the origin of the sounds.

It took a second or two to identify what he was looking at. The barely recognizable form of famed trial attorney Kevin Shands was wedged in next to the commode on the ceramic-tile floor, his body twisted into a fetal position. He clutched a gold, silk robe to his mid-section. He held a cowardly hand up. "Don't shoot! Please, don't shoot!" he wailed.

Steen could do nothing but stare, feeling competing waves of disgust and satisfaction building. "Don't worry, counselor. I wouldn't waste my metal on you."

Church entered the bedroom, quickly joining his partner to view the pathetic scene of the powerful lawyer hugging the commode, as if it were his best friend. Before either agent could speak, two shots rang out from the front of the house.

"Stay here," Church said. "I'll check it out."

Arriving at the foyer, Church found Shaw leaning against the bottom stair railing, a crimson stain beginning to ooze from a leg. Before he could say anything, she yelled, “It’s Weathers. I got a good look right before he fired.”

“Christ! You okay, Shaw?”

“I’ll be fine. Don’t think he hit bone.” She staggered slightly, gaining her balance against the railing. Receiving her first battlefield injury had dislodged her black cap, revealing a shock of cropped red hair. “He was upstairs... comin’ down. I got off a round just as he took aim, but think I missed. He disappeared into a room up there.” Her eyes were wide with excitement and adrenalin as she looked up.

Two more agents suddenly appeared from outside. Church barked at one. “Radio for an e. m. s., then make her as comfortable as you can. I’m going up.”

“Right behind you, chief,” the other agent said. He followed Church cautiously up the winding stairwell.

Church led the way toward the second level in search of Floyd Weathers, a former NFL journeyman who had bounced from team to team, while keeping his permanent home in Atlanta. Lincoln’s tip had included the fact that the one-time player was a steady client of the dealer who also serviced Shands, and would likely be in the house during the bust. It explained the other pro dropout found earlier; Weathers must’ve been a mentor of sorts, in more ways than one. He was known to carry heavy-duty weapons, so he had to be considered extremely dangerous.

Reaching the second floor landing, Church flattened himself against the wall, inching his way toward the one door that was open. He motioned for the other man to follow his lead. Reaching the door, he chanced a quick peak inside the room. Seeing nothing, he mouthed silently to his shadow. "Cover me."

Hitting the floor, he quickly rolled through the door, expecting to draw fire. Instead, he looked up to see a young black girl sitting up in a bed, no more than a teenager, a sheet pulled to her neck. She was trembling. "Please don't shoot," she pleaded. "I didn't wanna be here."

"Where is he?!" Church demanded.

She pointed by nodding to a sliding glass door, still open, the vertical blinds swaying in the light breeze. "Went out there."

Following her eyes, he managed to get to his feet. He approached the opening slowly, with the other agent trailing him. Taking a tentative step through the blinds, he found himself on a small, cement covered balcony. It took a second for his eyes to focus in the relative darkness, then discovered he was alone. Leaning over the wrought-iron railing, he could see a figure in the darkness below, streaking at a rapid pace across the back yard.

"Crap!" Church muttered to himself. The former athlete had shimmied down somehow, and was looking for a way out across the expansive lawn. He gripped his weapon at eye level, then thought better of risking a wild shot in the darkness. There were agents out there somewhere he might hit. But where were they? They were supposed to be watching the rear. He then realized they must have entered the house when they heard the shots from inside, as they had been trained to do.

"Watch her," he commanded the other agent, nodding toward the terrified girl, then retraced his steps quickly down the stairs, then out the front door, yelling at the agents gathered in the foyer. "Follow me!"

Circling the side of the large home, Church could see the man's racing form outlined against the tree line to the rear, evidently wearing only boxer shorts, still holding his weapon. He was approaching what appeared to be a chainlink fence, roughly a hundred and fifty feet back in the expansive back yard. The grassy terrain sloped gently downward to the fence. The agent recalled from studying the layout, there was a narrow creek behind the fence, which was the property line. Beyond the creek were thick woods, part of an undeveloped area behind the house. If the former football player was able to scale the fence, he might easily disappear into the dark forest.

Weathers suddenly stopped, turning to fire a round in the direction of his pursuers. Church ducked to the ground; the shot was wild, evidently only meant to slow him. Regaining his feet, he saw that the man had reached the fence, and was pacing back and forth parallel to it, looking for the easiest way out. Drawing closer himself, Church saw that the metal fence was nearly double the height of the former athlete, which must have caught him by surprise. He finally chose to begin his climb at one of the sturdy posts, wrapping his fingers through the openings in the chainlink fence, sticking his toes into the metal squares. In a flash he was halfway up.

Arriving within a few yards of the fence, Church lunged at the man's feet, managing to grab an ankle. Weathers had been an elusive wide receiver while playing, and was still in decent shape. With an athletic move, he was able to kick free, but in doing so, slipped a few feet down the side of the fence. Regaining momentum, he shot upwards again, quickly reaching the top. The agent jumped again, catching both feet this time, hanging on with all his might. Sweat on the man's ankles caused his grip to slip; he had to readjust, reaching higher on the leg. His pulling on the leg, plus the weight of the other man brought him down onto the top of the post, a sharp-pointed piece of metal. Weathers screamed as the post top gouged into his stomach. He tried to kick free once more, but Church had a firmer hold this time. Pulling with what strength he could muster, he dragged the man back toward him. He could hear the sounds of something ripping. Weathers screamed louder, obviously in severe pain.

Two pairs of hands now joined Church, helping to complete the task of pulling the drug addict into custody. With a final torturous cry, the man released his grip on the fence, falling to earth among the circle of DEA agents. As the man lay on the soft ground writhing in agony, one of the agents pulled the weapon from the elastic band of his shorts, tossing it to the side.

"Ahh!" Weathers bellowed. "Shit! Look what you did to me!" He ran a hand across his stomach. In the darkness, there did appear to be blood starting to flow. The post apparently hadn't punctured his body, but had dug deep enough to tear away a layer of skin as he was pulled away from the fence. As another agent rolled him onto his side to apply restraints, he glared up at Church. "I'll have your fuckin' badge for this. This is police brutality, man, plain and simple."

Church immediately wanted to classify the statement as ludicrous, but knew better. The wound was obvious. He knew from past experience it could be used to the addict's favor if, and when, it came up in court, and he thought there was little chance it wouldn't.

He suddenly became aware of activity behind him; there were more people coming. One pointed a camera lit by a bright light above it. The media had arrived, most likely tipped off about the drug raid on a high-profile figure by his own department — an attempt to show a federal law enforcement agency on a successful maneuver. But they had a way of appearing at the worst possible times.

As the team of agents pulled Weathers to his feet, he yelled directly at the camera. “You see what they did to me? I was tryin’ to surrender peacefully, and look at what they did.” He nodded his head toward his stomach. They got it all, focusing the light of the camera on his mid-section.

“Get him outta here. Read him his rights and see that he gets stitched up,” Church said loudly, in what was most likely a vain attempt to put a humane spin on things.

A young female reporter accompanying the camera man stuck a microphone in Church’s face, asking for a statement about the man’s claims.

“No comment,” he answered, starting to turn away. He paused, then faced her again, “What we have here is our attempt to put your hard-earned tax dollars at work, trying to keep the streets of Atlanta safe.” He knew immediately the words sounded canned — a clumsy afterthought.

He followed the procession of the agents escorting Floyd Weathers back up the hill, trailed by the camera-toting news team. He then returned to the house, and helped the agents inside with marching the other captives out to waiting vehicles. In the end, seven were apprehended, with the only casualties being the ex NFL player and rookie agent Brenda Shaw. The good news was no fatalities, always the goal. Somehow, he knew that positive fact, as well as the injury to a young DEA agent bravely doing her job, would get very little attention by the tabloid-crazed media. They had their own agenda, which was one hundred and eighty degrees apart from his.

Chapter 9

The following morning, in a part of Atlanta far to the north of the scene of the drug bust the night before, a carrier delivered a package, or at least, attempted to deliver it. It was an area that reeked of affluence, or at least, the appearance of affluence... all brick, stucco, and field stone. The white van with no markings pulled a short distance into the driveway of the house at the address listed on the package. A close look at the address scribbled on the wrapping paper would have shown crudely drawn numbers and letters, but no one would be getting close enough to look. A man in a light brown uniform, actually a cheap jumpsuit purchased at a local discount store earlier, and also lacking letters of identification, stepped from the driver-side door holding the small box covered with manila-colored paper. He was a rather thin man, with blond hair combed back neatly in place. A light mist was beginning to fall, adding to the lingering dew in the fashionable neighborhood. He made an exaggerated show of flipping the package over to protect the address from the elements.

Halfway up the driveway, he came to a halt. Scanning his eyes across the front of the large, bricked house, he knew things didn't look right. The lawn and shrubbery were unkempt. No edging had apparently been done for some time; runners of centipede grass invaded the walkway with the coming of spring's initial growing season. It took only a minute for him to realize the house was vacant, as he had expected it to be — it had that look. Completing his approach, he turned onto the sidewalk leading to the front door.

Standing at the door, he was now close enough to read the yellow sign taped to the frame. It was a notice that read:

NO TRESPASSING:
PROPERTY OF THE UNITED STATES GOVERNMENT

He had more or less expected such a warning, so he ignored it, and followed the agreed upon plan. He began to ring the doorbell, giving the non-existent occupants a minute or two for a response. When it became obvious there would be none, he stepped away from the door. Looking at the package with a puzzled expression, then shaking his head with a little more animation than was called for, he retreated to the driveway. He made another show of glancing toward houses on both sides, as if deciding which way to turn. The front door of the house to the left suddenly opened, and the decision was made for him.

"Pardon me, ma'am," he yelled to the woman who appeared, carrying a water-spout pitcher. Apparently not hearing the man, she proceeded to sprinkle water over the plants near the front steps.

Walking rapidly in the direction of the woman, fearing she might dart back inside, he called out again, “Excuse me, ma’am.”

Startled, the woman looked up. Barbara Blackburn wasn’t dressed for gardening, wearing her standard realtor garb: slacks; silk blouse with matching scarf. It had been a dry winter, and the morning mist notwithstanding, she made it a point to keep her favorite perennials hydrated, spending a few moments before heading to her office.

“Yes?” she answered, looking warily at the man.

“Sorry to bother you, ma’am,” Cesar Javier said, giving a hopeful look as he broke out his perfect English. “I’m trying to deliver this package to a Mr. And Mrs. Frapiana, but it appears no one currently lives there. Would you happen to have their forwarding address?”

The woman could only stare for a moment, surprised to hear the name again after so many months. She ran a hand through her straw hair, affected more than a little by the man’s striking good looks.

“Whoever sent them that must not know them well. Or what’s happened to them.”

Javier stared back with a confused expression. “Ma’am?”

“Well, Mr. Frapiana died back last year. It was very tragic.”

“Oh?”

The delivery man gave the impression he didn’t know what to say next, so she continued. “Let’s just say it was a mysterious death, and leave it at that.”

He looked back at the house for a second. “Well, how about Mrs. Frapiana?”

She shifted the water can to the other hand, raising her free hand to shield her eyes from the mist that had begun to taper off. "Well, she went back to Savannah, but I didn't know that until a couple of months ago. She was up here gettin' a few of her personal things ... you know, clothes and some of her daughter's things. We visited for a while in the driveway." Blackman shook her head sadly. "Such a poor, sweet girl. Such a sad story. It was humiliating for her while she was in there."

"Ma'am?" Javier gave a confused look.

The woman nodded toward the vacant house. "They stood guard while she got her things out. I felt so sorry for her."

"Ma'am?" Javier's confused expression remained.

"The federal guys. Drug agents, or whatever they were."

"Oh, okay. Why'd she go to Savannah?" Javier immediately wanted to kick himself; it was not the kind of question a deliveryman would ask. She didn't seem to recognize his mistake.

"That's her home. Her parents are there."

"Maybe I can forward this to her there. Would you happen to know her parents' last name? Better yet, their address?"

She put a finger across her lips, thinking. "I know she told me when I first met her..." She shook her head. "Sorry, it escapes me now."

Javier had no more ideas, and he felt more prodding would raise red flags. When he didn't respond, the woman spoke again.

"Just wish they'd do something about mowing, or weed-eating... anything to make the house look less of an eyesore."

He started to turn to leave, dreading reporting the bad news to Angel X, who sat crouched in the rear of the van. At least the mist had subsided, but that didn't improve his mood, or make his failure any easier to accept.

"Say," she said, stopping him, "give me your card, or the name of the sender. If she comes back to deal with selling the house, I'll let her know."

"Oh, no ma'am. We don't carry business cards, and we're not allowed to give out information on our customers." Holding the package upright now, he covered the return address, which was fictitious anyway. "But thanks for your time. We'll return the package to the sender."

"Sorry I couldn't help," she said, observing him as he walked away, concentrating appreciatively on his compact behind.

Javier had his hand on the door handle of the van when he heard the lady yell something through the humid air. "Love-something," is what it sounded like. He turned to look. "Ma'am?" he yelled back.

She cupped a hand over her mouth. "Lovejoy. I just remembered. Her maiden name. It's Lovejoy."

Javier waved a thank you to the woman, allowed himself a satisfied smile, then tossed the package on the seat as he closed the door behind him. He turned to look at the large figure in black, looking ridiculous squatting in the rear of the van.

"I got it," he said, with a cocky air of victory.

Angel X gave no reply, not even a grin.

Chapter 10

The crowd was sparse, considering the decent weather, which made Michelle feel even more conspicuous on what was her first real date in over a decade. She had never thought of outings with her late husband as dates, more like an afterthought on his part to keep him company. Tonight, she felt all eyes were trained on her, and to a large extent, it was true. And while a few may have recognized her from her early days in Savannah, or perhaps from more recent pictures in the local news, most were likely admiring the stunning beauty in their midst. But her bruised ego wouldn't let her accept the fact that her looks were anything out of the ordinary, so her comfort level was being severely tested.

Other than that, she gradually found herself actually enjoying the evening, and the company of the others. Sandi had been right — Dr. Royce Glynn *was* nice. And he was funny, with a quick wit. Tall — about six-four, with sandy brown hair and an easy smile, he resembled nothing of the distant memory she had of him from high school. During introductions earlier in the evening, it was pointed out to her he had actually been two years ahead of her, so their school connections had been vague at best.

With the high-decibel, funk-rock band perched on a makeshift stage adjacent to the downtown Hyatt finally taking a break, the group of four strolled aimlessly down a connecting street to the brick-paved River Street. The street, primarily a pedestrian walkway paralleling the Savannah River, had developed into a tourist and entertainment center over the past few decades, with restaurants, bars, and boutiques lining the river front. Sandi and Jeff Michaels, her real estate developer boyfriend, led the way with arms linked together, while Michelle and the dentist followed a few yards behind, doing their best at awkward small talk.

A steady breeze, heightened as it always seemed to be near the water's edge, brought whiffs of diesel fuel from a passing cargo ship moving slowly in the dark. The river, forming a border between Georgia and South Carolina, had been a major channel of growth during the region's early economy, and remained an important artery in the southeast, linking shippers from Augusta to the north, with the port of Savannah, then eventually, on into the Atlantic.

Sandi whirled to face the stragglers. "What do y'all say to stopping in at Dub's Bar for a drink?"

Michelle and Royce looked at each other. Receiving a nod of agreement from the woman, Royce answered, "Sure. If you'll let me buy."

"No problem there," Jeff replied. He pulled Sandi by the hand toward the popular watering hole, a rustic store-front café with a maritime decor and a history dating back to the beginnings of the nineteenth century. Legend told tales of thieves and pirates visiting the establishment, which wasn't hard to imagine, given other handed-down tales of a rough existence along the river's edge during those early times.

Settling-in at a table, the group of four placed their orders; wine for the women, beers for the men. They took a minute checking out the activity in the historic saloon, letting their eyes adjust to the dimness. Sandi, who seemed to be in high spirits with the apparent success of her match-making, eyed the other couple with a beam of approval. "So, Royce," she said, "what do you think of our girl?"

Michelle stared in astonishment. "Sandi!" There were times, in spite of her dearest friend's loyalty, she could strangle her.

Jeff shook his bushy head, looking at his date with arched eyebrows. "Even *I* know that's a ballsy question, sugar."

"Just tryin' to get the conversation started," she said defensively, eyeing Michaels with a hurt expression.

"Yeah, but good grief. There's something to be said for subtlety."

To Michelle's enormous relief, Royce tried to cover up her unease with a hearty laugh. He then turned and squinted at the gorgeous blond to his left. He leaned across, cupping her perfect chin gently in his hand. "Hmm. Well, let's see. She's got good jaw alignment, far as I can tell. Upper and lower centrals and laterals look fine." He moved his head from side to side, as if examining. "Can't say about her bicuspids and molars 'til I get her in my chair."

Sandi and Jeff both roared, causing others in the bar to stare over. Michelle turned an instant dark shade of red. She wanted to say something — anything to play along with his attempt to diffuse her discomfort. But she'd been away from the game too long; the words didn't come easily.

"So, Doctor Glynn," she managed to say. " Is this how you find new patients? Having Sandi arrange blind dates for you?" Her smile felt more pronounced than she intended.

Royce now joined the other couple in laughter. Sandi slapped Jeff on his arm. "See there. I know what I'm doing."

The drinks arrived, then the foursome fell into a more harmless discussion of Jeff's latest project, an upscale development of loft apartments and condos in an abandoned row of warehouses on the edge of downtown.

"It's perfect," he pointed out. "They're close enough to have a view of the river, plus within walking distance of everything downtown. People who grew up in town but moved to the suburbs for various reasons, or left for bigger cities, are wanting to move back now. It's happening all over the southeast. Been going on up north and in the Midwest for awhile, Chicago in particular, but with southern cities startin' to age, a lot of buildings such as the ones I'm re-doing are prime for development. We'll see more of it, and I intend to do my share."

The others listened politely as he droned on for awhile, covering advantageous tax breaks, government grants for rehabilitating distressed inner-city properties, and the impact his projcct would have on life in Savannah. He was enthused over the prospects, and it did sound interesting. But the others had more social reasons for the outing, and were finally able to turn the conversation to other topics.

Michelle gradually found herself enjoying the evening more and more, as the wine helped loosen the stress and uncertainties created when she had agreed to the arranged date. The feeling of being with people she could actually relax with was something she hadn't enjoyed during that same long, dark, miserable decade. Sometimes, looking back, she wondered how she had managed to survive it. If it hadn't been for Allison, perhaps she wouldn't have. Observing the people at the table with her, a warm feeling of restrained euphoria enveloped her. Even the memory of the worried look on her father's face about the possible source of her mysterious windfall was starting to fade, at least for the night.

Following a second round of drinks, the group decided to return to the brick streets, with the thought of catching what remained of the band's performance. Once outside, Sandi changed everybody's plans.

"Jeff, would you mind if we call it a night?" she asked, stroking his arm with a hand.

The developer gave a blank stare, then glanced at his watch. "But it's barely ten. The night's early."

"I know. But I've had a busy week, and I sorta promised the sitter's parents I wouldn't keep her out too late tonight. Do you mind?" she added with a pleading look as she tugged at his arm.

The man wasn't happy, but he had no choice but to agree.

"I should probably be getting back too," Michelle followed up. "Hate to burden my parents too much. It's past their bedtime, I'm sure."

"Oh, no," Sandi quickly said. "You two stick around. Enjoy the night." She beamed a mischievous smile at her friend, giving no attempt to hide her motives for leaving the other couple alone. "I'm sure Royce won't let you turn into a pumpkin." Leaving no time for any objections, she took Michaels by the hand and started to lead him away.

"Goodnights" were exchanged, and Michelle and Dr. Royce Glynn were left standing at the river's edge, helplessly watching the other two depart.

Another awkward moment followed before the dentist was able to break the silence.

"Looks like we're stuck with each other for awhile."

"Yeah. Thanks to Sandi. She has an infuriating way of setting things up exactly as she wants them." Michelle smiled as she spoke, then they both laughed. She brushed away a leaf that had blown from a nearby oak onto her ivory mid-calf length skirt. An aqua-blue, sleeveless blouse highlighted the sheen of her golden hair. The combination was one she had salvaged from her home in Atlanta — her first chance to put it to use. The breeze, although not a chilly one, still managed to produce goose pimples on her arms.

"Hope you don't mind," he said.

"No, of course not. But I'll get even tomorrow anyway. I'll drop the largest book I can find on her toes."

He took a closer look to make sure she was kidding. Satisfied she was, he laughed, then said, "Say, Michelle. Instead of going back to the hotel and having our ear drums punctured again, could we just sit and talk for awhile?"

"I'd like that." She meant it, suddenly realizing she *would* like to get to know the man better, just as long as their discussion steered clear of certain areas.

Spotting a bench nearby, well lit under a pole-mounted flickering gas light, they took their seats. They again grew quiet, while watching with detached interest as another freighter continued its journey toward the Atlantic. The ship was so large, it appeared to be not moving at all. The sounds of the band in full swing again drifted down toward the river, the drum beats standing out loudest as they reverberated between walls of surrounding buildings. The noise was thankfully muted by distance, and what sounds there were seemed to rise to the heavens and not flow down the hill. There were very few people strolling across the bricks, so there were no interruptions; no excuses not to talk.

"So, are you enjoying being back in Savannah?" Glynn asked.

She breathed out, again trying to relax. She found herself wishing for a third glass of wine. "Yes. A lot more than I thought I would. I've become adjusted to the slower pace, and it's kinda nice." Looking down at her hands, folded tightly in her lap, she continued. "And having my daughter and my parents have a chance to get to know each other has been a blessing hard to measure."

"How old is your daughter? Allison, right?"

"Right. She'll turn six in a month."

Glynn smiled and nodded, then gazed into the dark layer of mist hovering over the water. "I'm sure she's everything in the world to you."

"Right again. Especially since she occupies so much time in my world."

"I can only imagine the feminine mystique at that age. I come from a family of three boys, and my brother has two sons, so it's something I'm entirely unfamiliar with."

Michelle suddenly realized she knew little else about the man. She was curious about his history, but was hesitant to ask, not wanting to embark on a closeness that might not develop any further. Asking about his history might prompt him to inquire about hers. The cloud was still there, constantly hanging over her. It might never disappear completely, but this was not the time to try and break it apart.

As if interpreting her thoughts, he said, "In the interest of full disclosure, I think its only fair to mention I've been married before. Back in dental school. She was a dental student too, and it lasted just long enough for us both to realize we weren't ready."

"Oh. I'm sorry."

"It's okay now. Can't say it was a happy ending — divorces never are, I guess. But it turned out for the best for each of us. She's in practice up in Athens, her home town. Doing well, as best I can determine."

Michelle loosened her hands, rubbing them across her skirt. "Looks like we all end up back in our home towns eventually, but for various reasons."

He nodded agreement, then looked at her for a moment, as if trying to determine if she wanted him to explore *her reason* for coming home. Evidently he decided not, choosing a safer topic instead. "Any brothers or sisters?"

"Nope. Only child here," she said, pointing at herself. "I guess that's why I'm enjoying being near my parents again. And of course, they spoiled me rotten while growing up."

"I'll bet that goes double for them. Having you both here, I mean."

They touched briefly on his practice, then the book selling business, before growing quiet again, finding it difficult to find subjects worthy of carrying the conversation. During those lulls, when she glanced at the man, the image of Brent Musso's sunken, bearded face appeared. His appearance when last seen was forever trapped in her memory.

When the silence became too loud, Michelle concluded it was time to call it a night. "I've really enjoyed this, Royce. More than I can say. But I think I'd better go relieve my folks."

"Sure. I'll walk you up to your car. Downtown Savannah can be a little rough late at night, especially on weekends."

As they neared her Nissan, parked on a side street near the hotel, Michelle had a final point to make. “I hope you didn’t feel pressured by Sandi about tonight. I mean, the date and all. As you’ve noticed, she can be pretty impulsive.”

“Absolutely not.” He feigned a hurt expression. “This was more my idea than hers. And by the way, just to clear something up, I’ve got plenty of patients, so no problem there.”

They both laughed at the reference to her earlier comment, then parted on a good note, agreeing to do it again soon. Her mood was so light, she dispensed with her habit of checking out her surroundings. The precautions simply didn’t seem necessary.

It was almost 11:30 by the time Michelle arrived at her parents’ home. Allison was in a deep sleep, and the decision was made to let her stay the night rather than disturbing her. Silas had also given in to the late hours.

“I’ll be back to get her about nine tomorrow morning,” Michelle said.

“But don’t you have to work tomorrow?” Mary Lovejoy asked. A few inches shorter than Michelle, her trim frame was swallowed up by a housecoat. Close-cropped salt and pepper hair outlined a still attractive face, echoes of an earlier beauty that had matched her daughter’s at one time.

“I don’t go in ‘til one, so I’ll have plenty of time.”

“Dear, why don’t you just bring over a change of clothes for her in the morning? She can stay here until later in the day, then I’ll bring her to the store so you can ride home together.”

It sounded tempting. She liked having Allison at the store with her, and Sandi seemed to enjoy having her around. “If you’re sure it’s not too much trouble.”

"Of course not, honey. It never is. Then it's settled." Mary paused, looking hopefully at her daughter. Curiosity was creeping through. "How did things go tonight?"

The question made her think again about how things did actually go. It had been a clumsy first step, but one that seemed to have gone well. "Went just fine. We all had a good time. I'll tell you more in the morning. Right now, I need some sleep," she said, not attempting to stifle a somewhat forced yawn.

As she drove slowly away from the colonial-styled home, Michelle's thoughts were definitely trained on the night's events. So this was what it felt like to be nearly human again. A promising jolt of excitement, countered by the fear of the unknown. Even though it had been a long, long time, she recalled that things didn't usually fall into place so easily. Doctor Royce Glynn was a decent, funny, good-looking guy, somebody she wouldn't mind seeing again. She knew it was still too early to make decisions about her future. But maybe, just maybe, a ray of light was beginning to shine through. The sudden promise of unexpected fortune didn't hurt.

She relaxed her tired, yet tingling body as she pulled out into the street, ready to actually enjoy the ten minute drive to her apartment. It was a brief, simple pleasure, the kind she was hoping to get accustomed to again. Her mind still juggling the possibilities of her new life, she was totally oblivious to the dark compact car that turned on its headlights and fell into place behind her.

Chapter 11

Angel Xminez and Cesar Javier had traded in the van for a rental car at the Atlanta leasing office earlier in the day, then headed straight for Savannah, a long, boring drive across the heart of Georgia, taking most of four hours. Text messages between Xminez and Luis Torres during the ride had the big man's spirits high, with the notorious drug lord voicing his approval of the clever work done in Atlanta. Arriving in Savannah by mid-afternoon, they had checked in to a Best Western motel on the edge of the city. Studying the local phone book in their room, they found three Lovejoys listed. A quick look for the name, Frapiana, had revealed nothing, which was no surprise. The woman would certainly have an unlisted number, given her cowardly husband's reputation. Plus knowing she would want to remain hidden from men such as them, she might have changed her name. But that would mean only a slight delay. Using the internet capabilities of the cell phone, it was a simple matter for Xminez to Google the addresses of the three Lovejoy names listed, then map their locations.

"This is our target," Xminez announced, throwing the phone book on his bed. He was pointing at the map on his phone screen illustrating the location of the last name. He had saved the listing for last, since he knew from the phone book information this was the most likely location.

"How can you be so sure, Angel?" Cesar had asked, leaning on an elbow on the other bed. "We haven't checked out the houses yet."

Xminez responded without looking at the other man. "Two reasons. First, the other two addresses don't fit. One is in what is surely a lower middle class neighborhood, near this very motel as a matter of fact. The second is close to the city's airport. It seems to me these are not places our Mrs. Frapiana would have grown up."

"What makes you so certain?"

"You saw her home in Atlanta. A woman who lived in that luxury would certainly come from the same background. That is the way it usually works, especially in America."

"So what does the third house here tell you?"

Xminez threw his legs over the side of the bed, sitting up. He hadn't bothered to take his black snake skin boots off when settling in to the room. Looking disdainfully at the blond man, he answered, "It appears to be in a neighborhood of winding streets, possibly a nicer area. And the name of the street itself — Avalon Way — indicates a lifestyle she was surely raised in."

Javier yawned widely, still not looking convinced. "You're jumping to conclusions, Angel. Shouldn't we check them out first?"

The large, sullen hit man tried to ignore his companion. He was growing very uncomfortable with the man anyway. He was useful, yes, but he felt uneasy due to the rumors he had heard about the man's sexual preferences. Whether they were true or not, he had felt it wise to keep an eye open. The weapon obtained in Atlanta had been kept close by while he slept in the motel room in the Georgia capital city the night before. He would do the same later this night.

"We will, Cesar. We will look at all three houses. But the other reason I am sure Silas Lovejoy is our man is the way he is listed in the phone book. He has a residence *and* a business listing, meaning he is a professional. The initials, C.P.A., are listed beside his name. That is the kind of man the woman would have as a father."

"Perhaps," Javier said. "So, what do we do now?"

"We look at all three houses, to make sure I am right. We'll start with the two I'm sure are wrong." Xminez unwrapped a stick of gum, placing the folded-up wrapper in the usual pocket — a man of habits. "Let's go, while we still have daylight."

Xminez's predictions about the first two houses proved dead-on. The one near the motel appeared abandoned. A leaning "For Lease" sign was wedged into the ground in front of the faded brick structure. The second one near the airport wasn't much better. An ancient-looking cinder block building, it looked lived-in, but not by anyone with an interest in yard work.

With Javier behind the wheel, three passes were made in front of the Avalon Way house, an impressive brick and stucco home with white columns and a well-landscaped lawn. It was located on a deep cul-de-sac, with twenty or so equally nice residences spread among towering oaks. Angel X peered closely at 570 Avalon way, noticing the large entry door, and the drive leading to what was certainly an enclosed garage in the rear. When he began to fear their presence might be noticed, he ordered Javier to leave the area. "We'll return after sundown," he said, as Javier put the car into gear.

"You are certain she will come here?" the doubtful sounding Javier said as he drove the navy Corolla from the neighborhood.

Xminez nodded his massive head slowly. He seemed quite sure of himself. "Yes. If she is not living here with her parents, she will come to see them eventually."

"Eventually sounds like a long time."

His black eyes squinting under a furrowed brow, Angel X glared at the smaller man. "And what is *your* plan to find the woman?"

Javier knew better than to chance a reply, even if he had an idea. He gripped the wheel tightly and grew silent.

Shortly after 7:15 p m, when dusk had finally settled enough to obscure vision from more than fifty feet, they took up their position four houses down from the Lovejoy home. Before returning to their stakeout, a trip was made to a convenience store, where a cooler, a bag of ice, and drinks were purchased for the open-ended surveillance. Javier had waffled over his selection of caffeine-based juicers, making Xminez antsy by his indecision. As a result, they had missed Michelle's trip to her parent's home to drop off her daughter by less than fifteen minutes. It would result in more than a four hour wait until they saw her return.

With the hours ticking by, each man grew more miserable by the confinement in the small vehicle with the other. Sharing few common interests, their discussions were truncated. Xminez now occupied the position behind the wheel, wanting control of the car. Two hours in, more from boredom than a real interest, Javier reached into the glove compartment, extracting the Glock nine millimeter pistol Angel had arranged to be waiting for them in Atlanta. He pulled out the silencer that had been part of the deal, remaining unattached to the barrel. “It’s a beautiful thing,” he said, admiringly. “Do you really plan on using it?”

“If I have to,” Xminez answered with another hard look. “Put it back.”

Taking one last look, Javier did as ordered. He clasped his hands in front of him and stretched out his arms. “You know, Angel. If the other parties Torres was concerned about finding the money have been looking, they may have already found the Frapiana woman... and the money. It’s been over six months”

The thought *had* crossed Xminez’s mind several times. But if they had found her, and discovered her with the money, the chances were good she would no longer be alive. So if she was still breathing, either they hadn’t looked for her, or if they had, hadn’t found her. Or she convinced them she didn’t have the money — a troubling thought that might be true, leading to a dead end. Either way, he planned on getting answers soon.

When the woman had finally pulled in to the driveway just before 11:30, they were shocked to attention. Sitting up, they watched as she pulled halfway up the driveway, enter the house, then surprisingly re-appear ten minutes later, alone.

“What the hell’s she doing?” Javier asked.

“How should I know? Didn’t Torres say she had a child? A daughter? Perhaps she is in the house, with her parents. But that *is* her. There is no question.”

Falling in behind the Nissan, they trailed her for the two mile drive to her apartment complex. Parking three buildings down, they watched as she entered her unit.

Javier searched Angel X's face closely , looking for clues. "What now, Angel?"

"I think it is time for us to get some rest. We must be ready early in the morning. I want to see where she goes, what she does."

A half hour later, before launching a fitful attempt at sleep, Xminez sent another triumphant message to Luis Torres. They had reached their target. Finally kicking his boots off, he turned to lie on his side, keeping a wary eye on the man across the room.

Chapter 12

The extra hour of sleep came in handy Saturday morning. Michelle threw back the quilted sheet slowly and sat on the edge of her bed, giving her fuzzy brain time to review the events of the night before. As pleasant as the evening had been, the shock to the murky equilibrium her life had fallen into caused by the blind date left her feeling confused — disoriented. She had slept surprisingly well, no doubt having a lot to do with the two glasses of Chardonnay. Alcohol of any sort had been a non-existent part of her life the past months. Her parents were tee-totalers, and since her social life was in mothballs, there had been few occasions. Due to the sudden influx of wine, her body was rested enough. It was all in her head, a myriad of thoughts at war with each other.

Even her bedroom felt strange, as if she were waking in unfamiliar territory. She spent a moment gathering her senses before rising to her feet. Making her way to the small bathroom, she downed a couple of Extra

Strength Tylenols, something she should have done before hitting the sack. Shuffling to the kitchen, she started a pot of coffee, then returned to her inner sanctum for a quick shower. Slipping on jeans and a light-weight sweater, she laced a cup of black coffee with a packet of Splendor, then nibbled on half of a banana nut muffin. She finally felt the morning rounding into some sort of warped shape.

From a corner of the kitchen table, under a stack of newer mail, she pulled out the letter from the mysterious lawyer in Houston. Scanning it once again, she let a hopeful grin crease her face. The letter had arrived only three days earlier, but she felt as if she'd had it much longer. According to the letter, the money would begin arriving soon. *But how soon was soon?* Would it be next week? Or the next? Her grin suddenly reversed to a frown, as a troubling thought hit. What if it was a hoax? A horrible, sick joke someone was playing? She had heard of mail scams before, But those were mostly from foreign countries. Promises of great wealth; if only you would follow instructions that would be soon delivered. If that were so, the ones responsible had been entirely successful; raising her expectations and dreams to a level that would cause severe pain if it all came crashing down. And if that was what it was, there was nothing she could do about it. All she could do was wait — and hope.

A few minutes later, she carried the letter into her bedroom, tossing it into a drawer of a bedside table. She tried hard to dash it from her mind; otherwise, she would go crazy obsessing about it. Grabbing the things for Allison to take to her parents', she left the apartment, which now seemed even smaller, confining, and more depressing than ever. She would make a morning of it at her folks' house, then head to Liberty Lady in time for work.

The afternoon seemed to creep along, most of the small book store's activity being directed toward making arrangements for a book signing set for the coming Tuesday. A south Georgia nature photographer had put together a series of his prizes for publication. It amounted to a coffee table book, the kind that would draw narrow interest, and even narrower attendance. But he was well known throughout the area, and Sandi saw it as an important and necessary P R move. Most of the signings in the small store were of the sort, with occasional best selling authors stopping by during the year to make only collateral appearances while in town for publisher-arranged autograph sessions at the bigger chains.

Michelle's most stressful chore was in trying to ward off the smarmy I-told-you-so grins from her boss throughout the afternoon. Memories of high school came roaring back; conversations shared between classmates about secret yearnings involving the two friends and the countless boys who lusted after them, mostly for the untouchable blond princess. In the cozy confines of Liberty Lady, it was impossible to hide from the self-satisfied glances. Fred Huth chipped in his share of teasing, having received an earful of the Friday night outing from Sandi earlier.

She finally decided to face it head-on, hoping to put it to rest. "Okay, so I had a good time. Guess I owe you one."

"Damn right you do." Sandi folded her arms across her chest, rocking back on her medium-high heels. "You can repay me by letting me be the matron of honor. That is, unless you two decide to elope."

Michelle shook her head in frustration, but couldn't resist a smile. "You never quit, do you?"

"Not when I know I'm on to something."

"Sandi. It was just *one* date," Michelle said, hoping to stem the tide. She stepped toward the coffee nook, trying to change the subject by looking busy. Sandi followed close behind.

"So, what happened after we left? What did y'all do?"

"We sat and talked for awhile," Michelle sighed. "Sat on a bench down by the river. Then he walked me to my car, and we went home."

"Oh, really?"

"Me to my home, Royce to his. Sorry if that disappoints."

The silly grin re-appeared. "What'd you talk about?"

"Sandi, Please!" Michelle's face turned bright crimson; once again, strangulation seemed warranted.

"Okay, okay. I withdraw the question, your honor." The book store owner finally adopted a serious voice. "I was just wondering if... you know, if the subject came up."

There was little doubt what she was referring to. Michelle reacted likewise to the more subdued tone. "No, it didn't. There was a moment when I thought he was going to bring it up, but I guess he didn't want to pry." She leveled a wry smile. "Unlike some people."

"Touche," Sandi said, feigning a hurt, guilty look. "I figured he'd be a gentleman about it. Maybe he's waiting 'til the second date."

"Oh? You're that sure there'll be a second date?"

"It's up to you, my dear. He'll call... and soon, if I know anything about men."

"We'll see."

"Yes, we will."

Concentration was finally mercifully applied to work, as a few customers straggled in and out. The subject of Michelle's social life faded, much to her relief, and things fell into the usual routine. None-the-less, she was glad when Allison made her appearance just after 4:30. Mary Lovejoy stayed just long enough to hand off the girl's things to her mother. As she always did, Sandi told Allison to pick out any book she wished, and the women watched in admiration as she took her seat at the small table in the nook to begin paging through a picture book of fairy-tale princesses.

Just before 5:00, Sandi shooed Michelle and her daughter from the store, assuring her that she, Fred, and the other part time employee could handle things. The store closed at 6:00 on Saturdays anyway. It was mostly a matter of locking up.

Leaving the store, Michelle suggested an alternative to going home right away. "What say we go hang out in the park for awhile? Then we'll stop by McDonald's on the way home." It was an easy sale, and another attempt to bring normalcy into their lives.

Thirty minutes later, sitting on her usual bench-of-choice, Michelle watched as the girl explored the upper limits of the jungle gym roughly fifty feet away, marooned in the middle of a large sand box to cushion falls. Her blond pony-tail swished back and forth as she went higher and higher. They had climbed it together for awhile, until she had decided to let her offspring explore the restricted world on her own. A slightly younger boy soon joined her. A woman she assumed to be his mother took a seat across the way.

Keeping a close eye, Michelle took time to once more consider the ebbs and flows of life. The extremes of high and low points, periods of happiness, and the sometimes gut-wrenching agonies of bleak times, could provide a roller coaster of a ride. After an extended period when it seemed as if happiness would never return, she had survived a six month window of being in limbo... perhaps a stage of purgatory, waiting to see if she was worthy of a return to better times.

She honestly believed the things that had occurred in her life — both good and bad — were not of her own making. They had simply happened. She had taken no action to cause them, or prevent them, and that bothered her. Dickie Frapiana had moved into her life so quickly, and taken control so completely, she had found herself easily swallowed-up by his domination. When her escape from his murderous web of deceit presented itself, it *too* was arranged by someone else.

The cycle of events would continue, she saw all too clearly, unless she began to take charge of her life, set out on her own path. How to do that might take time, and she wasn't at all sure how to go about it. The counseling Sandi had suggested could be a first step. Surely the money, assuming it materialized, would help.

She opened the book she had brought from the store, the collection of nature photos by the photographer doing the upcoming signing. She wanted to familiarize herself with his work before Tuesday. The pictures were impressive, some actually spectacular, but the written descriptions accompanying them were too droll for such a pleasant early spring afternoon, and of little interest to her.

Her attention was drawn to the jungle gym. Allison and the boy were talking, and laughing. A good sign, while it lasted. The boy's mother soon called out, and he went running to her, leaving the girl to herself. She continued watching, and was only slightly concerned when a man entered the picture, walking casually toward the lattice-like metal bars. He appeared young, maybe her own age, trim, not unattractive at all, with wavy blond hair. Wearing jeans, a polo-styled golf shirt — tail out — and sneakers, he fit the image of a father spending time with his child in the park. But canvassing the area, she saw no other child.

Alarmed, but not exactly sure why, Michelle started to rise, ready to call out to her daughter. A voice from behind stopped her.

"Please sit down, Mrs. Frapiana."

The surprise of the words coming from nowhere struck her first, before she could recognize the sharp tingle of fear that immediately followed. The sound itself hit harder than the actual words that took a second to register. She had been on alert for so long; how could she let her guard down after all this time? Turning quickly, she saw a hulking, dark-complected man circling the bench from behind. She was vaguely aware he was dressed in something black, but her eyes didn't stray from his broad, pock-marked face.

She stepped away from the bench, taking a flash-glance back in Allison's direction. She was still there... climbing... singing something... no cares.

"I said, sit down."

"Who are you?... what do you want?" She made no attempt to keep the trembling panic from her voice. *But she knew.*

The man was beside her now, only feet away. His face had no expression, his black eyes spaced wide apart over a blunt, brown nose. "Who I am doesn't matter, Mrs. Frapiana. But I must ask you once more to sit down."

Michelle leaned to peer around his bulk, wanting to see her daughter. She was there, but the view created a sickening feeling in the pit of her stomach. The blond man was leaning onto the jungle gym, within feet of Allison, looking directly at Michelle. A grin resembling a smirk was plain on his face.

The implication, and indeed the threat, was all too clear.

With legs too weak to stand, she complied, falling back onto the hard bench, never taking her eyes off the girl. The book fell from her limp hands, falling unnoticed to the ground.

Angel Xminez turned to look himself, then shifted his gaze back. "Don't worry, Mrs. Frapiana, my friend does not wish to harm your daughter. And I will not do so either, unless you make me."

Her hands gripped the bench seat tightly, her knuckles showing white. The period of happiness embraced only minutes earlier evaporated instantly, floating away like the dandelions in Crawford Square being puffed along by the warm breeze. The park began spinning like a horrific merry-go-round, with the bench at the center of the vortex. Allison was on the periphery, seeming to float farther and farther away, with no fear about her circumstance. The sense of vertigo told her the nightmare caused by her husband wasn't over. There was no doubt in her mind these two were somehow connected to the business of illegal drugs and the death of her husband.

She finally managed to speak, but her voice was constricted to a whisper, strained through the bile forming in her throat. "What do you want?"

The man took a seat beside her, towering over her even while seated. He stared squarely into her eyes. "I believe you know what we want."

The money!

" They may come looking for it. " But she didn't have it. The payments she expected to receive soon — she had no choice now but to assume it was related to Dickie's crime spree. Despite the vapor lock taking control of her brain, she instinctively knew it would be dangerous if this monster knew

about it. It was no challenge to appear confused. "I don't have any idea what you're talking about."

Angel X looked closely at the woman. Her fear and concern for her child might be overriding what she did or did not know about the money. But it didn't really matter to him; his method was to always assume they had what he wanted, and to press ahead with blinders on. "The money, Mrs. Frapiana. You have our money."

She hesitated for only a second before answering, adjusting to the man's clipped accent. He was Hispanic, possibly Mexican. "What money? I have no money."

He saw the pause, knowing it was a tell, her way of hiding something. "The money your husband had with him when he died. You were with him in Florida when he was killed. I know he gave it to you." Xminez was judicious with his use of words, using them only as a lever to pry information from its source.

Michelle shook her spinning head rapidly, searching for words that might make sense to the man. "No... no. That's wrong. Yes, I was in Florida waiting for my husband to return. But I never saw him, and he never gave me any money. I had no idea what he was involved in, until I was told ... until I found out before he returned. I left before he arrived back at the beach. I swear, I know nothing about any money." Through tears that were forming, she took another look at Allison, shocked to see her actually talking to the blond man. The distance to her daughter now seemed to be lengthening even more, as if she were at the far end of a long, dark tunnel.

She stared pleadingly at the dark, hulking man. "Please don't hurt my daughter. She knows nothing about what her father did. She's an innocent child." Sobs were in her throat, ready to spew out.

"It is hard for me to believe you, Mrs. Frapiana. Sixteen million dollars does not simply disappear. Where is it?"

Sixteen million! It was the first time she had heard the amount; it stunned her. The DEA men had not mentioned the figure, if in fact they had known. The number also told her immediately that men such as these two wouldn't quit until they had found it. The mysterious letter again flashed into her mind, tying a tighter knot in her stomach. She took a hand away from the bench, swiping at a tear beginning to leak from her eyes. "You have to believe me! I never saw it! I didn't even know the amount until you just said it."

Angel X took a glance around the park. Darkness wasn't far away, but a few people still lingered among the oaks. He had to be careful. He stared hard at the woman. "Who was the other man?"

The question made no sense at first, causing her to pause again. "The other man?"

He remained calm, but leaned in toward her slightly. "The other man in Florida? Or was it a woman, perhaps?"

Brent Musso. It could only be him. But why would the man ask about him. "If you're referring to the man who helped me escape, his name was Musso — Brent Musso." It was safe to say his name now, she thought. They couldn't harm him. The monster's scent suddenly struck her senses. He stank not only from musky sweat, but also from the threat of danger she was trying not to think too deeply about. She then quickly realized some of the sweat was her own, generated by numbing fear.

"He was with your husband when he died. Did he take the money?"

She simply stared, mouth hanging open. "No. That's wrong," she said emphatically, shaking her head again. " He couldn't have been there. He had already left, on his way home to Texas."

Xminez knew he was on the right track now, since she admitted to his presence. "I believe you are the one who is wrong, Mrs. Frapiana. We know he was there." Leaning in closer, his voice became more forceful. "Where is he now?"

She looked down, not wanting to say the words again. "He's dead. He was dying as he helped me and my daughter leave the beach before my husband returned. Only I didn't know that at the time."

It was Xminez's turn to be quiet. He was trying to decide if what she said might be true, and what affect it would have on his quest if it were. He filtered the information through his cunning mind. "Where did he go? Where was his home?"

"I just told you. Texas. Houston, Texas." Saying the city's name reminded her again of the letter. *He mustn't know...*

Xminez studied her face, trying to read the expressions that came and went. She was not the kind of person who hid things easily, and she was definitely hiding something. If only she knew of the kinds of things he had done to others who had tried to conceal secrets, she wouldn't think twice about revealing what she was thinking. She *was* a beautiful woman, and Luis Torres had insisted on moderation. But in order to find the sixteen million, there was nothing he wouldn't do to her perfect face if she tried to stand in his way. He was beginning to think of the money as his, just as much as Torres'.

The park was filling up with late comers, evidently desiring the coolness of dusk. Other people began to come closer, invading what Xminez saw as his safe space. He wasn't done with her yet; there would be more time later.

Leaning even closer to her, grabbing her wrist firmly... firmly enough so she would feel pain, he said, almost in a whisper, "You see how easy it is for my friend and I to get close to you and your daughter. So I would suggest you rethink what you have told me. You will see us again soon." He rose to leave. "And do not be foolish enough to contact the authorities. We will be watching." With a nod to the blond man, he circled the bench again, disappearing into the shrubbery behind.

Michelle stood on rubber legs, walking as quickly as she could to the jungle gym. She saw Allison waving and saying goodby to the other man as he walked quickly away. Grabbing and pulling the girl from the apparatus, she held her tightly.

"What's wrong, Mommy?" the puzzled girl said, wincing under the hard squeeze.

"Nothing, honey. We just need to go." Forcing a narrow grin, she kept her daughter close as she walked rapidly to her car two blocks away. Allison had to practically run to keep up. It seemed to take forever to finally reach the car.

So much for taking control of her life.

Chapter 13

Sunday would prove to be one of the longest days of Michelle's increasingly tortured life, filled with dread, made even worse by a total lack of sleep the night before. The encounter in the park Saturday left her with the belief her entire world was crumbling, torn apart at the seams. After Allison had gone down the night before, she had remained fully clothed, sitting on her sofa, using the kitchen light to keep her company in the darkness of her small living room. She sat clutching the only weapon in the apartment — a butcher knife, eyes glued on the door, expecting it to come crashing in at any moment. There was a dead-bolt, plus a chain lock, but she knew if they wanted to get in, neither would stop them.

When would they come? Why were they waiting? Sometime around 4:00 a.m., when her sleep-deprived mind began playing tricks, imagining each faint sound from within and outside the apartment to be approaching footsteps, she came to the conclusion they were playing a sadistic mind game.

When they finally *did* come, she would be a complete basket case, almost ready to admit to things she had no knowledge of. What choice did she have if they refused to believe her? But that would open up another round of helplessness; having to produce money she didn't have, and didn't exist, as far as she knew. She suddenly realized she was again being naive, closing her mind to the possibility the letter from Houston was somehow related to the money Dickie had stolen. But she had no control over it, no access to it other than that expressed in the letter.

She continued to cling to the belief they *must not* learn of the impending payments; that would give rise to a new layer of suspicions about her. Her mind soon drifted to her parents. Were they in danger too? In any event, they had to be told. There was no room for more secrets. Maybe just her dad; her mom wouldn't be able to handle the strain. Eventually, her eyelids began to sag from their own weight. A picture formed of the four of them: her; Allison; her mother and father, all strapped into chairs in a stifling dark room, her tormentors threatening with pointed guns, pouring gasoline at their feet, torches being lit, ready to end it all, weary of her denials.

A bang, actually more like a thud, shattered the picture that was actually part of a shallow sleep, though deep enough to produce the terrifying dream. In her stupor, it sounded like a gun being fired! Her body convulsed as she emerged from the vivid images. The noise proved to be the newspaper being thrown against the front door. Rubbing her eyes, she let her breathing begin to even out. Finally, as the first muted rays of sunlight filtered between the blinds, she managed to start a pot of coffee, ready to try and make something of the frightening day ahead.

Later in the morning, she called to beg lunch for her and Allison from her parents, which was always a sure thing. Shortly before noon, feeling more asleep than awake, yet with nerves on edge, she tentatively led her daughter to her car, feeling naked to the danger she knew was out there. Her eyes worked overtime checking out the surroundings. It dawned on her she didn't know what to look for, since she had no idea what their car might look like. They could be anywhere, in any vehicle. It was safer to assume the worst about each one she didn't recognize. Remembering something she had seen in a movie, she took a serpentine path to the house she had grown up in; an attempt to lose them if they were indeed following. When there was no one in sight who appeared to be trailing her on the nearly empty streets, she adjusted her path.

"Where are we going, Mommy? This isn't the way to Granma and Granpa's house." Allison stretched from the seat belt to peer through the window during the detour, confused.

"I know, honey. Just taking a little Sunday drive."

The child gave a puzzled look, then settled back in her seat.

The once familiar neighborhood of her youth looked eerily foreign now as she neared the house, as if it were all new; another sign that life had been turned inside-out over the past twenty-four hours. There was the Jeffords' house, where she used to play with Emily Jeffords, who was now living in Charlotte — last time she'd heard. Emily's home offered no security now as it had then. Most of the people she had grown up with had moved away, seeking adventure in their adult lives. Savannah was an idyllic place to live as a child, but didn't offer the excitement of bigger cities. With a cynical grin, she doubted if any of those old acquaintances were experiencing the level of drama she was facing, although she would gladly trade places with the unhappiest of them.

Following lunch involving her favorite comfort foods, a full belly providing the only solace she had enjoyed since the encounter in the park, she managed to pull her dad to the side. Allison stood on a chair in the kitchen, chattering away while helping her grandmother load the dishwasher. The sight made Michelle wonder why the girl could converse so easily with her grandmother, while being so reticent with her. A tinge of jealously was replaced instantly by one of guilt, realizing it most likely had to do with the chaotic life she had dragged her daughter into.

"What is it, honey?" Silas Lovejoy asked as Michelle closed the study door behind them. "I could tell the minute you arrived something was wrong. Your mother noticed it too, I'm sure."

Michelle ran her eyes all around the bookcase-lined room, stalling, trying to decide how to begin. This would shatter his world almost as much as hers — maybe more. She finally dove right in, attempting to recall every word the man had said, even though her mind had been in panic mode.

When she finished, she watched as his face switched from fear to anger, then evolving into an expression she couldn't quite identify. Removing his glasses, he looked down, rubbing his forehead and shaking his head slowly. "No matter what he said," he began, now looking up, "you've got to tell the police. Or *we've* got to tell them."

"But, Dad! I think he meant it. I'm certain they're watching. It wasn't an idle threat."

"Oh, I'm sure you're right. But..." His words were halting. Whatever he was going to say, he obviously didn't want to.

"But what, Dad?" She leaned to look closely into his face. With a deep sigh, Silas Lovejoy sat back in his chair, his body sagging.

"There was a time we didn't contact the police. The results were... horrible."

"What're you talking about?" For a second, she was afraid her news had pushed him over the edge... into a fantasy world. But Silas Lovejoy was not prone to fantasies.

"It was a long time ago. You were about Allison's age, maybe younger."

Michelle shook her head in confusion, hoping for clarification.

He swivelled to look through the window at nothing in particular. "There was a man, a man who lived nearby, an elderly man. He was the kind of person everybody liked, the kind who would do anything to help folks in a bind. Because of that, he was trusted by everyone — until he violated that trust."

"How?" None of this made any sense to her relative to the problem at hand.

He looked sadly at his daughter. "You were always pretty, Michelle, even as a child." Another sigh, this one deeper. "Early one afternoon, while I was still at the office, and your mother was in the living room doing something...sewing, I guess, she heard the back door opening. It had a squeak in the hinges she had tried for months to get me to oil. Thank God I was too lazy to get around to it. She went to check, and saw the man leading you by the hand out the door. She stopped him, but was so shocked, she didn't think about the implications. He apologized for coming in unannounced, saying he was just taking you outside to look at a bird's nest in his back yard. She had her doubts, but accepted his story. He promptly left, appearing embarrassed, according to your mother."

Michelle could only stare; she remembered none of it. But what did it have to do with her current dilemma... or the police?

"When I got home that night, Mary told me about it. I was livid, reading more into it than her. We argued for hours over alerting the police, just as a precaution. In the end, we decided not to. We were young, and perhaps naive. We didn't want to accuse someone so respected of something that might've been evil. From then on, we avoided him, and he avoided us.

"Then, about a month or so later, I'd say, he did the very same thing at another house several blocks away. Only this time, he took the young girl. Took her back to his house, where he did things... things we could only imagine, since she was too young to tell. Her parents were in a panic. They *did* call the police, leading to a neighborhood hunt. Acting on a neighbor's tip that she may have seen him with the girl, they went to his house. The girl was still there. Evidently feeling trapped, the man secluded himself in his bathroom and shot himself. Took his own life."

"Oh my God! The girl?" She was almost afraid to know.

"Other than emotional scars I'm sure she still has, she recovered okay. But the point is, if we'd done the right thing and spoken up, it could've all been avoided."

"But Dad, you don't know that. That was, what, over thirty years ago. Things were different then. The authorities most likely would've only given a warning, since nothing really happened to me." As the words escaped from her mouth, a chill worked its way down her spine. She was thankful she had no recall of her narrow escape — none whatsoever. Maybe she had blanked it out of her memory. Regardless, it did somehow add a new blanket of grief to her miserable situation.

"But don't you see, we can't take that chance with what you're facing," her father countered, a pleading look on his face. "This is now. Things are different these days. We have to talk to them. They'll know what to do."

As Michelle considered the pros and cons of the advice, she posed a stalling question. "Did I know the other girl? Did we grow up together?"

"I don't think you did, and no. The family moved away soon after. Probably to distance themselves from the memory of what happened."

Michelle squeezed her brow with her fingers. "I don't have any memory of any of that at all."

"I'm sure you don't, honey. It probably seemed so innocent to you, it didn't register."

Silas then had a question of his own, evidently wanting to close off his own memories of the event. "You didn't mention the money you'll be receiving to the man, did you?"

"No. I thought that would be dangerous. They would never accept that I have no idea of the source."

"Good. So, will you agree to go to the police with me?"

"When?"

"Now. We can't waste any time."

Succumbing to his wisdom, she agreed. "But you'll have to explain to Mom where we're going. And why. She'll be upset."

"Of course. But she'll find out soon enough anyway."

The matter settled, Silas Lovejoy ushered his wife to a back bedroom to break the news. They emerged minutes later, the woman making little effort to hide her distress. Swallowing-up her daughter in an embrace she didn't want to release, she whispered words of concern and encouragement into her ear. "Silas is right, dear. We can't make the same mistake twice, especially since it involves you and Allison. I'll keep her busy while you're gone."

Leaving the house a few minutes later, Silas admonished Mary not to open the door to anyone until they returned. He accepted Michelle's belief the men were most likely aware of her visit to her parents' home. They would be watching her no matter where she went.

Exiting the driveway, Michelle hunkered down below the window level as her father drove his Buick sedan out of the driveway, not surfacing until he assured her no one was following.

Sunday afternoon proved to be an understandably slow period at the nearest precinct, meaning they were given an audience by the sergeant on duty instead of the precinct captain. He listened patiently to their story, then placed a call to his captain, who recalled the earlier patrols established months earlier to provide protection for the drug dealer's widow when she first returned to Savannah. From their end of the conversation, Silas and Michelle could tell the superior wasn't too crazy about the request, evidently convinced the previous efforts had been a waste of time and taxpayer money. To his credit, the sergeant hung in, apparently struck by the old man's determination, but more so by the pleading look on the gorgeous woman's tormented face. The young officer couldn't remove his eyes from her during the length of the phone call. His points won out, and the two emerged from the small brick complex thirty minutes later with assurances there would be a police presence visible as soon as possible. During the slow drive home, Michelle snuck glances at her father's face, trying to measure his mood. He didn't deserve what she was putting him through. If she'd only listened ten years earlier...

"I'm sorry, Dad, for getting you and Mom involved in all this. It's my problem, not yours."

He took a quick look over at his daughter, then smiled a smile only a doting father could. "Honey, we became involved the second you were born. You should never forget that. Everything since then... well, that's just life happening. It's not always easy."

Fighting back tears, she rubbed his shoulder, then thought about what might lie ahead. She had to admit, she did feel some comfort from the sergeant's actions. It set her mind at work, thinking about someone else she might call, although she had no idea what he could possibly accomplish.

Returning to her apartment later in the afternoon, she was actually surprised to see a patrol car exiting the complex. They were at least in the area. Entering her unit, she flinched when she saw the message light blinking on her machine. Two calls had been recorded. Staring at the device, she couldn't decide whether to listen to the playback or not. Although both calls had the local area code, neither number was familiar to her. If the man had somehow obtained her unlisted number and called, she didn't want to hear his voice.

Making sure Allison was occupied with the dolls she had salvaged from their Atlanta home, Michelle sat with a finger hovering over the playback button. Taking a quick breath, she lowered the volume of the speaker, then pushed the button and listened to the first call.

"Hi, Michelle. It's Royce Glynn. Listen, I got your number from Sandi. Hope that's okay. Just wanted to say again how much I enjoyed Friday night, and getting to know you. Should've called Saturday, but I got busy with weekend patients, and the day kinda got away from me. Hope we can do it again soon. Uh... you're welcome to call me, but if you don't feel comfortable with that, I'll call again later. Thanks." Reciting his number, hr hung up.

On top of the muddled terror she was facing, the call left her with a strange mix of feelings. She *did* want to see him again, but knew it wouldn't be possible until her newest cloud was removed — assuming it ever was. Jotting the phone number down, she stuck it in a drawer. As she did so, she spied the letter from Houston she had placed there after sharing it with her dad Thursday.

She moved on to the second call, which turned out to be not a call at all, but was enough to put her nerves on edge once again. The only sounds she could distinguish were a man's heavy breathing, accompanied by a lighter cough in the background. There was no doubt it was the man in the park, with his sidekick listening in close behind. It was more psychological mind-games, chipping away at her already brittle armor. How did *they* get her unpublished number?! The fact that they had told her all she needed to know about how determined they must be, how threatened her life had become. For a brief moment, she considered taking Allison and heading back to her parents' home. They had tried their best to get them to stay, but she didn't want to stress them any more than she had already.

Quickly erasing both messages, she retreated to her sofa, wrapping her arms around her knees, forming her trembling body into the smallest ball possible. Against the girl's objections, she made Allison go to bed much earlier than usual. She then resumed her Saturday night position on the sofa, butcher knife at the ready. It would be another long night, with even less sleep.

Chapter 14

Walter Church shifted uncomfortably in his chair, taking another look through the window behind the desk facing him. The lightly-tinted glass framed the outside world, where he longed to be at the moment. Anywhere out there would be just fine. The desk before him belonged to Richard Joyner, the senior agent in charge of the Atlanta Regional DEA office. He watched as Joyner's face flared a shade of crimson once again, hearing words neither man would like. The phone etched what appeared to be a permanent place in the wedge formed between his shoulder and ear. He shook his head, giving Church a preview of the results of the conversation. It was the third call the man in charge in so-called Hot-lanta had fielded by 9:30 Monday morning, all involving the men he considered to be two of his top agents.

The first had been from a reporter with *The Atlanta Journal-Constitution*, wanting a reaction to the claims made by the new attorney of Floyd Weathers. The lawyer had wasted no time in arranging a televised press conference to claim injuries to his client due to excessive force applied by DEA agent Walter Church. The former athlete stood next to his mouthpiece-for-hire, holding his shirt up to reveal a red mark for the world to see... no doubt smeared with rouge. The next was from a junior partner of Kevin Shands, having the gall to accuse agent Chris Steen of threatening to shoot his associate as he tried to surrender. There was no doubt in Joyner's mind the two esteemed counselors had compared notes, then synchronized their actions to heap as much misery on the agency as possible.

This second call held little concern for Joyner, knowing it would fizzle out as the facts in the raid on the scumbag attorney's house became known. But the first phone conversation, and the carefully choreographed announcement that led to it were troubling. After all, there *were* noticeable wounds on the former NFL player's body, which he was only too happy to expose to reporters. Weathers qualified as a semi-celebrity, and there were many fans in the Georgia city who worshiped sports heroes over actual role models. The accusations were heading in the direction of the kinds of publicity all federal agencies feared.

The final call was the one Joyner was enduring now, letting his superior in Virginia vent his spleen over the events from his lofty perch hundreds of miles away.

"That's not entirely accurate," Joyner said, managing to slip a word in. "And you're forgetting Weathers fired on our agents first, wounding one."

Joyner closed his eyes, running his free hand through his stubby crewcut, kept short since he'd left the field a few years earlier. He winced as he continued to listen, his argument apparently having little effect. He tried another.

"But, Phil. There wouldn't've been a peep about this if the man hadn't been a sports celebrity. He's taking advantage of his notoriety. And his reputation's been tainted in the past, I might add."

The voice from a command center somewhere outside D. C. could be heard escalating in tone. Church wondered if the man had taken exception to being addressed by his first name. Rank had its privileges... doubly so in federal bureaucracies.

"Yes sir. Yes sir." And then, one last, "Yes sir," as Joyner hung up the phone. Neither man in the modestly-appointed office spoke for a moment, letting the bad vibes settle.

Easily judging the frustration on his boss's face, and sensing what was coming, Church broke the ice. "And all this time, Richard, I thought we were the good guys."

Joyner removed his wire-rimmed glasses, squeezing his eyes shut with his fingers. "I remember when we were, Walt. Seems like a long, long time ago anymore."

Church had listened, trying to exhibit patience, while doing a slow burn deep inside, as the station chief had explained to the voice on the phone how the man had actually impaled himself on the fence post; how his wounds were caused by his own attempt to escape. All to no avail. Facts didn't seem to matter when measured against negative community moods. He appreciated the other man's attempts at lessening whatever was coming. They were contemporaries of sorts, he and Joyner. Both had been candidates for the position of station chief a couple of years earlier, although Church hadn't actively sought it. At the time, he hadn't been so sure he could handle the political bullshit that came with it. Now, he knew without any doubt the right man had the job.

"So, what's it gonna be, Richard?" he asked, knowing some form of atonement was expected. "A pound of flesh? I can accept almost anything, short of you saying they're going to ask the federal attorney to let him walk."

Joyner stared for a beat or two, rocking slowly in his chair. "You really mean that?"

"What? Don't tell me he wants to let him plead down, which is nearly the same as letting him off."

"No, nothing like that. He shot one of our own — a female at that. No way he's not serving time — a *long* time." Joyner rocked a little faster, emitting signs of reluctance in having to give bad news. "Grantham wants you out of the field, wants you to pull desk duty for a few weeks, maybe a month or so."

Church felt the neck hairs under his brown ponytail bristling. It wasn't the worst of possible punishments, but it was humiliating to a veteran agent, and it would go in his permanent file. "Christ, Richard. Don't you think that's a knee-jerk reaction? The guy hasn't even been arraigned yet, but it'll appear the department's admitting *I'm* guilty of something." He took a second to exhale the anger from his system. "That was a clean bust all the way around, and you know it."

"Doesn't make any difference what I know, apparently."

"And that crap about Steen. You've known him almost as long as I have. He's never threatened an unarmed suspect before, even ones like Shands who deserved it."

Joyner gave a thin smile, waving a hand across his desk top. "That's just a smoke screen. Shands probably knows his practice will dry up, even if he gets off. He's tryin' to save face. It'll die down."

The station chief paused before bearing the last tidings. He stared across. "One last thing. I'm sorry, Walt, but I'll have to announce your suspension from field assignments to the media. Grantham insisted. And he may be right. Might be the best way to smooth things over. But you know me well enough that kinda crap wouldn't come from me."

Walter Church *did* know the man across from him well; well enough to trust his sincerity — not that it mattered much under the circumstances. Desk jobs with any law enforcement agency for a field-trained jock were tantamount to insanity. His immediate thought was it might be time for a vacation. But with the cloud hanging over him, it wouldn't be an enjoyable one.

With his penance decided, and with no apparent chance for rebuttal, Church excused himself. He had to remove himself from the man's presence, before he said something he might regret later. Arriving back at his cubicle two floors down, he avoided the questioning stares of Steen, who wheeled his chair out from his desk to get a good look at his partner. Although he had been thankful to be left out of the meeting, he none-the-less felt short changed, sure he had missed something important.

"How'd it go?"

"Well, I've still got my balls, but they're pretty well chewed up." Church did what men do; made it sound worse than it actually was. His partner would expect no less.

"Exactly how chewed?"

"I'm benched for awhile. He wants me outta the field for a while."

"Holy crap! Doesn't sound like Joyner."

"More Grantham than Joyner. Richard didn't have much choice but to go along."

"For how long?" Steen raised his eyebrows.

"Didn't say. Guess he wants to monitor how far Weathers intends to take this. Could be a month or so."

"Well, hell. That stinks." Steen winced, showing sympathy, while a narrow smile indicated he agreed with Church's assessment; it could've been a hell of a lot worse. "Guess I'll have to break in a new runnin' mate. What a hassle."

Church feigned a hurtful scowl as he fell into his chair. "How friggn' inconvenient for you. Don't know how I could've been so thoughtless."

Steen widened his smile, leaning back with his hands clasped behind his head, smoothing out his jet-black ponytail. The contrasting shades of hair color, grown out and ratted-up for undercover assignments, was the only way some agents could distinguish between the partners. There were other obvious differences in the two, but few took the time to notice them. "Say anything about me?"

"You mean, beside the fact you're a flaming asshole?" Church made a show of ignoring his partner, turning his back, shuffling meaningless files on his desk.

"Yeah, besides that. Understand Shands is making like his shit doesn't have an unpleasant odor."

Church helplessly let a grin creep from the corner of his mouth, hiding it from the other man. "Don't sweat it. Joyner thinks that's all for show. I think he's right."

Steen let the news sink in, then the two partners were quiet for a second.

The muted sounds of phones buzzing and other conversations in the open area of their department filled the void. The cubicles spread throughout the large room had sound-absorbing padding, but couldn't eliminate all offending noises.

"Hear anything about Shaw while I was in the principal's office?" Church asked, still without looking at his partner.

"Just that she's in Grady. Be laid-up for a day or two, then home rest for a week. She'll be okay."

Church pursed his lips and nodded. "Good news. Tough way to be broken in, though. We'll have to drop in on her. It seems I'll have plenty of time to check on her progress myself."

"Hope what happened doesn't sour her any on the agency. Taking a shot like that can make you think about other possibilities, especially with her being so young. Could've been a lot worse."

Church thought about it for a second or two. What Steen said was true; Shaw was young, with a lot of living ahead of her; living she could easily do in a safer environment. And it was a rare woman who could stand the nature of the workload the agency had to offer. But she was bright... finished at the head of her class. Plus, she appeared steadfastly committed to the path she had chosen.

"I think she'll be fine," he finally replied.

He rested his elbows on the arms of the chair, looking absently at his desktop with a sinking feeling he would be seeing a lot of it in the coming days, or weeks, or whatever. Pushing his chair back, he said, "I'm going down to Caribou. Clear my head a little."

"Mind company?"

"Was hoping you'd ask."

Five minutes later, they were huddled over a table at Caribou Coffee, a trendy coffee bar a block from their office building on Peachtree Street, just north of the downtown area. It was more-or-less an unofficial satellite office for the various federal agencies housed in their building. The unwelcome humidity of early spring kept them from the inviting patio, preferring the inside a. c.

"Don't let it get you down, partner," Steen said, attempting a toned-down pep talk after they had received their orders and hunkered down at a table. "A couple of months from now it'll only be a memory. We'll be out bustin' down doors, chasing bad guys again."

"Easy for you to say." Church sat slouched in his chair, taking a draw on the black coffee. "You'll be chasing them with somebody else for a while."

The agents were quiet for a moment, staring around at the other mid-morning java drinkers, some reading, some on laptops, some talking loudly on cell phones. What did these people — the civilians — do for a living? Church wondered. But then, here he was in the middle of a workday, so who was he to talk. Besides, there were a few he was able to recognize from other areas of his building, so they weren't all slackers.

"Tell me, Chris, how did things ever get to the point where low-lifes such as Shands and Weathers have so much say in how we do our jobs, and in my case, whether or not we can actually do them?" He made no attempt to conceal his anger and frustration, directing a scowl toward the tinted plate-glass window, which represented the outside, screwed-up world.

Steen shook his head slowly. "No easy answer for that, Walt. Short version is that the criminal justice system has more or less been turned upside down, due to court decisions influenced by lawyers who are willing to talk the longest and loudest to have things go their way. Some of the problem stems, in my view, and you and I have to accept this as truth, from the fact enough innocent people have been tried, and in some cases incarcerated, that it's hard for a judge or jury *not* to view each suspect with more than the normal degree of innocence, no matter how much evidence we... meaning us and the prosecutors... can haul into court." He paused and leaned forward, lowering his voice slightly to avoid being overheard. "And I'm not just talkin' about cases like O. J. There was a little of what I just said in that case, but in my opinion that was more a racial thing involving the L A Police, and the celebrity aspect of it. Been several like that out in Lala land. But the outcome of those did have an affect on other cases. Just enough doubt to start looking at things differently."

Church simply shrugged, not wanting to hear the logic, but silently agreeing with it.

"Makes our job almost futile... even impossible at times."

"I agree. It does. But we've gotta keep at it. Even though it's like keeping those plates spinning on those wooden rods, we've gotta keep enough of them spinning so they don't all crash and break into a million pieces."

Church shook his head and grimaced at his partner's strange way of using metaphor-like comparisons. It was always plain what the man was trying to say, but he chose odd ways to express himself. In this case, he was referring to the never ending, constantly growing war on drugs. Most thought it was a losing proposition; but what was the alternative?

Sensing it was a good time to change the subject, Steen asked, "What're you goin' to do? Got any time saved up?"

"Right. Might take some. Don't want to leave you hanging, though. What's pressin' now?"

"Only thing on the immediate horizon is that nest up in Doraville. But it's been there so long, and grown so large, we need to plan our attack on a bigger scale than we've been talking about. May take a while, but it's not going anywhere. Still be there when you get back. Then there's the tip we got about the shipment coming our way from Jacksonville, but as you know, the details have been sketchy so far. Guess what I'm tryin' to say is we can manage without you for a little while."

The mention of the Florida city stirred up memories of a large drug buy the two agents had been involved in the previous year— the largest of their careers. It had been thwarted, and the impression had been that activity in Jacksonville had been put to bed as a result. Evidently, another player had managed to put things together in northeast Florida.

Church mulled his options for a minute. He had no idea what he'd do with his time off. He had no hobbies — his work was his hobby, but the thought of being a desk-jockey seemed a slow death. Travel might be nice; maybe a trip to the mountains of Tennessee, drop in to see his folks in that arca. He was way overdue.

"I'll give it some thought," he finally said. Seeing Steen's blank stare, he realized he was actually talking to himself. He stopped talking and raised his cup.

They discussed whatever else they could come up with, drained their coffee, then headed back to the office.

Chapter 15

The two DEA agents had barely settled back in to their respective cubicles, adjusting to the constant drone of the department noise, when a voice could be heard a few desks away repeating Church's name, interrupting his muddled thoughts about his immediate future. "Hold on, I'll transfer you," the voice said.

His phone buzzing, Church picked up. "Church," he answered curtly, and with no enthusiasm, half-expecting a rogue reporter to have somehow snuck through the system, seeking a comment on Weathers' claim of abuse.

There was a pause before the caller said anything, then a thin female voice spoke haltingly. "Uh... Agent Church?"

A sliver of recognition from the past, but not too far back. "Yes. This is Walter Church." His mind was busy assimilating tones... inflections. Somehow the combination was pleasant, but he couldn't put them together.

"I have a card you left with me," the woman said before hesitating again.

"You may not remember me. My name is Michelle Frapiana. You and another agent came to talk to me last year. In Savannah."

Church felt a current of electricity, more like a thunderbolt, rushing through his body, an undeniable, exhilarating tweak to his memory banks. "Of course. How are you, Mrs. Frapiana?" But he knew without a reply she wasn't doing well. Otherwise — no call. Answering the call as abruptly as he had hadn't helped any. Having announced the woman's name, he became aware that Steen's gaze suddenly swivelled in his direction. He could feel the stare boring in.

"Fine... well, really not exactly fine. Something you said when you were here last August, or maybe September, I can't recall exactly when now."

The woman's voice sounded desperate — stressed. He paused a second; she seemed to be having a hard time putting her thoughts into words, so he gave her a little time.

When she didn't speak, he did. "Oh? What was it we said?"

"That someone might come looking for the money my husband stole. The money that went missing in Florida."

Church sucked in air, waiting for the punch line he knew was coming. "Yes?"

"They're here."

Chapter 16

Church felt his body instantly tensing, legs beginning to tighten, a condition that usually occurred when he faced sudden stress. Phone calls representing impending danger were nothing new in his life as a DEA agent, some ultimately leading to scenes representing the worst of human decay, all due to the massive, illegal drug trade. Wasted bodies, broken families, and even death sometimes came with the territory. In the usual case, such calls would put his sensory mechanisms on alert, a strange feeling of hopeful excitement taking form, anticipating the hunt. As dreary as the job could be, he found it satisfying, and was the reason he would miss it during his forced Purgatory. The irony instantly struck him that it had been those very senses he had felt when leading his team to expose the large cocaine operation in which the woman's husband had been a major player.

But this call was different. He could still see the devastation in the woman's otherwise beautiful face, and the innocence she portrayed during the interview he and Steen had conducted. The agents had left her parents' home in Savannah that day satisfied she knew nothing of her husband's murderous crime spree, or the money that disappeared with him. Now, gripping the receiver tightly, his only thought was a strong feeling of dread for her safety.

"Take a deep breath, and tell me exactly what happened."

A sigh led off. "This weekend, Saturday afternoon, my daughter and I were in a city park, killing time before going home. Two men suddenly appeared, almost out of nowhere. One hovered near my daughter, like a threat, while the other made me sit on a bench with him." She had to stop; a choking sound accompanied her recall.

"It's okay," Church said, leaning close in to the receiver. "Take your time."

She collected herself, cleared her throat. "He said he knew I had the money Dickie stole, and he wanted it. I told him... like I told you when you were here... I don't have it, that I know nothing about it."

Church could feel Steen's eyes staying on him. He tried to shift away from his glare.

"And I'm sure he didn't believe you."

"No. Not at all. He said he would be back to see me. Said I should see how easy they could get to me... and Allison, my daughter." Light sobbing sounds were now beginning.

"So they simply left?" Church could tell from the brief delays in her answers, and the lack of clarity in the connection, she was on a cell phone. Probably felt safer.

"Yes. But he said they'd come back. I'm terrified they will."

They definitely will, Church thought to himself. "What did they look like?"

"The big one, the one sitting next to me, was Mexican, I think, or maybe from some other Central or South American country. He spoke decent English, but with a pretty thick Hispanic accent."

"And the other?"

"He looked different. Smaller, blond. He never spoke, at least, not to me, so I never heard his voice. He did say something to Allison, but she said he sounded like anybody else, so I don't know about his accent. But he could pass for American, going by looks."

The "Mexican" description was troubling. The drug cartels south of the border were brutal — violent. So much so, he had to wonder why the men backed off so easily. They weren't known to be the patient sort. "You're still in Savannah, I assume."

"Yes. It didn't seem like there was anywhere else for us to go after what happened in Florida."

"I understand. Have you spoken to the police?"

Another sigh, this one deeper. "Yes. The man warned me not to, but my father insisted. They said they'd assign a patrolman to monitor my apartment for a few days and nights, and I have seen them a couple of times." She paused, picking her words. "When I first came home, last year, they were good about having patrols out all the time. But after a few months, I think they just got tired of it. Guess they felt it wasn't necessary, and I can see their side. But now..." The sentence didn't need finishing.

Yes. But now. Church leaned back, rubbing the back of his neck, trying to think things through. She interrupted his thoughts.

"Oh yes, they... I mean the big man... said something else that sounded strange."

The way she drew the words out activated his antennae. "Something strange?"

"Yes. About Brent Musso. You may not recall, but he was the man I mentioned to you that made sure we were on our way to Savannah before Dickie returned to Destin. He introduced us to the couple from Tennessee that actually brought us here."

"I remember him. What about him?" Church sat up straight.

"He said he knew that Brent was with Dickie when he died at that marina, but I told him that couldn't be. He had left for Texas long before the shooting, and a full day before *we* left. He insisted I was wrong about that. But I *know* I'm right."

"Wait. Are you saying they knew his name? Who he was?" His antennae stretched another few inches. In their talks with her the previous year, they had agreed *not* to broadcast Musso's name, something she had begged them not to do, for his protection. How could these men know his identity?

"I'm sorry. No. They didn't know his name, they weren't even sure if the person was male or female, just that *someone* was with Dickie. I told them it was Brent... Mr. Musso, but that *he* was wrong about him being there."

So she didn't know about Musso's deeds. Somehow, the cartel *did* know, or at least suspected there was someone else involved. At that moment, Church realized there were many questions still unanswered, but now was not the time to address them.

He decided not to respond to her view of what the man had told her. It would be impossible to explain over the phone. He needed to think. A question did occur to him. If she had been so worried about Musso's identity last year, why had she given up his name to these men? The only answer was she knew of the poor guy's fate. He interrupted his own meandering thoughts to respond.

"I see. Are you calling from a cell phone?"

"Yes. I'm afraid to use my home phone. I'm afraid they'll get my number, although it's unlisted. In fact, there was a message left yesterday... well, not really a message. Just somebody breathing heavily before hanging up. So they may already have it."

She was learning quickly. "Maybe, or maybe not. But you're thinking right. Give me your cell number. I'll call you back within ten minutes."

"What for? I'm really not sure why I called you in the first place, and I'm sorry for bothering you with this. Guess I thought you might have advice about how to deal with people like this." But she read him her number quickly anyway.

"It's no bother. Just give me a few minutes, I need to give this some thought." He hung up before she could respond, then sat and thought about her last comment. *"How to deal with people like this*". She had no idea what dealing with them meant.

Without looking, Church knew his partner was continuing to bore a hole into the side of his head.

"What's going on, Walt?"

Still deep in thought, Church gave his partner a sideways look. "That was Michelle Frapiana, Dickie Frapiana's widow. You remember her."

Steen answered showing a sarcastic-looking grin. "I got that part, genius. What I mean is, what did she want?"

Church now looked straight at his partner. "Somebody's come lookin' for the money her husband stole. Sounds like a cartel bounty hunter."

"Christ. What happened?"

"Evidently nothing. They said they knew she had it, and they wanted it. She tried to convince them she had no idea about it. They didn't believe her, but they left."

"They just left?" Steen was equally puzzled.

"Said one was Mexican-looking. Or something like that."

"Crap. That's not good. Could be the cartel Carlos Medina belonged to."

Church nodded, but didn't respond. His mind was twisting in several directions, trying to home in on a decision.

"What was the other thing she asked about?" Steen asked, rubbing a hand across week-old stubble. "Who was the 'him' you mentioned? As if I didn't know."

"Brent Musso, the guy from Houston. The man that did all the talking told her they knew Musso was on the pier with Dickie when he took the bullets. She told him no way, but the man insisted."

Steen blew out a sigh, calculating what was coming, hoping he was wrong. "But you didn't set her straight just then, did you? And you also didn't tell her the Musso guy was dead. May I ask... why?" He quickly raised both hands, waving them back and forth before his partner could answer. "Never mind. You don't have to answer that. You didn't tell her then because you plan to tell her in person. Am I right?"

Church could only stare in Steen's general direction, glassy-eyed. "Maybe."

Steen leaned in close to the other man, zeroing-in, wanting his full attention. "Walt, please tell me you're not thinkin' what I'm thinkin' you're thinkin'."

"She might need help, Chris."

"Hell, partner. Aren't you in enough trouble already? Besides, we have a satellite office in Savannah. Let them handle it."

"From what I know of their operation, it's a two-man shop, working out of what amounts to a closet. And this doesn't fall under our normal duties. There's no drug operation here — nobody dealing or buying. This just involves protecting someone." He was aware his argument was coming across as grasping at thin straws. The matter settled in his mind, he was searching for rationale that would fit his purposes.

"Walt, I remember how the woman looked, how impressed you were with her. Aren't you afraid you're letting your libido get you *too* involved? I mean personally?"

The all-too accurate remark brought the first sharp reply. "Give me a little credit, Chris," he said emphatically. "Don't you think there might've been more we could've done last year in providing protection. We pretty much left her high and dry."

When his partner didn't immediately respond, Church thought for a second about mentioning Steen's marriage that had gone south a couple of years back, and that his opinion of his evolving plans to help the woman in Savannah might be tied up with his current view of women in general, based on the breakup. The two agents had talked things out several times over salted-in-the-shell peanuts and late night beers at Manuel's, their east Atlanta bar-of-choice, during one of such conversations, Steen had pointed out it was no coincidence "acrimony" rhymed with "alimony". Church thought better of it, swallowing the idea of bringing up the bitter memories.

"So you're feeling a touch of guilt," Steen finally said. "I get that. But what is it exactly you think you can do?"

Church softened his tone, gazing down at his hands clinched tightly in his lap. "I'm not sure, Chris. I won't know 'til I get there."

Steen simply stared for a second, then spit out the first thing that came to mind.

"Dumb-ass."

"Smart-ass."

"Half-ass."

"No-ass."

Unsure if the last foray was intended as an insult or not, and with the immediate topic having being exhausted, Steen continued to stare. "So, you've already decided. Anything I can say to talk you out of it, convince you it's a major mistake?"

Rubbing his calloused hands across his knees briskly, Church didn't answer directly, choosing instead to voice his plans. "I've got three weeks of leave built up. Rather spend it trying to be useful than sit here and develop hemorrhoids. And if I'm gonna do it, I've gotta leave now. Those guys are probably planning to make their next move as we speak."

Church quickly reached for the phone, dialing Joyner's office. The man had stepped out, so he left a message with his assistant stating his intentions for a last minute vacation, hanging up quickly before repercussions could flow downhill. Time-off not requisitioned in advance wasn't appreciated by federal law enforcement agencies. Hopefully, his banishment from the field would raise fewer eyebrows in regard to his absence.

Observing his partner of seven years busying himself gathering-up a few items he planned to take with him, and shaking his head with dismay, Steen could only watch as DEA Agent Walter Church begin a step that could threaten his career. He wanted to point out that no woman was worth the risk, but evidently thought better of it, sure that Church would bring up his *own* dirty laundry, which still had a lingering, foul odor about it.

"Later, partner," Church said, giving a nod as he left the bull ring.

Steen stopped him with a parting comment. "Hey, Walt. I think... no... I *know* this is a huge mistake. But if you get your ass in a bind, you know where to reach me."

Answering with a nod, the agent headed for the stairwell, forsaking the elevator. Even the added seconds of waiting for the lift seemed like time he didn't have to waste.

Stepping into the still muggy, overcast morning, he quickly returned to the nearby coffee house, this time setting up shop on the patio for privacy. Pulling out the notepad he had recorded her number on minutes earlier, he dialed Michelle Frapiana's cell with his own.

"What's your address?" he asked as soon as she answered.

"My address? Why?"

"I think you need more help than the local police."

She hesitated. "Are you saying you're coming to Savannah?"

"Yes. And if you have a job, give me that address too."

She gave him both, then paused again. "Are you sure you want to do this? I thought, from your comments last year, the DEA couldn't provide protection."

"The Agency can't. I'm doing this on my own. Can't promise how much help I'll be, but I can try."

For a second, he thought she was going to object to his offer, but the weight and helplessness of her situation had evidently broken whatever resistance she might have. “Do you know Savannah?” she asked.

“I’ve been there. I’ll find my way around.”

“Well, okay. And thanks.”

“Don’t thank me yet. I haven’t done anything yet. And don’t answer your home phone if you get there before I arrive. Do you have caller I D, or an answering machine?”

“Both.” She thought once more about the non-call from the night before.

“Use them to screen your calls. And keep your cell phone powered-up and with you at all times.”

Hanging up for the second time, Church glanced at his watch; eleven twenty-five; he needed to get going. Hurrying to the parking garage for his vehicle, he was all too aware of the fact he had committed himself to going out on a limb that could easily snap beneath him. He knew everything Steen had said was correct. But the Houston stock broker’s job of protecting the woman from the trauma of her husband’s world had only delayed the inevitable; maybe he could extend things, or even end them. He only hoped he would have a job waiting when he returned.

Chapter 17

The noon-hour lethargic pace of traffic heading east on Ponce De Leon Avenue did nothing to erase Church's angst, knowing valuable time was being stolen. There was no choice in his route; it was the only way to North Highland Avenue without getting stuck on cramped side streets. The delay meant un-wanted time to consider once more what he was doing. The echoes of Steen's warnings were still fresh. A new thought entered his mind, one involving his partner. While the mission he was undertaking was his own idea, it could easily have repercussions for his fellow agent, causing him collateral harm. Questions would be raised, especially if his efforts failed: why didn't you stop him?; why didn't you at least tell higher-ups what he was doing?; and the things he took with him, they were government property. Boiling it all down, there was no excuse for his actions, other than the fact he was human, with emotions and longings... however misguided they might be... just like anyone else.

Shaking the thoughts from his brain, while cursing the slow moving bus ahead, he pictured her beautiful but tortured face again. *He had to at least try.*

Pulling his GMC Yukon to a stop in front of his North Highland Avenue townhouse condo five minutes later, not taking time to negotiate the narrow alley behind, where he normally parked, he hurried toward the front door. North Highland was in the center of an aging area east of downtown Atlanta, referred to as Virginia-Highlands, an area attempting the labored process of re-establishing itself as a trendy neighborhood, a flashback to its appeal in the early part of the twentieth century. It suited him, being fairly close-in to his base of operations. Plus, the lure of the rebirth project worked on him. When he'd been re-assigned to Atlanta from the battle ground along the Rio Grande River over a decade earlier, it seemed the ideal place to settle in order to regain some semblance of a normal life, to reconnect with humanity again.

Unlocking the front door, taking a step inside, his key chain hadn't made it back to his pocket before he was struck in the mid-section by a fierce body blow. A dark missile — a compact seventy pounds of well toned muscle, was quickly all over him, slobbering with excitement and affection.

"Down, Char," he commanded, pushing the animal away. The excited dog responded by placing his front paws on Church's chest, sniffing around his shirt pocket for a treat that didn't exist this time. Escaping the onslaught, Church bounded quickly upstairs to his bedroom to get the few things he would need. The dog followed, taking his position on the bed, watching with panting anticipation.

A two-year old black lab, Char was a rescue from an animal shelter, adopted when he was six months old. Actually, he wasn't entirely black, the

Stansky, flipped his welder's mask up, then turned.

"Hi', Walt." The man extinguished the welding torch, placing it on a table supported by two saw horses. "What brings you home this time of day?"

Church snuck a glance at the man's project, appearing to be a young boy riding a bicycle. The man could fashion works of art from anything of a metallic nature, a talent envied by his left-brained neighbor, or was it right-brained?

"Got to make a short, unexpected trip. Had to come home to pack." He took a closer look at the other man's work. "Looks like you've outdone yourself this time, Elliot. Very impressive."

Stansky examined the sculpt critically, as if seeing it for the first time. "Nah. Wheels aren't round enough. Gotta work on it some more."

Church shook his head. "If you say so. Looks fine to me."

The other man removed the mask completely from his head, wiping away beads of sweat.

"What about Char?"

"Well, I was wondering if..."

"Say no more, Walt. Send that bad boy on over when you're ready." A smile sprouted under Stansky's ratty grey moustache.

"Thanks, Elliot. Shouldn't be more'n a couple of days."

"Where to? Or is this one of those secret missions?"

"Not this time. Actually something more of a personal nature." Church rolled his wrist to read the watch he wore when he could remember to strap it on — almost 12:30 p m. He felt the day was rushing by like a freight train. "Listen, Elliot. I've got to hit the road. You know where the key is. Can you just let yourself in to get his food and water bowl?"

"Sure thing, Walt. I'll come over and get him when I come to a stoppin' point. Better that way anyhow. I think my welding sparks kinda upset the old boy."

Church thought about that for a second, sure that the dog's reaction had something to do with his past.

"Okay. And thanks, Elliot."

"Anytime. Oh, okay if I take him out to Piedmont Park later today?"

"Sure. He'd love to run for a while. Leash is hanging on back door knob... usual place."

"Good enough. We'll be fine."

Within a few minutes, Church had his GMC Yukon negotiating the frustrating traffic once more, looking for the closest entrance ramp to I-75 south, the first leg of the route he had chosen to Savannah. There were two ways to go to reach the Georgia city to the southeast, only one of which made sense to him: I-20 east to Augusta, located on the border of South Carolina, then a series of state highways south that would take forever; or I-75 south to Macon, dead in the center of the state, then merging onto I-16 for a direct line into Savannah. Neither route was quick, or exciting, but at least the latter was interstate all the way. He steeled himself for the drive alone, hoping apprehension and adrenalin would keep him alert.

Chapter 18

Michelle punched the button ending the cell phone call. The DEA agent had hung up without giving her a chance to find out what his plans are. She again wondered if her desperation was giving her false hopes. Easing her way out of the cramped supply room in the rear of Liberty Lady, she glanced at her watch. Eleven-thirty. Counting the time she had waited for the DEA agent to call back, she had been in seclusion for close to half an hour. Mentioning to Sandi she needed to make a personal call, she had never intended to stay sequestered that long. Simply making the call had required an entire morning of mind-changes. She had started toward the back room at least three times earlier; so often she was sure Sandi must think she had something sinister going on in there. Each time, she had chickened out, deciding it was crazy to bother the DEA agent.

Her boss eyed her closely as she made her way to the store front. From the knowing grin on the other woman's face, Michelle was sure Sandi thought she was returning Royce's call. A relay message had no doubt made its way from the dentist to Jeff, then on to the match-maker, passing along that a phone call had been attempted over the weekend. It was as if matching the two together had become the book store owner's only reason for being; an obsession she wouldn't let go of.

As well-intentioned as the woman was, Michelle was in no mood for talks of potential romance, having already spent an awkward half-hour earlier in the morning at Allison's preschool. Explaining to the administrator and her daughter's teacher why it was vitally important for no one other than she or her parents to be allowed to pick the child up, without giving the entire reason, had been a challenge. Thankfully, Allison's teacher was quick enough to read between the lines, giving private assurances it would be taken care of. Somehow, the stout, pleasant woman seemed to be able to grasp Michelle's precarious situation with a minimum amount of questions. Even with those promises in hand, it was doubly tough leaving her daughter behind, more so than on any other day.

Sleep had been impossible to come by Sunday night, leaving her body constantly exhausted; nerves on edge. In spite of it all, there was a sense of security within the book store, a sanctuary of sorts where she felt protected from the evil residue of her husband's dark life. Ratcheting up a confident smile, she decided to face Sandi head-on, give her the disappointing news.

"Sorry I took so long, Sandi. Had to get something straightened out at school." The best lie she could come up with.

"Oh. No problem," Sandi replied, having to adjust her grin. "Just thought it might be something else."

Noticing the look of disappointment, Michelle laid it out. "I know you know Royce called me yesterday. I was with my parents all day, so we missed connections. We'll make contact soon enough."

"Sure, sweetie." Sandi searched her friend's expression closely, started to add more, then apparently decided to leave well enough alone. "Okay, troops," she said instead, "let's get ready for our signing tomorrow." By troops, she referred to Michelle and the only other employee in the store, Mandy Russell, the second part-time worker. Fred Huth had a full class load on Mondays, so preparations would be handled by the women. Mandy was a newly-wed, and an avid reader. She had been one of Liberty Lady's best customers before being hired, now searching for extra money to furnish the house she and her new husband were planning to buy soon.

Getting ready for the book signing didn't actually involve much effort, the only physical part being unpacking the forty books the author had shipped to the store in advance, stacking a few on the counter near the register. Recognizing the appeal that applied to only a few ardent readers, all nature lovers, Sandi fully expected the *Birds of the Okefenokee*, the book illustrating a collection of photographer Justin Fortson's nature photos, would sell less than half that number. It would then be up to her and the photographer to wrangle over how many extras she would keep on hand for possible future sales, and how many he would take back. Since she split the proceeds of the sales with authors on a forty/sixty basis, it was always a sticky moment, sometimes causing hard feelings.

Other than unpacking, the only other chore was setting up the pricing in her register to record the sales. On Tuesday, before the 4:00 p. m. signing, the store owner would make sure coffee, wine, and cheese samplings were in place to entice shoppers.

Monday then soon fell into its usual pattern, with customers coming in and out of the store, most simply browsing. Michelle summoned up her best efforts to treat the day as any other. From time to time as the hours drifted away, she considered bringing her best friend into her little world of misery, but chose not to. She knew without question, Sandi would be supportive, offering whatever she could to help — possibly even time off. But this is where she needed to be; a place to stay busy, keep her mind off the many unpleasant things that could easily spring to mind. And there was no point in putting the other woman on a downer also. Thoughts of Allison were impossible to dismiss, as she took occasional glances through the front window to survey for danger signs. The girl's safety was the overriding factor in all scenarios playing out in her brain, though her own safety was important too.

She stayed in for lunch, digging in to her brown bag, accompanied by bottled water kept in the tiny fridge in the rear of the store. The park was off-limits for the time being. In fact, she felt it might forever harbor haunted memories.

Early afternoon found Michelle stuck between two bookshelves with a customer, answering question after question about a book she knew nothing about. The elderly woman seemed intent on impressing the attractive young woman with her knowledge of the latest work of an author who had written a series of novels involving a heroine whose exploits were set in western mountain ranges. Michelle had indeed read one, several years earlier, but had all but forgotten the plot line, and was definitely not an expert on the female writer's collection. The customer appeared surprised that an employee of a book store was not familiar with the subject matter of *each and every* bound copy lining the shelves in the establishment. Politely demurring to the older woman, she held her own, while beginning to wonder if the lady was actually going to buy the book, or simply be satisfied with demonstrating her vast wisdom.

Michelle couldn't help letting her mind drift, becoming aware of the sounds of voices belonging to other customers who had made their way into the store. She silently wished she could walk away and help any one of them. As if in answer to a prayer, Mandy Russell suddenly entered the aisle, leaning a hand on a shelf to support her trim body. She had one of her easy grins on her freckled face, waiting for an opportunity to break in. When the elderly woman took a breath, she managed, "Sorry to interrupt, Michelle, but there's a gentleman here who wants you to wait on him."

Hoping to keep her grateful smile hidden from the "fountain of knowledge", she answered as calmly as possible, "As soon as I've helped this nice woman." She crossed her eyes and gave Mandy a far-too-wide grin, hidden from the customer, trying to send a message. The younger girl had to cover her mouth with a hand.

"That's okay, my dear," the woman said. "I'll just browse for awhile. I can find what I want on my own." Her tone gave the impression the employee had been of little use.

Giving Mandy a pat of thanks on a shoulder as she exited the stacks, Michelle looked around for the customer who had asked for her. At first she saw no one, then her eyes came to rest on a man leaning over a table of books near the front. All she could see was a pair of thin legs in faded denim jeans. His back was to her. As she approached, he began to straighten up, allowing her a view of a shock of blond hair.

She began to slow her pace as something took on a familiar, unsettling look, then froze as the store started to cave in around her.

The man who had stood guard menacingly over Allison in the park Saturday — had it only been Saturday? — turned and gave her a disarming smile, revealing perfect teeth. Still ten feet from the man, she wanted to go no nearer. She could feel the color draining from her face, her legs changing to jelly. Helplessness and rage came together at once, but neither could shake her from her paralysis. At least able to use her eyes, she scanned the windows to locate the other man, failing to spot him.

Realizing she wasn't going to come any closer, Cesar Javier picked up a book, then approached. "Mrs. Frapiana. Nice to see you again. Could you please help me with this book?" he said loudly, in perfect English. He was within a few feet of her now, holding the book up as if he really had questions. Taking darting glances behind her, he satisfied himself no one was eavesdropping.

She didn't answer at first, letting her mind rush through all possible things she could do, or say. Taking her own hurried look back, trying to maintain some composure, she also recognized that she and the man were being ignored. She was on her own. Finally, through clinched teeth, she whispered, "What do you want?"

He smiled warmly, as if talking to an old friend, then replied with an even tone. "You know what I want, Mrs. Frapiana. The same thing my friend wants. The money your husband stole."

"How many times do I have to tell you? I don't have your money." Her voice had risen to a higher level than she intended, her anger getting the best of her. Catching herself, she toned it down again. "And I know *nothing* about it. You have to believe me."

Javier's toothy smile seemed to be cemented in place. "I simply *don't* believe you, Mrs. Frapiana... may I call you Michelle?" When she didn't answer, he added, "And my friend doesn't believe you either, Michelle. And *that* is what you should worry about."

"I can't help that. I can't help what you believe... or don't believe." Somehow, she was gaining a degree of confidence, which she was certain had a lot to do with not feeling as threatened by this man as the other. She took another look outside, just in case.

The man followed her gaze for only a second, then looked back. "Oh, he's not out there now. My friend is busy checking out the charms of your lovely city. Right now... I believe... yes, he is keeping an eye on your daughter's school, making sure no one who would do her harm tries to take her."

Michelle had to lean a hand on a nearby table, her legs were of no use now. She summoned up just enough volume to say, "Please don't hurt her. Do what you want with me, but she's not..." Unable to continue, her voice tailed off. Her father's story from the day before came rushing back.

Javier ignored her, making a show of thumbing through the book. He actually had no idea what the book was about, or even the title. He then stared at her. "By the way, Michelle," he said, placing emphasis on her name, "my friend is also very angry that you have involved the police. You were warned not to."

The comment caused her to take a deep breath. She now knew they definitely were watching, probably all the time. Finding new momentum, she responded as forcefully as she could. "I don't give a damn *what* he told me. I'm going to protect myself, and my daughter."

The man now turned on a sinister, evil smile, evidently enjoying her defiance. "Oh yes, your daughter is certainly worth protecting. What a beautiful little girl. I enjoyed my chat with her the other day. It would be a shame to see something happen to her. But you see, my friend and I are very different. I am a very peaceful man. I don't wish to cause harm to anyone, especially children." He shook his head slowly to show empathy... the smile vanished. "However, my associate is not like that." He leaned in close to whisper through his pearly whites. "If I told you what I have seen men like him do to people — men, women, and children — well, I would rather not say. But I *can* say there is nothing he will not do to anyone who stands in his way."

Some of her resolve instantly evaporated; she believed what he was saying. She had seen into the other man's eyes, seen the deadness there. Unable to keep the tremor from her voice, she said, "I'm not standing in his way. Why won't you listen to me?"

"We're listening, Michelle. We're just not getting the right answers."

Michelle heard footsteps on the wood-plank floor coming in their direction. Sandi! For her friend's own sake, she needed to get rid of him. "Please, you've got to leave. I can't help you."

Noticing the other woman drawing near, Cesar Javier tossed the book back on the nearest table, not bothering to return it to the one he had taken it from. "Don't think I want this book after all," he said loudly. " Doesn't have the information I wanted. So long, for now, Michelle. See you soon." Blowing an air kiss in her direction, he turned to walk casually through the front door, setting off the chiming bells. For some strange reason which made so sense under the circumstances, she noticed his swaying hips produced something short of a manly stride.

Michelle stared at the door as it closed behind him, unable to move. She then felt the presence of Sandi standing next to her.

"Hell, I guess when it rains it pours," the auburn-haired woman said, nudging her friend's shoulder playfully.

"Huh? What?"

"You've been holding out on me, sweetie. Who's the golden hunk?"

Michelle had to think fast. Her friend's mistaken assumption generated a sudden queasiness in the pit of her stomach. "It's... it's not what you think, Sandi. He's just somebody I met. No big deal."

Sandi eyed the other woman closely, beginning to pick up on the negative vibes. Her face was ashen; a slight tremble was evident in her body. "What is it, honey? You look like you've seen a ghost."

Michelle's mind was hard at work, creating a believable story. "I met him through someone in my apartment complex. I guess he thought he knew me better than he really does. He got a little fresh. That's all."

The book store owner continued to stare. She came close to mentioning that Michelle had never talked about meeting anyone where she lived. In fact, she had made it a point to avoid everyone, due to her clouded history. Deciding it might come across as an interrogation, she let it drop. Placing a hand on the arm of her friend of over twenty years, she said, "Well, he's gone now, so the hell with him. Come on. Let's get ready for Mr. Fortson's visit tomorrow."

"Sure."

Following Sandi slowly to the store's interior, Michelle angled a last look through the windows. She saw nothing. Nothing — other than a dark, terrifying world, ready to tear the lives of her and her daughter to shreds. In fact, it already had.

Chapter 19

Angel Xminez was a quiet man... a patient man, perfectly willing to sit for hours without uttering a word. Silence was golden to his way of thinking, and it bothered him to have someone chattering away like his companion on this trip continued to do. The trim blond man, with the effeminate vibes, was driving him nuts.

He shoved a new stick of gum into his mouth, then absentmindedly folded the wrapper neatly as always, before dropping it into his shirt pocket. There it would remain until he would use it later to hold the twisted residue after being chewed into nothingness. The whole process was by reflex, a habit by now. As habits go, it was benign. There *were* worse habits: smoking; drinking to excess; unhealthy diets — none of which he practiced. Killing was another sometime habit. And at this, he was proficient.

On assignments such as the one that had brought him to Savannah, a city he never expected to visit, and hoped to never again, the willingness to kill without a second thought was very useful, although Luis Torres had cautioned him against using violence, at least unless absolutely necessary. That warning was becoming harder to heed by the day. Cesar Javier would be first on his list if he didn't shut his fucking mouth.

It was now mid-Monday afternoon. He and Javier had been in the sleepy southern town since Friday, with nothing to show for it, other than locating the woman. He wanted to make a move; either snatch the daughter, or maybe her parents — anything to make their target break down. The visit to the book store two hours earlier had surely shaken her world, but still had produced no results. He had sent Javier into the book store, knowing his own appearance would raise red flags. In his entire sordid, violent life, he had never had reason to set foot inside a book store, and his awkwardness would've stood out like a bull in a china shop. Now, as he considered the two confrontations with Michelle Frapiana, he knew more drastic moves were needed.

As if reading the monstrous man's thoughts, Javier ceased talking long enough to stare across the front seat of the rental car. They were parked a block away from the entrance to Frapiana's apartment complex, with the large, frightening man behind the wheel. They observed as the patrol car rotated in and out of the complex parking lot from time to time, making only a brief, cursory show of monitoring the situation.

"You know, Angel," Javier said, shifting his body sideways to ward off possible repercussions. What he was going to say wouldn't be welcomed, but shouldn't bring blows. But you never knew with the big man. "I'm startin' to think maybe the woman doesn't know anything. Just like she says. I don't picture her the type to stand up under much pressure, especially with her daughter at stake."

Xminez didn't answer right away, but absorbed what the other man said as perhaps having a layer of truth. He judged the mettle of Frapiana the same way. She would gladly give up secrets if it meant saving her life, or more certainly, that of the child. But it didn't really matter one way or the other to him. The woman, the child, and even the grandparents were nothing more than items to check off from his shopping list. Whether she was hiding the $16 million or not, he wouldn't hesitate to waste them all if the mood struck him, regardless of Torres' warnings.

He glanced down at the time on the Samsung's screen, preferring its accuracy over his watch. The patrol car was exiting the lot once more... right on schedule. Twenty minutes between drive-throughs. Still not answering the other man's comment, he turned to another troubling thought. Torres was becoming impatient as well. He was aware of their progress, or lack of progress, by a steady stream of text messages back and forth. From the words the cartel leader had used, it was clear he was unhappy with the pace of things. He wanted answers. He wanted his money.

Javier couldn't deal with the man's silence any longer. He spoke up again. "Say, Angel. Did you ever think that if we don't come back with the money soon, Torres may send somebody after us? You know as well as I the man doesn't trust anyone."

"What?" The dark assassin glared at the little man. His words had struck a chord. That possibility *hadn't* occurred to him... at least, not consciously. "Are you loco, Cesar?"

"Just think about it. He might think we have found the money, and decided to keep it for ourselves." He paused for a second. "And why should he believe us even if we go home empty-handed. He could still think we found his millions and hid it somewhere in the U. S., planning to come back and recover it later."

Xminez shifted again uncomfortably in the car seat, the vinyl sagging beneath his bulk. The things Javier had mentioned made more sense than he wanted to admit. If they didn't deliver the money, they might be walking into Torres' death trap. And he was well aware there were other hit men at Torres' disposal, maybe not as resourceful as him, however equally brutal. Things had to be brought to a head, one way or the other.

"Give me the gun," he said, holding out a meaty hand. "And keep your ideas to yourself."

Javier hesitated for a dangerous second. "What... what're you thinking about?" The smaller man's face registered sudden fear, belying the existence of a thrill hidden deep in his belly. Angel X's dormant thunder was emerging, creating what could only be described as a tantalizing rush.

"Just hand me the gun and keep quiet."

The trim blond man did as he was told, reaching for the glove compartment.

Officer Jerrod Murphy pulled the black and blue Savannah Police Department cruiser to a slow stop, choosing to find a resting point this time. He would pause for only a few minutes. The other five times he'd entered the parking lot, he had simply circled through slowly, never coming to a complete halt. This was horseshit, a monumental waste of time. He'd been assigned to the earlier detail months ago, keeping watch on the woman's parents' home. That assignment had lasted a month or so, and he and the others slotted for it had breathed a collective sigh of relief when it was finally called off. The only two redeeming aspects had been the time spent on the patrol kept him away from the more dicey duties in the seedier parts of town, plus a chance now and then to view the fantastic looking Frapiana woman.

Savannah was basically viewed as a benign city... crime-wise, with a reputation filled with history, well-kept parks, tourist attractions, including several nationally famous restaurants, and possessing an overall genteel lifestyle. A silky-smooth, lazy existence, with a somewhat mysterious, spiritual ambiance, brought to light by the book, *Midnight in the Garden of Good and Evil*, several years earlier. But there were enough hot spots in poverty-stricken areas to keep the Savannah PD and the Chatham County Sheriff's Department busy, just like in any city of its size. A hunger for drugs, and the willingness to do whatever it took to procure them, led to disproportionate crime statistics in those areas.

Parked next to a row of waist-high boxwood bushes lining the entry into the apartment parking lot, he knew his presence was way too obvious for a real stakeout. But he had ceased to care. Any criminals worth their salt had spotted him long before now, so what was the use in being discreet? Taking a sip of his third cup of afternoon coffee, he powered his seat back, then stretched his long legs to the max. He would stay in position for no more than five minutes, then circle back out. What a crappy deal.

Shaking his head with a self-satisfied smirk, he knew too well why the detail had been ordered. The weekend duty sergeant who had fought for it saw himself as a ladies man. When Murphy had again gotten a look at the woman as she left for work earlier in the day, he was convinced the other officer was positioning himself as the Frapiana woman's hero, maybe leading to something. In his dreams. What a friggin' jerk.

Movement suddenly caught his eye; someone was approaching from behind the driver side of the cruiser. It was a light-skinned man, strolling casually along the edge of the parking lot, whistling as he walked. He wore jeans, sneakers, and a golf shirt... tail out. He had his hands in his pockets. Murphy tilted his cap back and lowered his dark glasses to the tip of his pug nose, taking a closer look in the side-mounted mirror. Most likely a tenant, out for a walk. The officer's alert status was on hold; the suspects he was to keep an eye out for were Hispanic, or so the duty sergeant had said. He moved the glasses back to the bridge of his nose.

The man reached the patrol car's window, then leaned in, gesturing for the patrolman to lower the glass. Murphy did so, staring up at a head full of moppish blond hair.

"What's going on, officer? Somethin' happen out here?"

"Nothing at all to be concerned about, sir," he replied in the polite, monotone voice he'd been trained to use with citizens. "Just a routine patrol."

"Oh I see. Had me worried for a minute there." The trim man smiled a nervous smile.

Murphy continued to stare, starting to feel a little uneasy with the man's strange demeanor. He might possibly be looped on drugs. "You live here, sir?"

"Yeah. Right back there." He pointed generally in the direction of two buildings in the rear of the complex, but at neither in particular.

"What apartment number would that be, sir?"

The man didn't answer, instead raising his eyes to peer over the officer's head, across the roof of the car. Murphy suddenly recalled a detail of the description of the men he should be on the alert for; one of them was blond...

perhaps American looking...whatever that meant. As he looked up at the man again, he detected the reflection of movement in the dark lens of his glasses. He turned to peer through the opposite window, and saw the blur of someone stepping from behind the bushes. The officer was a fraction of a second too late recognizing it to be a man moving toward the cruiser quickly. The far window shattered from the blow of the butt of Angel Xminez's Glock, sending shards of glass scattering through the car. The startled policeman barely had time to put his hand on his holster before Xminez leaned in and put two silent rounds into the man's skull. His aim was directed toward the thin-skinned section of the cranium, carefully placed to produce a minimum of blood. But it didn't eliminate all of the splatter that resulted, as blood and brain tissue splattered into the rear of the cruiser.

Reaching in quickly to release the lock, then climbing into the passenger side of the car, Xminez calmly collected the police-issue cap and sunglasses that had flown off at impact, then used his brute strength to shove the still twitching body into the rear before climbing behind the wheel. It took several thrusts before no part of the patrolman's body was visible outside the car. Reaching under the dash, and yanking out any wires that appeared to be connected to communication or positioning devices, he then turned to glare at Cesar Javier.

"Why are you still standing there? Get your ass moving."

Javier, who had fallen to the pavement to avoid being a collateral target, now stood on shaky legs. The thrill of seeing his big companion in action had been overwhelmed by the casual brutality of what he had done. He'd seen it before, not by Angel X, but by others in Torres' web of brutality. The apparent ease of their actions never failed to amaze him. He began a rapid retreat to reach the rental, still parked a block away.

Wiping them clean, then placing the cap and shades into position on his own head, Xminez cranked the officer's vehicle, putting it into gear. Slowly backing, then circling, he eased from the parking lot, taking a last look around to assure himself there were no witnesses. Seeing none, he waited at the mouth of the lot for Javier to fall in behind.

The mapping application on the phone had proven useful once more. While waiting for the patrolman to return to the apartment, he had devised a route that looked promising, one that appeared to lead to a rural area outside the city. A place to ditch the car, with the body inside, was the goal. It had to be found, and soon. He would soon discover that the GPS mapping system only illustrated routes of roads, but no other three-dimensional features, such as vegetation and surrounding pieces of civilization. Nothing was as it appeared on the flat display.

Over thirty minutes later, having traveled a distance far greater than he had anticipated being necessary, Xminez finally spotted a side road that looked promising. He had stayed clear of the two interstates that bisected each other just west of the city, sticking to surface roads to avoid the likelihood of being spotted by other law enforcement. Even then, he sweated each mile, fearing encountering another city cruiser. He knew it wouldn't be long, if it hadn't happened already, before someone would be attempting contact with the officer, which would create suspicions.

The first leg had taken him out State Highway 26, with Javier keeping him in sight as he followed. Later, the two cars had veered right on smaller Highway 17, then another ten minutes until he saw it, almost passing it by. A narrow dirt road led to what appeared to be an abandoned shack, a hundred yards or so down the road, barely noticeable behind a thicket of pine trees. Pulling onto the road, he approached the small wooden lean-to structure. Before forcing the car through the thick underbrush, he scanned the surroundings again for anyone who might be in the area. Satisfied, he positioned the car at one end of the shack, put the car in park, then stepped from the vehicle. It took a degree of effort to open the door to the building, lodged into place by settlement and rust due to time and the lack of use. With a loud creaking groan, the door finally gave in, then flew open. Placing a nearby stone as a wedge to keep the un-level door open, he returned to the car, then drove into the protection of the structure.

Tossing the cap into the car, deciding to keep the glasses, he closed the door. No need to worry about fingerprints, since he was fairly certain his were un-matchable by any American authorities. Even if they were, he would be long gone by the time they were identified. He then went to join Javier parked on the dirt road. When they arrived back on 17, he looked back to admire the success of his work. Perfect. It couldn't be seen. By the time it was found, he and Javier would be back across the border, assuming they found the money. If not... well, that was trickier. The possibilities Javier had mentioned earlier were still resonating in his head. Positioning those thoughts in the rear of his active brain, he anticipated his next move. Dispatching of the patrolman now left a clear path to his next meeting with the woman.

For his part, the blond man drove in silence, evidently coming to the conclusion it was best to keep quiet. He had known it was only a matter of time until Angel X's true nature would emerge. Contrary to the cartel leader's instructions, Angel X was now in full kill mode. In spite of the enormous danger sitting beside him, he felt an undeniable turn-on

Chapter 20

When she arrived at her daughter's pre-school to pick her up, Michelle was still shaken to the core from the brazen afternoon encounter with the second of the two men who had come to threaten her existence. The school was only blocks away on Victory Drive, but when the fair-haired man had told her the more threatening man from Saturday was watching the school, it seemed miles away in her mind. And she had no doubt the monster had been there, while his sidekick toyed with her. *But were there only two of them*? She couldn't be sure of that — she couldn't be sure of anything anymore, other than the fact she and Allison were in constant danger. It was now five-thirty. The blond man had accosted her somewhere around 1:00 p. m., leaving her with plenty of time to screw her insides into a taut ball of worry. She had placed a frantic call to the school during the afternoon, trying to moderate her voice while asking the principal to take a quick look into Allison's class... just to make sure. Everything was fine, she was told. Hiding her fear from the girl as they left the confines of the school parking lot wasn't easy. She tried to carry on a normal conversation, but was sure it was stilted — rambling.

The girl appeared to be observing her mother's mood and tone, watching her with an innocent, questioning expression. She seemed to be utilizing the built-in sensing device all children seem to possess, understanding far more than adults realized. She sat belted-in next to Michelle in the passenger side front seat. Michelle knew she was pushing the limits on child restraint laws in Georgia, but since returning to Savannah, she had always wanted her daughter next to her. Plus, she would be six within a year, the cutoff age. She would chance it until then.

"Mommy, is everything okay?"

More than a little effort was needed to keep tears from bubbling to the surface, but Michelle managed.

"Just had a busy day, honey. How was yours?"

Her mother's answer appeared to be accepted, but the gaze remained locked-in for a moment. The girl then reached into a satchel she carried to pre-school each day.

"Okay, I guess. Mrs. Suchet gave us homework to do." She beamed, apparently proud to have received an assignment normally given to older students. She held up a handwritten piece of paper.

Glancing down quickly, then back into the rearview and side mounted mirrors, ever on the alert, Michelle answered, "Oh, what's it about?"

Allison sighed. "I'm not sure. You'll have to read it. Something about the alpha... alpha..."

"The alphabet?" Her mother helped out.

A real smile now. "Yeah. We're supposed to put this list of animals in order."

"Oh, you must mean alphabetizing. Putting them in order using the first letter in their names. Okay. That should be fun. We'll start soon as we finish dinner."

Michelle peered at the reflection of the fading sunlight behind her, seeing a vehicle approaching at a rapid rate of speed. She had lost her focus for a second, and wasn't sure if she had noticed anyone falling in behind earlier. Alarms went off instantly in her head. Before she could decide what to do, the vehicle, proving to be a battered pickup truck, honked its horn, blinked a headlight, then sped by in a no-passing zone. A teenaged girl floated a hand out her window to wave bye-bye, then punctuated it with a middle finger.

"Nice girl," Michelle mumbled under her breath, or so she thought; the words had evidently crept out.

"What, Mommy?"

"Nothing, honey."

It took a few seconds to calm herself, stabilizing her heartbeat again. It could've easily been them. She felt entirely vulnerable; exposed to the world. The time of day had her on edge too. She longed for daylight savings hours that would be arriving in a few weeks. Her world was dark enough without the gathering gloom of night making its appearance so early in the evening. She was beginning to view the evening darkness as her enemy.

The incident put her mind at work, thinking about Allison's safety. And what about her parents? There could be no doubt the men threatening her knew about them too. Something had to be done to protect them. But what? They were all at risk due to her. Not because of anything she had done, but because of what she had allowed to happen to her. Dejectedly, she realized it was her life-long dilemma again; letting her fate be determined by others. It was a simple thing to vow once more to change that, but in her current situation, that was a thin promise, full of holes.

She had debated with herself over packing a few things and heading to her parents' house for the night, but ultimately decided against it. There was no doubt now the men would track her wherever she went, and she was still determined not to put them in danger too.

Arriving at the apartment complex, she pulled in to her usual parking spot, and was ready to switch off the ignition when a screeching noise coming from somewhere behind made her pause. It was the unmistakable sound of rubber on asphalt. Taking an instinctive look in the mirror, she was instantly paralyzed by a new terror, seeing a car turning into the complex and barreling directly toward her. She leaned over the console separating the two front seats and twisted her body to get a better view. It was a small, dark car, about the size of her own. Two men inside were visible in the gathering darkness. It was them! There could be no question.

She needed to get her daughter out of the car and into the apartment. In a desperate panic, she unsnapped her seat belt, then hovered over Allison to remove hers. With a sickening feeling growing in her stomach, she fought with the clasp. It was catching again. Oh Christ! It wouldn't release. She tugged fiercely.

A quick glance back saw them within fifty feet now. There was no more time to waste — no time to re-clasp her own belt. Speaking rapidly through a dry mouth, she yelled to the girl. "Sit tight, honey!"

"What's wrong, Mommy?"

There was no time to expend energy on answering. Shifting the gear stick into reverse, she backed out hurriedly, creating her own squealing sound on the pavement. Braking when clear of the adjacent cars, she turned sharply to the left, preparing to circle past the oncoming car, then exit the complex. Before she could straighten out, she watched in horror as the other car shifted its path to strike the Nissan. It managed to clip the left rear bumper, sending her car spinning around in the parking lot. Her unrestrained body felt the jolt of the glancing blow, knocking her sideways in the front seat. Her ribs struck the armrest with enough force to cause her to scream, causing Allison to began crying in fear. It took her a second to regain control of the car.

Allison was now screaming and sobbing non-stop, terrified and confused over what was happening. From her protected vantage point, her only thought was her mother had gone mad... driving like a maniac. Michelle had to ignore her, knowing her efforts had to be spent on finding an escape route. Hopefully, there would be time to explain and apologize later, or at least try. The Nissan finally ceased rocking. She put the accelerator to the floor. In the gathering dusk, she didn't see the curb she was about to jump, carrying the car across a freshly planted flower bed, jerking the pain through her body once again. The damage to the landscaping didn't matter... it was the quickest way out. Her tires churned up the soil violently. Shc could smell the damp, earthy odor of mud as it spun up from the lacerated ground. Finally, she cleared the bed, gaining traction on the paved parking lot.

Almost afraid to look, she checked the status of the other car. It was turning to begin the chase. Sparks were visible beneath the tires as it headed toward her. The brief collision must've knocked a piece of molding loose, the metal now hanging to the pavement. Turning her eyes back to the business at hand, she realized she was running on adrenalin alone, unsure of what to do — where to go.

She exited the parking lot on Abercorn Street, then used precious seconds trying to decide which way to turn. Her mind was a jumble of cold, debilitating fear. Should she try to reach her parents' house? No. She couldn't lead these monsters to them. The police precinct she and her dad had visited the day before was a greater distance, but her feverish brain knew that made more sense. Pumping the gas again, she turned right in that direction. Quick acceleration was not a selling feature of the Altima; the car seemed to her as if it were moving in slow motion. Looking in the mirror, she saw the other car hit Abercorn and follow. She could make out the face of the big Hispanic man behind the wheel. The blond man sat next to him, a dwarf by comparison.

In her panicked state, she had forgotten about the police patrol she had spotted a few times since the previous afternoon. Now that she remembered, she realized they were nowhere in sight when she really needed them. Contacting them had been a complete waste of time. Her pursuers would be on top of her within minutes, and she would be powerless against them. Shaking off thoughts of inevitability, she concentrated on avoiding other vehicles as she drove like a crazed lunatic through the streets of her home town. Allison was sobbing hysterically, her thin, tiny voice screaming as she squirmed in her seat.

"I'm sorry, honey," she said, her own voice choked with fear. "We'll be okay." The shaky words probably did little to convince the girl, and certainly not herself.

She soon spotted East 73rd Street ahead, the connecting street over to White Bluff Street where she needed to be. Slowing to make the left turn, she saw the car behind gaining on her, coming to within a few car lengths. It was easy guess work to know the man driving the chasing car was the more experienced driver. She would have to use her knowledge of the surroundings to stay ahead of him.

Making the turn at a speed far greater than she thought possible, the small Japanese car felt as if it were turning on its two right side wheels. A car passing through the intersection had to brake hard to avoid hitting her, veering to the right as it slowed to a near halt, blowing its horn at the idiot driver. She was momentarily gratified to see that the offended car had come between her and her pursuers — but not for long. Almost as if the other vehicle wasn't there, the dark compact blew by it, and resumed the chase.

Michelle tightened her grip on the wheel, as if trying to wrench it in half.

The frantic drive on East 73rd lasted for only one long block, as the two cars rushed by a small shopping center on the right. Narrow misses in the growing darkness caused stops and starts. The distance between the two remained the same with the trailing vehicle unable to gain ground. A right turn onto White Bluff Street would be next, which would soon morph into Bull Street. The precinct stood several blocks down on Bull. How many blocks, she couldn't recall. To her horror, she saw the intersection of 73rd and White Bluff had a signal light, now showing red facing her. Right-turn-on-red didn't help much, with a steady flow of traffic during the afternoon rush-hour visible passing through the intersection. If she came to a complete stop, they would be out of their car and smashing their way into hers. That couldn't be allowed to happen.

Sitting fourth in a line of cars from the intersection ahead, she pulled out suddenly into the oncoming lane, moving at a speed moderated only by a fear of colliding with another car head-on, which would also bring the chase to a frightening end. She barreled out into the cross street, then turned right on White Bluff, managing to find an opening in the traffic, forcing her way in. Again, she was bombarded with horns and angry looks. She ignored them all, and resumed her speed. Certainly her desperate driving would bring the police soon, and they would be saved. But it hadn't happened yet.

The small blue car behind had negotiated the second turn as well, and was making up a frightening amount of distance. It took only two blocks for the car behind to come up directly behind her, continuing to throw up sparks from the dangling molding, more visible in the surrounding darkness. She begin to believe she wasn't going to make it. If she only felt certain about the distance! But in the gloom of night, matching the terrifying gloom in her life, she had no bearings. Whatever knowledge she'd had about the city had evaporated over the years.

Looking desperately through the windshield, trying to spot the police building, she was jolted into the steering wheel when the car behind suddenly rammed her. Allison screamed louder. Michelle recovered, then pushed the pedal down as far as it would go, gaining precious distance. Fear was all that allowed her to ignore the pain in her rib cage.

She steeled herself for another violent nudge from the rear, beginning to wonder how many more onslaughts she could withstand. Gripping the wheel firmly with white knuckles, she prepared her body to cushion the next blow. Suddenly, there was a loud sound of metal on metal, followed instantly by another screech of tires on asphalt. Peering into her mirror, she saw headlights gyrating from side to side. She questioned her vision as she thought she saw four beams of light, meaning two sets of headlights. The chasing car must've crashed into another motorist. The thought brought instant feelings of guilt, laced with those of hope and deliverance. She should be worried about the other innocent driver, but could only view it as a means to a chance of survival, if only temporary.

Continuing to look through the mirror, she again had to question what she was seeing. The blue car was turning, retreating in the opposite direction down Bull Street, working its way through traffic. Forcing herself to take deeper breaths, she finally felt the tension in her body subside somewhat. Allison was still convulsing in stark fear; she needed comforting. Spotting an entrance to a strip shopping center parking lot on the right side of the road, she eased the Nissan in, then pulled into the nearest slot. Shifting into park, she was finally able to release the girl's seat belt, then reached to grab and hold her.

"It's okay now, Allison. Everything's fine." She stroked the sobbing girl's hair, something she always did to settle her down, although at that moment, it was uncertain who was comforting who the most. Michelle turned her head slightly to determine exactly where she was. She still planned to go to the police precinct, but it would have to wait for a few minutes. The pain in her side was now working its way across her body. She didn't think any ribs had been broken, but the throbbing couldn't be any worse if they had.

Her relief was suddenly interrupted by a dark form moving toward the car from somewhere in the dark lot. She saw it in the mirror. It was the form of a man approaching from the rear; a man who seemed to be carrying something. From her vantage point, she could only see as high as the chest. The *something* was now visible. The glint of metal. It was a gun! He tried to cover it with a free hand, but she could see it.

"Oh no! Oh, God. No!" He was so close, now standing beside the rear of the car. It wasn't over after all. She began to tremble all over again, knowing it was one of the hunters... or perhaps a new threat that had joined the chase. Her fear there might be more than two of them was correct. There was no time — nowhere to go. Her body was wasted; she didn't possess the will to run. Sensing her mother's fear, Allison's desperate sobs grew louder again. Michelle held her daughter as tightly as she could and closed her eyes, and waited.

"Mrs. Frapiana?" a voice rang out.

It was a voice she thought she recognized. But from where?

The voice spoke up again, yelling from right outside her window. "Mrs. Frapiana? Are you okay?"

Then she remembered. It was a voice from earlier in the day, and also from those many months before. She relaxed her grip on her daughter, then opened her eyes. Looking through the window, she could see him silhouetted against the backdrop of the street lights. The remainder of her stress then drained from her body, and she began to cry real tears — a bottomless reservoir of indescribable relief.

DEA agent Walter Church holstered his weapon, then leaned in and tried to open her door. The power lock was still engaged. He thumped on the window to get her attention, and she hit the release button. Opening the door, he kneeled in and let her tears flow for a second before speaking again.

"Walter Church, Mrs. Frapiana. Sorry it took so long to get here. Are you two okay?"

She could only manage a thin grin, accompanied by a nod of her head. Allison leaned to look around her mother at whoever was talking to her. Her small body was choking back the remains of her distress.

Peering in at the woman, he was able to get only a muted view of her tear-streaked face, with only the dome light illuminating it. But it was enough... enough for the DEA agent to know without question he was doing the right thing.

Chapter 21

It was only a car; a big one; an expensive one; but still only a car. Well, technically an SUV. Church had rationalized things out as he bore down on the car that appeared to be chasing Michelle Frapiana. It could be replaced. Using a technique employed in several drug dealer chases, one learned early in his agency training days, he had side-swiped the rear of the blue compact in a manner just enough to destroy its momentum, actually only a nudge, without destroying either vehicle, or causing a major pileup. Only this time, it was his own vehicle, not one belonging to the U. S. Government. It was a price he was willing to pay for his perhaps foolhardy adventure. He had seen confusion evident in the face of the other driver as his car's spinning finally ceased. It was a dark-skinned face, possibly Hispanic. It had to be the man she had mentioned on the phone earlier. The other man... the passenger... had shown only wild-eyed fear. Thankfully, the tactic had achieved the purpose the DEA agent had intended, causing the hit men... bounty hunters... or whatever they were, to call off the chase. At least for the time being.

Arriving in the city barely an hour earlier, he had used his Blackberry to Google the addresses she had given him: the book store; and her apartment. Mapping both locations, he first made a quick re-con of Liberty Lady. Parking near the front of the business, he strolled by, but hadn't spotted her inside. He had chosen the clandestine approach in order to keep his presence in the city as private a matter as possible, not only for the woman's benefit, but for his as well. He was walking a narrow tightrope, one that could become quite slippery if his extracurricular activities made too much of a splash.

He next went in search of her apartment, which took some doing. The mapping app was good up to a point, but with so many turns on the city streets, it took longer than it should have. He had pulled within a block according to the coordinates, when he had spotted the two cars leaving the complex at breakneck speed. Instinct told him it had to be her, and her tormentors. Keeping his distance at first in case he'd been mistaken, he finally managed to get close enough to view what could only be a desperate escape attempt. When he pulled in line behind them after the final turn onto Bull Street, he saw the danger of what was happening ahead. They had rammed her once, and were apparently closing in for another try. Knowing he had to act quickly, or watch the woman's car be smashed into submission, he had made his move.

They now sat in an IHOP, located not far from the scene of the chase. He felt confident they were safe here; the woman's pursuers were probably far from the area by now, trying to distance themselves, but no doubt regrouping. They sat in a booth, Church on one side, Michelle on the other with Allison, both observing the girl as she tore into a short stack of pancakes. Her fear had dissipated into hunger, which was much easier to deal with. The two adults toyed with cups of coffee, neither having much of an appetite.

"How in the world did you ever find us?"Michelle asked, still wrung out, slowly decompressing. She winced occasionally from the pain in her ribs.

"Simply used a little modern technology. That's why I asked for your addresses this morning." Church pulled his Blackberry from his pants pocket, turning the side with the screen toward her. "These new gadgets are unbelievable. Basically anything you can do with a p. c. can be done on this, maybe with the exception of printing. But you can probably hook it up to a printer somehow... not sure about that. I was able to pull up your apartment and work addresses on a map using something called Google Map."

Michelle stared at the device. Allison looked up for a second too, then dove in again. "My cell phone is old fashioned, I guess," Michelle said, appearing slightly embarrassed. "All I can do is make and receive calls."

The comment silenced Church for a moment. He sat back in his seat, staring at the device in his hand. Why in the hell hadn't he simply called her when he arrived in town? He had her cell number trapped in his phone. If he had known where she was sooner, he might've saved her some grief, along with a blemish on his Yukon. Feeling more than a little dumb, he realized he enjoyed using the capabilities of the device so much, he had forgotten to use it for its most basic function — phoning.

"That's probably all most people need," he admitted, trying to hide his embarrassment. "A lot of the functions built into mine are used in my work. Don't have much use for them in the real world. The Department gives us several toys to play with."

They were both quiet for a moment, each collecting their own thoughts about the event that had brought them together for a second time. It was awkward. Unsure of what to say, they took turns watching Allison as she devoured the pancakes. Michelle finally looked at him.

"I'm sorry about your car. I'd like pay for the damage?"

He shook his head casually, trying to show a lack of concern. "No big deal. I'll think of a way to get my insurance to cover it." He wasn't at all sure about that, wasn't even sure if he wanted to go that route, since it would be a bogus claim. It was a deliberate hit. He had other things on his mind, needing to get an idea of where things stood. He wanted to know if there had been more threats since her phone call, leading up to the chase he had interrupted. "Sounds like you've had a busy day," he said.

She didn't reply right away, instead glancing down at the child. "Can we talk about it later?" she mouthed silently with a hopeful look.

Church nodded, recognizing her intent on keeping the gory details of her suddenly dangerous life hidden from her daughter's ears. When he'd leaned into her car after rescuing them less than an hour ago, he had heard her explain to the girl some bad drivers had been chasing them. Having no children, in situations such as this he had learned to defer to the judgement of those who did. His mind wandered back over the last seven... or was it eight... months. He'd lost count now. He was picturing what the woman and her child must have lived through. Most of it, he could only imagine. Then he realized it actually went back further than that. Her marriage must've been holy hell for her, for a long, long time.

Continuing to sit in silence, letting Allison finish eating, he felt a strange, warm feeling of contentment wash over him. A feeling that told him he could sit right here, in this spot, all night, and shove the danger somewhere to the back of his mind.

He noticed occasional questioning glances directed toward him from the girl. She was trying to decide who he was — what he was doing here. From her youthful, narrow frame of reference, she surely had no choice but to see him as a threat. He read more into it than curiosity, seeing her furtive looks as a way of telling him he was out of his league if he possessed ulterior motives. How could he argue?

He went for what he hoped was a safe, yet vulnerable spot.

"Do you have any pets, Allison?"

A slow shake of the tiny head, then, "No, but I'd like a kitten."

"How about dogs? I have a dog. Name's Char. He loves kids."

She seemed to consider what he'd said for a second, then replied, "I like kitties more."

The girl, purposely or not, had thrown a roadblock in front of him. He pressed on one last time. "I think you'd like Char, and I know he'd like you."

Her small mind was obviously churning away, giving the subject some thought. A grin almost snuck through, but she quickly withdrew it. She looked up at her mother instead. "Can we get a pet, Mommy?"

Michelle shot a tired, unhappy frown across the table, evidently not appreciating the subject, then smiled at the girl. "We'll see, honey."

Church decided to surrender, knowing any follow-up would only make things worse. He realized she might not only resent his putting ideas in the girls' head, but also using it as a possible ploy to ingratiate himself into their lives, which he had to admit was true. The agent had been trying not to stare, but Michelle Frapiana was as every bit as beautiful as he remembered, though in a strangely different way. Desperation had somehow given her a vulnerability that made her all the more appealing, giving encouragement to his reasons for being here. But reality was a cold, relentless, unforgiving force, and he understood clearly some form of hell would have to be dealt with — and soon. He had managed to talk her out of going to the police right away to report the latest attack, saying he wanted to size things up first. But he had other, ulterior reasons to steer clear of the locals for the time being. Her rather quick agreement with his reluctance to involve the authorities came as something of a surprise. It puzzled him, but he wasn't quite sure why.

Michelle was busy checking him out at the same time; actually, trying to *figure* him out. Still unable to grasp why he had come, she was none-the-less grateful. She reasoned there was a chance he felt things had been left undone the first time he had traveled to Savannah, and was harboring a feeling of guilt. She didn't know enough about how the DEA functioned; whether they normally offered protection or not. And then there was *him*... his appearance. Rough around the edges, but with a degree of rugged, masculine good looks, she assumed his pony tail was designed to give him the look of being able to blend in with the people he went after. In fact, if she hadn't known for a fact who he was, what he did for a living, she might lump him in with the criminals her husband had dealt with.

"I'm through, Mommy," Allison announced, interrupting their individual thoughts. Her face was streaked with sticky syrup, causing the two adults to laugh.

Michelle led her to the restroom, then stood outside waiting while she washed up. Church took advantage of the alone time to join her in the short hallway so they could discuss what to do. He had more to tell her, but there wouldn't be time now.

"I don't think you should stay in your apartment tonight," he began. "They're getting more aggressive. Might try again, soon."

"I was thinking the same thing. I've been thinking about going to my folks' house."

Church considered that before asking, "Do they know what's going on?"

"Yes. After the first man approached me in the park Saturday, I had to tell them. It was my dad who made me contact the police."

He nodded. "I'd forgotten you'd mentioned that this morning." He paused again, wondering about something. "What happened to the patrol this afternoon?"

She shook her head. "No idea. They've been there since yesterday afternoon. But not when those two showed up this afternoon." She was going to add something, but Allison emerged from the restroom, shutting down the conversation.

Church then settled the check, over Michelle's mild objections, and they headed for the door. The DEA agent was still mulling the missing patrolman. His past case experiences caused him to question it. He had a troubling thought; it was his nature to think the worst, influenced by his past observances of the drug cartels. They were capable of anything.

As they headed toward their respective battered vehicles, Michelle turned to Church. "We need to go by the apartment first to get a few things. Could you follow us there, and then to my parents'? You met them last time, as I recall."

"Yes I did. Nice folks. Sounds like a plan to me. Lead on." He was instantly aware his mood was a little too upbeat, given the situation. He couldn't help himself, still filled with the electric feeling of being in the woman's presence. "Is your car okay? Driveable?"

"I think so. Made it here without any trouble. Think I picked up some mud underneath in my apartment parking lot, but it'll wash off, I'm sure."

Later, while he stood watch in the parking lot, Michelle and Allison entered the apartment to take what they would need for the duration, whatever that duration might be. During the drive, she had called to alert her parents they were coming. As she closed the apartment door behind her to leave, she remembered to check the mailbox.

Church continued to observe the two of them, Michelle holding the girl's hand as she unlocked the box. Grabbing a stack of envelopes and junk mail, she took a moment to flip through it. He thought he saw her pause when looking at one particular envelope, but paid little mind to it. Stuffing the mail into her purse, she lead her daughter to their car. He noticed her own mood had altered slightly; she had more bounce in her step, which didn't seem to match her predicament. As a light rain began to fall, they were soon back in their vehicles; Michelle and Allison in the dented Nissan, and DEA agent Walter Church trailing in his dinged-up black GMC Yukon.

Chapter 22

Angel Xminez sat on the edge of his bed, deciding on the words he would use when placing the mobile phone call. Texting wouldn't do in this situation. He had too much to say. Actually, too much to ask. Posing questions to the powerful, ruthless drug lord required careful planning, and a degree of diplomacy that might be beyond his abilities. Plus, he needed to hear the tone of the voice on the other end. See if he could detect any sense of deception. Cesar Javier's words about the possibility of Torres' duplicities were still lodged in his brain, too troublesome to ignore.

Javier had cleared out, wanting to remove himself from the potential volcano he was sharing the cheap motel room with. As Javier had readied to leave, Xminez grabbed the rental car's keys from the bedside table, pocketing them. He didn't want to give the man a chance to move the car. He had backed it into a tight parking spot in the back of the Best Western motel earlier, hiding the damage to the rear bumper from curious eyes. The front molding, still hanging from the first clipping of the woman's car, had been popped back into place, and wasn't quite as noticeable. His fearful blond companion told him not to worry, he planned on hanging out in the lobby, which would prove to be a lie. He instead wasted no time in making his way through the lobby, exiting the front door, then proceeding on foot through a steady drizzle to the bar he had spotted when they had arrived four nights earlier, located only two buildings away. Judging by the quick glimpses of the clientele he had noticed since, going in and out of the club, he thought it could be the kind of place he might be welcomed. He glanced at his watch, knowing it would be foolish to stay for more than one drink... two at the most... or risk Angel X searching for him. But his inner desires were driving him, longings having been placed in hibernation far too long. Entering the bar, he immediately caught the attention of two customers, who eyed him as if he were strapped in gold. Yes, he would feel quite at home here.

Back in the room, Xminez ran through the possibilities once more before calling Luis Torres. There were four scenarios that made sense in regard to the person who had thwarted the attack on the Frapiana woman a little more than an hour ago: the police, but that didn't stand to reason, or else they would've pursued; a friend of the woman's, or private security — but where had they been before?; another drug family coming after the money, the most likely answer; or, the scenario that had his blood boiling. Torres had sent someone else, dissatisfied with his performance. It made sense for two obvious reasons: Torres wouldn't care *who* brought him his money; if two teams were better than one, why not send a second, and let the best team win. There would surely be a reward for the winner, and most likely a miserable end for the laggard. And in the murderous, dangerous world of drug trafficking, especially in the region where the state of Sinaloa existed, the region so familiar to him, there was no such thing as honor or loyalty. If his suspicions were true, he had to assume the new team would strike soon, hoping to get results first. The cartel leader wouldn't hesitate to double down. It was the same mind set that had made Torres first suspect the Medina family as being responsible for the sabotage at the huge drug buy, sacrificing one of their own in the process.

He finally punched the key to automatically dial the only number pre-programmed on the cell phone's key pad, and waited for Luis Torres to pick up. When he did, he began speaking without a greeting.

"Yes, Angel. What do you have to tell me that you could not text?" Torres sounded angry. He did not like speaking on any phone, even one as secure as the one he had provided his bounty hunters.

"We have a problem, Sènor Torres."

"Oh? A problem you cannot handle?" The tone reeked of impatience and suspicion, perhaps trying to disguise his deception.

"Sì, I can handle it, Sènor Torres. I am only trying to locate the source of the problem."

Torres sighed. "What are you talking about, Angel?"

"No more than an hour ago, we were very near the Frapiana woman. We were closing in on her... on the truth," Xminez said, choosing to exaggerate his success, "when someone rammed our vehicle from behind. We were thrown off course, and found it wise to retreat. We were in a populated area, and did not want to engage in close combat. Those were your wishes, were they not?"

"Sì, unless it was absolutely necessary. Are you certain it wasn't an accident? Perhaps you are becoming paranoid, Angel."

The words stung, and raised more suspicions. "No, sénor, it was meant to stop us. I am quite certain of that."

"But who were they? Who sent them?"

Xminez hesitated. "I do not know. Perhaps someone else is searching for the money as well."

Torres now paused, then spoke slowly. "That was always a possibility. We discussed that before you left. Could it be the mystery man from the Florida coast? Helping to protect her secret?"

Xminez considered this new possibility. The woman had said the man was dead. If she was lying about the money, she might be lying about that also. But he was growing doubtful.

The line had grown silent for a few awkward seconds. Receiving no response from his bounty hunter, Torres followed up, his tone altered.

"Was there something else on your mind, Angel?" The drug lord spoke slowly, almost making the words sound like an accusation. He was aware Xminez was a cunning, clever warrior, who was most likely thinking the same doubtful thoughts *he* would be if the situations were reversed. Never-the-less, Torres would not allow anyone to question him. The allowances he made for himself weren't extended to others.

Xminez paused, listening to the man's heavy breathing, then chose his words carefully. "It may have occurred to me that you were not trusting Javier and I to complete our mission. It would be understandable if you have chosen to send others."

"Are you accusing me of something, Angel?" The voice was now icy. He didn't wait for an answer. "If you are, I will *tell* you if I did decide to send another team to do what you have been unable to do, I would not be afraid to inform you. Is that clear enough for you? *¿me entiendes*."

Xminez exhaled a huge breath of air. There were few people he feared — Luis Torres was at the top of a very short list. "Sì, Sènor Torres. I understand. Forgive my mistake."

The remarkably clear connection spanning two countries was quiet again. Angel X could only imagine the thoughts passing through the cartel leader's head. Finally, Torres spoke again.

"Are you saying you are no closer to finding my money?"

"That is hard to say, Sènor Torres."

"And what does that mean?"

"Cesar and I are beginning to believe the woman knows nothing. She is terrified of what we might do to her and her family. But still, she does not change her story. She lives very simply, in a small apartment. Surely if she had the money, she would choose a better existence. I think it is time we search elsewhere. Perhaps the man Musso did go to Houston, as she said, and took the money to Texas with him."

"But you said he was dead."

"That is what the woman said. But perhaps he is still alive, or gave the money to someone in Texas, or hid it before he died." He voiced the scenario he had been considering. "It could be *she* is protecting Musso, lying about his death."

"Possibly." Torres breathed a deep sigh into his end. "I might agree with you about the woman's innocence Angel, if it weren't for the party who interfered tonight, as you have said. And you must realize there are people who can live as paupers for many months, perhaps even years, waiting for others to stop searching, until they can enjoy their stolen riches. Perhaps she has found someone to help hide her secrets." He paused for a second, evidently exploring options. "Exhaust every possibility with her. If you still feel she knows nothing, we will discuss going to Texas."

After the connection had been broken, Xminez sat for several minutes on the edge of the bed, the seat he usually preferred. The flimsy chairs in motels such as this could not hold his bulk comfortably. He replayed the conversation in his mind, phrase by phrase, word for word. It was now clear to him that he and Javier could not return to the Sinaloa region of Mexico without the money, or what was left of it. Cesar had been right. Torres did not trust anyone. He would certainly assume they had found and hidden the money.

Thinking of his accomplice, he began to wonder why he hadn't returned. It was still relatively early in the evening, but they needed to plan their next step. Aware the Frapiana woman had described his appearance to the police by now, he disguised himself with the only prop at his disposal, a baseball cap, and headed for the small lobby. No Javier. Stepping through the lobby door into the rain that was starting to subside, he peered across the parking lot, the pavement glistening from the reflections of the motel's lights on wet surfaces. Only half-looking for his traveling companion, he was already concentrating more on his choice of locations where he would feel safe from Torres. Such a place probably didn't exist. At least, not in Mexico, or anywhere in the U. S. If he could somehow obtain a passport, his options would be greater. Perhaps his contact in San Antonio could help once more.

He was still deep in thought when he spotted him, walking on unsteady legs, exiting through the door of a bar a few buildings down. He started to approach, ready to berate the man for his apparent drunkenness, then stopped when another person from the bar stepped out behind him. The stranger wrapped an arm around Javier, who responded by curling an arm around the other man's neck, pulling him into an embrace. They were talking loudly and laughing, their words muted only slightly by the damp conditions.

Xminez felt rage and disgust building within his belly. He had seen enough. Not only had the weakling most likely endangered their presence, but he had done so in a manner repugnant to the big man's very nature. Managing to stifle his anger for the time being, he knew he dared not make a scene; it would draw too much attention. Quickly retreating to the motel, he decided he would deal with Javier when he finally arrived back in the room. It just might be that the little man had ceased to be useful, and was in fact a liability. He had a way of dealing with liabilities. Luis Torres' words and voice tones were still ringing in his ears, which only added to the gloomy outlook for Cesar Javier's future.

Chapter 23

When Michelle and Walter Church arrived at the home of her parents, after re-introductions had been completed, she pulled her father aside, asking for a minute in his study. It was important she talk to him alone first, before a full discussion of the past few days took place in the presence of the DEA agent. As the door closed behind them, she immediately filled him in on the details of the narrow escape she and Allison had survived, thanks to Church's sudden appearance on the scene. Since she hadn't talked to her father all day, she also covered the visit to the book store by the second man.

Silas stared incredulously at first, horrified and angered by what she told him. Trying to digest the sequence of events, he stared at the closed door, as if he could see right through it.

"Where did agent Church come from? How did he get involved?"

"I didn't tell you about it last night, Dad, because I really hadn't decided for sure until this morning. I called him."

"You *called* him?" Silas said, staring. There was more surprise than question in his words.

"Yes. I'm not sure why, but I kept his card from the time he and the other agent were here last summer. I was hoping he might have ideas on how to deal with those men."

"And his *idea* was to come here?" Silas quickly adjusted his tone. "Not that I'm complaining, of course... he may have saved your life... Allison's too. I'm just surprised he would do that. Sounds like he got here just in time."

"Yes, we were lucky. A few more minutes, and I don't know what might've happened. From what he's told me, he didn't come on official business. Just wanted to help out. Other than that, I'm not at all sure why he decided to come."

They had both been standing. She fell into a chair, feeling the exhaustion of her ordeal overtaking her. Rehashing the day's events caused her to relive them, but it also gave time for the remaining adrenalin rush she had felt during the chase to continue to fade, and along with it, her energy.

The man slowly took a seat across from her. He smiled a gentle, knowing smile. "I've got a pretty good idea why he came."

She was fairly sure she knew what he was hinting at, but was too tired to give it more than a passing thought. She started to speak, but Silas held up a hand to interrupt.

"Wait a minute. I just remembered something. What happened to the police patrol we arranged yesterday? Where were they?"

Michelle shrugged. "Don't know, Dad. They were around earlier, but not when those men came after us."

She saw a rare flash of anger appear on his face, along with determination.

"I'll find out. And they'd better have a damn good excuse."

Shocked at what for Silas Lovejoy was an uncharacteristic outburst, she put a hand on his arm. "I've been thinking about that, Dad. Those two may have just gotten lucky and timed it just right between patrols. Or it could be they saw the officer's patrol pattern, and took advantage of it. Besides, they can't be everywhere at once."

"Doesn't matter. I'm going down there first thing tomorrow and talk to them."

"Okay. Just try not to get your blood pressure up too much." She grabbed her purse she had brought with her into the room, opened it and pulled out one of the pieces of mail she had gathered at her apartment mail box. "Listen, Dad. The real reason I wanted to talk to you in private was this." She held it up. "I haven't had a chance to open it yet, but I'm sure it's the money."

The man managed to calm himself, then stared for a second, then said, "Well then, go ahead, open it. Let's take a look."

She did so, then spent a moment scanning a cover letter, wrapped around a check made out to her in the amount of $6,500. At any other time of her life she would've been exuberant, overcome with joy and excitement. None of those emotions surfaced while reading the numbers on the check. Her only conscious thought was again spent wondering about the source of the windfall. It worried her more each time she considered it, especially after the events of the last few days.

Taking it from her tired hands, Silas Lovejoy examined the check for authenticity, as would any accountant worth his salt, while Michelle read the letter more thoroughly out loud. It was from a bank in Texas, drawn from a trust account, appearing to have a generic name. Just as the attorney had promised in the letter, there were also instructions from the sending institution, a bank located in a place called The Woodlands, Texas, covering automatic deposits into her bank of choice. The Woodlands rang an indistinct bell for Silas, but he had no idea where in Texas it might be.

"Looks legit, honey," Silas said, handing the check back. She handed him the letter, giving him a second to scan it.

Michelle summoned up the energy to sit up straight, looking intently at her father. "Here's the thing, Dad. We agreed yesterday"*...God, was it only yesterday?...* "not to let those men know about this money. I don't want Church to be aware of it either. At least not yet."

"Oh?" His face showed surprise, but he nodded as if he understood.

"I hate to be so secretive, but we have to remember, he *is* DEA. I'm sure his motives are well intended. About helping us, I mean. But part of the reason he's here could be that he's curious about the money too, and what happened to it. If he knew about this," she held up the check, "it might change everything."

Silas scratched his chin, thinking. "Hadn't thought about that," he said. He then looked squarely into her eyes. "But if I'm any judge of people, or at least men — I've *never* been able to read women — I believe you might have him pegged wrong. One of your faults, honey, though its really not a fault, has always been that your humility won't allow you to understand the affect you have on men. I think he's here only because of you."

"Dad. Please! We have to take this seriously." Michelle shocked herself by the force behind her reply, immediately feeling she had lashed out too strongly once more. She chalked it up to frayed nerves.

Holding up both hands defensively, equally stunned by her tone, he backed off. "Okay, okay. I'll do whatever you say. So, how do you want to handle the money?"

"Would you mind depositing it in my account tomorrow? I'm not sure what Church's plans are, but I may not be able to get to my bank without raising his suspicions. He might be keeping a close eye on me."

"I'm sure he will," Silas said, with raised eyebrows.

"Dad." Her response was a little softer this time. "Anyway, I'm sure those other men will be watching me."

"We have to assume that's the case. Okay, I'll take care of it. What about the automatic deposit request?"

"I haven't decided what to do about that yet. I'll let you know."

This all felt so strange to her; holding secret meetings, plotting against people who might do her harm, and a man whose motives she was unclear about, *with* the man who had taught her how to ride a bike, helped with her math homework, chauffeured her to soccer and ballet practice, and helped her bury several pets. They had conspired often in this very room years earlier about surprise birthday and Mothers' Day gifts for Mary Lovejoy. The comfortable study seemed different now. Her entire world had been turned inside-out, leaving her in a place she never dreamed possible; a place you only read about in novels, or saw in movies. All because she couldn't say "no" to Dickie Frapiana ten years ago.

"One other thing, Dad. I don't like having you, Mom, and Allison exposed to this kind of danger. Is there somewhere you can take them 'til this is over?"

Silas rose, took a few paces, then turned to look down at his daughter. "I'm not sure, honey. Do you really think that's necessary?"

"I think so. And we can't afford to take chances." She thought about it for a moment. "Maybe Agent Church can give us his opinion. After all, he probably deals with these people... these situations, all the time."

He nodded. "Makes sense. But I can't see how I can go anywhere now. We're right in the middle of tax season. Most of our clients can be handled by my associates, but I have a few I can't neglect. They'll leave the firm if I do. Been with me for decades. Besides, I can take care of myself. But if the agent agrees with you, I'll see to it that your mother and Allison go somewhere." He looked at her again, stroking his moustache. "Any ideas?"

"Maybe one. Let's go talk to him first."

Silas put the check and the accompanying information in his briefcase, tapping it. "I'll see to this first thing tomorrow."

Mary Lovejoy was doing her best to entertain her five-year old granddaughter and the strange looking guest simultaneously, which was a unique challenge for her genteel southern social charms. The three of them sat in the well-appointed den; the woman and the girl on the sofa, and DEA Agent Walter Church in a wingback chair, hands on his knees, feeling as out-of-place as a person could possibly feel. He had crossed his legs when taking his seat, until now he was starting to lose feeling in his upper leg. Putting both feet on the floor, he placed his hands on his knees, letting his eyes wander around the den, checking out the ivory and forest-green color schemes, obviously chosen carefully to fit the woman's refined tastes. Their mutual discomfort made it a toss-up as to who was the most relieved when Michelle and Silas finally re-entered. Michelle couldn't suppress a grin noticing the expression on Church's face; it was his turn to be rescued. He rose to meet them.

"Mom," she said, "why don't you, Allison and I raid the refrigerator while Dad and..." She looked at the agent for help, unsure of how to refer to him. She hadn't bothered to ask him earlier. Agent Church seemed too impersonal, but she wasn't sure of alternatives.

"Walt. That's what my friends call me, and I hope you all consider me that." He smiled a silly, awkward grin, knowing this evidently tight-knit family may not be ready to accept him as such.

The older couple seemed to take it okay, but the only reaction that mattered to him was a faint smile on the younger woman's face, managing to extend from her lips to crinkles around her eyes. She blushed slightly from his obvious stare. Her dad's opinion about why he had come still echoed in her head, and would for awhile, even though she found it easy to dismiss the idea.

"Okay, Walt it is," Silas said, taking control. When the others were out of earshot, he motioned with a hand. "Please, be seated. Make yourself comfortable, Walt." He said the name with pointed emphasis, trying to adjust to it.

He sat across from the agent. "First off, I don't think there's anyway possible to thank you enough for what you've done tonight. These last few days have been hell for all of us, but mostly for Michelle." He frowned, then turned his gaze toward the floor. "Hate to think what would've happened if you hadn't showed up when you did."

"I'm sure it's been pretty rough. Don't think I've run across any civilians who've faced exactly what she's had to deal with. And not just lately. I can imagine the entire past year's been a nightmare for her. She may have told you, but when my partner and I were here last year, we warned her this could happen, although we both held out hope it wouldn't. I'm just glad I got here in time."

Silas nodded, clearing his throat. "Well, just so we know who knows what, how much did she tell you when she called this morning?"

"Just that one of the men approached her Saturday afternoon in a park downtown, somewhere near where she works, I think. He asked her for the money her husband had stolen, while another man stood guard near Allison to emphasize his point. She tried to convince him she knew nothing about it, but he didn't believe her. Said they'd be seeing her again." Church paused, then recalled something else. "And then there was the call she received yesterday."

Silas squeezed his eyes almost closed. "Call? What call?"

"It was on her machine. Not actually a call, just somebody on the line who didn't speak. Could've been a crank call, but she's sure it was them. I have to agree with her."

The older man rolled his eyes at the ceiling. "My God. She didn't even tell me about that."

Church felt for the man. He wasn't equipped for this kind of stress. "Probably didn't have time to. She's had a lot on her mind today. Plus, Mr. Lovejoy..."

The older man stopped him, raising a hand to interrupt. "Silas. Please call me Silas. I think we've both earned a first name basis."

"Okay, Silas. I was going to say you and your wife are experiencing something you haven't been trained to handle. She's aware of that, and wants to limit your exposure."

The thought struck Silas that the man had no idea what his "exposure" already was. He couldn't resist a telling glance at the briefcase he had brought with him from the study, but simply nodded. "I'm sure you're right." He shifted gears. "Has she had a chance to fill you in on what happened today? Before they came after her in her car, I mean."

"I'm not sure what you're getting at, but we didn't have much time to talk earlier. She didn't want Allison to hear how bad things really were."

"Yes, I see. Well, this afternoon, while she was at work, the other man, the one who had stood near Allison Saturday in the park while the other one terrified Michelle, came into the book store, repeating the same things the other man had said."

Christ! Church was surprised at such a brazen move. They must be desperate, becoming impatient — a very bad sign. "What happened?"

"Nothing, really. Just more threats. He told her they didn't believe her. Said they knew she had the money. But what really terrified Michelle was the man saying the other man was watching Allison's school while he was taunting her. I have to admit, that bothers me more than anything. When Sandi... that's the store owner... appeared, the guy left."

Church mulled this latest news, knowing it meant things would surely escalate soon. His brain was grinding away, trying to use his experience to come up with a plan that might relieve these people of the danger they faced, a danger much more threatening than even they realized. It had to be a plan that wouldn't pull him into a quagmire *he* might never escape from. He could see the headlines: *Rogue DEA agent goes undercover, on a freelance assignment; causes mayhem and bloodshed in peaceful Savannah, Georgia. End of career.*

He shook the image from his thoughts. One idea did emerge, an idea that at least might identify the people he was up against.

Silas had been watching the agent, waiting for a response. Receiving none, he suddenly stood. “Walt. Michelle thinks it would be a good idea if Mary and Allison go somewhere for awhile, just to be on the safe side. Wanted me to go too, but that’s not going to happen. We wanted your opinion.”

“Yes, I would recommend it. It would have to be somewhere that your family has no known connections to. And the sooner the better. Hopefully, it won’t be for too long a period. I would say Michelle should go too, but they’re watching, and would track her no matter where she goes.”

Silas nodded again, now with a heavy frown. “So, you think they’re that dangerous.”

Church paused for a second, rubbing a hand across a denim knee. He had chosen the jeans for travel when he’d rushed by his condo before leaving Atlanta, along with a golf shirt and light windbreaker. The humid conditions that had greeted him in Savannah told him the jacket was overkill. He had wanted no trappings of his occupation visible. He thought carefully about what he was about to say. He didn’t want to alarm the man to the point of hysteria, but he wanted to paint a clear picture.

“Silas, let me tell you a little about my work... and what I’ve seen.” He shifted in his seat, leaning elbows on the arms of the chair while clasping his hands. “I joined the Drug Enforcement Administration just over fifteen years ago. Trained at Quantico in Virginia. That’s the FBI training facility. Back then we used their place to get broken in. We have our own place now, also in Virginia. When I graduated, my first assignment was pulling border duty along the Rio Grande, sort of like advanced basic training... or punishment, depending on how you look at it. I had..." He paused, deciding how far to go... " many chances to observe what the Mexican drug families are willing to do to their enemies, and sometimes to some of their own people.

"I was stationed there for four years, which seemed like twice that. When it came open, I jumped at the chance to grab a slot in the Atlanta Region. I'm originally from east Tennessee, so it was an opportunity to get closer to home. It's taken a while to get those images of pure evil and brutality out of my head. Don't think I completely have, actually."

He hesitated again, looking intently at the older man. "When Michelle called this morning, she said the first man who had approached her looked Hispanic, possibly Mexican."

"Yes, she told me the same thing." Silas' voice was thin, as if someone had their hands around his throat, choking off his air.

"In that case, yes. I think they should leave, the sooner the better."

Chapter 24

Michelle spent a few minutes putting Allison down for the night before rejoining the others in the den. She received little resistance; the adventure earlier in the evening, followed by the pancakes stuffed into her tiny body, had played havoc with the girl's stamina. Silas then gave his daughter and his wife an overview of the discussion he'd had with Church, careful to omit certain parts they didn't need to hear.

"I think Walt and Michelle are exactly right, Mary. You and Allison are leaving first thing in the morning."

"But, Silas. What about you and Michelle?" Mary Lovejoy's expression appeared to be equal parts fear and confusion. "You'll be in danger too."

"Perhaps, but I don't think so. As Walt pointed out, the danger would follow Michelle wherever she goes, and I simply can't leave the office now." Noticing doubts remaining on her face, he quickly added, "I'll be fine dear. I'm going to have a talk with the police first thing in the morning. See if they can't do a better job of keeping tabs. And I'll make sure I'm never alone."

Not allowing more time for his wife to question how things had to be, he turned to Michelle. "You said you have a suggestion about where they could go."

"Right. The Martins. The last time I talked to them they kept insisting we come for a visit. I can't think of a better time. I know Allison would love seeing them again, and vice versa." She addressed Church, reminding him of who the Martins were. "They were the couple from Chattanooga who Brent recruited to bring Allison and me home last year. I'm sure I mentioned them to you when you and your partner were here."

Church nodded, but had his doubts. "Are you sure their names weren't included in any news stories? If they were, you can be sure these people will know about them."

"No. I'm absolutely sure their names were kept out of everything, just like I did with Brent. I made certain of it."

"Can you call them tonight?" Silas asked. Now convinced, he was anxious to move things along.

Michelle glanced at her watch, surprised to see it was still only 9:15. As traumatic as the night had been, it seemed to have lasted forever. "I'll give it a try." She returned to her father's office to use his phone.

Ralph Martin answered on the third ring, his cheery voice sounding as full of life as ever. After exchanging greetings, she got right to the point.

"Ralph, I have a big favor to ask."

"Well then, ask away."

She could picture the tall, angular, white-haired man, probably with the same friendly smile he had seemed to carry with him during their brief time together the year before. His impish bride, still perky despite her advanced age, was surely hovering nearby. “Would you and Flora mind if Mom and Allison flew up to spend a few days with you?”

Martin reacted immediately, expressing his delight. He then hesitated, evidently picking up on the stress in her voice. “This have anything to do with what happened in Destin?”

“Yes. I’m afraid so.”

“In that case, you don’t even have to ask. You get them on the next plane, and we’ll pick’em up at the airport here. Just let us know the flight number.” He paused. “Wait, why just your mom and Allison? Aren’t you coming?”

“I can’t ,Ralph. I’ve got something to see to down here. But I’ve got help, so don’t worry about me.”

“Well, Flora’ll be disappointed. Me too. But she’ll be chompin’ at the bit to show Allison the sights of our mountains.”

“Thanks, Ralph. You two are going to be our guardian angels again. I don’t know how to express...” Her voice trailed off, choked with emotion, recalling their unselfish kindnesses from before. They had gone hundreds of miles out of their way to bring her and her daughter home. She realized they had only known her and Allison for parts of two days, yet they were willing to help once more. How lucky she had been... or more truthfully... Brent had been, to find them.

Martin cleared his throat. “Now hush about that. Call us when you know something about the flight. And you better take care of yourself, ya hear?”

Ending the call a second later, Michelle immediately dialed a second number, booking two tickets out of Savannah/Hilton Head International on Delta to Chattanooga, with the obligatory stop-over in Atlanta. The earliest flight out the following morning was at eight forty-five.

When she rejoined the others in the den, the Lovejoys decided enough was enough. With an early drive to the airport looming, they announced they were retiring for the night.

Church took it as his cue. "I'll see all of you first thing in the morning," he said, standing to leave. "I'll be here in time to follow you to the airport, just in case."

"Why, you're staying here, aren't you?" Mary Lovejoy asked, looking surprised, as if it were a given that hadn't been discussed.

"No ma'am. Thought I'd get a room somewhere. Don't want to burden you folks."

"Nonsense. You're staying." She wasn't taking no for an answer. "Michelle can sleep in her old room with Allison. That leaves our guest room for you. Just get your things and Silas will show you the way."

"Mary's right, Walt," Silas jumped in. "If you've come all this way to guard our daughter and granddaughter, you can't do that from some motel. You ought to be here."

Encouraged once again to see an agreeing smile visible on Michelle's face, the DEA agent did as he was told. And it did make sense. He went outside to the Yukon to retrieve his things, spending a few minutes checking for signs of danger. He walked to the front of the house, following the curved driveway, then peered in both directions down the peaceful street. The earlier rain had settled into a fine mist. The night showed signs of leaving foggy conditions for the following morning. But for now, all appeared to be quiet.

After the older couple had disappeared to the rear of the house a few minutes later, Church and Michelle finally had a few moments to themselves, a chance to compare notes and collect their thoughts. They sat on opposite ends of the sofa, while she filled him in on what her life had consisted of since her return to Savannah. She asked about his job, wanting to get a picture of his past experiences with the type of people who were lurking out there somewhere, possibly waiting to do her harm. His answers glossed over the parts that might be too intense for her to accept. She wondered, but did not ask, how long he had tracked her husband, and whether his observations of Dickie's drug dealings had included watching her. She decided those were questions better left untouched, since they weren't important anyway. This whole situation was weird enough as it was.

As she talked, then listened, her mind drifted occasionally to her dad's opinions about why the agent had come. She knew it didn't matter. He could've been the perfect Adonis — which he surely wasn't, but it was beside the point. Her mind was a maze, filled by the dark men threatening her and her child, memories of her brief time with Brent Musso, her miserable existence with her late husband, and even Royce Glynn. My God! She had forgotten all about Royce; she made a mental note to call the dentist soon. Aside from all that, this man was just *so different* from anyone else she had known; his life was entirely alien to hers, filled with dangerous situations and people — people like Dickie Frapiana. The memory of her late husband gave her a slight shudder.

Church broke into her thoughts with a question. "Michelle, do you have access to a p. c. somewhere, one with internet capability?"

"Well, there's one at the store where I work. And my dad has one in his study, plus several at his office I'm sure you could use. Why?"

"I may need to email something to someone, probably tomorrow. Could be something that might help us."

She eyed him closely. "Should I ask what?"

"Probably not. But only because I'm not sure if it'll work or not. If it does, then I'll tell you. Otherwise, I'd rather not give you false hopes."

"I think you should use one in Dad's office then. I'd rather not disrupt things at the store. So far, Sandi... my friend who owns the store... isn't aware of what's going on. I'd just as soon keep it that way as long as I can." She suddenly remembered the book signing set the next day; another layer of stress and concern. She rubbed her forehead, again entertaining hopeless thoughts about ever having anything resembling a normal life.

Church nodded. During more than one lull in the conversation, he had come close to telling her about Musso's full involvement in her husband's death. The fact that it wouldn't make the current situation any easier caused him to stifle the urge. And there was another reason. While some might consider such an heroic act Musso had planned to be the ultimate sacrifice, there were others — and he was almost certain she would fall into this group — that would be repulsed that someone would plot to take a life, even one as twisted as her husband's, to save their own. He would keep it to himself unless revealing it became absolutely necessary. He also chose not to break the news of Musso's death. There was a better than even chance she already knew, but he didn't want to be the one bringing it up in case she didn't.

"Okay then. Listen, I may be gone when you and your parents wake up. If I am, I promise I'll be back in time for the trip to the airport."

"I'm sure we'll be okay if you're not here. We'll be careful. What will you be doing?"

"Rather not say. Same reason as before; it may not work. But it's part of why I may need a p. c. By the way, what time does your dad usually arrive at his office?"

"This time of year, during tax season, he likes to get there by seven-thirty. But tomorrow, by the time we make the run to the airport, it may be well after eight." She gave him directions to her dad's office, then paused briefly; another detail she had forgotten to cover popped into her head. "Oh, I failed to mention, the man who approached me first in the park told me the amount that was stolen. You may already know it, but it's sixteen million. Needless to say, I was shocked when I heard the amount." She watched his face closely for a reaction.

Nodding slowly, he tried to apply his best poker face. "No, we didn't know for sure. We had estimated from fifteen to twenty, based on the street value of the cocaine we confiscated. One of the bigger deals we've heard of. Certainly the biggest I've been involved in." He regretted the words as soon as he had spoken them. The magnitude of the crimes her husband had been involved in could only make her feel worse. Her only response was to put her hands to her face and stare at the floor with a helpless look. He hoped her reaction was due more to the stress of the day than any guilt she harbored, which would be ridiculous.

With very little else to talk about, they soon ended the awkward silence and said their goodnights, then headed to separate rooms. Neither slept much; Michelle due to the danger filling her every moment — every thought, wondering what the next day would bring, and Church due to the knowledge that the most alluring woman he had ever seen, a woman he was risking an important part of his life to protect, was lying in a bed only yards away, separated by thin walls.

While he tossed and turned in the strange but comfortable bed, alone with his thoughts for the first time all night, the DEA agent had too much time to digest fully what he was doing, the risk he was putting himself and his career through. It was easy to question his own actions and motives, and where they might take him. Then, he would think of the woman, almost within arms reach, and how vulnerable she would certainly be without him. There were no guarantees he could stand in her tormentors' way of getting to her, but there didn't appear to be anyone else. It was knowledge that finally enabled him to drift off.

Chapter 25

Angel Xminez had to wait a few hours for the darkness of the night to fully envelope the outlying areas of Savannah. The rains continued off and on, spitting occasionally, hopefully keeping those who might wish to venture out late on a Monday night indoors. When Javier had drifted in a few hours earlier, smelling of tequila and cigarettes, Xminez had pretended to be asleep, not wanting to engage in conversation with the man. If he had, he would not have been able to restrain his temper. He would have demanded to know what he had told the man he had met in the bar. Perhaps there had been more than one person he had warmed-up to in the dingy-looking place. He would've probably lied, denying anything harmful, which might actually have been true. But it didn't matter. Sooner or later, the man's urges and carelessness would no doubt cause trouble.

Javier was completely under, sound asleep, dreaming his final dreams. Xminez grabbed the cell phone, then made his way out to the parking lot to size up the conditions. Twelve-thirty, and all was quiet. The parking area was empty... only silent vehicles. He breathed in the warm, damp air, steadying his mind, assuring himself he would be doing the right thing. He really didn't see any other choice, if his beliefs about Javier's dangerous weaknesses were correct. And if he was reading Luis Torres correctly, the man lying peacefully back in the room would not fit in with the plans he was beginning to form in his mind.

Returning to the room, he shook the other man's legs, rousting him fom his sleep.

"Come, Cesar. I've just had another talk with Sènor Torres."

Javier managed to push his upper body up from the bed, disoriented by the sudden wake up.

"Umm...what? I didn't hear the phone ring."

"Of course not. I placed the call after I received a text from him. I went outside to use the cell phone. I did not want to wake you."

Javier rubbed his eyes. "Then why are you waking me now?"

"Because we are going to make our next move. Torres continues to grow impatient. We have agreed to a night visit to the woman this time. This should end her stubbornness."

"But... didn't you talk to him earlier?" The effects of alcohol lingered.

"Yes," Xminez answered impatiently, making an effort to control his anger with the other man. "He wasn't satisfied with that conversation. He wants us to make something happen."

"Give me just a little more time to..." Javier started to lie back down.

"Now!" Xminez bellowed. "There will be time to sleep later."

"Christ," Javier muttered, again rubbing a hand over his eyes, then slowly climbing out of his bed. Xminez watched with burning eyes as the man splashed water onto his face, letting his hatred and disgust build. Every word the man spoke... every move he made, inflamed him more. It would only make his job easier.

Arriving at the rental car a few minutes later, Javier was about to climb into the passenger seat, when Xminez, who had proceeded him to the blue compact, walked to the rear. He inserted the key and opened the trunk.

He suddenly called out to Javier. "*Oh Dios mio*!"

"What is it?" Javier said, looking toward the back of the car. With the trunk open, he couldn't see the big man hidden behind the lid, obviously disturbed over something.

"Come here, Cesar. What is this?" The words were a command, though spoken in hushed tones.

"What is what?" Leaving the door ajar, the blond man slinked his way toward the rear of the car to join Angel X. He was still more asleep than awake. He yawned as he stood facing the trunk. Xminez stood back, allowing the other man room to see into the cavity, lit by only a dim bulb. Staring in, Javier said, "I don't see anything, Angel. There is nothing in there except some of the clothes we have worn."

"Oh, but you are wrong my friend. Look closer," Xminez said evenly, removing the Glock, with silencer in place, from his waist band. As Javier leaned in, he put a round into the base of the man's skull. The force of the discharge jerked the body forward, face down into the trunk, his legs still dangling over the dented bumper. Xminez used one of his legs as a fulcrum, levering the man's now useless legs into the compartment along with the rest of the body. Javier's face turned awkwardly towards him as he fell into the trunk, eyes wide, his mouth in a strange, crooked grimace of shock. Sounds resembling gasps were escaping from the man's lips. The massive hit man suddenly cringed. He had no problems with causing death; he had done it many times. But he never particularly relished staring into the face of death. He saw it as a spiritual thing. Leaning in quickly, he held the gun to the man's head, putting one more round between the eyes. Turning, and then shoving the motionless body as far as possible into the small trunk so that it faced inward, he closed the lid.

Closing the passenger side door and locking the car, he surveyed the lot. Still no one in sight. Unwrapping a stick of gum, he put the paper into a pocket, stuck the gum in his mouth, then headed back to his room.

Torres had said use violence only if necessary, and in Angel's mind, both the cop and his drain of a traveling companion had been obstacles standing in his way, so they had met the description of "necessary". He would finally get a good night's sleep, then make one more run at the woman — this time alone.

Chapter 26

Church didn't sleep the whole night through, waking twice. Strange beds, no matter the conditions, usually led to fits of uneven rest, leaving his body somewhat depleted of energy... energy he would likely need during the coming day. When he finally gave it up and crawled from the bed, he did what he needed to do in the adjoining bathroom as silently as possible. He wet a wash cloth, using it to gouge the sleep from his eyes. He then took great pains in easing quietly out of the Lovejoy home early in the morning, not wanting to wake anyone else. Nor did he wish to create noises that might be interpreted as an attack by the men he was going in search of. It was 5:30 a. m., and the still leaded grey skies weren't quite ready to give way to what was promised to be a better day weather-wise. He checked once more the surroundings for evidence of the men who had pursued Michelle the night before. All seemed to be clear, except for the slowly lifting fog that had settled in overnight. Before pulling out of the crushed pea graveled driveway, he examined once more the damage to the left front of his GMC. On second look, it didn't seem to be as bad as his first glance the night before, and well worth the risk.

Finding the two bounty hunters in a city unfamiliar to him might be compared to a needle in a haystack, but he had a few things on his side. First, he was virtually certain they weren't local talent. The pool of Hispanic hit men from the Savannah area couldn't be large — most likely nil. And since they were from out of town, and probably from out of the country, they had to be staying in a hotel or motel. Motels were cheaper, especially ones on the outskirts of town, probably one of the lower end chains. They also offered the added benefit of a low profile. Using his Blackberry again to map the locations of motels that might be candidates, he found a nest of similar establishments west of the city, nearly ten miles out. Gateway Boulevard appeared to be a frontage road of sorts, roughly paralleling Interstate 95. There were at least five in that area that matched the category he sought. He would troll the area, and maybe get lucky.

Stopping first at a convenience store on the way, he purchased a large cup of coffee, black, and since he hadn't eaten since lunch on Monday... a quick drive-through at a Burger King somewhere between Atlanta and Savannah... a bear claw. Heading west on State Highway 204, it took only fifteen minutes to locate Gateway Boulevard, which intersected with 204. The first two motels, an Econo Lodge, and a Days Inn, proved fruitless. A slow drive through the parking lots of each turned up nothing that seemed to match the compact he had struck the night before. In the remaining shades of darkness, now giving way to morning, he made two circles around the buildings to make sure, and then exited. According to the image on the small screen of the magical device in his hands, his next candidate, the Best Western, was only a minute away.

The sun soon began to burn away the last remnants of dawn, and with it the fog, as it eased over the horizon, making it easier to navigate his way through the unfamiliar surroundings. Within seconds of entering the parking lot of the Best Western, an older version of the chain, built around a center courtyard without interior hallways, he was sure he had hit pay dirt. Toward the rear of the parking area, he spotted a dark blue compact, a Toyota Corolla, nestled in among a row of cars, pick ups, and SUVs. The front of the car was facing out, which was a possible tell. Needing to see the rear of the car to determine if it fit, he turned the corner of the lot, and parked in a vacant slot.

The cold front that had brought the rains in, then ushered them out of the area the night before, had left a slight chill in the slowly brightening morning air. Church grabbed the jacket he had brought from the back seat of his GMC and put it on. He strolled casually around the corner of the motel building. Not wanting to stray too close to the suspect car in case the men were early risers, he walked to the rear of the line of vehicles surrounding it. It gave a clear view of the back of the Corolla, revealing a dent in the proper place on the passenger side bumper. A black streak smudged just above the bumper was more evidence. It matched the scrape on his own vehicle in both color and height.

In the few seconds before side-swiping the car, he had managed to read the first three characters on the license plate. Creeping a few yards nearer, he was able to read the two letters and one number that clinched it. An insignia of the car rental company stuck in the rear window was further evidence, but hardly necessary.

He hurried back to his vehicle, climbed in, then circled the motel once more, looking for the ideal spot to observe whoever would show up to operate the small Toyota. He was able to find a parking space next to an island of palmetto bushes and pampas grass, separating his space from the one next to his, and roughly a hundred feet from the Toyota. The vegetation would provide cover, while allowing an opening between the grassy tentacles of the plants for what he had in mind.

It was still only 6:15 a. m. Knowing it might be a long wait, he made himself as comfortable as possible. This was all too familiar; lengthy stakeouts were a major part of his work as a narc. One such extended surveillance had been the many hours spent observing Dickie Frapiana and his boss as they set in motion the huge cocaine deal that ultimately led to the theft by Frapiana, followed soon after by his death. The fact that the previous assignment had resulted in him being here now seemed surreal, when he allowed his mind to wander over the entire path.

His thoughts returned to the money again, now knowing the amount, an amount that was certainly worthy of having someone sent to retrieve it. The only question was, why it had taken so long? Surely they had known Frapiana had a wife, a likely candidate to have the money. In the end, he decided it didn't matter; they were here now. Demolishing the stale pastry in three bites, he took a few sips of the coffee which had turned tepid, losing its bite. He poured the contents out the window, putting the bear claw wrapper in the Styrofoam cup and placing the container in a holder.

An hour passed, and he began to realize he wouldn't be back at the Lovejoy home in time to accompany the family to the airport. But he knew it didn't matter, since he was sure the men who might try to cause them harm were still in the motel. To assure himself there would be no confusion, he placed a call to Michelle's cell phone.

"I won't make it there in time to follow you to the airport," he told her. "But you should be okay. I'm pretty sure I've got them under wraps."

"Under wraps? Is that a DEA term for something *else* I shouldn't ask about?"

Church knew he was sounding too dramatic. "Sorry. Just means I'm keeping an eye on them."

"How did you find them?"

"I can't divulge all of my tricks," he chuckled, then realized his mood was now too light again. She didn't want to hear his clever remarks, any more than the buzz words of his profession. "I'll explain later." He changed his tone, and the subject. "What are you and Silas going to do after your mom and Allison are safely aboard the plane?"

"I'll head on in to work, and so will Dad. I told him you might be coming by to borrow time on a computer. He'll be expecting you."

"Okay. I'll catch up with you later in the day." Ending the call, he could only hope he'd have a reason to use the p. c.

Another fifteen minutes passed. Church suddenly sat up when a large, dark-complected man wearing a baseball cap and dark glasses emerged from an exterior hallway separating two sections of the building, moving in the direction of the blue Corolla. He had managed only a brief glimpse of the man the night before as their vehicles played tag, but it had been enough. The man appeared to be checking out his surroundings as he walked. He definitely appeared to be Hispanic, which could mean from anywhere, Mexico on down. The face reminded him of many he had encountered during his years on the border. There was no choice but to assume he was an extremely dangerous sort.

Church quickly grabbed the HP digital camera he had commandeered from his office, the second device he had brought with him. The Blackberry was useful for other tasks, but the camera was state-of-the-art, with all the bells and whistles, including a built-in GPS system. “Borrowing” it from his department had been a risk, but Steen had a back-up in case it was needed. If things went well... whatever that meant... he would be back in his Atlanta office before higher-ups knew he had taken it. He stepped from the SUV, finding a vantage point behind the frond-like sprouts of the bushes. He started shooting images of the man as he neared the car as fast as he could refocus and click. At one point the man seemed to stare directly at him. He instantly lowered the camera, worried the glare of the low sun might reflect off it. The man looked away; he didn’t think he had been seen. Before raising the digital device again, Church began to worry about something. Where was the second man? He glanced back at the hallway the huge man had exited from, expecting to see the other one following behind, but no one else was coming. Maybe this one was retrieving something from the car, and would be returning inside the motel to rejoin his friend.

But that turned out not to be the case. The big man folded his girth into the compact, then cranked the engine. As he exited the parking lot, Church ducked down in front of his GMC, then hurried to get behind the wheel to follow the other car. It was just past 7:30, too early to head to Silas’ office. He would stick with the tail for awhile, see what he was up to. What passed for rush hour in Savannah hadn’t reached its peak yet, so he had to allow the man ahead plenty of space in the sparse traffic. It would be relatively easy to spot a trailing vehicle in these conditions, especially one with a bruised front end.

It didn't take long to figure out where the man was going. The farther the tail went, the closer it came to Michelle's apartment. When the Corolla finally came to rest a block from the apartment, Church parked well back, prepared to wait once more for the next move. It didn't come, at least not while he watched. The man simply sat there. He was still puzzled by the second man's absence. Michelle had said there were two, and he was one hundred percent certain he had seen two figures in the compact the night before. It bothered him not knowing, but felt the man ahead posed more of a threat. Eight a. m. rolled by, and knowing that Michelle was either still at the airport or on her way to work, and fairly confident the rest of her family was safe, he decided to head to Silas Lovejoy's office. Taking one last look at the other car, he eased out into the light traffic, then made a u-turn, a move he hoped wouldn't be spotted. But it was either that, or drive right by the other man.

On the way, he placed a call to his partner, relieved to find him already in his cubicle.

"You in Savannah?" Steen asked.

"Yep. How're things there?"

"You mean you're still interested in the daily grind of us poor working stiffs?" Steen replied dryly.

Church sighed, not entirely surprised at Steen's attitude. They had been partners for so long, they had developed something of protective yet competitive relationship with each other. They squabbled like siblings at times. "Of course I am, Chris. Cut me some slack, will 'ya."

"Whatever you say." Steen paused, then brought his partner up to speed. "To answer your question, Shands is keeping a low profile, but Floyd Weathers — not so much. He's really gettin' the black leadership of Atlanta riled up. Maybe it's a good thing you're out of town."

It wasn't the kind of news Church needed to hear, and he didn't wish to hear more. He jumped right to the business at hand.

"Say, Chris. I'm going to email you some pictures in a few minutes. Just shot 'em this morning. I haven't had time to review the images yet, but I'm hoping I got a few that will be clear enough to get an I D."

"Somebody we might know over here?"

"I seriously doubt it. But I was hoping you might be able to forward them to our counterparts in south Texas, somewhere near the border, or maybe even the Mexican Drug authorities. See if the face I'm sending rings any bells."

"Christ. You're not asking for much, are you?"

"Come on, Chris. You *did* tell me to let you know if I needed help. Remember?"

"Yeah, but I was just being nice. You know, just something you say."

"Cut the crap, Chris. This is important. And I'll owe you big time."

Steen sighed. "You're damn right you will." He paused for a moment. *"This* is what I'll do. I'll send them to an agent I know in the San Antonio office, then have *him* relay them to the Mexican federal police in Mexico City, if he's a mind to. Any requests for I D's down there I want coming from him, and not me. Make more sense for him to be making inquiries anyway." He paused, then added, "This is all unauthorized, Walt."

He was right, Church admitted to himself. The Atlanta regional office had enough to worry about without doing personal favors. But he wanted to know the people he was dealing with... know what they were capable of. “I realize that, Chris. If I had another way, I’d use it.”

When Steen didn’t respond right away, Church assumed he would help. He quickly changed the subject. “Anybody come looking for me yesterday?”

“Yeah. Well, only a phone call. Joyner’s assistant called wanting clarification of the message you left before splittin’.”

“What did you tell her?”

“Just you had some personal things to take care of.”

Which was exactly the truth. “Okay. Thanks, partner. I should be in front of a computer within thirty minutes.”

“I can’t wait,” Steen said sarcastically. “I’ll sit here all tingly with excitement until it comes across,” he added, then hung up.

Chapter 27

Silas Lovejoy hadn't made it to his office by the time Church arrived. He was concerned about that at first, but then decided the man may have stayed at the airport until the plane departed. The receptionist, whose nameplate on her desk read Shirley Kinnebrew, hadn't been expecting any visitors, let alone a DEA agent, so early. That, along with the agent's ratty appearance had her staring occasional darts at him while he waited in the reception area. Fully expecting the woman to call the police at any moment, Church had to pinch his mouth to keep from smiling. He squinted his eyes and stared back a few times, causing her to quickly avert her eyes. It was a common reaction to the look he needed to maintain for occasional undercover assignments. Now it was providing cheap entertainment, helping to fill the time.

When the C. P. A. finally walked through the door nearly half an hour later, he did so with a noticeably worried look on his face. Church thought the worst as Silas waved him back to his office, while telling the woman to hold all calls until further notice.

"What's happened, Silas?" Church reluctantly asked as soon as the door to the accountant's office was closed. He wasn't sure he wanted to know. His mind raced. *The second man*! They had somehow tricked him, sending him to watch the big man, while the other pulled a sneak attack. That had to be it.

Silas Lovejoy fell into his chair behind his desk, then motioned for the agent to take a seat across from him.

"I've just come from the police precinct station... the one that assigned the patrolmen to keep watch on Michelle and Allison. I wanted to know what happened to the man that should've been on duty." He chose not to mention he had also made a brief stop at Michelle's bank to make her deposit, honoring his daughter's request for secrecy.

Church had completely forgotten the man had said he was going to talk to the police.

"And?"

"They wanted to know the same thing." Lovejoy paused, then stared at Church with a dazed look. "They haven't heard from him since yesterday, around mid-afternoon."

The idea that something might've happened to the officer *had* flashed into Church's mind the previous afternoon when Michelle had wondered why the patrolman hadn't intervened.

"That's not good. I assume they've started a search for him."

"Of course. Been confined to the city limits so far, but they think they may have to enlarge it soon. There's been no report — from anybody. They checked with his family. They said he never came home last night either. The chief of police is preparing an announcement to release to the media within the hour." The man paused again, his frown deepening. "And they've called off any further patrols at Michelle's apartment, at least until he's found. All their personnel are tasked to find him."

Church didn't think that mattered much, since Michelle wasn't going back to the apartment any time soon. He was trying to make sense of it, wondering if the media getting involved was a good or bad thing. His instincts were solidly behind the likelihood the man had been taken out by the bounty hunters. Would they be scared into hiding by the announcement? Or become more desperate? He started grasping at straws.

"Did they mention if they had interviewed the tenants at the apartment complex? Find out if anyone saw anything?"

Silas nodded. "First thing they did. Nobody saw a thing. He's simply disappeared." He then gave the DEA agent a strange look, as if he wanted to ask something but was unsure of how to begin. He finally said, "They wanted to know more about these men, the ones threatening Michelle."

Of course they did; it was an obvious question. Join the club, Church thought. The comment reminded him of the images he needed to transmit to Steen. It was way past the time he had promised to send them.

"That's why I need to use one of your p. c.'s, Silas. I've been able to take photos of one of the men. I'm going to email it to someone in my office. See if we can get an I D on him."

Silas sat up straight, staring in surprise. "You mean you saw one of them?"

"Yes, I was able to locate where they were staying."

"And you didn't do anything?"

Church cringed, knowing how that sounded. It was a mistake to tell the man what he had been up to. He needed to explain himself — and quickly. Spreading his arms, he said, "What could I do, Silas? I have no arrest authority here. Especially since I'm technically on leave, here on my own. I've come here to do my best to make sure these people don't harm your daughter and your granddaughter. But legally, it's all outside my jurisdiction." He wondered if the rationale sounded as thin to the man as it did to his own ears.

"And even if I had notified the local cops I had spotted them, technically, they haven't broken any laws yet. At least, none we're aware of."

"But they threatened her! Attacked her and Allison in her car!"

"I know, Silas. But Michelle didn't see them, and I couldn't positively identify them based on what I saw last night. In these situations, you have to catch them in the act... and it has to be done by the local police."

The accountant was rubbing his forehead, while keeping glaring eye contact with Church. Suddenly, it dawned on him that identifying the men might in fact cause his daughter problems. Pointing them out to the authorities, including Church, could somehow lead to disclosing the payment she had just received... the first of many, supposedly. It might possibly heap more suspicion on her about her involvement with her worthless husband in the drug money theft. That's why she had wanted to keep it hidden. He quickly softened his tone. "I suppose that does makes some sense. But still, they've threatened my daughter and grandchild. I can't let these men harm them."

"I'm with you on that, Silas. And I knew as long as I had the man in my sights, he couldn't harm your family. By the way, did Mary and Allison get off okay?"

Church received only a half-hearted nod in answer. The man was still clearly troubled by his daughter's so-called protector's lack of action, or so it would appear.

"Good. That's going to make it easier to monitor things, since the threat of kidnaping is gone." Once more, Church thought he was setting the wrong tone, sounding too optimistic. "Listen, Silas. If I can email these pictures, maybe, just maybe there'll be outstanding U. S. warrants on these two, and we'll get the locals to take some sort of action."

The older man nodded again, but he had more to say. "When I told the police about you... what you did yesterday to help Michelle, they wanted to know about you too. What you're doing here. I mean, in what capacity."

Church felt his body sagging. Of course they would want to know that too. It never occurred to him Silas might mention his presence to the police. "My capacity is what I just told you. Did they want to talk to me?"

Silas shook his head. "Didn't say so, but I got the impression they may want to." A hint of a narrow smile poked out from his moustache, more ironic than anything else.

"I explained to them your history in all this. How you were here last summer interviewing Michelle, on behalf of the DEA. I think I convinced them your interest now is more of a personal thing."

Church could only stare. "Oh," he managed to say.

Lovejoy managed another smile, in spite of his misgivings toward the agent."It's okay, Walt. I've got a pretty good idea why you're here. I tried to explain it to Michelle last night, but I don't think she wanted to hear it." He leaned his elbows on his desk. "There's something you have to understand, she's been through so much over this past year... well, really, over the past ten years. She's been damaged, especially in regard to her emotional side. I doubt if she feels she can trust anybody. And now, she's dealing with these threats. So she probably won't be receptive to..." Silas now looked slightly embarrassed. "Well, I think you get the drift of what I'm trying to say."

Michelle's protective father had seen through his motives, which shouldn't come as a surprise. "Of course I do, Silas. And I understand completely." He decided to come clean. "That's partly why I'm here, I'll admit it. But some of it has to do with how we left things last year. I'm afraid we didn't offer her much in the way of ideas in how to guard against this kind of thing happening. It's bothered me ever since."

Before either man could say anything else, Church's cell phone started ringing. It was Steen.

"What happened to your email?" the voice on the other end asked impatiently before Church could get a word out. "I've been waiting over an hour."

"Sorry, partner. I've been busy. I'll do it now." He looked expectantly at Silas, seeking approval. The man nodded.

"Well, you'd better hurry. I've got other things to do, ya know."

Church hung up. "The computer...?"

"There's a vacant office next to mine," Silas said. "You can use the one in there. It's new. Should have what you need. And I've got to get busy myself." He pulled a file from a stack, powered-up his own p. c., and busied himself with work.

Church wanted to say more to the man who now had doubts about him, but took the hint and went to the vacant office. Within a few minutes, he had hooked up a USB cable he had stuffed into his jacket pocket, running it from the HP camera to a portal in the computer's central processing unit, the brains of the p. c. Thankfully, the Dell computer had the software needed to house photos and videos. As the images were imported onto the computer screen, he was able to view them clearly for the first time. Most were probably unusable, offering a limited view of the man in profile. One, however, did give a fairly good view of the face when the man had started to turn in his direction. The cap covered part of the forehead, but perhaps there was something there. Putting the cursor on the image, he clicked, and it instantly enlarged. Should be enough there, he thought. Modern digital technology didn't require much; only a small section of the face was needed, isolated to match the same spot on another image, assuming there was another digital photo of the suspect somewhere in cyberspace. Attaching each of the photos to an email addressed to Steen, he clicked on the "SEND" button, transporting the images via the internet. All he could do now was wait.

But he couldn't wait here. He needed to go check on the man he had left outside of Michelle's apartment, see what he was up to. Putting the USB cable and the camera back inside his jacket, he took a minute to lean in and wave goodbye to Silas, who returned a token wave without speaking. Church knew the man was busy, but also detected a degree of unease, or perhaps disappointment, in the body language.

Pausing long enough to give the receptionist a parting wink, evoking a new frown, he rushed outside to his Yukon. As he pulled away, he decided to make a quick run by Liberty Lady before heading to the apartment complex. If the second man had been there yesterday, he might return. He continued to worry about this mystery man, perhaps a joker in the deck.

Chapter 28

A quick drive-by in front of Liberty Lady produced no indications of danger. In fact, peering through the front windows, Church could make out Michelle's perfect frame as she waited on the first early customers, showing no signs of stress. From his vantage point, she appeared to be able to keep the underlying currents in her life hidden from her face. He could only imagine what was circling through her mind, though her smile remained inviting. Perhaps knowing her daughter was safely removed from the scene was relieving a certain degree of tension.

As he sat in a parking space across from the quaint store, it was impossible to filter out the conversation he had left behind at Silas Lovejoy's office. He tried to put himself in the man's place, tried to see things from his perspective. Michelle's well being was being handled by a federal agent he hardly knew, but an agent he *did* know was here mostly due to the fact he was attracted to his daughter. Naturally, there should be suspicions and doubts about the arrangement. That went without saying. Church attempted to recall the words Silas had used to describe his motives. Although the man hadn't expressly discouraged his intentions, he had made it crystal clear he would be fighting an uphill battle. That also went without saying. In fact, he wasn't at all sure he was capable of scaling that slope; it seemed entirely beyond his reach.

He surveyed the street in both directions, trying to pick out anyone who might fit the description of the blond man, possibly lurking in the morning shadows to spring another surprise attack. No one rang any alarm bells. Next, he circled the block to determine if there was an alley behind the store providing a hiding place. There was one, but it was clear, except for a few scattered boxes and trash cans. Satisfied there were no immediate problems at the store, he decided it was time to return to the apartment.

Navigating his way again through the streets of Savannah, which took some doing even with the help of his GPS in the still unfamiliar surroundings, he managed to again find Abercorn Street. From there, it was a simple matter of following the thoroughfare to the complex.

Nearing his destination, he saw the blue Corolla was no longer parked on the street where it had been earlier. Scanning the block, it was nowhere to be seen. That bothered him at first, because if he wasn't here, he had no idea where else to look. Entering the parking lot, he knew he had to be certain the man was no longer in the complex, having moved on. But to where? With Mary Lovejoy and Allison out of the picture, there were only three locations the supposed hit man could do damage: here; Liberty Lady; and Silas' office. Well, four, if he counted the Lovejoy home, but there was no one there. The book store seemed secure, but he would make a rapid return downtown, just in case, as soon as he was convinced the apartment parking lot was clear. Silas should be okay. He was surrounded by people — too risky for a daylight attack there anyway. But then he remembered; there was a second man out there — somewhere.

Just as he was completing the loop through the lot, he saw it. The blue compact was parked in a corner slot, almost hidden from view, again facing out. It appeared to be empty. Craning to look in all directions, failing to spot the man, he knew he would have to do a foot search. He backed the GMC into a nearby slot, leaving it in position for a quick getaway, then stepped from the black SUV. Keeping an eye peeled, he walked over to the compact, placing a hand on the hood. Only slightly warm. It had been parked for a while.

The morning sun was fully engaged now, bringing with it temperatures that had to be approaching eighty. The jacket had become excess baggage. Removing it, he wrapped it around the camera, then returned to lean in and place it under the front seat of his Yukon. He kept the Blackberry in a pants pocket, and the third piece of equipment he had brought... his Beretta... tucked in his belt. Pulling the tail of his golf shirt out to hide the weapon, he began his search, knowing it could only lead to one place.

A dusting of fresh yellow-green early spring pollen floated through the warm air, beginning to blanket the damp roofs and hoods of the vehicles drenched by overnight showers that had washed away earlier deposits. It was a tough time of the year for allergy sufferers, Church mused as he moved cautiously toward the building containing Michelle's unit. Thinking about such extraneous subjects was a mind-relaxing trick he played on himself, a habit he had developed over the years, letting his thoughts drift to trivial things while in situations such as this; a way to keep his entire system from locking down as he zeroed in on his target. It was similar to preventing your knees from locking up when standing in rigid formation too long during military training. But when engagement actually presented itself, it was all synapses on deck.

Stepping to the front of the building, he was alarmed, but not at all surprised, to see the door to Michelle's unit slightly ajar. Squinting to get a better look, he could see splintered wood from the frame around the lock. The door had been jimmied. He knew the man was still inside, since his car was in the lot. He flattened himself against the wall of the building, beginning to edge toward the damaged door. Reaching inside his shirt, he wrapped his left hand around his gun, then held it tight against his leg.

He flinched, then came to an abrupt halt at the sound of a door slamming somewhere above him. Footsteps could be heard descending the exterior stairway from the second level of the building. The iron-bar and concrete stairs were the kind that extended outward from the building until halfway down, then turned back toward it after reaching a small landing. A young man, possibly only a teenager, bounded from the bottom step, bringing him face-to-face with a strange looking man wearing a ponytail, leaning at an odd angle against the wall. Evidently surprised to see anyone standing there, he also came to an abrupt stop.

"How's it goin', my man?" he said, with only a slightly puzzled expression.

Embarrassed at being caught off-guard, Church gave a clever reply. "Okay, *man*." He kept the gun hidden behind the leg, away from the other man's sight.

The boy nodded, gave a disinterested look, then turned and left.

Giving him time to reach his pickup, climb in and drive away, Church then put his mind back on the task at hand. The door was only a few yards away now, open a few inches, displaying a streak of darkness along the vertical edge next to the frame. He wondered about that, but then realized the lights inside were out, and the person he assumed was still inside couldn't close the door behind him since the latch was shattered. There were no sounds from within as he drew within a couple of feet. For the first time, he wished he had Steen with him. Entering a potential trap such as this one was better suited for a team, or at least a second man.

Switching the gun to his right hand, he put his left on the facing of the door, ready to enter. Easing it open with his free hand, alarmed by the crimped, creaking hinges, he knelt down, making a smaller target of his body. He knew the apartment had to be small inside, probably no more than three or four rooms, so whoever was in there was no doubt fully aware of his presence. He wished he'd gone inside the night before while Michelle grabbed what she needed. At least then he would be familiar with the interior.

Pushing the door slowly until it was all the way open, he now felt entirely vulnerable, fully exposed against the back-lighting from outside. Duck-walking with knees bent, gun held before him with both hands, he stepped a few feet inside, then came to a halt, letting his eyes adjust. The only illumination came from the sunlight streaking in between the vertical slats of the blinds, along with the light streaming through the open door. A definite scent of something he recognized seemed to permeate the stale air of the tiny unit. It was a sharp, sweet smell that took only seconds to identify. It was cinnamon.

He accepted the fact danger was close at hand — very close, given the confines. Any other time, he would be experiencing a cheap thrill, rummaging through the woman's digs, seeing the things she saw every day, which he now could see were strewn about. The man had also been searching. But for what? He suddenly stood, then focused on listening; listening for breathing — movement — anything. There was nothing. That bothered him. The place was so small, and his presence so obvious, the man *had* to be within yards, drawing a bead on him. But for some reason, he was holding back.

Two doors were visible leading from the den where he now crouched. One had to be a bedroom, and the other appeared to be a kitchen. A short, narrow hallway led to what must be a second bedroom... probably Allison's room. Still holding his Beretta with both hands in front of him, he chose to move toward the kitchen. Then he noticed there was no door at all, just an arched opening connecting the den to the kitchen. He removed his right hand from the gun long enough to place it on the edge of the opening, ready to swing his way in.

Immediately inside the kitchen was a refrigerator to his left. A stainless-steel handle ran vertically on the side nearest him. He reached to grab it to continue his way in. Wavy reflections only barely noticeable in the handle suddenly indicated movement behind him. A rush of air accompanied the movement. Instinctively he ducked to his right, swinging his gun hand at whatever or whoever was approaching. Contact was made with the right rib cage of an enormous figure, who grunted only slightly at the impact while swinging wildly over the crouched agent's head. Before he could take a glance upward to make out the face, though he really didn't have to — there was no doubt who it was — Church was propelled across the kitchen floor by a mighty kick to his back. His head made an impression in the bottom door panel of an oven a few feet away, stunning him enough to cause him to drop his weapon. He thought he made another swing toward his attacker, but wasn't sure in his dazed state. Trying desperately to gather his wits, he started to push himself up, but was stopped by an even more ferocious blow to his lower back, literally knocking the remaining wind from his body. Kicking backward at where he thought the man's shins might be, he caught nothing but air. He started to gasp for breath, but his efforts were interrupted by a third blow, this one a crack to the back of his head. His head exploded into a flame-filled star, which was quickly extinguished, along with all conscious thoughts.

Xminez leaned over the man, examining his handiwork. He considered for a moment whether to waste a couple of rounds to make sure he would cause no further problems. But he had found what he was looking for, even though he hadn't known what it would be until he had happened upon it; there was nothing this person could do to stop him now. And he would be long gone by the time the man... whoever he was... recovered.

He started to turn and leave, then decided he had to satisfy his curiosity, wanting to know if it was indeed someone Torres had sent, or a member of a drug family in the U S. He bent to reach inside the man's bulging rear pocket, extracting a wallet. Another thought struck him; he wouldn't have been shocked for it to reveal the man's identity as the woman's friend from Texas, the third possibility. Musso, she had said his name was. The Drug Enforcement Administration I D was a puzzling shock. He stared down at the motionless body, trying to make sense of a narc being here. From his knowledge of their way of doing business, he didn't think they worked solo. They traveled in packs; not as lone wolves. The card indicated an Atlanta location, which was another puzzle. But there was no time to reason it through to a conclusion. His discovery now told him where he had to go, and time was critical. Tossing the wallet and card onto the man's back, and cramming what he'd found into a pocket, he hurried out.

Chapter 29

The annoying sound seemed to come from another world. A nightmare world. A world filled with pain. He wished it would stop, because it only added to his throbbing misery. Then he felt a tingling sensation below, also seeming unreal, something tickling the upper part of his leg. Whatever the source, the combination of the two stirred him to life, or as near to life as possible with his head pounding like a kettle drum. By the time he realized it was a device of some sort... a cell phone, ringing and vibrating in unison, it was too late. It had stopped.

His next challenge was to recall where he was, try to recognize the surroundings. Managing to sit up, leaning against what he thought was a wall, he looked around. It had to be a kitchen, since he was staring straight ahead at the bottom half of a refrigerator. His back was resting uncomfortably against a railing of some sort; it was digging into him. He turned his head only slightly to identify the handle of an oven door. The movement sent arrows of pain through his brain. The drumming in his head made it hard to concentrate, while he began to try and remember where he had been before his world turned dark. Slowly it came to him; Michelle's apartment. He had been looking for something. No — someone. The bounty hunter — the Hispanic man, who had ambushed him from behind, judging from the searing pain in the back of his head. He ran a hand back there, feeling a sticky matting in his thick hair, working its way down into his pony tail.

He pushed himself up gingerly, continuing to use the oven as a prop while he gained his balance. As he stood, something fell to his feet. A wallet. His wallet, he assumed. Next came his credentials, bouncing across the linoleum floor in its plastic case. Ignoring them for the moment, he stood still for a long moment, trying to work the dizziness from his head. He then staggered to the nearby sink. He ran the water until it was warm, then grabbed a paper towel from its rack. Dabbing at first, then loading up a second towel with cold water and holding it firmly in place, he reached for his pocket to extract his cell phone with his free hand. He was impressed by the fact it was a fancy device — a Blackberry. The number that had been ringing was still displayed. He wouldn't've recognized it by itself, but the identity of the caller was also shown. It was Chris Steen, the man he *was* able to recall as being his partner. Why would he be calling? Then he remembered having talked to him earlier in the day. How much earlier? What had they talked about? The current time was also displayed on the screen: 11:35. Since he could see light through the window, he knew it couldn't be p. m. But 11:35 a. m. was bad enough. He had been out for a long time, maybe an hour, but probably more.

The rest slowly came to him. He had emailed pictures to Steen. Maybe that was the reason for the call. He hit the "CALL" symbol below the number that had jarred him awake.

"Steen."

"Chris, it's me," Church said in muted tones, rationing his words, knowing talking would cause more pain. "Couldn't get to the phone."

"You sound like you just woke up. You takin' a nap over there? I knew Savannah was a sleepy little town, but in mid-day?"

"I wish." A clever come-back would take energy, and would hurt. "Had a run-in with one of the hit men."

"Jesus Christ! Are you okay?"

"Don't know yet. Your call brought me outta the funk he put me in. Head's about to explode."

"Sounds like you'd better get help, partner."

"I will. Why'd you call?"

"I got something on the name of the guy that matches the face you sent over. And from what I got back from San Antonio, it's amazing you're still kicking."

What face? Right... the bounty hunter... the man that had battered him like a rag doll. "They talk to the Mexican officials?"

"Nope. Didn't even have to. They know this guy. Names' Angel Xminez...aka...Angel X. He's one of the baddest of the bad, partner. One of Luis Torres' men. He's made a few forays into the country before, but most of his activity has been below the border. He's ruthless, Walt."

Normal brain function, or at least, something resembling it, was slowly being restored. The Torres name was easy to recognize. He was head of one of the best known, most notorious drug families in Mexico. Instantly Church knew Steen was correct; it was a mystery why Michelle was still alive. If they had found her with any of the money, she wouldn't be. And the reason she was still alive was most likely due to the fact they weren't sure if she had it or not. And why hadn't the man finished him off? There had to be a reason.

Steen continued. "It makes sense, Walt. The Torres and Medina families did a lot of deals together. My guy in San Antonio said they've had reports of some of Medina's leaders gettin' wiped out. The one that survived was sent home in a body bag, but still alive. Appears Torres held the Medinas responsible for the deal here in Atlanta going bad. Now he must be lookin' for the money. Appears you just got in his way."

Church asked Steen to hold on a minute, then removed the blood-soaked paper towel while placing the phone on the counter, then wetted another to replace it. He used the time to look around the kitchen. Every drawer was pulled out; the floor was littered. He was sure that was true throughout the entire apartment. Each movement was torture; his head was still pounding. The sucker punch to his back must've bruised a kidney. Pain was radiating through his body as he picked up the mobile device.

"Looks that way, Chris. Feels that way too." He recalled something else that had been bugging him. "Did your contact mention if this Angel guy works alone? Anything about an accomplice?"

"Didn't ask. But I'll try and find out and let you know." Steen paused. "Our folks in San Antonio are pretty pissed, by the way. They're dumbfounded that these two made it across the border without being spotted, let alone makin' it all the way cross country. They had to have flown outta somewhere in the southwest... maybe San Diego, Phoenix, or even San Antonio, right under their noses."

"That may be true, but I can't worry about that now."

Steen was silent for a beat before adding, “Walt, I know you shot this down yesterday, but don’t you think you should enlist the guys in the Savannah office. This has gotten out of hand, it’s serious now. For both you and the Frapiana woman.”

Michelle! The guy might’ve gone after her after finishing with him. “Listen, Chris, call them if you want, and have them call my cell. Maybe I can use their help. I’ve gotta hang up and check on Michelle now. Thanks.”

“So its Michelle now, huh? Crap. Sounds like you’ve gone all in, buddy.”

Church ignored the comment, ending the call without saying goodbye.

Punching in her cell number, it took a minute for Michelle to answer.

“Are you okay?” he asked, barely giving her time to say hello.

“What? Yes. Why? What’s wrong?”

His head throbbed even harder hearing her voice, but he felt enormous relief at her response. “He’s been here... the big guy. At your apartment. Hate to tell you, but he messed things up pretty bad.”

“Oh my God! Did you see him?”

“If I’d had eyes in the back of my head, I would have. He was able to catch me by surprise. Clubbed me, then took off.” Church noticed his breathing was constricted, causing him to speak in short gasps.

“Are you okay, Walt?” Her concern sounded sincere, although his head was clear enough to know it was due to the kind of person *she* was, and not who *he* was.

“I will be. But you may want to come and check to see if anything’s missing.”

“I’ll be there as soon as I can.”

“Okay. By the way, do you have any peroxide? any antiseptics or band aids?"

"Of course. I've got a five year old, remember. And there's Tylenol in the bath room too. Help yourself."

"All right, but listen, Michelle. Check things out as you leave the store. Have somebody walk you to your car. They could be anywhere."

Promising she would, she hung up.

While he waited, he walked through the apartment, using the time to get his legs back under him. Whatever order she had maintained before was scattered everywhere. If there had been anything here to satisfy the man's search one way or the other, it was impossible to know if he'd found it. He also wondered if the bounty hunter's success, or lack of success, bore any connection to the fact he was still among the living. Stepping outside, he then walked to the corner of the building, leaning to assure himself the blue compact was gone. The fresh air helped. The car was gone.

About to return to the apartment, his phone buzzed again. He didn't recognize the number, but the area code was the same as Michelle's. It was one of the local agents, introducing himself as Reggie Floyd. Church vaguely recalled seeing the man's name tag at a regional meeting in Atlanta some time back.

"We actually had a call about you before your partner called," Floyd said. "The locals inquired about you this morning. Wanted to check out the story a local accountant gave them about why you were here. Course, we didn't know crap about it, so we weren't sure what to say. They're curious about you, and why you're here. Have to say I am too. But right now, I think *they're* more concerned over a missing cop."

"Yeah, I'm sorry about that," Church said, knowing his secret mission was out in the open now. It made perfect sense for the police to check out Silas' story about a wayward DEA agent. "I know it put you guys in a bind. Hoped to be in and out before anybody knew I was here."

Floyd hesitated briefly. "Well, Steen vouched for you. Said other than being a royal pain in the ass and a love-struck doofus — his words, not mine — you were okay. What can we do to help?"

He thought about the question, as a narrow grin crept out due to Steen's description. But he was still finding it hard to put things in order. "One thing. You might give the accountant a call, make sure he's okay. Did the local cops give you his name?"

"Right. Silas Lovejoy. We've already looked him up. We'll check in with him soon as I hang up. Meanwhile, the local guys wanted to know if you being here had anything to do with their missing officer. Anything we should know?"

"Not at the moment. No evidence either way." Church knew that might be stretching the truth some, but thought he might be doing Floyd a favor by not divulging more at this point. Steen had just provided a name that *might* be involved in the disappearance, but there was no proof to go with it. And, he reminded himself he was not here on an active DEA case.

"I see," Floyd answered slowly. "Well, anything I can do for you now?"

"Can't think of anything now, but thanks. I'll hang on to your number, if that's okay."

"Sure." Floyd paused again. "Look, Church. We'll keep all this on the q. t. as long as we can. But, you *do* realize you're pretty far off the reservation. If the locals get too aggressive, or if the media finds out what's going on, we'll have to disavow any knowledge of your actions, which is the truth. Just don't do anything foolish."

"I understand. And thanks."

Ending the call, Church wondered what could be more foolish than what he'd already done. He went back inside to wait for Michelle.

Ten minutes later, she arrived. It took a few minutes for the equal shocks of seeing her apartment trashed, as well as the agent's bloody head, to wear off. As she took it all in, she shot an unsettled look toward the room he had assumed was her bedroom. Something was distressing her... something he couldn't read with an addled brain. When she was finally able to calm herself, she turned to examine Church's wound. Other than downing two, and then a third Extra-Strength Tylenol for good measure, he had been unable to address his battered head, since he couldn't see it to work on it. She carefully cut away enough of his blood-clumped hair to expose the gash, then drenched it with peroxide while he squirmed and winced in new agony. She had to squelch the odd sensation of wanting to lop off the man's dirty brown ponytail while holding the scissors. The flow of blood finally ceased, she taped down a wadded-up piece of gauze with cris-crossed bandages.

"You need to have this checked out at an E R," she admonished, while taking another glance toward the bedroom. Her voice was unsteady when she spoke. Something was nagging at her."I don't think there's any infection... yet. But I'd rather have someone that knows what they're doing look at it. You might have a concussion."

"Yeah. I'll do that later." He sounded unconvincing, since he knew he couldn't afford to spend time waiting in an emergency room. The man was out there somewhere, planning his next move. "Are you certain you didn't spot him? Or the other one?"

"No. And, yes, I was careful." She looked around the den where they were seated, noticing once again the items that were broken and scattered. Nothing was in the same place she had left it the night before. But that didn't seem to bother her as much as something else... something he still couldn't see. "Give me a minute, Walt. I need to check on something?" Not waiting for a reply, she suddenly stood and headed toward the inner room.

Her face had turned pale, taking on a look resembling fear; her eyes had widened as she headed toward the interior room. It was as if she expected a harmful presence to be waiting for her behind the open door. Church could hear her rummaging through drawers, then repeating to herself, *"Oh, no. Oh, no."* Then the sounds from the room ceased. She slowly re-appeared in the doorway, an ashen look indicating trouble. A hand was pressed across her forehead.

"What is it, Michelle?" His expression then mirrored hers, knowing whatever she had found, it couldn't be good.

She slowly turned her frightened gaze toward the DEA agent, hesitating for a moment before speaking. When she did, it was with a trembling voice, barely audible.

"We need to talk, Walt. There's something I have to tell you."

Chapter 30

Church could only sit and listen quietly while Michelle explained what she had discovered missing from her apartment. It was a letter; a letter she had never wanted him to know about; a letter that told her she would be receiving money from a trust; a letter sent by an attorney in Houston, Texas. Houston was the home of Brent Musso. The combination of those factors immediately told him one of the theories he and Steen had discussed nearly seven months earlier about what happened to the sixteen million was correct. Only he hadn't known the amount until the night before, when she had told him. Musso had somehow taken the money after her husband had been gunned down, and secreted it back to Texas. Technically, it was a crime, but one he had cared little about pursuing when it occurred, and even less so now. The millions were the residue of the sickening habits of weak, desperate people, who had thrown it away on something that could do nothing but ruin their lives, if not end them. To his way of thinking, no one had a claim to it that superseded anyone else's. Well aware not everyone in his office would agree with him, he simply didn't care.

He watched as she agonized over not telling him about the letter, and the reason she gave. She had been afraid he would think she was complicit in taking the money, or at the very least, a portion of it. After all, he was a federal agent, trained to track down drug dealers, and their money. Wasn't that one of the reasons he had come looking for her the previous year? To ask about the money? Her hands were squeezed together tightly in her lap, causing her thin knuckles to turn white; eye contact was avoided as she talked.

"I'm sorry, Walt. I guess at this point, I just didn't know who to trust."

His recall had returned enough to realize they were the same words Silas had used in describing his daughter's vulnerable situation a few hours earlier.

While he had listened, his emotions were busy taking a wild roller coaster ride, up one second, then down the next. Touched by her sincerity in pouring her heart out, framing her in a more sympathetic light than ever, he couldn't shake the fact she *hadn't* trusted him. If she had only known how he had fought to put an end to the search for the money after her husband's death, and then Musso's soon after, she would have no doubts. But then, there was no way for her to know about any of that, other than trying to convince her now.

They were sitting next to each other as she gave her reasons, perched on the sofa. He wanted more than anything to reach for her, hoping his touch would show her she was wrong. Instincts told him this was not the time; there might still be some misgivings.

Instead, he sighed, and said, "Michelle, I don't know how I can convince you I don't care about the money, except simply saying it. When you called me for help yesterday, the thought you might have it never entered my mind. As far as I was concerned, the money was forgotten when we learned about Musso's death late last year. It just didn't exist any longer."

She looked up quickly at the mention of Brent Musso's fate. "You knew Brent died?" Her pained expression was also one of confusion.

"Yes. I think it was either October, or maybe November, when we found out."

"But how... how did you find out?"

Church breathed in deeply, knowing what would follow would be hard on them both. He eased into it carefully. "Well, it was actually our north Florida office that discovered it first. They were attempting to get in touch with him for an interview, since the killings occurred in their neighborhood."

"An Interview? Why would they want to interview him?"

He stared directly at her. "They wanted to ask him about that last night in Destin."

She unclasped her hands, then fell back, as if succumbing to a heavy weight. The cushions of the sofa had been ripped open by the bounty hunter. She grabbed at one of the rips absently with a nervous hand, digging in."I don't understand."

Oh, Christ! He wished there were someone else here to tell her. But it was left up to him. He anticipated her reaction as he began slowly. "You see, Michelle. What that man told you, about Musso being on the pier with Dickie... well, he was correct. We have proof he was there."

She didn't respond. Her body seemed to be sinking into the sofa. Her hand gouged deeper.

Wanting to get it behind him and be done with it, he continued. “His fingerprints were matched to those found on a couple of the weapons involved in the shootout. At first, nobody could identify his prints, since he didn’t have a criminal record. Then they decided to check them against the prints that all security dealers — stock brokers, in other words — have to give before entering the industry. His were a match.

Michelle shook her head back and forth, appearing dazed. “No. That can’t be.”

“I wish I could agree with you, but prints are almost always conclusive. There are times when only one print matches, and there’s some doubt. But there were positive identifications of three prints... in other words, three fingers... on both guns. So there was no question.”

Church shifted in his uncomfortable seat. He had more to tell. “Here’s what I think happened, Michelle, actually, what I’m *sure* happened. Musso... er, Brent,” Recognizing her apparent feelings for the man, he decided to use his first name, “knowing his condition was terminal, and knowing he couldn’t allow your husband to involve you and Allison in his escape plans, plotted to remove the two of you from what he saw as a dangerous situation. Once that was done, with the help of your friends from Tennessee, he decided to make sure Dickie could never bother you again.”

Seeing shades of doubt mixed with horror creeping across her face, he leaned toward her and quickly added, “Just think about it, Michelle. Brent realized he had nothing to lose. Even if he was caught doing what he planned, he knew there was little harm the authorities could do him.”

He paused, keeping an eye on her face, by now, twisted into a confused mask. “After the Martins had you safely out of the way, he tracked your husband to the marina, where he planned to take his life."

Michelle's entire face sagged, losing some, but not all, of its appeal. An expression of disbelief covered it. "Are you asking me to believe Brent killed Dickie?"

"No."

"But you just said..."

"Oh, his intentions *were* to kill him, there's no doubt about that. But from the ballistics tests conducted on the weapons found at the scene, they were able to determine beyond any doubt the bullets that killed Dickie were from the guns of the two hit men a drug lord from Virginia, one of the men he stole from, had sent to find him. Turns out, the rounds Brent fired were the ones that took out the hit men. If he hadn't, they would surely have killed him. It was self defense, more than anything."

The small den, seeming even smaller by the clutter the man had left behind, and the tension in the room, fell into a few moments of uneasy silence. Church watched her closely, wondering what could possibly be running through her mind. She looked crushed. He needed to help her... no... *make* her, accept the truth of Musso's motives.

"You have to try and understand, Michelle. He must've wrestled with his decision before doing what he did. Brent wasn't a killer by nature... I think you'd agree with that. But he most likely felt that if Dickie lived to escape, or even if he was apprehended, you and Allison would never be free of him. In my opinion, it was a courageous thing he did."

As he summarized Brent Musso's actions from over seven months ago, describing to the stunned woman what his reasons must have been, Church began to see how close they were to his own purposes for being in Savannah.

His actions weren't as selfless as the other man's, but the goal was the same — protect the woman, at all costs.

Michelle finally came to life, yet with a muted voice resigned to understanding. "Looks like we both were keeping secrets."

She immediately followed the comment with a wave of a shaking hand, then used it to rub her forehead. "Wait. That's not exactly fair. They weren't the same at all. You kept yours to protect my memory of Brent. I'm sure it wasn't easy telling me the truth, but I'm glad you did." She looked away, unable to meet his eyes. "I kept mine to protect myself, to keep you from knowing about the money I would be receiving." She finally looked at him. "By the way, I received the first check yesterday, in case you were wondering. Dad was supposed to deposit it for me this morning." She made herself continue looking at the agent through bleary eyes. "So you must think Brent took the money?"

He nodded as gently as possible, keeping his throbbing head in check. "Yeah, I do. But it doesn't matter now. And it doesn't matter who was hiding secrets. Let's just worry about what happens next."

"What *does* happen next?"

"Well, for starters, I don't think you have to worry about those two anymore."

Her eyes widened, showing surprise. "Why do you say that?"

"Because of the letter. The man who took it now thinks the money is somewhere in Texas. Houston, to be exact. You said the attorney who sent it had an address there, right?"

She nodded. "Yes. Well, it had a Houston postmark, but he didn't list his address, or phone number. I think it was to insure I wouldn't try to reach him."

"The way I see it, Musso...Brent... turned the money, or at least part of it, over to this attorney. What was his name again?"

"George. Arthur George."

"Right. And that's where our friends are headed. They're probably on their way to Houston as we speak."

Michelle stood, beginning to pace the crowded floor, a hand over her mouth, deep in thought. She abruptly stopped and looked at Church.

"Shouldn't we do something to help the attorney? At least warn him?"

Now Church stood, still wobbly on his feet. He had been thinking the same thoughts. "Yes, we should. But since we don't know how to get in touch with him, I'm going there to find him." He reached for his phone, looking at the screen; it was the only timepiece he was carrying, forgetting to strap on his watch. "They've had at least a two hour head start on me, so I'll take the first flight I can get. One thing working for me is those two don't know where he is either, and I'll have the advantage."

"What advantage? How will *you* find him?"

"That's one of the perks of working in federal law enforcement. We have a pretty big network of agents to help out in searches. Houston just happens to be one of our largest and busiest offices. If Arthur George is practicing anywhere in the area, they'll know about him."

"Then why don't you just let them handle it? Surely, they can protect him."

"For the same reason I didn't contact our guys here. This is unofficial. It has nothing to do with an ongoing drug operation. Plus, from what I hear, those guys don't have time for guard duty." Those comments weren't exactly true. The organization he worked for would welcome the chance to take a cartel hit man down. But he still wanted to keep his extracurricular activities to himself. Self preservation was a strong motivator. He looked hopefully at the woman. She was pacing again. "And think about it, Michelle. If we tip our guys in Houston off about why we're trying to find the attorney, the existence of the money you're receiving will come into play. They may examine your connection to the money." He started to explain to her that not everyone in his office shared his lack of concern about recovering the money, but knew it would add to her misery.

"My God. I hadn't thought about that." She stopped pacing.

"Time is critical, Michelle. Could you give me a lift to the airport?"

She didn't answer his request, but posed her own question. "Let me ask you something, Walt. What happens if, for some reason, these guys don't find the money there? Is there a chance they might come back here?"

Church exhaled a labored sigh, admitting to himself there was slight chance it could happen, if for no other reason than to try and intercept her payments. "I guess there's always that possibility, but I don't think so, and I'm going to try and make sure that doesn't happen."

Michelle stared at him for a second at first, as if deciphering what that meant. It didn't take her long to decide it didn't matter. "Then I'm going with you." It wasn't meant as a request, but a statement.

Chapter 31

The Atlanta airport was jammed-up as usual, with passengers either arriving from, or heading in, every conceivable direction. Angel Xminez sat slumped in the uncomfortable molded plastic chair, barely able to hold his massive frame, suffering his surroundings in mute silence while waiting in his gate area. He had his choice of things that were barely tolerable. Concourse B in Hartsfield-Jackson International Airport was packed to begin with. The bratty toddler running in circles around the seated passengers waiting patiently for their flight to be announced, with his parents ignoring him, had everybody throwing fierce eye-darts at the oblivious couple. Then there was the loud, obnoxious conversation between three middle-aged women seated across from him, each with a tone more nasal than the other. Their frequent laughs cackled in his ears. The teenager behind him talked virtually non-stop into her cell phone, taking time-outs occasionally to no doubt text the same people she was talking to. At least she was quiet, but it still set him on edge. She was an example of one of the few things he didn't like about America; a sense of entitlement combined with the boredom of having too much time to waste on the many luxuries at their disposal. Her very existence seemed tied to the device. He liked having the phone Torres had arranged for him, but he could restrain himself to using it only when necessary.

These annoyances made it hard to concentrate on the important things on his mind. Propping his enormous boots on his carry-on bag on the floor in front to him, he ran a hand across a pants pocket, feeling no bulge where there should be one. He again felt vulnerable without a weapon. He would contact his man in San Antonio once more; surely he had a connection in Houston, where a replacement could be obtained. The Glock had been left in the parking lot of the Savannah airport three hours earlier. He had wiped it clean, then tossed it in the trunk of the rental car atop Javier's stiffening body, while holding his nose, then quickly slamming the lid on the growing stench. Removing possible prints was a habit, though it really didn't matter in this case. By the time his former traveling partner was found, and the gun traced back to its source in Atlanta, which he thought was a virtual impossibility, he would be hidden away where they would never find him.

And that was the second thing he was pondering — where to go; where would he feel safe? It was a sad thought knowing he might never see his home state of Sinaloa again. He would miss the rolling hills of his younger days, the dangerous, violent familiarity of it all. He had been protected there by his association with Luis Torres, an association that was now as fragile as the driest twig on the deadest mango tree lining the Fuerte valley. He could not return, he now knew that beyond any doubt. The letter in the pocket of his worn corduroy coat almost certainly ended any chance of that. And returning without the slimy Cesar Javier at his side would be certain proof to Torres that Xminez had eliminated the man who would otherwise share in the millions recovered, now stashed away somewhere in America. Perhaps when Torres has ceased to exist, which was always a possibility in his chosen, dangerous world; ambushed by a rival family, or finally caught in the cross hairs of the authorities, he might feel safe in returning there. But that was too much to hope for, and certainly too unpredictable to wait for.

California would be his starting point. He planned to spend as much time there as he thought practical, somewhere in the beautiful hidden valleys of the San Gabriel Mountains, north of the sprawling city of Los Angeles. Wise to the resources Torres had at his beck and call, he knew it would be a matter of time before he was hunted down. Two months — three at the maximum — would be his safe period in the cool mountain breezes of the secluded area he had visited once before. Then it would be on to another place, one far enough away to extend his life. For how long, he could only guess. Financially, he would survive, with or without the money he sought. In spite of his suffocating, dangerously domineering, paranoid nature, Luis Torres paid his subordinates well. Well enough that his prime hit man had stashed hundreds of thousands in various bank accounts throughout Mexico and Panama over the years. Living simply, he had spent only a tiny fraction on himself, leaving plenty for a new life, however long that life would last. Accounts established online would lead to simple transfers virtually anywhere he wished.

First there was business to attend to in Houston, which he now had reason to believe had an excellent chance of being a waste of time. Regardless, it would settle things, one way or the other. Then he would make the three hour drive to San Antonio to put his helpful contact busy at preparing a passport and other documents.

Which led to the one flaw in his plans. The shadowy figure that lurked in the darker parts of the Texas city, with such strong connections to his home country, would certainly not hesitate to inform Torres of the requests Angel X would be making. To *not* inform the drug lord might lead to instant death if discovered later. Torres might even pay handsomely for the information. So when the man's usefulness was completed, Xminez would see to it he would not be telling secrets.

The frenetic child suddenly crashed into his outstretched legs, bouncing off them like a ping pong ball. Still no reaction from the parents. Xminez leveled a glare at the grinning, drooling child that he normally used to cower his prey, but the boy only giggled louder and ran away. His natural urge was to grab the boy and pinch his head off; the uncaring parents might even thank him.

The big man removed his legs, grabbed the bag, and stood. There was still a half hour until boarding. Unable to tolerate the interruptions to his thoughts any longer, he stood and moved to the farthest group of seats he could find, actually out of his gate area. He would still be able to hear the boarding call from his outpost.

Falling into his new seat with an enormous grunt, he pulled the letter from his pocket to read it once more. There had been no time to examine it thoroughly in the woman's apartment, and very little in the Savannah airport. He had managed to purchase a ticket and clear the security gauntlet just in time to board a plane for a connection to Atlanta. He continued to use the fake I D and credit card issued under the name of Ron Martinez, a resident of Phoenix, Arizona, items that had allowed him to move about the country in relative ease. The one part of the letter that *did* register while in the apartment was the city the letter had originated from. Now he read it slowly, line-by-line, word-for-word. When he finished, he nodded his large head slowly, a silent reaction meant only for himself, fearing that he understood the implications all too well.

It was the structure of the payments it said the woman was to receive; he had seen such an arrangement before. Nearly six years earlier, when the Torres-Medina partnership was in full gear, raking in over a hundred million annually between the two families, he had been dispatched on a mission similar to this one. A native Panamanian who had legally immigrated to California several years earlier had settled in the outskirts of the City of Angels. Maintaining ties with former associates in his home country, who kept a modest stream of cocaine flowing north to the expatriate for his personal consumption, he was eventually matched up with the consortium of the two Sinaloa families. A shipment was arranged after the man had guaranteed to have $3 million on hand from well-heeled addicts in and around the L. A. area. Exhibiting the money to the cartel's emissaries at the meeting place, he promptly wasted the representatives from the south, then disappeared into the scenic mountains, apparently with the intentions of laying low, taking with him the money and the coke.

But he had severely misjudged who he was dealing with. Although the amount was only a pittance of the cartel's yearly sales, they would not be cheated by anyone, for any amount. Xminez was sent to reclaim the money and whatever was left of the drugs not distributed to the man's clients. It took only one week to find him. With his last breath, just before the big

Mexican put a crescent-shaped slice from beneath one ear to the next, the Panamanian emigrant screamed he had instructed his attorney to immediately put the money in trust for the benefit of the Spanish Seventh Day Adventist church he frequented, in the event of anything happening to him.

Unsure of exactly what the man meant, Xminez soon found out. The attorney was next to feel the wrath of the hit man, doomed by his client's greed, his tongue loosened by fear. Before two bullets were placed in his forehead, he quickly explained the money was indeed now in trust, administered by a bank, with no hopes of being broken apart. The man had shown a copy of the document to his assassin, evidently hoping it would show the depth of his cooperation and atonement. His efforts made no impression on Xminez, who promptly ended the attorney's life, due more to his anger at the small time dealer than the man cowering before him. Besides, *to not kill* the man would raise Torres' ire.

The words in the letter a lawyer by the name of Arthur George, somewhere in Houston, Texas, had sent to Michelle Frapiana were very similar to the ones he could recall on the letter sent from the California attorney to the church, a copy of which he had witnessed during that previous wasted trip. Savvy enough to estimate sixteen million would certainly produce far more than $6500 per month, he knew there was still money unaccounted for. What had happened to the rest? If his worst fears were realized, there were more trusts, with more beneficiaries. He would soon know. He only had to find the attorney, a chore he saw as only a minor problem. Soon after, he would start the process of having his money transferred from the current locations to a new bank, possibly one in California.

Xminez shifted his bulk once more as he attempted to find a comfortable position, while his dark heart pumped a little faster while picturing his future.

Chapter 32

It made no sense, based on either his training and experience, or purely from a safety angle, for a private citizen to accompany a drug enforcement agent on a mission, even one that was off the clock. The possible repercussions, all of which were bad, had Church questioning his own sanity. He had put up an argument, although not as strong as it should have been, explaining to Michelle the danger she might be facing in Houston. The discussion lasted for only a few minutes, with the agent firing off a few rounds of logic, followed by her adamant objections. This was *her* problem , she had insisted, caused by her own bad judgments, and she intended to see it through to whatever end may come. He had weakened much sooner than he knew was wise, but his true understanding of how wrong it was stood no chance with his heart pounding like a sledge hammer against his chest cavity. The mental picture of her traveling with him, even on a platonic basis, was too vivid to overcome. The undeniable truth was there was a better than even chance he would accomplish little by making the trip, whether alone or with the woman. The gut feeling that he should stay as close to the bounty hunters as possible, and locate the attorney before they did, was his only justification.

There were phone calls to be made. The first was made by Michelle to Sandi Booth, as Michelle and Church pulled away from her apartment in his Yukon, explaining to the book store owner she would have to be gone for a while, hopefully, no more than a day or so.

"Sure, sweetie," Sandi had replied slowly, with obvious concern in her voice. "We can manage."

"I'm sorry, Sandi. I know this leaves you short-handed, especially with Mr. Fortson coming in this afternoon." Since hurrying from the store a little over an hour earlier, the book signing had never entered her mind, until now.

"Don't sweat it, hon. I'll get one of Dad's assistants next door to come down and help out. Probably won't even need that." There was a noticeable pause. "Should I ask if this has anything to do with that jerk who came in yesterday?"

Thinking that might be a good cover story for the true extent of her problems, Michelle answered, "Yes, in a way, it does. But not how you think." Michelle knew she wasn't managing to remove the stress from her voice. "I can't tell you anymore now, Sandi, but I will as soon as I can. I've got to go now." Feeling rotten about hanging up so abruptly on her friend, she knew she simply had no choice. Sandi would surely have more questions, but there wasn't time for them now. Every minute seemed crucial.

The next call was placed to Silas Lovejoy, and was much, much harder. It took a few moments before she could make herself key in the number. She summarized rapidly what had transpired at her apartment, leaving out the severity of Church's injuries. If she'd described them completely, her father's desperate pleas would've been much more pronounced, fearing the agent was too incapacitated to protect her.

"Michelle, honey, are you sure you know what you're doing?"

"It doesn't matter, Dad. This is something I have to do."

"Why? I don't understand why you feel that way. Let Walt handle it. That's the reason he came. That's what he's trained to do."

"I know, Dad. And I know this is hard to explain, but if I don't follow through with this, my life is never going to change. I'm not sure I understand it entirely myself. You'll just have to trust me on this." She found herself choking back tears; not from fear for herself, but for the emotional strain she could feel in the man's voice over the phone. She had caused him such pain over the past ten years, and now she was adding more.

"I'm not sure what you mean by 'change'," he said.

"Dad. Please. I don't know how else to put it."

After a moment of extended silence, Silas said, "Let me talk to Walt."

The Yukon was pulling into the Lovejoys' driveway when Church reluctantly took the cell phone, dreading talking to the man almost as much as Michelle had. "Silas."

"Walt, can't you talk her out of this?"

A flood of guilt poured over him. The anguish in the gentle man's voice was palpable. "I'm afraid not, Silas. I've tried every argument I can think of." *But probably not as strenuously as I should have.* He could feel Michelle staring resolutely at him as he spoke, arms crossed in front of her. "She evidently feels very strongly about this." He looked at her for one last assurance. She squeezed her arms tighter and nodded. "I think there's a better than even chance this will be a wild goose chase anyway, Silas. They've had such a big start on us, they'll most likely have been there and gone by the time we arrive."

There was silence for a moment. The older man's voice sounded constricted when he spoke. "Walt, you've got to promise me you'll take care of her. Please don't let anything happen to my daughter. I thought we'd never get her back, and I don't want to lose her now."

The flood was now a tidal wave crashing over the rogue agent. He had chosen not to share the information Steen had given him about Angel Xminez with Michelle, and would not be relaying it to her father either. He suddenly felt like a fraud, harboring something inside him approaching cowardice. But the only way to cover up his misgivings was to press ahead.

"You have my word, Silas."

Michelle took the phone back. "Don't worry, Dad. I'll be fine, " she said with all the confidence she could muster. Ready to end the call, she added, "I love you, Dad."

Silas Lovejoy said a few words in response, and they ended the call. Taking one last look at the DEA agent sitting next to her in his vehicle, she nodded. "It'll be okay."

They entered the empty house to pack what she would need for a trip of unknown duration. She had taken her essentials there with her the night before. His bag was in the rear of the Yukon, where he'd placed it when sneaking out of the Lovejoy home early in the day. Having Mary Lovejoy tucked away safely in Chattanooga prevented a prolonged stay at the house. Likewise, there was little conversation during the drive from her childhood home to Savannah/Hilton Head International Airport. On the way, Michelle made one more call on her mobile, only this one not to a live person. Punching in a series of numbers, then putting the phone close to her ear, she was glad to discover the deposit her father had made earlier was already reflected in her checking account, giving it a much-needed boost. There would soon prove to be a need for it.

Since money seemed less important than time, Church parked in the pricier short term lot nearer the terminal. They grabbed their bags and rushed inside the terminal much faster than necessary; the next flights out weren't for another couple of hours. Studying the flight boards, their choices were American to Miami, or Delta to Atlanta. It came as no surprise there were no direct flights to Houston. The hop to Atlanta was chosen, since it gave more options for connections to the Texas city. When it came time to purchase the tickets, Michelle tried to insist on paying for both, explaining the windfall in her account. Plus, she reminded him, she was the reason they were making the trip.

Church quickly pulled her away from the counter, out of earshot of the ticket agent. He needed to explain things in private. "Believe me, I'd like to take you up on that," he replied, "but we have to purchase separate tickets. We need to make it appear as if we're not traveling together."

She stared. "What're you talking about?"

He patted the side of his travel bag. "I'm armed. In order to carry my weapon on board past security, I've got to fill out some paperwork showing I'm a federal agent, cleared to take it on flights. Then, I'll have to check-in with the pilot when we board. Just some of the hassles we have to go through now, mostly due to 9-11." He shrugged.

"I still don't get why we have to travel separately."

"If they suspect we're together, it won't look like I'm on official business. Might make it harder to get authorization for the gun. It'll look like we're on a pleasure trip. Like a date, or something." He felt a cheap thrill just from the words.

She actually gave a bemused smile, one of the few times he had seen her guard lowered to any extent. "Would that be so bad?" she asked in a surprisingly teasing manner.

His pulse quickened at the thought. Her harmless words together with the faint smile set his heart-rate soaring. "Not at all. But I don't know what we'll find in Houston, and I don't want to walk into a confrontation at a disadvantage. I need the gun. The only other option would be for me to cuff you, treat you like a prisoner transport, but I can't see that happening." Another inticing image.

Finally convinced, she approached the counter first, and purchased a one-way ticket, since there was no way to predict when they would return. Church then fell in line a few spaces behind, and did the same.

Later, they were camped in a much smaller, but less crowded gate area than Angel Xminez currently occupied a few hundred miles to the northwest. Michelle's bag was perched on a hard plastic chair between them, with his at his feet. The positioning of her overnight was another attempt to create a ruse of coincidental passengers on the same flight. After a period of awkward silence, feeling no eyes were on them, they managed to carry on a semblance of normal conversation over her luggage.

"I know this is personal," she said, "but have you ever been married? I've just realized I know nothing about you, other than your job. Unfortunately, you know my history all to well. Turn-a-bout's fair play." She had been sneaking what she hoped were hidden glances, making a more earnest effort to size him up.

He adjusted the baseball cap he was wearing, tilting it back slightly. She had borrowed it from her father's collection to help him hide his scalp wound. Even that small movement sent stabs of pain through his skull. The Tylenol he had choked down were slowly beginning to take affect, but aches and pains were still there. He was resigned to the fact his ribs would grow more tender over the next few days.

"Nope. Did come close near the end of my senior year of college. She called it off when she discovered I was serious about what I planned to do with the rest of my life."

"Drug Enforcement?"

"Actually, the U. S. Marshal Service at first. After a couple of years, jumped over to DEA. But it wasn't that exactly. The branch didn't matter to her. It was the idea of having a spouse whose job caused a reason for constant worry." He paused, recalling distant memories that had been painful at one time. They were long since forgotten, or at least, moved to the back recesses of his mind.

"Looking back, I can see her point. My partner went through a nasty divorce a couple of years back, and I can count on one hand the number of happy marriages in my office. Haven't come close since," he concluded, with only a hint of sadness. The words were hardly out of his mouth before he realized he was painting the wrong picture for any possible future they may have together. Just as quickly, the futility of those wishful thoughts came crashing home.

She had no response to his admission, knowing he probably wasn't expecting one. Instead, for the lack of anything better, she asked, "What college?"

"Middle Tennessee State. Just south of Nashville. You?"

"Georgia Southern. Folks wanted me to stay near home. The only-child syndrome wouldn't let me wander any farther. They nearly died when I told them I was moving to Atlanta after graduation. Seeing how it worked out, they were right, as usual."

"I can see that. A lot can happen in Hot-lanta." Again, he wanted to kick himself for being too flippant. Besides, there was nothing he could tell *her* about the evils of the capital city. Most of her married days there must've been pure misery.

"How about your family? Any siblings?"

"An older sister in Nashville... a teacher... married, with two kids. A brother, two years younger than me... divorced. He's a high school basketball coach in a town near where we grew up. I guess you'd say we're moderately congenial toward each other — we get along fine when we get together at Christmas, or Thanksgiving." Church thought for a moment what being an only child must be like. Probably pros and cons.

They then grew silent again. She was thinking about something else; something that had crossed her mind several times the past two days. It seemed like a good time to ask. She leaned slightly in his direction.

"Walt, just out of curiosity, while you were investigating Dickie, what he was up to, were you watching me too?"She looked at him with an expectant expression.

"Only in the beginning, when we were trying to get a picture of his daily routines. But you were never a suspect, if that's what's on your mind. After the first few weeks, we pretty much ignored you." The words sounded strangely harsh, but she surely wouldn't see it as an insult. No one could ever completely ignore her.

She nodded slowly, but had no reply.

The mention of her husband brought up a subject *he* had been wondering about. Turning his head gradually in her direction to avoid a new jolt of pain, he said, "I can only imagine how tough it's been since you've been here, Michelle. In Savannah, I mean. The name, Frapiana, must've caused a few problems along the way. Any thoughts about changing it?"

"Yes, I have," she answered, almost apologetically. "I've had the documents prepared for Allison and me for a few months now to take back my maiden name. For some reason, I just can't seem to make myself throw the switch. I know it doesn't make any sense, and I can't explain my reluctance. I guess it has something to do with her. It might be strange for a girl her age to suddenly have a new last name. One thing I have to bear in mind is, she doesn't have the same memories about Dickie that I do. I shielded her from most of his doings. And not being called Allison Frapiana all of a sudden could be confusing, maybe even psychologically harmful."

Church was getting the strong impression she felt she had to explain herself to him, which was ridiculous, yet somehow encouraging. Another thought suddenly occurred to him, but one he would never utter to her. Changing her name might've made it harder for the bounty hunters to find her. Then realizing if they knew she was in Savannah, the rest would've been a matter of time; they could find her through her parents. He shook it off. He looked at her gorgeous face, the strain still there, but having little effect on her beauty. “I can understand...”

He was interrupted by the chirping of his phone. Viewing the screen, he thought he recognized the same alien number he had seen a few hours earlier, but couldn’t quite recall all of it.

“Church? Reggie Floyd again. You still in town?”

“On my way out.” He was sure his leaving would be welcome news. “What’s up?”

“Thought you might want to know. The missing cop’s been found. Happened just after lunch. A rural mail delivery gal caught a reflection of sunlight from a shack a few miles west of town. She goes by there every day, and knew she hadn’t noticed it before. She’d just heard a report about the search for the officer on the radio, so she checked it out. Crammed into the back seat of his cruiser. Two rounds in the head.”

Church could feel his insides turning over, his early fears about the patrolman’s disappearance coming true. He rose as quickly as his aching body would allow and stepped away, out of Michelle’s hearing range. He felt her eyes following him. “Jesus Christ. Sounds like a professional job?”

“Sure looks that way. As you can imagine, the locals are up in arms.” Floyd hesitated. “Given any more thought to what you can tell us about a possible shooter?”

He had no choice now, and no reason *not* to tell what he knew. “The name’s Angel Xminez, Floyd. Hit man for a drug cartel out of Mexico.” He repeated the information Steen had given him earlier, adding the fact he had emailed pictures for identification.

There was a lengthy sound of breath being exhaled on the other end. “I’d say there’s an excellent chance it’s about to hit the fan. Not with us, but the

Savannah P D. Why the hell didn't you pass that along earlier?"

Feeling deflated, Church leaned against a plate-glass window looking out over the tarmac. His sprits were sinking lower and lower, even though he knew it wouldn't have mattered if he *had* shared the information. The man had been dead for over a day. He quickly corrected his own flawed thinking. That's not the way it works in law enforcement. If preventing a crime wasn't possible, then finding the perp quickly was all that mattered... Criminology 101. Double that when a cop's the victim.

"Listen, Floyd, I didn't have the man's name until about the time you called, and that's the truth. The reason I didn't call back to clue you in is that the guy's probably long gone by now." It was weak; there was no way he wasn't looking bad on this.

"Gone? Where to?"

"I'm pretty sure Houston."

"Houston? What the hell's in Houston besides a lotta friggin' heat and humidity?"

"The reason those guys came here looking for Michelle Frapiana was they thought she had money her husband stole from their drug cartel. She doesn't, of course, but one of the guys... just before he clubbed me... found a letter in her apartment indicating it may be in Houston. How it got there's kinda complicated, Floyd, and I don't think it matters much now."

"That may be true, but it ain't gonna help the feelings of the police chief, and he may not agree with you. I'll give your partner a call and ask him to send the information on this guy Xminez to the locals here. This'll most likely be handled as a local homicide case, since no drugs are involved. A short pause followed. "Wait. Did you say *guys*? As in more than one?"

"Right. A smaller guy, blond. Don't have a name or any other info on him." An idea suddenly struck. "Say, Floyd. You might want to have someone check out the airport parking lot. Look for a blue Toyota compact... Corolla, I think. It'll be a rental, with a scrape on the rear right bumper. If my guess is right, the second guy could be sleepin' in the trunk. I think there's a chance this Xminez guy has decided to go it alone."

"Should I ask how the scrape got there?"

"I couldn't say." How many lies had he told over the last two days? He was losing count. Some were lies of omission, which seemed less serious, like not telling Floyd he was also headed to Texas. Another possibility hit him. "There's also a chance the second guy might be in a room at The Best Western northwest of town if he's not in the car."

Another pregnant exhale on the phone. "Okay, I'll pass it along. But if he's in there, housekeeping might find him before we do." Floyd adjusted his tone slightly. "Church, don't be surprised if your chief in Atlanta gets a earful from the Savannah police. Richard Joyner's your guy, same as mine, right?"

"Correct. And he's got my file on his desk at this very moment. So tell the chief he'll have to take a number and get in line."

That actually produced a snort from Floyd. "Don't suppose you'll be coming back this way anytime soon?" It wasn't really meant as a question.

"No plans to"... *another possible fib...* "but if I do, Floyd, I promise, you'll never know about it."

With a parting snicker, Floyd ended the call.

As he punched the button to end the call, something he'd just told Floyd lingered in Church's head. Continuing to stare through the tinted glass, he wondered about the second man, and whether or not Xminez *had* actually eliminated his partner, and if so...why? Why would he do that? Experience in dealing with the cartels told him there could only be one answer: Xminez was going rogue... dealing for himself. Any money he recovered would now be his... he would turn on his boss, and keep it for himself. Thinking about that possibility, he wondered if there was a way to use that to his advantage, but couldn't see how based on where things now stood. The man might already be in Houston, or getting close, while he twiddled his thumbs here.

Rejoining Michelle, he saw her punching the "END" button on her phone.

"Calling my landlord," she said. "Told him to send me the bill for the damage to my apartment." She gave a questioning look. "Who was that?"

He sat his battered body down gently before responding. "That was a local DEA agent my partner asked to check in on me. I'm afraid he gave me some bad news."

A new mask of dread fell across her face. "What?"

He told her about the patrolman's fate, giving her a few minutes to absorb it. He expected her to fall apart, sink deeper into what was by now an apparently bottomless pit of despair. However, she didn't fall as far as he anticipated. She did express her sorrow over the loss of the man's life — lost while trying to protect her. And she winced at the horror of the brutality involved in the murder. But she didn't break down; she didn't cry; and she didn't seem to lose her sense of purpose. Her resolve seemed to be strengthening. Or maybe it had all been too much, and she had become numb. At least now, she had an idea of what Xminez was capable of, without him having to describe to her the details Steen had given him.

They sat still for a while, again lapsing into silence. Boarding time was now within thirty minutes. He thought of one more call he needed to make.

Feeling she knew all there was to know, he decided it was okay for her to hear this one. He remained seated.

"Steen. It's me. Glad I caught you before you left."

"Hell, it's only 3:40. Where you think I'm goin'?"

"Don't know. Nowhere, I guess. Listen, I need your help on something else."

"Crap, partner," Steen sighed. "You're a bigger pain in the ass when you're *not here* than when you are. Didn't think that was possible."

Church ignored the comment. "Chris, I need a name in Houston."

"That's a big damn city, Walt. Must be millions of names. Which one do you want?"

"Okay, wise-ass. The name of an agent in our office there. Know anybody off the top of your head?"

Steen didn't respond right away. When he did, he said, "Houston? Wasn't that where our boy Musso was from?"

"Yeah," Church replied, hoping he wouldn't have to explain too much to his partner. Broadcasting the reason for a search in the Texas city could conceivably reactivate the questions about the missing money in the Atlanta regional office. He needed to short wire that possibility. "Listen, Chris, if you'll do me this one last favor, I promise you won't hear from me again 'til I get back. And I promise I'll give you the whole story then. Right now, I just want a name. Preferably, one who's been in that office for a while. Somebody who knows the territory."

"Don't worry. Not sure I wanna know what in the hell you're up to." Another pause. "Does this mean you're going to Houston?"

"Possibly." Another lie, or maybe only a half-lie. There was no reason for this one, since his partner could care less; he just seemed to falling into the habit. “So, can you help?”

“Man, oh man.” Steen stretched the words out. “ She’s got you in so deep now you can’t get out. Don’t say I didn’t warn you.”

“Look, never mind about that now.” There were times his partner’s cynicism went too far. He wished now he had stepped away again, afraid she may have heard the words over the phone. Michelle was surely at least picking up the tone on the other end. “You gonna help or not?”

“Okay, okay. I’ll see what I can come up with. McCarley was assigned to that office before transferring in. I’ll quiz him about possibles. Want me to call or text you?”

“Whatever. Just try not to let McCarley know why you’re asking.”

Steen gave a sarcastic laugh. “That’ll be easy, since I *don’t* know why I’m asking. Just as soon keep it that way. Ignorance *can* be bliss, you know.”

“*Then you must be in a state of Nirvana*,” Church wanted to say, but didn’t. “So I’ve heard,” he said instead. He took a glance at Michelle. She was occupied checking out the status of their flight on a message board. He moved away again, not wanting her to hear the rest. “ Oh, and by the way, you’ll be getting a call from Floyd, our guy in Savannah, asking you to forward the picture and scoop on Xminez to the local police.”

There was a much longer pause now. So long, Church though Steen might’ve hung up.

“I’m positive I’ll be sorry for asking... but why?”

“It’s possible Xminez may have killed a cop over here. At least, he’s the likely suspect. They’ll be looking for him.”

“Tell me you’re kidding. Are you for real, Walt?”

"Relax, partner. This had nothing to do with me being here. Matter of fact, it happened before I got involved." *That was true*, wasn't it? The man had to have been killed before he interrupted the high-speed chase. It was becoming hard to keep his lies and truths separate.

After a long sigh, Steen agreed to providing whatever the Savannah PD needed.

Saying thanks was harder this time, given Steen's attitude, but he said it anyway while ending the call.

Michelle had a strange look on her face when she turned to face him.

"Was that the other agent who came with you last year?"

"Yeah. Chris Steen."

"Didn't sound like he was too happy about what you're doing, from what I heard."

"Don't worry about him. He's just a hard a... a little different." Church caught himself in time, taking stock of who he was talking to now. He chalked it up to being tired. Thirty-nine didn't seem old to him, but he was beginning to recognize he didn't have the stamina he did ten years earlier. For the first time since arriving, he began to feel it, not having slept more than an hour since Sunday night. Strange beds, like the one in the Lovejoys' guest room, always led to lost sleep. He had been operating on adrenalin alone. Sneaking out of the house early in the morning for his search hadn't helped any. Nor did the crease in his head.

Her eyebrows were raised, a narrow grin appeared. "Maybe he's right. This could be considered a foolhardy thing you're doing, getting involved in my problems." She chose not to ask him his reasons, since she was starting to see some truth in her dad's assessment. Even though she had no idea how she felt about that, she felt a certain comfort in his company, thankful he was willing to be here.

Church's contented feeling soon returned; he let his body relax in the uncomfortable chair as much as possible. He could tell by her tone she understood some of why he had come, and that he felt he had no other choice. "Doesn't feel foolhardy to me," he said. "Just wanna see that you and Allison are okay. And I'm as anxious as you are to find out what's waiting for us in Houston."

Whether she accepted his answer or not, she didn't respond. They sat silently, waiting for the boarding agent to make the announcement.

A little over two hundred and fifty miles away, Angel X stood in line at his boarding gate, loading for his flight to Houston.

Chapter 33

Angel Xminez stood stock-still in the motel shower, letting the water cascade down his body. The water was as hot as he could stand, hoping to wash away the filth of the cramped ride in the belly of the border patrolman's SUV six days earlier, the time spent searching for the money in God-forsaken Georgia, then the final leg to the outskirts of Houston. But most of all, to wash away the thoughts of Cesar Javier's leering glances. He hadn't chanced a shower as long as Javier had been rooming with him. The only reason Xminez had insisted on one room was to keep tabs on the other man and his twisted weaknesses. Remaining static in the shower-tub, while relieving the pressure on his bladder, he craned his neck to watch the rusty water combine with urine as it circled the drain. It was his version of multi-tasking. Stepping back to clear himself from the putrid whirlpool, his feet made the cheap fiber glass buckle and warp under his mass.

Later, he lay naked across the threadbare sheets of the lumpy bed. It was the first night he would feel it safe to sleep the way he preferred — au naturel, without the hungry eyes of Javier creeping him out. The little man had tried to pretend he wasn't looking, but Xminez could tell.

The night was still relatively early, but he was tired, and his belly full. Tex-Mex restaurants seemed to be on every corner in the Houston area, but he had held out until discovering a small, modest appearing establishment with the word Taqueria in its name. He knew from past trips into the country, those market-type establishments were the ones with more authentic dishes of his homeland. He had left with two Styrofoam boxes stuffed with food, the first *real* food he'd had since crossing the border.

He stared up at the stained plaster ceiling of the stale room, wondering if this might be the last night he would have to endure such a Spartan existence. The mid-eastern desk clerk... most likely Indian or Pakistani... had promised a non-smoking unit, but it reeked like an ashtray that had never been emptied. Too tired to return to the office to make the sandal-wearer understand the error of his ways, he chose to ride it out. Besides, if the man who lived nearby, the man whose name his friend in San Antonio had given him, could provide a lead on the anonymous attorney, along with supplying a gun, he would bring things to a crashing head the following morning, and soon leave the Channelview Inn behind, a place whose memory would quickly fade.

The motel fronting I-10 was located logically in Channelview, one of the many indistinguishable communities along the expressway east of the massive Bayou City, each seeming to funnel into the next. The establishment appeared to be the kind that wouldn't hesitate to rent rooms by the hour, or by the day, or any other method a customer might be willing to pay.

Ordinarily, it would fit the mold of those frequented by semi-tractor drivers, but lacked the space to park the big rigs. When he'd checked in an hour earlier, he had noticed a decided Hispanic presence in the others staying there, spotting them lounging near the small lobby and in the parking lot. Construction crews, he assumed — cheap labor. He exchanged brief nods with a few, who stared back at the enormous man, but only for a second. Something in the way their eyes were quickly averted told him they instinctively knew he was to be given a wide berth. Their reaction was something he was quite familiar with. Occasional sounds of *tejano* music, or its earlier incarnation, *norteno* style, drifted through the open doors of the rooms in the courtyard of the decrepit motel. The familiar strains produced a surprising touch of longing for his homeland — one that quickly dissipated when he set his mind on his future.

Earlier, before heading to the shower, he had texted Torres to inform him of his arrival. He knew he had to, since the man would be waiting. He was quite sure the drug lord could track him through the GPS in his cell phone, and couldn't afford to take chances until his future travel plans had been decided. There had been no choice but to tell the man about enlisting the help of the San Antonio connection to find a friendly contact in Houston. Torres questioned that, but Xminez explained he needed a source with local knowledge to locate the attorney. A quick check of the mammoth city phone book when he checked into his room proved no listings for the lawyer, and information had been no help, so it was the only way. He of course neglected to tell Torres the man would also provide him with a new weapon, and subsequently, a passport. During the messaging, he was glad there were no questions about his now former traveling companion. The fact he was no longer part of the search would surely set off alarm bells in Torres' suspicious mind.

The outdated air conditioning unit emitted more noise than cold air. Eventually, the mechanical, rattling sound became rhythmic enough to lull him into near-sleep. Before succumbing, he allowed himself a hopeful thought. He believed there was a better than even chance he was now alone in his search for the money. The unfortunate man whose skull he had put a dent in some eight hours earlier in Savannah was not the threat he had imagined; not another bounty hunter as he first suspected. And Xminez did not think he had been there looking for the $16 million. After all, the agent almost certainly knew about the information in the letter, and had not acted on it. Why he *was there* was still a mystery, but one that he didn't think he had to solve. Angel X was not the kind of man who would envision any man doing something so loco simply for a woman — any woman, so that idea never entered his mind. His only remaining mission was to determine if there was indeed any money to be found. It was a slim hope he held onto.

Other than that, the only thoughts in his head as he drifted off were more images of the vistas of the San Gabriel Mountains. It shouldn't be long now.

Chapter 34

The Boeing 757 with the Delta Airlines logo on its fuselage was buffeted about by sudden turbulence, hidden within a dark hundred-foot cloud layer as it made its approach into Bush Intercontinental Airport. Positioned roughly ten miles to the northeast of the huge city, Bush is the larger and newer of the two major airfields serving Houston, the other being Hobby to the south. Less than ideal weather is a common feature in southeast Texas, especially in spring, when low pressure cells often coil like a tightly wound spring over the great southwest, then are released by westerly wind currents to barrel across the southern states, including southeast Texas, creating havoc. It serves as the onset of tornado season in the region, as these fast moving systems meet up with others coming from different directions, and with varying temperature gradients. Walter Church and Michelle Frapiana had no way of anticipating the bumpy ride, neither having flown into the area before. Nor did they have any way of knowing it could've been much worse.

The second leg of their journey, from Atlanta to Houston, had produced a less than full passenger load. After the seatbelt light had dimmed, Church had left his seat three rows back, and slid his way into the vacant middle seat next to Michelle's window view. An attendant, no doubt informed by the pilot the man was a gun-toting federal agent, noticed the move. She started to approach him about it, but when sizing up the person he had chosen to move in on, decided to accept it as a case of raging hormones. When serving the pair drinks later in the flight, she leveled a cynical, knowing smile at the man, as if to say, "*I know what you're up to, but I'll let it slide, just this once.*"

After an unnerving few minutes, the Boeing aircraft managed to clear itself from the underbelly of the cloud layer, and things smoothed out considerably. Michelle, finally able to relax, was busy peering out into the nighttime darkness.

"Wow, it's huge."

"What?"

"This city. I know Atlanta's big, but this place goes on and on. The lights are as far as I can see." She scanned the small window to take it all in. Slashes of raindrops begin to streak across the glass, blocking her view to some extent. They were being welcomed to Texas by steady showers, produced by the thick clouds above.

He leaned across her to view what she was seeing, getting a whiff of her aromatic hair as a bonus. He wasn't sure if she'd had a chance to spray something on it during a restroom break in Atlanta, or if it was just her natural fragrance. "I read somewhere it's the fourth largest in the country," he said, trying to concentrate on the dark vista peppered with far-reaching, glistening lights.

"I can believe it."

The pilot soon announced they had been cleared for landing, and one of the attendants gave her rote warning to have "seat belts securely fastened, and all trays in an upright position." For his part, Church wished the flight would go on indefinitely into the night, stoked by the exhilarating feeling of having the woman by his side. It brought back vague, long-ago memories of finding a seat next to the prettiest girl in high school assembly, and with it, the same nervous apprehension. Only now, it came with a dose of real-life adventure.

Following a knuckle-whitening landing in a last minute pocket of brisk wind, they had to wait out a prolonged taxiing before pulling their bags from the overheads. By the time they entered the terminal and approached the Enterprise Car Rental kiosk on the bottom level, it was within a few minutes of 9:00 p m., Central Standard Time. Gaining an hour between time zones did little to make the day seem shorter. It had taken almost nine hours to get from Savannah to Atlanta, then to Houston, which the DEA agent saw as a reason for concern. There was no way to tell how far behind Xminez they were, and he could only hope he hadn't already located the attorney.

While Church went to negotiate the leasing agreement for a vehicle, Michelle stood and observed him with arms crossed. She thought back to the last time she had planned to rent a car. It had been at Destin, the morning following the night her husband's life came to a violent end, although she hadn't known about his death at the time. Brent Musso had left the Martins in charge of helping her with the lease, since she had never attempted it on her own, always letting Dickie handle it. The plan had been for Michelle to drive herself and Allison to Savannah. But after Brent had left for Texas... or at least she thought he'd left... which she now knew wasn't true... the Martins had double crossed her, in the kindest way possible. They instead had chosen to drive the two of them home, cutting their own vacation short, going those many miles out of their way.

And now, after Brent, then Ralph and Flora Martin, a fourth person had appeared from nowhere to protect her. Well, not exactly from nowhere; she *had* called him. But the point was, he had come. Watching him as he finished up at the counter, she couldn't deny the existence of a warm feeling, bordering on tenderness toward the man. She wiped away the mist from the corners of her eyes as he approached, hoping he wouldn't notice. If he did, he covered it up nicely.

"The rental guy said there's a La Quinta near by. That okay with you?"

"Sure. Sounds fine."

Catching the shuttle to the off-site parking facility, they were soon driving through the steady Houston rain, covering the short distance to the motel, proving to be one of the chain's more upscale Inn and Suites. There was no further need for the pretense of the two of them traveling separately, so she insisted on paying for both rooms, which he agreed to after judging the intensity in her eyes.

As they began to part ways to find their separate rooms on the same floor, he stopped her in the hallway. He was bone-tired, but there was something he needed to explain to her. "Look, I need to show you how to operate my gun, just in case it becomes necessary."

Her eyes, appearing turquoise in the hall lighting, narrowed, a frown appearing. "I'm not sure, Walt. I've never fired a gun — never even held one.

Frankly, the thought of it makes me ill. Do you think it'll come to that?"

He shook his head wearily. "I have no way of knowing, Michelle. Of course, I'm sure it's highly unlikely. But things don't usually turn out the way you plan. It's only in movies and detective books where people seem to be able to predict what their enemies are going to do." He wanted to tell her he actually had a plan, but that would be another lie, and he didn't want them to pile up any deeper. "It'll only take a couple of minutes, and I think it's important. We may not have time in the morning. Your room or mine?"

She smiled another tantalizing smile, teasing him over his question. He instantly realized how it had sounded. "I guess that wasn't the best way to phrase it."

"No, it's okay," she laughed gently, "I knew what you meant. Give me a little time to dry the rain from my hair. I'll see you in your room in fifteen minutes."

As she turned to walk away, Church watched her leave, unable to take his eyes from her. He realized she had made the sensible choice for a woman traveling with a man possessing questionable motives. Coming to his room meant she could leave whenever she wanted, not that he would give her reason to.

He had the dark steel-grey Beretta 96 lying on his bed when she arrived. A clip holding eleven rounds was next to it, but it was only for show. If he was going to teach her one of the tricks of his trade, may as well show her everything.

She stared at the gun as if it were a serpent, wincing when he first picked the weapon up. It was toxic as far as she was concerned, a lethal device designed for one purpose — to end someone's life. She didn't view it as a means of protection; instead a weapon that would cause someone to *need* protection. Dickie had kept one in their Atlanta home, but she had never seen it, making it a point to never ask where he kept it hidden.

"It's a semi-automatic, Beretta 96," he explained, picking it up and holding it flat in the palms of his hands. "Go ahead, hold it for a second."

Reluctant at first, she took it from him. The weight, or lack of weight, surprised her. "It seems lighter than I thought it would be. How much does it weigh?"

"Barely two pounds. It's a newer version... new technology... new materials. Makes it easier to handle, though some agents prefer the heavier, older models. They feel it gives them a sense of power." He shrugged. "Go figure."

Repulsed, but unable to remove her eyes from the dark piece of metal, she asked, "Does semi-automatic mean what I think it does?"

He picked the clip off the bed. "Right. When this clip is inserted," he said, taking the gun back, then demonstrating where the clip was housed in the butt of the weapon, without actually clicking it in place, "and the safety is turned off, you have eleven rounds to fire, simply by pulling the trigger again and again. No need to re-cock or reload."

The very thought of the weapon firing even once produced a shiver running through her body. She could never see herself in the position of pulling the trigger period, let alone eleven times. It was impossible *not* to let her mind float back to the carnage her husband had left behind when he'd killed all those people. How many times had he pulled the trigger? *Fourteen deaths in all*, plus that poor doctor in Alabama during his escape. If she let her thoughts linger, she would become physically ill once more, as she had several times over the past months.

Hoping to remove the unspeakable images, she asked, "Have you ever used all eleven...what did you call them? Rounds?"

He grinned only slightly at the awkward way she asked. "Nope. Not even close. Fortunately one or two warning shots are usually the most I've needed." He still saw doubt written on her face; her hands were shaking with unease. There was no way he was going to describe to her the few actual kills he had on his record. This was all so foreign to her. But he'd rather be safe than sorry, tell her what she needed to know, and no more. Silas' words about taking care of her were still adhered to his brain cells.

"Michelle, I know this is distasteful to you, but you need to know how to fire it. Probably won't have to, but just in case..." His voice trailed off, feeling he had said enough.

"Okay." She peered closer than she wanted to at the piece of metal. "You said, turn the safety off, then pull the trigger. Is there more to it than that?"

"I'm talkin' more about how to actually fire the weapon, and how to position yourself before taking the shot. Assuming there's time, of course."

A blank stare was her only answer.

"See, like this." Church stood away from her, bent his knees slightly, and held the gun with his arms outstretched, right hand on the trigger, left hand supporting his right wrist. "This steadies your body, gives you more control." He held the gun out for her to take. "Here, you try it."

Staring at the Beretta for a second, as if it might bite her, she took it, holding it limply in one hand. Both hands trembled as she put them on the weapon, trying to copy his demonstration. Her hands were much smaller, making it hard to replicate his grips. Seeing her reticence, he moved next to her, supporting her hands with one of his own. He would've accomplished more by standing behind her, wrapping his arms around her, stabilizing her body, but was certain neither of them could withstand that, for entirely different reasons.

Standing close to the man, their bodies actually touching, she snuck a glance up at his eyes, noticing for the first time how brown and deep set they were. He had a musky, manly scent that struck a surprising chord. He was roughly the same size as her late husband; just over six feet, solidly built. His chin was well defined, but not sharp. She was able for a milli-second to shift her gaze from his ratty tail long enough to notice specks of beginning grey in his hair, still covered by the cap to hide his scar. But unlike Dickie Frapiana, his rough exterior belied an inner gentleness she easily detected. Shaking the strange, unsettling thoughts from her head, she realized that whatever feelings she was experiencing, they were most likely just in-the-moment, but they were scaring her.

"Okay. I think I've got it," she said, stepping away quickly while he dropped his hands from hers. Her face showed splotches of crimson red. Taking a few paces, she then turned and looked at him. "I'm sorry, Walt. It's just that..."

He shook his head rapidly, forgetting it would bring the pain back. He grimaced slightly, then said,"You don't need to explain anything, Michelle. I know this whole thing is weird for you." He would've thought her awkward retreat comical, if only his heart wasn't palpitating so wildly.

"No, it's not that." She was recalling what her dad had said; the reason he gave for the agent's willingness to help. He had to understand where she was, where her life was. "It's just what I've been through over the past year or so. Married to a man who turned out to be a monster, with the only way of freeing myself from him was by his own death. Then rescued by someone who I knew for only three days of my life, but I will never forget. Who's now dead himself. Then my life with my daughter, the most special thing in my life, surviving in Savannah, waiting for the day when men like these might come." She paused for a second, allowing the emotion and anger to fade from her voice, then refocused on him. "And now you come, willing to risk your job, and certainly your life — for us. There's no way I can tell you what that means to me, Walt. But... I just need time. Everything in my life is so complicated... so unsettled, I just don't know..." Her voice tailed off, as if in hopeless resignation.

Church's heart was pounding harder, now like a jackhammer, right along with his throbbing head, as he tried to decode what she was saying. It wasn't the gun that was making her uneasy — it was *him*. He wanted to say something, anything, but could hardly breathe, close to hyper-ventilating.

When he didn't speak right away, she filled the uncomfortable silence. "I've probably said too much. I just thought it was only fair you should know."

"Okay." He managed to say, exhaling, then added, "I understand." But he didn't really, and was having a hard time believing that what he *thought* she meant might be true.

She started to leave, embarrassment written across her crimson face. Reaching the door, she turned again. "Exactly what will happen tomorrow? What are our plans?"

He gathered himself, trying to get back down to Planet Earth. "While I was waiting for you, I checked the local listings," he said, still reeling. "As

I suspected, there's no entry for an attorney by the name of Arthur George. Nothing in information either. So we have no phone number or physical address. I'm hoping whoever Steen puts us in touch with will have something on the guy." He shrugged. "We're kinda at a stand still 'til then."

She started to say something else, but evidently changed her mind. Nodding, she told him goodnight, and left.

As the door closed behind her, Church stood motionless for a few seconds, letting the echos of her words reverberate through his head. He knew he was in trouble. On a night when his body was beyond exhaustion, needing sleep in the worst way, it was clear he would have a hard time calming his brain into submission.

Returning to her room, Michelle fell backwards onto her bed, and began rubbing her forehead briskly. What had she just done? What had she just said? She had let the emotions due to her gratitude for the man get the better of her — that *had* to be what it was. It couldn't be anything else. Could it? For the first time, she was questioning the wisdom of joining in the race with Walt and the bounty hunter to find the mysterious lawyer. She didn't belong here. And the thought of holding that gun, actually firing it at someone — that wasn't going to happen.

Whatever her true feelings were for the DEA agent, she realized the following days... however many there were... would be awkward. They would be joined at the hip until the journey somehow came to an end.

Her stressed brain wandered back over the events of the day, and the truths she had learned. The full depths of the sacrifice Brent Musso had made, the sacrifice of the brief time remaining in his life, had been made clear to her when she and Walt had bared their souls in her ransacked apartment. The stark heroism the stock broker's deeds had exhibited, as voiced by the DEA agent, was also now all too evident to her. The memory of Brent's actions were jumbled up with her thoughts about the man who was *now* trying to protect her, the very same man who had been involved in the chase and ultimate demise of her own husband.

She felt as if she were a marionette, with strings pulling her body and mind in various directions. Taking control of her life was still elusive. She began to sob tears of utter confusion, which slowly ebbed as the emotions of the day gave way to dreamland.

Chapter 35

A virtual steam bath greeted Xminez when he stepped from the rental car just after 9:00 a. m. the following morning. It was the fourth different vehicle he had used during his trip across the southern part of the U. S. Still wearing the sunglasses taken from the Savannah patrolman, along with the baseball cap, he wiped the line of sweat that beaded up instantly on his forehead. He took a moment to size up the strange surroundings he now faced. The building he was about to enter stood almost directly beneath a high-arching overpass. He knew from the map he had pulled up on his handheld device displaying Houston that it was part of the enormous, spaghetti-like interchange of I-10 with the Sam Houston Tollway encircling the spread-out city. The bar was an aged cinder block structure, actually lying adjacent to the frontage road underneath and paralleling the toll road, indicating the seedy-looking place had remained hunkered down while the massive interchange was built around it. The constant overheard traffic created a cacophony of noise, seeming to fall all around him.

His mood was dark and unsettled, as close to virtual panic mode as the stoic man would allow himself. Before leaving his room in the musty motel ten minutes earlier, he had been stunned to see his picture flashing across the t v screen. It was a local channel covering the morning news. There was an APB alert, identifying him by name, as well by the alias he had used when checking in to the Savannah motel, as being wanted for a murder in Georgia. Not just any murder, but that of a cop. The alert indicated he was thought to be in the Houston area, and should be considered armed and dangerous. No mention was made of why he had chosen to come to the Texas city. His mind raced as he tried to assimilate how they could possibly have I D'd him. And how did they get the picture? It had been taken in Savannah, of that he was sure. He was wearing the same cap in the photo, and he had only had it while in the Georgia city. No one except the Frapiana woman and the narc he had put down had known he was in the city, so it must've been taken by one of the two... the man, most likely. But it was useless to dwell on it for long, knowing instantly his window of escape had just been narrowed considerably.

Stepping inside the structure, he discovered the thick, blocked walls did manage to somewhat buffer the outside din, but it was the only saving grace of the interior. A veil of cigarette smoke wafted through the dark room, mingling with the stench of beer. The single room occupied the entirety of the building, with the exception of two doors, one leading to a restroom, the other evidently to a supply room. Walls covered with chipped paint slowly came into view. A sticky substance on the concrete floor greeted his first few steps. He had noticed only three other vehicles in the lot, so it was no surprise when he could make out only four indistinct figures lurking, including the bar tender. The crummy aesthetics mattered little to the big Mexican, having been in hell-holes much worse during his lifetime. Besides, this was business, not pleasure; he could tolerate it for the short time he planned to be here. He removed the cap, then tried to pick out which of the shadows belonged to the man he had come to see.

A form sitting alone in a corner table silently nodded, indicating he was the one. The man eyed Xminez up and down as he approached.

"Jeez. Our friend in San Antonio said you were big. Just not this fuckin' big."

Angel pulled out a chair, then took his seat without responding or smiling. Glancing over at the other men standing nearby, he sized them up as associates of the man who had spoken, maybe bodyguards of a sort. He looked back. "You are Alonzo?"

"The one and only," he replied, seeming proud of his existence. He wore his own baseball cap, highlighted with an Astros emblem. Light colored stringy hair flowed out from all edges of the head gear. A sharp, broken nose sat above gleaming white teeth, the obvious result of a few thousand bucks of heavy duty dental work. It seemed wasted on his otherwise unattractive features. "And you would be...?"

"The man who has an appointment with you. I'm sure our friend told you my name is not important." He removed his dark glasses so that the man could feel the glare of his eyes.

Alonzo spread his thin hands apart, while displaying his pearly whites. "Hey. We're all friends here. Just thought, you know, since you know my name, only fair I know yours."

"I waste little time worrying about what is fair."

The other man stared across blankly, then cleared his throat, finally getting a good look into the stranger's dead eyes. He shot a furtive glance toward his companions.

Xminez followed the gaze. "Why don't you tell your friends to relax. Get lost for a few minutes. I get nervous when people hover around me." The drug cartel enforcer actually was never nervous about anything. He wanted to talk in private.

Alonzo started to respond, thought better of it, then nodded to the others. Xminez could hear the scrape of their feet on dirty, bare concrete as they moved to the other side of the room. He took advantage of the lull to pop a stick of gum.

He propped his thick elbows on the table, glaring across. "Now, Alonzo. You're supposed to have something for me."

The man showed his teeth again. "I do if you have the five hundred."

Xminez leaned across the table, coming within a foot of the other man, narrowing his gaze. "I believe you mean four hundred."

Alonzo's cocky smile all but vanished. He leaned back. "Why? What'd I say? Did I say five? I meant four." He found it hard to keep from watching the man's large jaw as it worked the gum.

The huge Mexican patted his shirt pocket with a hand. "I have it here. Where is my gun?"

Alonzo pointed with a turn of his head. "It's in the chair between us. Under the newspaper."

Xminez leaned to reach. Pulling the cold metal from its hiding place, he examined it closely. It was a Colt revolver — an older model. He squinted at the man across from him. "Is this the best you could do?"

The other man attempted to smile again, but it came out twisted. The other man's size, along with his piercing gaze was making his palms sweat. He rubbed them across his pants legs. "I didn't have much notice. The guy only called me late yesterday afternoon. If I had more time, I could..."

"You don't have more time, because *I* don't have more time." Xminez then leaned back, to the shaggy-haired man's immense relief. "This'll have to do." He dug in his pocket for the money and slid four bills across the table. As Alonzo reached for it, the Mexican covered the other man's hand with his own massive palm, pressing it down.

Alonzo looked up with cold fear in his eyes.

"There is something else I need from you. And I need it quickly."

Wincing in pain from the pressure of the meaty hand, Alonzo managed to say, "What? What the fuck you talkin' about?"

"Alonzo, I need the address of an attorney. His actual physical address. An attorney somewhere in the Houston area."

Alonzo stared ."An attorney? I know lots of lawyers in this friggin' city. Must be a zillion of 'em."

A little more pressure, a little more pain. "No. You do not understand. One *particular* attorney. His name is Arthur George."

"Never heard of him. Why do you need this guy?"

"Alonzo." Xminez increased the pressure on the man's hand.

The man's mouth flew open in pain. "Christ! Look, I don't know the guy. What do ya want me to say?"

"I want you to say you'll find out about him. Where his office is."

"But how?"

"Make a few phone calls. Surely you know many other lawyers in a city this size. They should be able to help."

Alonzo decided to risk more agony by asking, "What's in it for me if I do?"

"Let me put it this way, Alonzo. Get me something, and I'll give you the other hundred you tried to steal from me a minute ago. But if you fail, then the reward will be much different."

Quite certain he didn't want to know the answer, he asked anyway. "What...what are you talkin' about?"

Xminez leaned in again. "Did our friend in San Antonio mention who had sent me on my assignment, and asked for your help?"

Even in the hazy darkness, the man's face could be seen blanching. He nodded.

"Well, then, Alonzo, if you refuse to help me, you're refusing to help *him*. He'll chose a special way to reward you."

"Okay, okay. I'll make a few calls." Alonzo pulled his hand back quickly as the man released it. He rubbed it to get circulation going. "Leave me your number, and I'll get back to you when I get something."

The hulking man sat back, shaking his head. "No. I'll sit right here while you find it. I don't have time to wait for you to call me. I intend to leave here with the information I need."

Alonzo started to object, but instead rose from his chair. Producing a cell phone from his pocket, he flipped it open and quickly stepped outside, preferring to make his calls in the privacy of the stifling humidity. It took several calls to collect the information that would help him avoid sure torture.

Returning inside and taking his seat again, he gave the big man a questioning look as he handed him a piece of paper with an address written on it. “Seems this guy has a sorta special kinda practice. Only one lawyer I talked to knew anything about him. Made me swear to not tell anybody I got the address from him. And he didn’t have a phone number for him, or at least wouldn’t give it to me.”

“No problem. I only need the address.” He read the scribbling. “Where is this place? This Webster? Is it a street or a town?”

“Town. The other name is a street in Webster.”

Angel X knew he could find it on his mapping app, but wanted to save time by heading in the right direction. “Where?”

“South of here, about a half hour or so. Take the tollway around to I-45,” He pointed up, indicating the expressway above the bar, “then head toward Galveston. Just follow the signs. Can’t miss it.” He looked hopefully at the man. “We slick?”

Xminez started to rise. “Of course.” He produced another bill, tossing it on the table. “And, Alonzo. As your attorney friend said, you’ll tell no one about this.” He waved the piece of paper.

“No idea what you’re even talkin’ about.”

Alonzo had heard many stories of the merciless ways the Mexican drug cartels dealt with anyone they perceived as enemies. Of the many secrets he had kept, or deeds he had done during his days of dealing with various levels of the underworld, this would be one he would carry to his grave.

Chapter 36

In spite of the caffeine-like jolt Michelle's pronouncement the night before had provided, Church had managed to drift off fairly quickly; the body can only take so much sleep deprivation. Three more Tylenols also helped his brain fade to neutral at first. Colorful, convoluted dreams of distant and recent past events then took over, fading in and out, the last of which was interrupted by the obnoxious chirping of his cell phone. He awoke from his comatose condition, thrashing wildly in his bedding, until it was turned inside-out, again finding himself in a strange room. The curtains over the windows were closed, making it harder still to get his bearings in the relative darkness. Then he remembered — remembered what she'd said — remembered how it had set his juices flowing. She had spoken the words in a motel room, a motel room in Houston, the room he was now in.

He grabbed the phone on the fifth ring. "Hello."

"Walter Church?" the alien voice asked.

Reaching and fumbling for the switch on the bedside lamp, he looked at the clock radio. It read 8:45 a. m. He was alarmed to discover he had slept over nine hours. He had decided not to set the alarm on the radio, choosing to let his internal clock operate... but it had failed him. He had misjudged how sapped his body was.

"Yes."

"Charlie Gage here. I'm with the Houston regional office. A guy in Atlanta... Chris Steen... says he your partner... asked me to give you a call."

"Oh, yeah, right." Church sat up straight, squeezing his crusted-over eyeballs, trying to come to life. "Sorry Agent, uh... sorry, I didn't get the name."

"Gage. Charlie Gage." He sounded impatient, all business.

"Right, Gage. I apologize for sounding a little loopy. Had a pretty long day yesterday. Started out in Savannah, and didn't get in until late. I appreciate you calling."

"What exactly is it I can do for you?" The man asked with a heavy sigh. He obviously had more important things on his mind. Church reminded himself how active the Houston region was.

"Okay, I'll get right to it. I need to locate an attorney somewhere in the Houston area. All I have is the man's name. I was hoping someone in your office might have a line on him."

"The name?"

"Arthur George. No middle initial I know of."

Gage didn't respond immediately. Church thought he heard the man inhale, but he was still too groggy to identify the sound. For an instant, he was afraid the man might hang up, pissed at having someone start his day with such a waste of his time.

"Did you say Arthur George?"

There was a noticeable change of tone that sounded promising. "Right. The name mean anything?"

"Yeah, sure, I know the guy." Gage paused. "Actually, just know *of* him. But before I give you what you want, may I ask why you're trying to find him."

Caught off guard by the return question, Church switched the phone from one hand to the next, buying a second to decide how to answer. Judging from the apparent no-nonsense attitude of the guy, he made the snap decision to tell the man more than he had intended. He knew the type, by-the-book, willing to help, but not without good reason.

"It involves a case my partner and I worked last year. A major drug buy in Atlanta that was hijacked by one of the players. He took the money, then managed to make his way to Florida, where he was taken out by a couple of members of one of the customers he stole from, but not before he was able to waste them too. The money disappeared, and until the last couple of days, there's been no hint of what happened to it. We confiscated and destroyed the coke in the deal, and since every party involved in the deal, including the supplier, is dead, the case was closed." Immediately he knew that it was a mistake to tell the man that. If the case was closed, why the trip to Houston? "Actually, it's been treated as inactive." One more lie couldn't make things any worse.

"You try to track the money?"

"For a while. But there was nowhere to track it. Like I said, anybody we thought might've had it was dead. I'm afraid we lost interest after several months. You know how it is. Other cases kinda pushed it to the back burner."

"Yeah, believe me, I know." Gage paused again. "Okay, so what happened the last few days that stirred things up?"

Church had hoped those questions wouldn't be asked; he knew this would be the tricky part. There was no reason for Gage to ask the question, but to gain his cooperation, his curiosity had to be humored. He couldn't completely omit Michelle from his story, otherwise there would be no reason for him being here. "Two things. First, let me back up a little. The guy who did the deed, took the money, had a wife and daughter. After her husband was gunned down in Florida, we interviewed her as a possibility. Didn't take long to convince ourselves she was oblivious to his criminal activities, as well as the money."

The other agent interrupted. "How much we talking about?"

"Roughly sixteen million."

The Houston agent actually whistled, which seemed not to match his phone demeanor. "Yeah, I would've looked at the wife too. Go on."

"So, out of the blue Monday morning, the woman called me. We had warned her last year, whether she had the money or not, one of the cheated parties might re-surface and come looking for her, and the millions. And that's what happened. Two men from one of the families in Mexico showed up, threatening her and her daughter. They wanted their money, and she couldn't convince them she didn't have it."

"Any idea which family?"

"Pretty sure the Torres family. We think they were partnered-up with the Medinas on supplying the coke in the botched deal in Atlanta."

"Makes sense. They're both from the Sinaloa region. They're two of the worst, especially Torres. I'd say she's lucky to be alive, if in fact, she is."

"Yeah, they made a run at her, but she managed to escape."

"Okay. But I still don't see why you've come to Houston. And why you're looking for George."

Church now realized there was no way getting around the next part. "That's the other thing that's happened. Within the last few days, the wife received a letter from this attorney, this Arthur George, informing her a trust account's been established for her benefit. The trust was evidently drafted by him, and administered by a bank in this area."

"Well, hell. There's your money."

"Not all of it. The woman's dad's a C. P. A. In Savannah. Based on the income she's receiving, he's calculated there's only around a million and a half in her trust. My thinking is, George is handling *all* the money."

"So, you've come to... what... try and recover it from him?"

"No. Try to protect him. Or at least warn him."

Another hesitation. "I'm not following."

"Yesterday, one of Torres' hit men broke in to her apartment and took the letter. So my hunch is he's on his way to try and find the guy too, thinkin' he's got the rest of the money."

The man on the other end emitted a throaty chuckle. "Well, he'll most likely be disappointed if he is able to find him. How long did you say it's been since the heist?"

"Going on eight months."

"Then I think it's safe to say every penny is tied up in trusts scattered all around. He uses several different banks. That's why I was curious over your interest in George. It's his specialty, laundering big stashes. Sometimes legal... sometimes not. Sends the money off-shore for awhile, then pulls it back to do whatever with it. Hiding it in trusts that can't be undone is one of his tricks. We're pretty sure he's done the deed for a few drug kingpins in Texas, maybe Louisiana too. But we're never able to catch him with his hands dirty. He's smart — very careful — and very thorough." He couldn't resist a short laugh. "Sounds like Artie might get bit by the dogs he's been lying down with."

"I think you're right. If the bounty hunter finds him before we do, he won't care if the money's reachable or not. This guy's in a bad mood. He's already killed a Savannah cop who was guarding the woman, plus maybe the accomplice that came up from Mexico with him, so..."

"Hold on just a minute, Church. Since you just woke up, you probably haven't had time to turn your t v on yet."

"Why?"

"It's all over the local news. An APB's been issued for someone who's got to be your guy, because of the Savannah cop. The locals here think he's in town. Shows his picture too, 'cept I doubt anybody can pick him out from it... pretty vague."

Church was stunned into silence for a moment. Things had suddenly changed drastically... and probably in a bad way. The locals in Savannah hadn't wasted any time. Steen had sent them the photo he had taken, and they had sent it on to Houston authorities. If Xminez learns of the alerts, he'll be even more desperate, and speed up his hunt. He needed to wrap the conversation up, and quickly. "So, can you give me a lead on George?"

"It's a waste of time giving you his phone number. From what we've been able to determine, he only takes calls that his caller I D identifies as known clients, or referrals. I can give it to you, but he won't answer. Evidently docsn't have an answering machine. Just lets unknown callers get tired of waiting before hanging up. His office is down in Webster, just south of Johnson Space Center. Hang on a minute, and I'll get the address for you."

Gage was soon back on the line, reading the street address to Church. He jotted it on the note pad the motel provided on the night stand. It suddenly dawned on him that he was wasting valuable time. Over sleeping hadn't helped. He had no idea if Xminez had sources he didn't, but the big man was surely on the attorney's trail.

"You need directions?" Gage asked.

"I should be able to map it, but thanks just the same"

"You sure? This is a big damn city. Where ya staying?"

"Out near the Airport."

"Which one?"

"The one up north, Bush International, I think it's called."

"Actually, Bush Intercontinental. Well, let me at least get you started. You're near Hardy Toll Road. Should be able to find it okay. Take it south 'til you hit the 610 loop, then head east, and keep circling until you hit I-45 heading south. Webster's down in that direction, toward Galveston."

"Okay, thanks." Church wanted to hang up and get moving.

"You sure you don't need help?"

"Yeah, but thanks. Should be all right." Hopefully, not famous last words. A thought suddenly struck him.

"Say, Gage. Since there *are* attorneys whose calls George *will* accept, any chance your contacts can get in touch with them, see if they'll give the guy a heads-up call. Might help if he's got some kinda warning."

Silence said the man was considering it. "Might be worth a shot. I'll see what I can do."

"Thanks."

"One more thing, Church. How you reckon the money got here from Florida?"

It was the one bit of information Church had decided to keep to himself, as long as he possibly could. He still wanted to hide the role Musso had played. The man was dead. No good could come from dragging his name into it. Plus, Michelle would never forgive him, which was the overriding factor.

"Not really sure." Hopefully, the final lie.

Before either man could speak again, there was a knock on his door. Telling Gage to hang on, he pulled on his pants, and went to answer it, still holding his cell phone. Opening the door, he put a finger over his mouth a fraction of a second too late. Michelle said "Good morning," before she caught the warning.

Her words were clearly distinguishable on the other end. "Sounds like you're not traveling alone," Gage said. When Church didn't respond, an awkward silence hung in the air for a second. "Hey, wait just a damn second, Church. What the hell's going on here? When your partner told me to call you, I assumed another agent was with you." He paused again. "You're not on company time, are you?" There was accusation in the tone.

Staring at Michelle's beautiful face, he could tell she was reading the concern on his. She closed the door gingerly behind her. "No, I'm not, Gage."

An exasperated exhale, similar to the one he had heard from the Savannah agent, Floyd, and later from Steen, could be heard. A few muffled, "shit...shit...shit's", came next. Then a sound that could only be the tapping of a finger on the receiver. Then, "Assuming that's who I think it is, are you sure you know what in the hell you're doing, Church?"

Church thought about the man's question, rolling it around in his head for a second. "I may not be handling things according to the manual, Gage, but I know what I'm doing is the right thing. Just trying to end this thing with no one gettin' hurt."

"Yeah. That's what I was afraid of. I take back that offer to help. And, listen, do me a favor, will ya? No matter what happens from here on, you and I never talked. You got *nada* from me. Okay."

"I understand. And thanks, Gage."

"Yeah, right." Click.

Church punched the "END" button, hoping the guy would still follow through on trying to contact the attorney, then turned to face Michelle. In spite of how glad he was to see her, he felt himself falling into a deep, dark hole... hopefully not dragging her down with him.

Chapter 37

What was that all about," Michelle asked as Church threw his phone on the bed.

"The local agent Steen hooked me up with. He gave me the address of Arthur George's office." He rubbed a hand over his eyes, then changed the subject. "Afraid I overslept. Give me fifteen minutes to shower and dress. We need to get going. I'll meet you downstairs in the lobby. We can grab coffee and go."

"Shouldn't we call him first? Warn him about the danger he's in?"

He rushed through an explanation of the attorney's paranoid phone procedure, as well as the type of activity he was involved in, plus the request to get in touch through his "preferred" contacts. "The guy I was just talking to feels certain all of the money's been put in trusts, similar to yours. But as I explained to him, if Xminez finds him first, he'll...well, it'll be a dangerous situation."

She was suddenly looking hard at Church. “Xminez? You know the man’s name?” The blue in her eyes had given way to green as she tightened the muscles in her face.

He wanted to kick himself for letting the name slip. He had purposely kept it from her, not wanting to paint too vivid a picture of what the monster might do to her, not to mention, Allison. And if she was aware he knew the man’s name, he would probably know more about him.

“Yes. That’s why I needed Silas’ computer, to email pictures I took of him yesterday morning. My partner Steen sent them on to San Antonio, and they identified him.”

“You took pictures of him? When?”

With a sinking feeling he explained to her his early morning activities of the previous morning. He fully expected her to react the same way Silas had, but she instead seemed to be doing a slow, controlled burn.

She crossed her arms. “What did they say about him?”

The way she was looking at him, especially after last night, made him feel miserable. What anger she possessed had been bottled-up for a long time — maybe forever, and it was finally about to surface, at his expense. He fell back to sit on the edge of the bed. “It was as bad as I expected it to be, Michelle. He’s a butcher for one of the drug cartels in Mexico. The ones Dickie was doing business with. He normally wouldn’t hesitate to kill anyone. And that includes children.”

Her hand was over her mouth now, shock on her face. “Why didn’t you tell me?”

He could only shake his head slowly. “I didn’t want you to know. It’s as simple as that. I understand how you might feel, that I was holding out on you. But, when I saw the stress you, and your parents were under, I just didn't want to dump anymore on you. I was concerned about your psyche not being able to handle it." He rose again, approaching her. "Think about it, Michelle. What good would it have done for me to tell you. Besides, the truth is, I didn't know myself until right before you got to your apartment yesterday morning. And by that time, after you told me about the letter, I was sure they were gone. I felt the danger for you in Savannah was over. And that's one reason I didn't think it was a good idea for you to come along. I thought you would be safe if you stayed there."

Michelle didn't respond at first. She seemed to be piecing together what he had said, and how she should feel about it. Her face began to gradually dissolve from anger to something resembling acceptance. Finally she spoke in a level voice. "I guess I can see why you felt that way. And I had some idea anyway, especially after what they did to that poor patrolman. But I still wish you had told me. Having a name to put with his actions makes it seem... I don't know... more personal, I guess. Just from now on, don't keep anything from me. I'm in this as much... actually more... than you are. So I've got to know everything. There's no reason for me *not* to know it now."

With that, she turned for the door without giving him a chance for a reply. "I'll be waiting for you in the lobby."

As he had the night before, he stared at the door after it closed behind her for a few seconds, wondering if that brief glimpse of magic from last night had vanished forever. He rushed to the shower, hoping it would wash away an unsettled, sinking feeling.

Church drove for fifteen minutes enduring the uneasy silence in the car before either spoke. They were traveling south on the toll road Gage had advised him to take when Michelle broke the ice, leaning toward him.

"Listen, Walt, I'm sorry about what I said earlier. It was an over-reaction on my part." She paused, turning her head to peer out the car window at the steady drizzle starting to fall. She was beginning to wonder if the sun ever shined in Houston, but accepted that the dreary conditions seemed to fit her current stage of life. "I knew all along those men were dangerous. Hearing you voice it somehow made it seem worse, and it just..." Her voice tailed off.

"No need to explain. Or apologize," he said, feeling an enormous flood of relief. For a fleeting second in his still fuzzy mind, he had thought she might possibly be referring to what she'd said the night before. So anything else was a relief. "This is all new for you. You're experiencing things no one should have to. And I've never been in this situation either, getting involved with a private citizen on a search. I'm feeling my way as I go, and I'm making mistakes. But I'll try and keep them to a minimum from now on." He gave her what he knew was a silly, skewed grin, hoping to repair the mood.

She smiled in return, then gave him a questioning gaze. "I know you're in trouble, because of Allison and me."

"Trouble? I'm not sure what..."

"I heard enough of your conversation with your partner yesterday, and again this morning with that Houston agent, to figure out you're putting your job on the line for Allison and me, not to mention taking that blow to your head. He could've killed you. I keep telling myself you didn't have to come when I called. I can imagine by now you're probably sorry you did."

"Don't worry about that. My job will be fine, and so will I. It so happens, right before you called me Monday, I had been put on desk duty for a while.

There was an incident last week involving the arrest of a drug user in Atlanta. I was in the middle of it. It was only a minor injury, but he's something of a jock in the Atlanta area, and he's taking advantage of the publicity it's creating. And if it's a choice of riding my desk or being here with you, I'll take this any day."

"Even after what I said this morning?"

"Absolutely. And you were right about that anyway. We both need to accept the fact we have to trust each other."

He eased up to the second toll booth they had encountered, dropping correct change in the hopper, then getting a green light. Pushing the button to raise the window before the rain could blow in, he glanced across. "Speaking of Allison, have you checked in with her and Mary?"

"Yeah. Called before I left the room this morning. They're doing fine. Flora and Ralph are taking them down to the Chattanooga Choo Choo today, eat lunch at the Garden Restaurant in the old terminal building, then up to Lookout Mountain. I think their aim is to keep Allison occupied so she won't ask too many questions about what she's doing there, and why I'm not there with her."

"I guess it is a little confusing to her. But I think she'll enjoy being around the train depot. Used to go down to 'Nooga for field trips while I was in high school." Church split his vision between the heavy volume of traffic on the wide thoroughfare, and quick glances at his enticing passenger, still amazed she was right there, sitting within reach. If and when he and Steen were allowed to hit the streets together again, the adjustment might be impossible to stomach.

As she listened, Michelle was busy observing the endless warehouses and small commercial buildings pass by the window. They were traveling through an obviously blue-collar area that went on for miles, paralleling the toll road. She suddenly turned to the agent. "Walt, there's something I want to do before we leave Houston. Actually, something I *need* to do, because I may never have the chance again."

He gave a questioning look, but didn't reply.

"When you explained to me how you knew Brent had died, you never asked me how *I* knew."

"I guess I figured you checked up on him, somehow." He actually hadn't thought much about it, since it hardly mattered.

She nodded, and pursed her bottom lip before continuing. "I did. I called the cell phone number he had given me in Destin, and got a disconnected service message. Knowing how bad he'd looked when he left, I had a strong feeling about the reason. A premonition, I guess you'd call it. I couldn't recall the name of the company he worked for, so I started calling every listing for Musso in this area, until I found his son, Brock. He told me about the cancer, and a little about his dad's last days. Without getting into details, I told him that I was somebody Brent had met on the beaches in Florida, and he had saved me from a bad situation."

She paused for a moment, trying to collect herself, and her thoughts. Church said nothing, knowing she needed time.

"There's a daughter here too... Jana. She has two kids. Brent talked about them all while we were together. Funny; it was only three days, but it seems longer, looking back." Stopping again, her eyes were focused on something in the distance, beyond the rain drops. "In the end, I simply told Brock I thought his dad was a hero, and I just wanted him to know that."

"I'm sure that call meant a lot to him, even if he couldn't grasp what you really wanted to tell him."

"There was no way I could ever explain to him the whole story, about Dickie and all. That would've been too weird for him. Plus, things were still too fresh in my mind to go through it again."

Coming up on the 610 Loop that Gage had mentioned, Church had to strain to read the overhead directional signs in the elements, determining which ramp would take them on the eastern arc of the downtown area. Finding it at the last second, he merged with even heavier traffic, then settled in on the new expressway.

"So you want to meet them?" It was an easy guess.

She looked at him hopefully, glad he had figured it out. "Yes, if it's possible. I know we're here for another reason, and we have no idea how it'll turn out, but it's important to me."

"Are you sure that's a good idea?"

She leveled a look that was a mix of curiosity and suspicion before answering. "I'm not sure what you mean."

"Well, because of what you just said. How are you going to explain how you knew their dad? And what he did? Do you think they'll be able to handle it? Just because time has passed, doesn't mean it won't still be strange for them to learn their dad plotted to kill someone, even if it was the right thing, plus the fact he was unsuccessful. Especially since it was the husband of the person telling the story."

She watched the wipers rhythmically scraping moisture from the windshield, almost hypnotized by them while absorbing his logic. It did make sense. "I won't tell them everything. I'll just take it up to the afternoon I thought Brent had left for Texas. Even that much will show them what he did to protect me, and how unselfish he was."

He nodded, but voiced no reply. The way she spoke of Musso, it was almost as if he were still alive; competing against his own motives — a phantom rival. For the first time in a while, he let his mind drift back to the situation Musso had encountered the previous year, only this time, looking at things from the stock broker's perspective. When he'd first come in contact with Michelle, he'd probably been struck by two thoughts: she was one of the most beautiful, enticing women he had ever met; and he knew for certain he could have no future with her, due to his own doomed existence. Those two competing realities must have been devastating for him as he planned her rescue.

Now, reading Michelle's pained but hopeful expression, she seemed determined, so he let the subject drop, instead concentrating on the open-ended mission ahead. She had hit it on the head a minute ago. There was no way to predict the outcome of their mercy mission. The attorney could already be dead, as far as they knew. And if the hit man hadn't arrived yet, what could they do to deter him? He had a strange sensation of not only not having answers, but not really having a handle on the questions.

"Let's get through whatever's waiting for us at the attorney's office first, then we'll see."

Chapter 38

The white rental car was parked in the lot of an abandoned convenience store a few hundred feet from the target, in the middle of a puddle left behind by intermittent showers. Despite the gloomy, overcast conditions remaining as the rain took a break, the driver kept the dark glasses in place. They were more of a necessity now, along with the baseball cap. Xminez knew the odds against being spotted in a city this size were astronomical, but there was too much riding on staying incognito for another hour or so. And if anyone could pick him out based on the indistinct picture he had seen displayed on the tv screen two hours earlier, then perhaps it was his fate to be stopped. Time was also on his side; it would soon all be over. He would have the money — or not. Either way, he would be on his way to San Antonio within the next hour or so, the first stop on a new life.

His attention was concentrated on the two vehicles in the parking lot of the nondescript brick building a half block away. One of the cars was a cheaper model from Honda, belonging, he calculated, to the man's secretary. The bigger, more expensive car, a Buick sedan, no doubt belonged to the attorney. His plan was to wait out the secretary's break for lunch, then approach the man while he was alone. Of course, if they both left the building, or if they didn't leave at all, he would adjust his plan. He would simply ruin the day for them both. He would have no problem with that scenario, but it would be cleaner and faster with only the lawyer involved. If luck was on his side, the man was the type who preferred to eat in. It was nearing 11 a. m., so he would know soon.

Only minutes later, a stout middle aged woman, with thick legs showing beneath her plain-looking dress, topped by mousy hair shaped into a bun, walked out the front door. She surprised Xminez by climbing into the larger car. He watched as she exited the lot into traffic. Waiting until he was certain she had cleared the area, he cranked up the rental and drove into the office lot.

Arthur George tugged at his scraggly, greying beard, while reading through the outline of the documents he had scribbled out on a legal pad. He would soon enter the words in a more formal arrangement on the word processing program installed on his p c, filling in the important points as he went. It was the way he had done his trust document designs for years, preferring to see things written out before hitting the keyboard. He adjusted his gaze to focus through the bi-focal lens in the glasses perched on the tip of his pinched nose. It didn't match his rounded face, but was handy to hold the spectacles in place. The job before him was a rush project. It would be months before the divorce decree was finalized, but the well known, well heeled plastic surgeon wanted the millions his wife didn't know about permanently shielded from her reach before property settlement became an issue. The money had begun trickling back in from the Caymans into various accounts, where it would sit until he was prepared to fund and activate the trusts. Once in existence, the income from the trust investments would be accumulated until well after the marriage was history, then released to a separate, previously unfunded pour-over trust, all for the benefit of a new business entity the physician would establish at the appropriate time through his personal attorney, who happened to be the man who had recruited Arthur George. But before all that, George's work had to be precise, allowing for all contingencies.

This was his life, working alone, in an office that was rarely visited by anyone other than him and his trusted secretary. The existence of his practice, and its location, was known by only those with a need for his services. It was a unique specialty he had stumbled into some two decades earlier, when a client from his more traditional practice at the time wanted to protect his squabbling future heirs from themselves. The relatively modest amount of roughly eight hundred grand would be better utilized by a worthwhile charity than by his three children, who already possessed more than they deserved. He had performed well, word spread, and his career from that time forward was dedicated to similar projects. He felt strongly he had done right by that client; in fact, in almost all situations he had been paid to handle over the years, he found it easy to justify his work. And also easy to demand a handsome fee. It wasn't without risks, as he was well aware. For every client he had solved a sticky problem for, there was someone, somewhere who would feel they had been shortchanged through his clever work. Oh, there were a few questionable motives along the way, which had led him to adopt a principle he tried to cling to. He would refuse to handle funds that were directly a result of a *proven* criminal act. In other words, if a person wanting to hide money had been convicted of a crime, or appeared on the verge of being so, he was not the man for the job. But if not, then he would gladly help. It was becoming a slippery, sliding scale, with the scope of his work branching out into areas that could only be described as grey in recent years.

The building he occupied had been built for, and had room for, four small professional or commercial enterprises, but now housed only his unusual practice. Soon after the first few attractively large fees in his chosen area of the law had rolled in, he had bought the building, and as soon as their leases expired, he had evicted the other two tenants at the time. His services had to be performed in absolute secrecy... for obvious reasons.

His concentration was interrupted by a rattling noise, coming from the reception area outside his office. Betsy had forgotten something again. She was honest and dependable in regard to her work, but a little on the ditsy side otherwise. He stood his short, rumpled frame up from his desk to go meet her.

Before he could take the first step, his phone rang. He debated whether to answer or not, but knowing the caller could only be one of a relatively few — one who might have a lucrative project for him, he picked up without looking at caller ID. As he answered, the rattling sound was replaced by the sound of glass breaking. The alarm system was off during the day, so no security offices would be picking up a signal. He listened carefully with one ear, while the person on the line started speaking rapidly into the other, just as the bell ringing indicated the front door was opening. The outside door then could be heard closing behind whoever was entering. The alarm control box was in the hallway; no way to get to it without confronting whoever was entering.

He listened without actually concentrating on the words the caller was now speaking frantically into his ear, finally gaining understanding of what the man was saying, but knowing instantly it was too late.

Without responding to the caller's hurried words of warning, he simply hung up, then retreated to his desk, sat, and opened the top drawer on the right side, just a crack. Keeping his right hand hovering near the opening, he waited. Similar invasions had happened before: a cheated beneficiary; a sour ex-partner of a business gone bad; a vengeful ex-spouse, or someone hired by them. A few had managed to find him, and had come expecting to undo what he'd done. After venting their spleen, then finally becoming convinced his work was irrevocable, they all eventually left without accomplishing anything.

This, he now knew, would prove to be none of those. He wasn't sure *what* he had expected to appear in the doorway to his inner sanctum, but the massive figure he beheld truly unnerved him.

The man was dark-skinned, easily Hispanic, wearing dark western-style boots and all black clothing. His head was huge, matching the scale of the rest of his body. There was no smile beneath the cap and sunglasses as he entered. George attempted a brave look of confident defiance, but was certain it was failing.

"Can I help you?" he managed to say, his hand gliding into position above the drawer.

Angel Xminez reached the front of the desk, towering over the man, who looked like a child in comparison. "You are Arthur George?"

"Yes. My friends call me Artie." It was a pointless, idiotic thing to say, but his nerves were going.

Xminez only stared, boring holes into the other man's eyes. "I do not think you and I will be friends."

George tried unsuccessfully to clear his throat, looking for his voice. "Perhaps not. What is it you want ?"

"I am looking for money I believe you have."

The nervous attorney shifted slightly. He knew from the call this wasn't a simple shakedown? For some reason, that possible motive wouldn't have the same chill factor others might. But this man was no run-of-the-mill burglar. He appeared dangerous. "I keep no money in my office. I'm afraid you..."

"No," the man interrupted. "Don't take me for a fool. If I wanted to rob you, you would be dead by now." His large, brown face was expressionless as he spoke.

George's fear grew in intensity, more consuming due to the tone of the man's voice. He watched as the man moved a large hand toward a pocket. George stiffened. Knowing it might be a good idea to go for the gun in the drawer, his body was numb, unable to do what his brain was telling him to do. Instead of a weapon, the man pulled a folded-up sheet of paper from the pocket, tossing in onto the desk.

"Perhaps this will make things clearer."

George leaned to stare at the page, then quickly looked up, afraid to take his eyes away from the man for any length. "What is it?" he asked, his voice cracking.

"Read."

The attorney reached a shaking hand to pick up the letter, noticing right away it was one of his own doing. Straightening it out, he read the addressee, looking for clues. The name and city brought it back instantly. He had sent it only a week or so earlier. The woman in Savannah, Georgia. The dying man who had paid him to set up the trust for her benefit — what was his name? And how much money had been involved altogether? The name was Musso, and the amount was around fifteen million, six hundred thousand, after his fee was netted out. He had suspected the money was less than clean, but following his own guidelines, had agreed to take on the project. With a constricting knot tightening in his stomach, he realized his standards had been far too vague, and it was going to cost him. With a sickening, sinking feeling, he silently asked himself... *Why did I identify myself in the letter? There was no need to. If I hadn't, he never would've found me. Idiot*!

"Yes, I prepared this. What of it?"

Still without expression, the huge man said, "Where is the rest of it?"

George knew exactly what he meant, but grasped at buying time. "I'm sorry. The rest of what?"

At lightening speed, especially for a man of his size, Xminez snatched the revolver from his belt, putting a round into the upper left arm of the little man who was trying to play games. There was no silencer on the cheap weapon, and the sound of the discharge bounced off the walls of the small office, almost swallowing up the man's shrieks of agony. The attorney grabbed his arm with his right hand, his face twisted in pain.

"You know precisely what I am asking. This letter represents only a portion of the sixteen million. I want the rest." He shifted his aim toward the other arm.

"Wait!...Wait!" George gasped in desperation; his mind reeling. A bowel-activating realization told him the man would probably not leave him here alive. The woman in Savannah; he thought she was likely dead also, since this monster had the letter he had sent her. Who else had he drafted trusts for involving the money? There were kids... Musso's kids. They had received a portion. The largest share had been set up for the Children's Clinic at M. D. Anderson. He wasn't concerned about the mammoth hospital... they were too big to go after. But the kids... he had to protect them, or at least their identity.

"The money's all in trust. It's tied up. There's no way of getting to it." The shock of the bullet tearing into his arm seconds earlier was gone, replaced by searing, throbbing pain.

"Who is the trust for?" Xminez fired a second round, a warning shot, into the back of the leather chair, just missing the man's neck.

George screamed with terror. "A hospital! M. D. Anderson Hospital!"

"Why?"

The lawyer looked up with fear in his Yoda-like eyes. Specks of blood from the arm, along with foam from the chair had made their way into his beard. "I don't understand. What do you mean, why?"

"Why would Musso wish to give it all to a hospital? I think you are lying."

Hearing the monstrous man say the name shocked him. He wondered what he'd done to the woman to get his identity. "I don't know. I don't ask questions like that."

Angel X paused for a second, comprehending the undeniable truth that his search was coming to a crashing end, even though it was the end he had expected. At least, he would be free soon. One last thought came to mind... one last grasp at an unlikely fortune. "I want to see proof of what you say.

The documents showing where the money has gone."

George moved his bloody hand from his wounded arm, inching it ever slightly toward the open drawer. "I don't keep copies of what I do in my office."

Xminez waved the gun toward the p c. "In the computer. You have files where you keep records, correct? Documents? Open them. Don't play more games with me, little man, or your other arm will pay."

All resistance had evaporated from the lawyer. His body went limp as he accepted the fact he would not survive no matter what he did. His only hope of spoiling the man's hunt was to keep him from seeing the files. There were many names and many millions in those records — names and amounts no one must ever see — especially not *this* man. The small office reeked of the aroma of sweat, tinged with the paralyzing fear of impending death.

With the attorney hesitating, Xminez pulled back the hammer of the gun and pointed it at his head. "Open the files," he demanded.

George shifted again to face the keyboard. Having only one hand functioning well, it took longer than usual. He moved the mouse so that the cursor perched on "documents", then clicked. He then opened the file titled "AG tasks", a lame attempt to disguise what was within. AG stood for Arthur George, a simple code he never imagined would face being broken. As soon as the file opened up, he quickly moved his right hand to the left, holding the "CONTROL" down, then spreading his stubby fingers as far as possible, punched another key so quickly, the man hovering couldn't follow his move. In a flash, the file went blank, the hundred-plus cases within deleted forever, unless someone wanted to take the time to tear into the hard drive. With a muted feeling of satisfaction, he tried to relax, while accepting his apparent doom, waiting for the man's reaction.

"What have you done?!" Xminez bellowed, pivoting the p c monitor toward him and peering down at the screen, realizing instantly that whatever had been in the files was gone for good. His search was indeed over.

Taking advantage of the brief distraction, George reached in the drawer for his Derringer. Turning quickly, he fired without aiming. The desperate wild shot was only marginally effective, striking the behemoth in his left side, below the rib cage. The wound erupted in a spray of blood.

Roaring more from surprise and anger than pain, Xminez instinctively returned fire, putting a bullet in the man's head. His body fell slumped over the arm of his chair, quivering for a second or two before growing still.

Xminez held a hand to his bloody side. He could tell no internal organs had been damaged; the bullet had only penetrated the leathery layer around his mid-section. But it was beginning to bleed noticeably. Cursing, he searched the hall outside for a restroom. Finding one at the end of the corridor, he used paper towels to compress the wound, soaking several layers with cold water. He took a second to glance in the mirror as he dabbed, seeing a man who had come to the end of one existence, ready to enter another. He finally allowed himself a faint smile, anticipating Luis Torres' reaction to his vanishing act. The smile then evolved into a frown of concern, as he came to grips with the knowledge of the drug kingpin's likely *ultimate* reaction, all too aware Torres would eventually find him... hunt him down like an animal, as *he* had so often hunted others in his sordid lifetime. Realizing he was losing valuable time, he held another layer of damp towels in place, doing his best to quash the flow of blood. Trying hard to remove the images of how things would surely end, he headed for the front door.

Chapter 39

Church slowed the car to a crawl as he neared the attorney's parking lot. He was trying to make sense of the scene ahead. There were two cars in front of the rather plain, one story brick building. One showed signs of being a rental, the insignia of the company stuck in the rear windshield being a clue. The other, a Honda sedan, most likely belonged to someone inside... Arthur George was his guess. He leaned in over the steering wheel for a closer look.

"What do you see, Walt?" Michelle asked, following his gaze. She knew his experience was telling him something. She leaned with one hand on the dash while trying to see the same thing he did.

"I think he's here. He'll be driving a rental car, like that one. Could be someone else, but we need to assume it's him."

Michelle felt a flash of cold dread, fearing they were probably too late to save the attorney.

"So, what now?" she asked.

Church knew it was necessary to continue adjusting whatever ideas he came up with on the fly to include keeping his companion safe, a factor he wasn't used to dealing with. When he'd told her earlier this was all new to him, he'd understated things considerably.

"I'll pull in behind that car, blocking him in. You slide behind the wheel, and I'll go in and try to get a picture of where things stand. If he's in there, it may be too late to help George. But it'll be up to me to make sure he doesn't come out." He took the magazine filled with the nine millimeter rounds from the console, jamming it into the butt of the gun until it clicked in place. Pulling into the lot, he looked at Michelle. "If he comes out before me, and he's armed, forget about blocking him in. You gun it. Get as far away as you can, as fast as you can. Use your phone to call 911."

"I'm not leaving until you come out, Walt, no matter what."

Their faces were only a foot apart. He looked into her eyes, more deeply than at any time in their journey together, trying to drive home his point. She didn't look away. "You don't understand, Michelle. If he comes out first, then I probably won't be coming out at all. You've got Allison to think about. Your only thought should be to escape."

He took a quick glance toward the front door of the office, then back at her. Time was slipping away.

"Promise me you'll leave."

"But..."

"Promise."

"Okay. Just please be careful," she pleaded.

Pulling his own rental vehicle length-wise behind the suspect car, he exited. He waited until Michelle had positioned herself behind the wheel, then crept slowly toward the office door, again gripping the Glock with both hands. He could see the glass around the knob was broken, so the question of whether or not the hit man had arrived was settled. And if the rental was his, he was still inside. An oversight had been not to pack his Kevlar vest... but he wouldn't have been able to wear it on the flight anyway... but he then realized there would've been time to check it in his tote bag... but he couldn't have known... crap!...these useless thoughts, more ways of keeping loose, were wasting valuable time, sapping his concentration. He focused hard on the job at hand.

He was within ten feet when the door suddenly swung open, and a towering figure rushed out, a weapon in his right hand. Xminez and the DEA agent both stopped dead still upon recognizing each other.

It was a tossup as to which man was more stunned: Church by the mere size of the monster; or the bounty hunter by the fact the man he thought he had dispatched in Savannah was actually standing in front of him. In the split second before either man reacted, the DEA agent noticed the other man had been wounded; a crimson circle could be seen beneath his hand at the point of the injury. The attorney hadn't gone down easily.

The Mexican reacted first, tossing away the blood-soaked towel, and getting a shot off with a fierce growl. Church feinted quickly to his left and returned fire, managing to pull the trigger twice, a milli-second before the other man's round tore into his gun-hand arm extended in front of his body, causing him to drop the Beretta. He yelped in pain as it fell away from him. His arm felt like it was on fire. Fearing a follow-up shot, and aware he was an easy target, he quickly ducked behind the rear bumper of the hit man's car, then circled it as the other man advanced. He had no idea if either of his shots had found their target; his thoughts were concentrated on staying alive and retrieving his weapon.

Seeing his car boxed in, Xminez moved on unsteady legs toward the vehicle hemming him in. He had been hit by one of the rounds the agent had fired, this time in the right leg. Whatever pain he felt from both wounds was dashed from his mind; his concentration was on escape. Since he couldn't move his car without causing damage to it, he would take the one behind it. He saw someone sitting in the driver's seat of the car, which mattered little to him. Ignoring the foolish DEA agent still circling his own rental like a scared rabbit, he neared the other car with his gun pointed. Within a few feet of the vehicle, his cell phone suddenly started chirping. Pulling it from his pocket, he took only a cursory glance at Torres' name and number flashing. He growled impatiently, then tossed the phone angrily into the shrubs lining the front of the building, cursing as it left his hand. He had no use for it any longer. The cartel leader's monitoring of his travels would now end.

From his hiding place, Church observed the device as it disappeared into the greenery, then turned to watch in horror as Xminez approached the car Michelle still occupied. She hadn't left, as he'd told her to! He tried without success to get her attention, waving at her to go. She appeared petrified — frozen in place, her eyes transfixed on the other man coming toward her instead, evidently shocked into inaction.

"Michelle! Go! Go! Go!" he screamed. No reaction. She remained locked in position... a beautiful, immobile statue.

Xminez received a second shock when he peered into the passenger side window of the second car. He came to another sudden halt. The woman from Savannah sat behind the wheel, a terrified expression on her face, hands gripping the steering wheel. She sat staring back at him. Their eyes locked on each other for a second that seemed to stand still. Although his body was damaged, his mind remained sharp, computing instantly why she was here. She had lied — the dead attorney had lied — she knew more about the money than either had said. There could be no other reason for her to have come this far. But there was no time to address the question of her appearance. It didn't matter. His window of escape was closing rapidly. He leveled the gun at her.

She suddenly came to life at the sight of the revolver, yanking the car into gear, beginning to press the accelerator.

Xminez reached out with a long arm, grabbing the door handle. The sudden momentum of the car drug him a few yards as he hung on, his boots trying to dig in to the pavement. He raised his gun hand and swung mightily, smashing the window. The sound of metal shattering glass terrified her. She came to a stop, just as he aimed the revolver at her head.

"Take your foot off the accelerator, or I'll end your life here!" he roared through the broken glass.

Michelle had grown motionless again, except for a frightened shiver. Her hands remained tightly wrapped around the wheel.

"Drive!" he bellowed, as he climbed in and slammed the door shut. He had made the quick decision he was not in the best condition to drive, and with his blood loss, he might soon grow faint. He would use her to escape, make her tell him where the millions were, then rid himself of her.

Michelle could feel nothing; her body was numb. She could see and hear the man, but she couldn't make herself move. She took a chance to look back to find Church, but couldn't spot him. What had happened to him!? Was he hurt!?

"I said drive!" Xminez roared, reaching over to strike her roughly with the back of a huge blood-soaked hand.

Shocked into action by the sting of the blow, she put the car in gear once more, turning to exit the lot. Having no idea where he wanted her to go, she chose the direction she and Church had come from only minutes earlier. She was evidently driving too slow for his tastes, so he struck her again, this time drawing blood from her lip. "Quit stalling! Go!" he yelled into her ear and stuck the gun roughly in the side of her neck. She pressed the accelerator down, but not all the way. His own blood was now spurting from both wounds, spilling onto the seat and floorboard. He scanned the area desperately to get his bearings. Unless he could quickly locate a safe place to spend time halting the flow, he would lose strength rapidly as he bled out.

Church had made it to his feet, rushing to grab his gun with his left hand. As he did, he glanced inside the rental car belonging to Xminez, hoping the keys might be in the ignition. They weren't. In panic mode, he transferred the gun to his damaged hand, reaching with his left to grab his cell phone. Dialing 911, he waited for someone to pick up. The words of Silas Lovejoy were screaming in his head: *"Please don't let anything happen to my daughter."*

Holding the phone to his ear, he ran after the car as it began to leave the office lot. Knowing he couldn't chance firing for fear of hitting Michelle, especially with his weaker hand in control of the weapon, he felt helpless. His aim couldn't be trusted. Realizing he would never catch the vehicle on foot, he quickly retreated to the parking lot, remembering the other car parked in front of the building. It had to be the attorney's. He would rifle through the man's office...reach inside his pants if necessary...whether dead or alive, find his keys, then chase down the escaping vehicle.

He would never make it inside the building.

Michelle had been shaken by the second blow, but her anger quickly overshadowed her pain. Pent-up rage from somewhere deep inside was building. The man had done enough harm to her. He had threatened her daughter... disrupted the lives of her innocent parents. In a fraction of a second, her mind cascaded back to her miserable years with her criminal husband; the danger he had almost pulled her and Allison into before being murdered himself; the unbearable life she had endured waiting for *this* monster to come. It had to end. Enough was enough. She saw one chance to at least slow him — if only she had the courage. Knowing there was no other way, she prepared herself. If he wanted speed, she would give it to him. The vehicle she was driving was now a long block away from the attorney's office. She was gaining the speed the man had demanded. Spotting a delivery van about to emerge from a cross street ahead, approaching the next intersection, she allowed it to fully enter her street, then accelerated quickly toward it. She ignored the red traffic signal appearing huge in her eyes, aiming for the rear of the white panel truck. If she was going to endanger herself, she would at least try to avoid injuring the innocent driver. Drawing within a few feet, she prayed no one was in the rear section of the van. She saw the eyes of the terrified driver growing wide, staring at her in disbelief as she took dead aim on his vehicle. She closed her eyes just before impact.

Too late, Xminez saw what she was doing. He roared a warning, just as the car broadsided the rear section of the van. The sound of metal striking metal was deafening. Neither he nor the woman had seatbelts fastened, but she had the advantage of bracing herself, knowing what was coming. Another advantage she didn't know she had was a driver-side air bag. It deployed, swallowing her up. The passenger side didn't have one, or if it did, hadn't functioned. The man's body was catapulted, his large head lurching forward, colliding with the windshield, creating an instant spider web-like crack. Recoiling, it took a few seconds to shake the added pain from his head. It took a few more seconds to recover his senses. Blood from his battered head now joined that seeping from his other wounds. Reaching for the floorboard to locate the revolver that had been knocked from his grip at impact, he located it, then aimed it to end the woman's life. She wasn't there! A fierce rage engulfed him, as his dreams of freedom and a new life seemed to be ebbing away, all due to the stupidity of the woman.

Throwing the door open as soon as the bag deflated, Michelle had freed herself, falling out onto the hard, wet pavement. She heard the screech of tires braking all around her... horns blaring. A car came to a rocking stop only a few feet away, spraying oily moisture over her body. She could feel the heat from the engine on her back. Closing her eyes tightly for a second, she waited for another vehicle to crush her. When it didn't happen, she knew she couldn't wait for the sounds to subside. Realizing the monster could still come after her, she hurriedly scrambled to her feet, and began running toward the office lot, hoping to find Church. The block might as well have been a mile away; the building seemed to grow more distant the harder she ran... her legs like jelly. Her mind was a jumble of fear and confusion; horrific recall of the car chase two nights earlier came flooding back. But her thoughts were clear enough to accept that the man wouldn't let her escape if he could free himself.

The sound of the violent crash had stopped Church in his tracks as he headed toward the building. Cradling his damaged arm, Church threw his phone on the roof of the bounty hunter's car, then ran to meet Michelle halfway down the long block, grabbing her arm and leading her back to the office parking lot. They took shelter behind Xminez's abandoned car.

Noticing people in vehicles that had stopped, emerging to observe the scene, he yelled for them to return to their cars, then focused on Michelle.

"Are you okay?" he asked, noticing the blood streaked across her face.

"Yes. What about you?" She then saw his blood-soaked arm, horrified by the site of it. "Walt! You've been shot!"

"I'll be fine."

Suddenly there was a voice on the phone he had placed on the car; it was barely audible. Someone at an emergency command center somewhere had finally picked up, but he wasn't listening to the voice. No time to grab the phone and talk. His concern was for the woman — and Xminez. Looking over the hood of the car, he saw the man had left the rental car, lumbering unsteadily toward them. His head now also bloodied, the man had a wild look in his dark eyes, glaring animal-like through streams of red. He staggered in their direction. Church left the phone where it was, hoping whoever was on the other end might be able to trace the signal, while he dealt with the immediate danger coming toward them. Bystanders observing the frantic scene would surely be on their mobile phones too.

Reaching the parking lot, Xminez managed to spot the agent peering from behind the car. His battered head was filled with white-hot anger, knowing his escape to a new life was now gone. His only inflamed thoughts were directed toward punishing the two who had taken it from him. He fired a shot wildly, the bullet striking the outside wall of the building, sending a chunk of brick flying.

Church tried to hold his weapon in his left hand. It felt weak; he couldn't aim with his usual control. The right arm was of no help, having lost all feeling. Taking another glance, he recognized the gun Xminez held was a revolver — six rounds. He quickly did the math: two rounds fired at him; at least one to dispense with the attorney inside. So at most, three rounds remained. But that was enough to do harm to him and Michelle. He turned to the woman crouching next to him, trembling. There was only one way they could stop him. He kneeled next to her.

"Take the gun, Michelle. Use it the way I showed you last night."

She shook her head rapidly. "No! I can't, Walt. I can't do it."

"Yes you can. I can't get a bead on him with my left arm. You've got to do it!"

Shaking her head again, she was too horrified to speak. Chancing another look, Church was alarmed to see the man within ten yards. He was raising his gun, wiping away blood from his eyes, trying to take aim, ready to end their lives.

"Think about Allison," Church pleaded, growing weak from blood loss. "She needs you. This'll be over now. You two can have a life again." He had more arguments to give, but there wasn't time.

She looked at the Beretta for a second, despising the sight of it.

"Go ahead," he said as calmly as he could, for her benefit as well as his. "The safety's already off. Just fire it the way I showed you."

With reluctant, unsure hands, she took the weapon. She stared at it, then took a deep breath. Standing quickly to face the man who wanted to kill her, before giving herself a chance to think about what she was doing, Michelle held the gun the way Church had showed her. Her throat was filled with bile as she saw the enraged hit man point his gun directly at her, smiling menacingly through the blood stains. Her bile turned to rage again. Just as he fired, she pulled the trigger once, twice, then a third time, her hands jerking back violently each time. The sound of the man's round zinging through the humid air above her hardly registered. An ear-piercing scream, mixed with those of people in nearby vehicles, bombarded her ears. It was a second before she understood it was a scream from deep in her own throat; a scream of defiance; a scream of terror; a scream to cover up the horror of what she was doing. As suddenly as she had risen, she quickly dropped the weapon, then fell into Church's arms as he rose halfway to meet her. They leaned against the side of the car for a seeming eternity as she sobbed violently, her body trembling. Neither dared to budge.

After a few seconds, they could hear voices; voices of people slowly making their way into the parking lot, making murmuring sounds of morbid fascination. They had left their vehicles and were viewing the scene, tentatively approaching what appeared to be a body lying in a pool of blood. Sirens could be heard in the distance, seeming to come from several different directions. The street resembled a used car lot, arranged in demolition-derby style... vehicles strewn around the damaged panel truck and the car that had rammed it... more drivers emerging to discover the reason.

Church reluctantly removed his arms from around Michelle. He suddenly remembered something he had to do. Something that might be important. He walked over to the shrubs, digging around among them with his good hand. It took a few seconds, but he located the cell phone Xminez had discarded. Looking at the screen for a second, he powered it off, then returned to the car where Michelle still crouched. He shook her gently to make sure she was listening, then placed the phone in her hands, whispering, "Go get your purse in the car, and put this in it. Don't let the purse out of your possession. Hurry... before the police get here. I'll explain later."

She hesitated a moment, not wanting to visit the damaged vehicle, and not wanting to leave the security of Church's side. Judging it must be important, and aware she would need her purse anyway, she half-walked, half-ran to the car, not letting her eyes linger on the sprawled body as she passed it. She had barely climbed out of the vehicle with the purse in hand when the first police cruiser arrived.

Chapter 40

The boardwalk along the western shores of Galveston Bay was busy with locals and tourists alike, celebrating hump night, their spirits not dampened by the sticky, overcast conditions. The community of Kemah seemed to be the focal point of a booming hospitality industry set along the edge of the bay, with restaurants, hotels, carnival rides, and even a large aquarium drawing a sizeable Wednesday night throng. Michelle wondered about the odd name of the community. It might possibly be an Indian name, like several in her native state. But those wandering thoughts weren't important... she had to focus on the task at hand... the task Church had schooled her on earlier from his hospital bed.

She parked the replacement rental car on the edge of the parking lot of an enormous Cajun-themed seafood kitchen. Six p. m., and the restaurant was filling up rapidly, so the outward slots were all that were left, which was fine with her, since she had no plans to enter the establishment. The car had been delivered by the rental company to the hospital in nearby Clear Lake, where she and Church had been transported by a local e. m. s. unit.

Getting the substitute car had proven to be a problem at first. Church hadn't thought to list Michelle as an additional driver when filling out the paperwork for the now damaged car, but he *had* accepted the insurance that came with the agreement, since he didn't want to push his luck with his insurance company if he filed a claim on his Yukon. When it was explained to the leasing company she had been behind the wheel at the time of the collision, they had balked at providing another vehicle. Fortunately, a police officer had accompanied the two of them to the hospital. He took part in the phone conversation with the rental company, explaining the sequence of events, and promising to forward a police report. So after a four hour delay, the small economy car was driven to the hospital from Enterprise's Hobby Airport location.

She hadn't thought her minor injuries qualified for a trip in the rear of the van, but she didn't want to be separated from Church. Once inside the E R, the physician on duty soon discovered his earlier head wound, plus possible damage to his kidney. He ordered an immediate cat scan and x-rays to check out internal damage, both of which proved to show no serious damage. His wrist would most likely need surgery to repair the damage caused by the gunshot, all of which meant he would be kept for at least two nights until all tests were completed and the arm treated.

A few stitches were required on Michelle's lips; the type she was assured would leave no permanent scarring. Following an antiseptic being applied to her other wounds, she had covered the marks with makeup and released from the ER. Not wanting to leave the DEA agent's side, she was told she would have to wait elsewhere while he was being treated, then assigned a room. After spending time in the hospital coffee shop, then growing antsy in the comfortable main lobby, she decided to kill time by wandering outside the entrance to Clear Lake Regional Medical Center, a sparkling clean, evidently new facility located approximately ten miles southeast of Houston. The distance was only a guess, since she'd lost all perspective. Not only was she in a strange city, in a strange state she could never have imagined she would be visiting as recently as two days ago, it was more the enormity of the metropolis. It was even bigger than she had judged from the plane the night before. They had driven what seemed like forever in search of Arthur George's office earlier in the day. The adrenalin of her earlier adventure having worn off, she was suddenly feeling weary. Locating a bench, she had sat and tried to collect her thoughts about the day's events. Without knowing a soul in the enormous metroplex, other than the man being treated upstairs, she felt every bit alone as she had in Crawford Square in Savannah, yet somehow, without the same feeling of dread. She used the time to think back over the surreal, horrible day.

Thankfully, she and Church had been carted off before Arthur George's body was removed from his office, so she had avoided seeing him carried out. One lifeless body observed had been enough. When they arrived, the police had so many questions, they didn't seem to know where to start. A supposed dead cartel hit man from the state of Sinaloa, Mexico; a secretive attorney, who they all seemed to have heard of, but knew very little about, evidently slain by the hit man; a DEA agent from Atlanta, Georgia... a long way from his home territory; and a woman also from Georgia... this time Savannah... all made for a confusing mix. As to who had taken out the hit man wasn't clear, and although the DEA agent claimed it was him, he didn't sound convincing. After taking a few statements from the two of them, the investigating officers stood scratching their heads, assigned an officer to follow them, then released them to the e. m. t.'s, with promises they would continue the questions later. They couldn't give guarantees that charges in regard to the gunfire exchanged would not be forthcoming. Since neither Church nor Michelle had any idea where their night would be spent, the officers got the name of the hospital they would be delivered to from the emergency technicians.

Michelle felt terrible about the poor attorney. He hadn't deserved his fate. If only she and Walt could've arrived a few minutes sooner, it might have made a difference. She wondered if he left a family; her guess was probably not, given the secretive nature of his work. His secretary, who was at lunch when everything happened, was distraught when she returned to discover what she had missed. Her tearful reaction to the news about her boss told Michelle the man must've had more good traits than bad, although the whispers and innuendos among the officers said otherwise.

The cell phone in her purse buzzed. When she reached for it, she saw the other phone... the one Walt had told her to secret away, lying next to hers. It was still powered off. The call was from Church, using his own mobile device.

"Come on up," he had said, sounding slightly sedated. "Room 312."

When she reached his room, she walked to the side of his bed. Without thinking about it, she leaned and kissed him gingerly on his forehead. "How're you doing?" she asked with a crinkly, restrained smile, a subtle reminder of her own wounds.

"Okay, I guess. But now you've gone and elevated my blood pressure." He was groggy with pain killers, but not so far gone that he didn't feel something. "I'm more concerned about how you're holdin' up."

"Tired, but somehow relieved, now that it's all over." She smiled, then stared for a second. "You do think it's over, don't you?" His hesitant expression made her wonder.

"That's something we need to talk about. And we need to hurry in case the police make good on showing up for more questions. Do you have your purse... the phone I gave you?" She produced the phone, and for the next fifteen minutes he had explained what she needed to do, how to do it, and where to go to do it. While being treated, he had quizzed one of the nurses about the surroundings. With the information gleaned from her, he thought he knew the perfect place for her assignment. Now, with his mind being in neutral, he found it necessary to stop and start over a few times as he went through her instructions. But she finally understood. And it did seem to make sense. One thing that didn't was his insistence in telling the officers at the scene that *he* had fired the shots ending Xminez's life. When she asked him about it, he explained it was an attempt to keep the fact she had even been present at the shooting out of the story. What she was going to do based on his instructions was another step in that direction.

"You need to go now," he had said, seeing her confused look based on his rationale. "There's no time to waste. It'll be dark soon."

She took another chance with his pulse rate, planting another kiss on his forehead before hurrying from the room. "Get some rest," she said.

Taking her purse from the car, she walked from the restaurant parking lot, crossing the expanse of a manicured lawn in front of the restaurant, then across a frontage road, finally making her way onto the boardwalk fronting the seafood house and several other restaurants. The boardwalk had piers jutting out toward the bay every hundred feet or so. There were a few docking stations along each pier, but they appeared to be mainly observation points for tourists. She walked slowly, since she wanted a little more darkness to settle before completing her task, recalling that Walt had said things would go better under the cover of darkness, which she also understood. Passing by the aquarium, she thought about Allison, and how much she would enjoy seeing it. When this was all over... *really* over, she and her daughter would make more trips, try to enjoy life. They could afford it now. Maybe they would come here.

Finally, after meandering along the wooden walkway for nearly thirty minutes, she felt the time had come. Searching for a pier that no one else was occupying, she strolled casually out to the end, taking a moment to let the warm, moist air wash over her. The water below her was dark... murky. She recognized an odd sensation of exhilaration over what she was about to do coursing through her. It was a simple thing, but one that might be vital to her future. Walt had admitted there were no guarantees that it would end things permanently, but it was the best they could do under the circumstances.

Her other thought was the irony of the fact her husband's death on a pier a few hundred miles to the east, some eight months earlier, had now lead her to *this* pier, hoping to end what his death had put in motion. None of it seemed real.

Taking a look back down the pier to guarantee privacy, she removed the Mexican's phone from her purse, cringing from the idea of holding in her hands the device once held by the monster who had terrorized her. Powering it on, she watched as the screen slowly flashed to life. Following Walt's instructions, she pressed the key to display the numbers that had called from the phone. There were only two numbers shown, and one that had called the most recently, and the most often. That, he had told her, was the number to use. He had also taught her how to text, something she had never done. They had practiced on his phone in the hospital room until she felt confident, powering-up the Mexican's phone just long enough to make sure it had the capability needed, then quickly silencing it again.

Clearing the screen, she then punched on the button illustrating an envelope. A lined tablet of sorts instantly appeared. She put her thumbs to work entering her text message. Her fingers were clumsy... shaking... influenced by the weight of what she was doing. Then she thought about the evil man she was texting, and how crucial her message was. It gave her the impetus to complete the task. The message was short. It read:

forget about the money
the moneys gone
and so am i

Then scrolling down to the correct number, she hit "SEND" — then waited.

Walt had said the message should get immediate results, and she hoped he was right. She wanted to hear the voice of the man who had tried to destroy her, and her daughter. It would also be the voice of a man who had helped her husband drag her and Allison into the horrors of the past year. It took less than thirty seconds. The phone began vibrating and chirping, the shock of it almost causing her to drop it. It pulsated evilly in her hands. She was surprised at her sudden reluctance to answer the call, having the sickly feeling she would be exposing herself to the man, as if he could see through the phone. Realizing it was a ridiculous fear, she answered, hitting the correct key, but didn't speak.

A frenetic barrage of what she assumed was Spanish came pouring forth. The man was screaming loudly, without stopping, using what she knew were threats laced with cursing. She allowed herself a satisfied mental image of the rage in the man's face. It was hard resisting the urge to talk into the device, scream back at the man, even though Walt had cautioned her it would ruin everything if the man heard her voice. The only reason for waiting for the man to call was to assure her he had received the text. She realized with growing rage how badly she wanted to release her rage at the voice, tell him how she despised him for what he had attempted to do to her family; tell him he had failed, and she would never fear him again. She hoped that was true. She wanted desperately to believe it.

Instead, she did the final thing Walt had told her to do. Leaning back, she cocked her arm, then threw the phone as far as she could into the dark, hopefully deep water. The man's fading voice could still be heard as the device floated end-over-end through the air, the blue-lit screen glowing on and off in the darkness as it flipped again and again, before disappearing without so much as a ripple into Galveston Bay.

Chapter 41

The police kept their promise just before 9:00 the following morning. Two of the uniformed officers who had quizzed them at the crime scene were accompanied by detectives from the Homicide Division of the Harris County Sheriff's Department. Michelle had not arrived at the hospital yet, but the detectives, who took control, said they would interview her later. She had checked in the night before at a nearby motel close to one of the exits off I-45. Church was puzzled at first about her absence, then it dawned on him where she most likely was. At least, he hoped that was the reason for the no-show. He realized it was impossible *not* to worry about her. She was on his mind constantly now.

The two detectives, one white, one black, named Ross and Ladner respectively, pulled the two visitor's chairs next to the bed and produced their credentials, while the uniformed guys leaned against a wall, content to be on-lookers.

Church pointed with his good arm in the direction of the room's tiny closet. "My vitals are in my..."

"Don't sweat it," Ross said, appearing to be the senior man. "We've already checked you out. How're you doing, by the way?"

Church eyed the man closely, trying to judge his demeanor. Was he a threat? Or just doing his job? With his mind still somewhat in limbo, he couldn't decide. "As well as can be expected, I guess. They seem to have pretty good doctors here."

"That's what we're known for around here." Ross paused, adjusted his position in his chair, then started in. " Feel up to a few questions?"

"Sure."

"Good." The detective scratched his chin. "Well, to begin with, what my partner and I are having a devil of a time figuring out is what you're doing in our neighborhood. You and the woman gave our friends here," he jerked his head toward the uniforms, "a statement yesterday. Something about a drug cartel, a bounty hunter, a shady lawyer, and your search to find him. Would you humor us by elaborating? Filling in a few gaps?"

Church's head was clearer than the night before, thanks to the I V drip in his arm and a deep, deep sleep, but a few cobwebs remained. He spent a few seconds organizing the details in his mind, thinking things through. There were parts he knew he needed to tell them, but also parts he wanted to keep to himself. In the end, he decided to go as far as he could with his desired version, then hope for the best. He launched into his story, starting with the surveillance of Dickie Frapiana nine months earlier. The events he related took the detectives through the murderous rampage at the drug buy in Atlanta; the chase to find Frapiana during his escape to Destin; the night on the marina pier when the drug dealer, along with two hit men searching for him and the money he had stolen, were gunned down; the interview with Michelle in Savannah following her husband's death; the call earlier in the week from Michelle telling him the cartel hit men had arrived, thinking she had the millions; and then the events of the last few days in Savannah, including the stolen letter; and now Houston. For the most part, the detectives simply nodded or shook their heads while taking notes. Each took a turn or two at interrupting with questions. When he got to the end, he couldn't tell from the looks on their faces, and the glances they exchanged, if they were intrigued by the story, or thought he was flat-out lying, making the whole thing up. He wouldn't blame them if they felt that way.

Making one last notation in his notepad, Ross reached into his coat pocket, producing a plastic bag with a piece of paper folded inside. He held it up. "This the letter you say the woman received?"

Surprised to see it, Church leaned to look. He knew it couldn't be removed from the bag, but he could read through the polyethylene. "Yeah, I think so. But I've never seen it before." He peered up at Ross. "Where was it found?"

"On the desk top in the attorney's office. We can probably match a few prints on it to the bounty hunter if we have to, but don't think it'll be necessary. Ballistics should show he killed George." Ross paused for a moment, then frowned at the patient. "Where'd the woman learn to handle a weapon like that?"

Church simply stared back. "I don't... I'm not sure what you mean."

The frown remained. "What I mean is, it took some training to know how to handle a weapon even as stout as a Beretta. So, I was just wondering..."

"Nope. You've got it wrong, Detective. *I* took the guy down."

Ross and Ladner exchanged quick looks, then Ladner jumped in. "That's the way we thought it probably went down... at first. Until one of the witnesses told us different. Said he couldn't resist taking a peek through his windshield. Some folks are like that, you know. Like to look at car wrecks, bloody fist fights...that sort of thing. He's definite about seeing the woman pull the trigger. Said it was 'pretty damn awesome, seeing a woman shoot like that', I believe were his words."

The room was silent for a moment. Church looked away from the detectives, wanting to avoid eye contact while being caught in another in a litany of lies.

"Look," Ross said, leaning in toward the bed. "What the hell difference does it make? The shooting was flat out self defense...the witness made that clear. Plus, we know the guy killed our attorney friend, and had you and the woman in his sights too. There's no big mystery to solve here. We really don't give a damn about who fired... just trying to get our facts straight."

The DEA agent leaned back, forcing himself to stifle a satisfied smile. "Okay. I gave her a crash course last night. Just in case what did happen, might happen. She had never fired a weapon. She didn't wanna fire mine, but my injury didn't leave much choice."

"Good thing you coached her," Ladner said. "Too bad you aren't left handed."

Church gave a sardonic grin. Even that hurt a little.

"Why'd you decide to take the credit?" Ross followed up quickly. "Your higher-ups aren't gonna be too thrilled about it, you being so far from home."

Church knew the man was right, but didn't answer right away. He thought it was a better solution than Michelle's name being broadcast as the shooter. He suddenly realized the fact that it was known by some that she had fired the round at the hit man might keep her at risk. He set his mind at work looking for ways to undo the potential damage.

Ross was busy running his pen through his thick black hair, beginning to show grey around the temples. Since the guy wasn't going to answer, he posed another concern. "Something else is bothering me about your story, Church. I'm not questioning anything you've said, now that we got that part straight, but aren't you leaving out one tiny detail?"

Church cringed, hazarding a guess at where the question was leading. "I'm not sure what..."

"Goin' back to Florida, since the drug dealer and the hit men were all taken out on that pier, there must've been someone else there. There's almost always a last man standing."

Church's heart and stomach sank at once. There was no way to leave Musso out of it now. He sighed and began again, telling about the ballistics tests and fingerprints that proved the stock broker's role in the killings.

"Why'd you leave that out the first time?" There seemed to be more curiosity than accusation in the man's tone.

He had an answer prepared; the answer he had been ready to give the Houston DEA agent the day before. But Gage hadn't thought to ask the question. This guy was sharper.

"Two reasons. First, he had nothing to do with what happened yesterday. He was out of the picture months ago. Bringing his name up now will only cause his family unnecessary headaches. They're here, in Houston, by the way."

Ross chewed on the answer for a moment. "And the second reason?"

"The man's dead, Ross. Died of pancreatic cancer soon after he got back to Houston. My thinking is he knew he was dying, and that's the reason he did what he did, protecting Mrs. Frapiana." It felt strange referring to her by that name now, but thought it might sound better.

"Who was the guy. We may need to check out your story. Not saying we will, but just in case."

"Name's...or was... Brent Musso. He was a stock broker from here. Just happened to be on a last vacation in Florida when he somehow met the woman and her husband."

Ross made a few notes. "So he..." His face grew into a frown for a brief second, then brightened, putting it all together."So, *that's* how the money got to Houston, and in the hands of Arthur George?"

"I don't see how it could've gotten here any other way. But I don't think I'll ever know what he did with the rest of it. The attorney, I mean."

"Well, it looks like you're right about that. None of us will. We had one of our techies examine the man's computer. Seems he erased all of his files. Probably to keep the man he knew was going to kill him from viewing it."

Church felt a surge of relief coursing through his body, along with whatever the tubes were pumping in. He also felt a sense of admiration for the attorney's courage. Maybe there was still a chance to bring the trail to an end.

"However," Ladner jumped in, " there *are* companies that can extract information from a p c's hard drive. Takes a little time, but even stuff that's been deleted can be retrieved sometimes."

Church ran his gaze across both detectives, trying to gauge their dispositions. “You think that’ll happen?”

“That’s really hard to say,” Ross answered. “Maybe not, since it’s not critical to solving our killings here.” Before Church had a chance to get his hopes up too high, he added. “Thing is, though, George was suspected of doing business with a lot of... let’s just call’em... scum bags, for want of a better term. Might produce some interesting transactions. A ton of federal guys may want to dig in to ‘em.”

All three men looked at each other for a few silent seconds. Church knew it was in hands he couldn’t control.

“Tell you what,” Ross suddenly said, standing to leave. “We’ll talk to our boss, Sheriff Howorth. If he thinks it’s worthwhile to pursue it, we’ll pass along your concerns about keeping Musso’s name out of it. That’s the best we can do. No promises, though. And its not our call on the computer deal. I’ll say this, though, this is one hell of a story.”

Before the detectives could leave, Church had another favor to ask. “Listen, I know what I’m about to ask is counter to everything you and I have been taught about investigations... gettin to the truth of matters.” He hesitated, anticipating a less than favorable response.

“As I explained, Mrs. Frapiana’s been through a rough time, none of which was due to her actions. She and her daughter have lived every day since her husband’s death in deadly fear of someone like Xminez coming after them. If it’s revealed she pulled the trigger on him and the media puts it out there, the cartel who sent him will want to know why she did it, wondering what secrets she’s hiding. Her nightmare will continue.”

Ross furrowed his brow. “So, what are you saying? You want us to put you down as the shooter? You know that won’t fly, even if we wanted to.”

Church was desperate to win his point. "Why not?"

It was Ladner who answered. "For one thing, no way her prints aren't all over the gun. And what if the witness I mentioned talks to the media, tells what he saw? Or another witness confirms it?" He glanced at his notes, then thumped the pad with a finger.

"Witnesses get confused all the time... you know that. And it would be easy to claim her prints were from the night before, when I taught her how to use the weapon. And I'm fairly certain everyone was laying low during the action. Don't think anyone really saw clearly what happened in all the confusion... who did what." He looked hopefully at the two men.

Ladner raised his palms up. "Yeah, but she'll have powder residue on her hands. We can test her for that when we talk to her."

Church wasn't done arguing yet. "That's true. But only if you *have* to test her." He looked from detective to detective, pleading. "Come on, guys. Like you said, what difference does it make who did the deed. It would make more sense if I pulled the trigger anyway."

Ross stared hard at the agent, who just happened to be hundreds of miles out of his jurisdiction. "The difference it makes is the *truth*, Church. Like *you* said, we've all been trained to uncover the truth."

Church slumped in his bed. "You're right, of course. Not arguing that. But if the rules can't be bent this one time, an innocent woman, and her child, might be at risk the rest of their lives."

The room was again silent for a moment. Ross and Ladner shared quick glances. It was Ross who finally sighed, then spoke. "As I said before, can't promise anything. We'll give it some thought."

"That's all I ask." Church thanked them, and the four cops readied to leave.

Asking for the motel Michelle had selected, they also told him to have her call if she showed up at the hospital before they found her. They left their cards. He didn't push his luck by asking if they actually planned to test her for the powder residue, but he thought there was a good chance they wouldn't.

With the room empty except for the occasional nurse to administer a dosage and check his vitals, he had time to think... and worry; several hours, in fact. Having one of the nurses look up the number of the motel, he called twice, asking for Michelle Frapiana's room. No answer. He wanted to see her, or at least talk to her, for more than the obvious reasons. He wanted to tell her about his interrogation, and what he had asked the men to do, before they got her side of the story. She wouldn't be happy to learn what he'd told them, but she needed to understand it was for her benefit, and couldn't be avoided.

He also let his mind wander to what he thought the future might hold for the two of them. He was smart enough to know that when two people were thrown together in the manner they had been, it was easy to let emotions run amok. People might say things they wouldn't mean ordinarily... a closeness might be formed that would only be temporary, evaporating when the ordeal was ended. It could easily explain her words two nights earlier. *Still, since she was thinking of changing her name anyway...* he checked himself, thinking the drugs being wired through his body must be putting ridiculous thoughts in his head. He had to accept there may be *no future* for them beyond their shared adventure.

Chapter 42

His next visitor came shortly after 1:00 p. m. Following a knock on the door it opened to reveal a tall, angular man with a butch haircut, the kind that dated back to the sixties. He appeared to be in his late forties. The face was one Church had never seen, but knew the man's identity as soon as he spoke. The gravely tone was unique, but it matched his overall appearance. He was shocked the man had taken the time to come, remembering the way their previous conversation had ended.

"Church. Charlie Gage." The man moved his lanky body to the side of the bed. He made no effort to hide a bemused smile.

They didn't bother to shake hands. It would've been an awkward left-handed, un-manly shake anyway.

Church could only stare at the man for a moment, trying to assimilate why he *had* chosen to come. "Gage. I appreciate your coming. Have to say I'm surprised, though. Have a seat."

"Better not. Can't stay long." He ran his eyes around the interior as if he'd never seen the inside of a hospital room. "Your little adventure made a dent in the news last night, except none of these hippy-dippy reporters probably got the story right. They never do."

"Same way back in Atlanta. In their defense though, this one *is* sorta confusing."

Gage chuckled. "Yeah, I suppose so. That may be why they didn't spend too much time on it — didn't know what to make of it. Plus, we get so many events similar here each day, they get kinda jaded." He cleared his throat. "Actually, the reason I came was, had a talk with your partner again. I figured he'd want to know what you got yourself into."

"Oh? What did he say?"

"He was concerned at first, wanting to know how you were doing. I told him you were okay. At least, the reports I got from the folks here said you were. Then we had a good laugh, agreeing you stepped in it pretty deep down here."

Church's body shook with sedated pain, unable to hold in his own laugh... a laugh influenced more by the fact he was still alive.

"Oh, and he told me to give you a swift kick in the ass when I saw you. But looks like you've been beat up enough."

"I'd say so."

Following an awkward, brief pause, Gage added, "He asked me about something else too — something I guess you forgot to mention yesterday."

What little color Church had left drained from his face. It could only be one thing.

"Some guy named Musso. Steen wanted to know if his name had surfaced.

Wanna tell me about him?"

Exhaling a deep sigh, the injured patient came clean, re-hashing the same story about the doomed stock broker he had given the detectives earlier in the day, and giving the same reasons for not including him in the first explanation.

The Houston DEA agent nodded slowly, pursing his lips while he digested the story. "Steen did say you seem to have a thing for the woman. My guess is you wanted to keep the guy's name out of it because of what he did for her."

"I'll admit that's most of it. But I can't see any benefit to anyone by dragging his kids into something they had no part in. Their dad died from cancer less than a year ago. And now they get bombarded with the news he had planned to kill a man. Plus the fact he most likely came home with millions in dirty money. That would be too much for most people."

"Speakin' of the money, aren't your higher-ups gonna be curious over what happened to it?"

"I don't think so, Gage. Especially after what you told me about Arthur George's way of hiding things. Doesn't look like we'll ever be able to find it. At least, not all of it."

The other man slowly nodded again, evidently absorbing the logic. They grew silent for a moment. The man looked as though he was debating something. "I don't know if I should mention this or not, Church, 'cause I don't think it'll make you feel any better — maybe even worse."

"Go ahead." The sedatives blocked only some of his apprehension.

"I did what you requested, tried to have someone contact George to warn him. Seems like by the time one of our esteemed Houston lawyers would agree to call him, it was too late. Matter-of-fact, he was on the phone with him when Xminez barged in. That's the word I got back from my contact."

Church leaned his head back and closed his eyes. "Christ! That stinks. Yeah, I wish you hadn't told me. Another couple of minutes might've made all the difference." And it was one bit of news Michelle would *never* know of.

Gage didn't respond right away, spending a moment to stare through a window while shifting his stance. There was nothing he could add to the other agent's sentiments.

"Well," he said, clearing his throat, "it's not my case, so I'll let the local dicks sweat over it. Let me know if I can do anything while you're here." He tossed a card on the bedside table. "I'd better get going. I shouldn't even be here now."

"Wait a second, Gage. Are you big on doing favors?"

"Thought I'd already done one."

"This one's a little bigger."

Gage turned sideways and frowned. "Depends."

"You got any pull with the Harris County Sheriff?"

Gage hesitated, furrowing his brow. "Otto Howorth? We do each other a good turn now and then. He's a decent guy, as sheriffs go. What ya got in mind?"

"Two of his homicide guys were here this morning. I think I convinced them to try and keep Musso's name out of their investigation, along with Mrs. Frapiana being at the scene. And it appears to me, the cases they're concerned with, the killings of Xminez and the attorney, are pretty much solved. But if they were to somehow lose the Mexican's body, maybe delay getting the word out on Xminez's identity, it might help to put an end to the cartels coming after either Frapiana's widow, or Musso's kids. Luis Torres, or whoever sent him up here, may start thinking about going after his bounty hunter instead, believing he found the money and disappeared with it. So, I was just hoping his body might get pushed to the back of the morgue for awhile." It was a favor he had held back on while talking to the homicide detectives, feeling he had pushed them to the limit.

The Houston agent rolled his eyes at the ceiling. "Shit, Church. You don't ask for much, do you?"

Church shrugged. Even that sent a groggy pang through his body. "Thought it was worth a shot."

"Before I say yes or no, what makes you think Torres'll go after Xminez if he thinks he's alive? He sounds like one of the creep's main guys."

"Because, I'm pretty sure Xminez killed his traveling companion in Savannah too, along with the cop. The only reason he would do that would be to keep whatever he found for himself. At least, I think that's how Torres will see it."

After staring at the floor for a moment, Gage said, "Here's what I will do. There's no way they'll let it stay in limbo for long. But since the guy probably didn't have his true I D on him, that might stretch things out some anyway. And from what I hear, his face was pretty smashed up... might be hard for his own mother to I D him. I'll put a bug in the sheriff's ear about your concerns. Might depend on what kinda mood I catch him in."

"Thanks. That's all I'm asking."

"Yeah," Gage said sarcastically. "That's all you're askin'."

Church hoped, along with the homicide detective's earlier semi-pledge, it might be enough to buy time. Michelle's secret mission the night before would also help to put an end to her worries. The one drawback to his request to delay news of Xminez's demise would be also delaying the word reaching the Savannah authorities that their suspected cop killer was dead. Weighing all the factors, he still saw it as the right way to go.

Gage turned toward the door again, then paused and looked back. "Can I ask you something, Church?"

Church hesitated, wondering. "Yeah, sure."

"You still think this has all been worth it? I mean, everything you've been through? Puttin' your career on the line and all?"

Before Church had time to respond, the door opened wider, and Michelle finally made her appearance, coming face-to-face with the tall stranger. After a good night's sleep, she looked more radiant than ever. Her perfect face held a strange, serene expression. Gage looked at her for a long second, then back at Church. "Never mind," he said, with a wry grin. Nodding to the gorgeous blond woman, he said, "Ma'am," and left.

Taking a seat in one of the vinyl chairs, Michelle asked, "Who was that?"

Shifting to get a better look at her, he felt his body tingling from her sudden presence. "The Houston agent who called yesterday. Just checkin' up on me." He noticed what seemed to be a smile of contentment. "I was starting to get a little worried about you. Been calling all morning. But I've got a pretty good idea where you've been."

She nodded, with a bare hint of a shy grin. "I called Brock Musso last night. He was able to take time off this morning. Arranged for me to meet both him and his sister at her place. Her daughter was in pre-school, but her son, Cory, who just turned two, was there. Took me almost two hours to find her house, even with the detailed directions she gave me. She lives out in the western suburbs."

"How did it go?"

Michelle's eyes, now aqua again, glistened as she continued. "They were so nice, Walt. We all hugged. It was awkward at first, then we all relaxed; it was like we had met before, just from that one phone call last year. Neither of them seemed to exactly resemble Brent, but they each had features that looked vaguely familiar. Of course, I'm sure Brent's normal appearance had changed when I knew him, due to his illness."

Church didn't interrupt, unsure of what to say. The joy and emotion in her face was enough for him, telling him how much the meeting meant to her.

"They told me about his final days, and how close they had both come to him. Jana especially. She admitted Brent had drifted away from them after his divorce from their mother, and he indicated some of that to me in our brief time together. But that had all been washed away toward the end."

"How much did you tell them?"

She glanced at her hands clutched in her lap, then hesitated for a second. "I went in planning to mention just the part you and I discussed yesterday. How he helped me escape from Destin. Before I could even get around to it, Brock showed me a story from the morning paper about what happened yesterday. Somehow, my picture was included with the article. It wasn't a very clear image of me, and I can't imagine how it was taken. I don't recall any reporters being there."

"With phones like the one I brought with me, photos are easy to take. Somebody in the crowd must've taken it, then sold it to a reporter later. Or maybe a police officer snapped it; they always take pictures at crime scenes."

"Well, anyway, you can imagine how confused they were when they saw the article, then matched the photo to me when I showed up this morning. That kinda opened the floodgates. I had to tell them why you and I were here."

"Yes, of course. I never thought about that possibility."A troubling one suddenly did occur. "Michelle, did the article mention you had been the person who shot the bounty hunter? Did it use your name?"

She frowned. "No. In fact, the only name mentioned was Mr. George. That's how they made the connection. They couldn't have possibly recognized me from the photo... it was only a side view. It went on to say an unknown Hispanic man was also killed, and the fact he was suspected of being responsible for Mr. George's death. Why?"

"So it didn't identify the Mexican? No name was mentioned?"

She frowned. "I'm pretty sure it didn't, but I didn't read it that closely. Why?"

He then spent a few minutes explaining his conversation with the two detectives and Gage, and his requests. She still objected at first, for the very reason he had predicted. She didn't like pretenses of any type, even those that might actually protect her. Following a brief argument, she finally accepted his reasons. She then started to continue her recounting of the meeting with Musso's kids.

"Wait a minute," he interrupted. " You said they made the connection when they saw the attorney's name. I'm not sure I follow. How did they connect *him* to *you*?"

She answered with a smile that was hard to decipher. "Not to me... to them. After I explained about the letter from the attorney, and why we had come here, they both looked at each other strangely. For a moment or so, I thought they had heard enough, didn't like the idea of me receiving the money, and might even ask me to leave. Then Jana got up, and went into her husband's study. She brought back a copy of a letter both she and Brock had received, similar to mine."

"Christ! Of course." Church knew he shouldn't be surprised. It made perfect sense. "So *that's* where the rest of the money went?"

Michelle shook her head. She was displaying a grin that was even harder to decipher. "Not all of it, if we can believe what that monster, Xminez, told me. Their payment amounts were each about the same as mine, so based on what Dad showed me, there was a lot more still unaccounted for."

He simply stared, assuming she had more to tell.

"It was used to set up a trust fund for a hospital, M. D. Anderson, here in Houston. Arthur George set that one up too. Actually, it's for the benefit of the Children's Cancer Clinic wing. Brock and Jana didn't know about it until a couple of months after Brent died. His doctor had them meet him at the clinic to show them what their dad had done, and explain why. It was a month or so later when they received their letters about what Brent had done for them."

Church had heard of the clinic she had mentioned. He knew of at least one agent in Atlanta who had sought treatment there for his child. "Not that it matters, but how did they feel about him doing that for the hospital? After all, I recall you saying he wanted to take care of them. And it must've been...what?... around nine...ten million?"

"I guess. I didn't ask. But I don't think they actually knew, since like me, until that monster told me, they had no idea what the total amount was. And they were more than fine with it. Seemed happy with what they got. Jana teared up when she talked about it. According to the doctor, he had taken Brent on a tour of the clinic soon after giving him the terrible news of his own diagnosis, right before he left for Florida. It must've had a tremendous effect on him." She paused, then looked at Church with moist eyes. "So what you told me about his motives for helping me last year make perfect sense now."

The room fell into a prolonged silence, the only sound being the faint beeping of one of the devices hooked up to his arm. But there was one last part she hadn't mentioned, and it was only his curiosity that made him ask, since it mattered little to him.

"Did they ask, or did you tell them, exactly how Brent ended up with the money in the first place?"

She exhaled a sigh of relief. "Thank God, no. I think that maybe they didn't want to know, and possibly sensed I didn't want to tell them. So that's where we ended it."

He could clearly see the impact the visit had had on her; her eyes were now covered with a moist film. He wanted to reach and wipe it away, but still felt it wasn't quite the time.

"Michelle, the more I learn about Brent, the more I like him. I can see why he was so important to you. And why you had to meet his kids. It probably brought him back, if only for a few minutes. I hope it did."

She gave him the tenderest smile he had yet seen. "Yes it did. And I haven't forgotten it was you who brought me here, Walt. You made it all possible. And everything else you did for me... and Allison. I'll never be able to repay you." The film now became a flood as the sum total of what she had learned, along with what she had done the last few days rained down on her in torrents. He reached and handed her the tissue box on the table, while noticing a hollow feeling inside. Something about the words she had used contained a hint of "*thanks for everything; you've been great; it's been nice, but...*". He hoped he was reading too much into them.

When she'd dried her eyes, she went on. "Jana asked me if I wanted to see his grave site, and of course I said yes. It wasn't far from her home. She offered to take me, but I wanted to go alone. So she wrote out directions for me, then gave me the location of a florist shop. I placed an arrangement at his headstone, and thanked him again." She let her soft voice hang in silence for a moment. "So, in a way, I guess you could say that part's all over, and I'm glad I did it."

She took a glance through the window at skies that were beginning to brighten, then spoke again with a touch of regret. "They wanted us to stay in touch, and maybe we will. But I know how those things usually work out."

They remained silent for a few more minutes, each having their own separate thoughts, many of which probably diverged away from the other's. Church wished he could read her mind, find out where she wanted to go from here. Then again, he may not want to know. But there was something about what she had just told him that gave him hope for *her* future. If and when the attorney's computer's hard drive was dissected, revealing the clandestine deals he had orchestrated, the fact that one beneficiary of his handiwork was the hospital so important to the city would never be disclosed, because it would be a public relations nightmare to try and bust up the trust favoring it. And if that was the case, the other parties benefitting from the same funds would probably be ignored too. He couldn't tell her that, since it wasn't guaranteed. But he felt good about her chances.

Something else had been crossing back and forth in his mind. He recalled how Silas Lovejoy had described his daughter's lack of ego had prevented her from realizing her affect on men. That character trait was at work again, and she was still not able to recognize her role in what had transpired over the past two days. She needed to be aware... and he needed to be the one to explain.

"Michelle, I appreciate you giving me credit for leading you here, and I'll accept as much as you want to give me, but you have to understand, that's all I did. It was all you, Michelle. You kept Xminez from escaping... and *you* ended the threat he represented. All I did was put you in position, and even *that* was because I couldn't seal the deal myself. If it weren't for you, we wouldn't be here in this room thanking each other. I think it's important for you to understand all that."

Her only response was for tears to start welling-up again, and to nod her thanks. Other than that, she seemed to be having a hard time accepting the truth of his words, and probably also trying to rationalize the death of the Savannah cop and the unfortunate attorney — perhaps even absorbing blame for them, which was entirely wrong.

He then decided to make things a little easier for her, tell her to do something she was likely thinking about already. "Michelle, I think you should go see about Allison. And your mom. I don't think there's any way they will have heard about what happened here yesterday. But just in case, you need to show them you're okay. I'll be fine here."

She looked hopefully at him. "I've been thinking about that. And I've talked to them this morning — Dad too. But are you sure? You might need help getting home."

"No. They won't let me leave unless they're sure I can travel. Shouldn't be more than another day or so. But would you do me one favor?"

"Anything."

He allowed the word "anything", and the possible options wash over him for a second, before snapping back to the real world.

"Would you take my keys, get my Yukon out of hock at the airport when you fly home. Hate to see that parking fee mount up. You can drive the three of you home in it. I'll come pick it up first chance I get."

"Of course. Anything else?"

"Can't think of anything now. Oh, I almost forgot. The detectives that were here this morning want to talk to you." He gave her the card Ross had left. "Law enforcement types don't like it when folks skip town without giving an interview. I think they'll be decent about it, but you should call. And don't forget what I told them about the shooting. I think it's important."

Nodding, she gave her promise, then rose to leave. She leaned down, gazing directly into his eyes. She whispered one more teary thanks, then kissed him, this one moving down his face to land softly on his lips. She let it linger gently there for only a few short seconds, but it was enough to revive his fading hopes. Then she was gone.

Within seconds after the door closed, a nurse rushed into his room, alarmed by the sudden increase in his heart-rate monitor reading at her station. She was greeted by a strange grin.

Chapter 43

She sat alone again...only this time, she didn't feel alone.

When the seasonal heat finally arrives to stay in southern cities such as Savannah, it usually shows up without much notice, virtually moving in overnight. Crisp, cool mornings that tease the region in March and early April disappear, not to return until late September at the earliest, replaced instead by a steam bath that seems to make even the wispy strands of Spanish moss sweat. There were often years in which winter would morph directly into summer, bypassing spring all-together. Citizens that frequented the city parks at lunch and other times would now migrate to what shade they could find under the majestic oaks.

It had been slightly less than two weeks since Michelle had visited Crawford Park for what she thought would be the last time... the time her world was turned upside down by Angel Xminez and his friend, whose body had indeed been found at the airport, in the trunk of the rental car they had pursued her in. But the change had already come; a blanket of heat and humidity had settled in with a vengeance.

The unmistakable smell of freshly-cut grass and wild onions permeated the air, badgering the senses into recognition of the rude changing of the season. The lawns covering Crawford Square had received their first cuttings of the early spring, enhancing the display provided by the emerging azaleas blossoming in flower beds scattered at the base of trees throughout the park. The stifling heat would end their short life spans sooner than the norm. The human population in the city park was still impressive in number, as if they were trying to deny the suddenly uncomfortable conditions. Leisurely lunches had a way of extending past the usual allotted time, putting workers in a languid funk when finally returning to their tasks.

Michelle took her place among the others just before noon on a Friday, managing to find her customary seat on the usual bench unoccupied. She had considered a change in location due to the memory it held, but decided that would somehow be giving in to the men who had come to destroy her. She also continued to brown bag it, even though she could now certainly afford a more substantial lunch. She enjoyed the excuse to continue to experience the charms of the genteel city, charms she had left behind in her former, miserable life, then re-discovered, before almost losing again. The sights and happy murmuring sounds seemed more precious than ever; sensations she had missed more than she realized. A thin bead of perspiration began to form on her forehead, but not enough to wipe away. The heat didn't bother her; she didn't mind the touch of premature summer. In fact, she didn't mind anything that would normally bother her, as long as she was allowed to participate in what she saw as an ordinary life.

But there was another reason she chose to convene in what she saw once more as an oasis in her daily life. When Silas Lovejoy had grilled into her the wisdom of getting back aboard her first bike over thirty years earlier, after a few humiliating, sometimes painful falls, the lesson had come back to her several times during her life. None more clearly than now. She reasoned that if her life was ever going to reach the normalcy she sought so desperately, it would never happen unless she faced the memory of her last visit to the innocent looking, peaceful park. The monsters that had so terribly threatened her and Allison must not be allowed to control her future. In fact, she was determined to not let *anything*, or *anybody*, control it. She felt different, in ways she couldn't put description to. It could only be expressed in ways she made decisions from here on; how she responded to challenges and questions posed to her. In that regard, she knew it would be a day-to-day process... a journey, rather than a destination. She didn't see herself as Michelle Frapiana any longer, and perhaps, not even as Michelle Lovejoy. But who she *would be* was now entirely up to her.

Which was not to say she didn't continue to observe her surroundings with a still wary eye. It was a habit that might stay with her for a long while, if not forever. Walt, while not giving any guarantees, felt strongly the message she had transmitted to Mexico, along with the hopeful cooperation of the authorities in Houston, would throw all suspicions about the missing millions toward the brutal hit man. Only time would tell. Unfortunately, the time frame might be open-ended. The best she could hope for was to enjoy her life, and do her best to move her fading fears to the back of her mind, until one day, they might vanish for good.

Placing the bag and water bottle on the bench next to her, she looked around at the others in the park, letting herself smile at their enjoyment of the day, and the fact she was here again to witness it. She couldn't deny a degree of melancholy; the events in Texas remained with her. Most of it had to do with the meeting involving Brent's kids. When she thought of them, she pictured their faces, which made her picture Brent's face; his face as she had known it. She wanted the emotion of that visit to overshadow the memory of firing the gun — *actually taking a man's life*. It was a life that had to end in order to save her own, and that of Walter Church. Erasing that memory would also take time.

And then there was Arthur George, the attorney whose life ended so brutally. She was genuinely sorry not to have had a chance to meet him, let alone save him from his fate. He had been paid by Brent to draft the documents that now meant so much to her, and her future, but he would never know how important his work would be to her. And based on what Walt had told her in their one phone conversation since, which he had in turn learned from the authorities in Houston, the attorney had died hiding the knowledge of the existence of Brent's children and their share of the trust. So his brutal death was not entirely in vain.

But yet, there was something else. She couldn't deny another feeling; a feeling something was missing, something that was rendering her joy incomplete. It wasn't her daughter; Allison was fine; she had thoroughly enjoyed the few days in the mountains of Tennessee, as had Mary Lovejoy. The three of them had flown home together from Tennessee the Friday afternoon following her adventure in Houston, with tales for all to tell. Sandi had stood open-mouthed Saturday while Michelle related the events that had occurred since she'd called in Tuesday of the previous week, saying she needed time off. It was one of the few times she could recall her class mate's voice being completely silenced. When her story was complete, her boss could only resort to a tearful hug, glad her friend was okay.

No. The missing part was something else; an unsettled feeling she couldn't quite put a name to, since she wasn't at all sure about it. Except that it came to her time and time again. There were moments during the last few days when she would grow quiet, as if her mind was elsewhere. When Silas had noticed it the day before, he had given her the strangest smile and shaken his head. But he hadn't said a word. With her apartment and most of her belongings trashed by the bounty hunter, she and Allison were staying with her parents again while she looked for a new apartment, so it wasn't the first time he had reacted that way.

She unwrapped the sandwich in her bag, then unscrewed the bottle of water. Taking a bite, she glanced over at the jungle gym where the blond man, whose name she never learned, had stood... a threatening guard over Allison, on a day like today, not so long ago. No one lurked there now that appeared dangerous. In fact, she saw no threats anywhere.

As she continued to stare, a shadow began to move across the ground in front of her. A figure was approaching from the west, her blind side. The memory of the last time someone approached from behind the bench shocked her from her reverie... her nerves instantly at the alert. She turned quickly in that direction. The early afternoon sun was hanging slightly in that direction, so she had to squint. It took a minute. He was roughly ten feet away, walking with a silly grin, his bandaged arm in a sling, still wearing her dad's baseball cap.

"Any room on that bench?" Church asked, trying to be nonchalant, while his heart felt as if it was being squeezed by a straightjacket, constricted by Silas Lovejoy's words of caution nearly two weeks earlier, as well as by Chris Steen's caustic opinions of the risks he had taken. Over his career, he had faced life-threatening danger several times, including two near-fatal brushes with the monster who had been the catalyst for his re-connection with the woman who now held a hand over her eyes, trying to identify him through the blinding sunlight. None of those occurrences generated the same stomach-twisting terror he now experienced. He had no idea what her reaction would be to seeing him, fearing it wouldn't be as he hoped; fearing the brief closeness achieved in Houston would have disintegrated. Separation could cause changes — feelings could ebb. He held his breath as he neared her.

The emptiness was instantly solved, the nagging hole filled in. She stood slowly at first, then shocked herself by the speed with which she dropped the sandwich and ran to meet him, to embrace him. She had known what was missing the whole time; she simply couldn't admit it to herself; it was too scary, too frightening, too unfamiliar to even *think* it might happen to her... a luxury that hadn't applied to her life. Careful to avoid his injured side, she held him for a full minute, letting her joy rain kisses on his shocked face until her own still-tender lips started to ache.

She took him by the hand, leading him back to the bench. They sat and talked for nearly half an hour, bringing each other up to date on the time spent apart. She gradually felt what tension remained falling away, as their conversation flowed easily now, no longer filled with awkward periods of silence or uncertainty. He told her more about his stay in the hospital, how he had watched the local news and read the local papers each day. Nothing had been written or broadcast as to identify either her or the bounty hunter by name. So he felt all that could be done had been done to protect the future for her and Allison. She then explained how the phone conversation with the Houston detectives had gone before she had left the city.

"I didn't feel like Ross, the one I talked to, believed me when I told him you fired the gun. But I also got the impression he really didn't care. That's good news, isn't it?"

"I'd say so."

"What about your job?" she asked. "Are you in trouble?"

"A little. Nothing I can't live with. My leave from field duty's been extended some. Only this time, without pay."

"I feel terrible about that, since I'm the cause of it. I'll loan you money if you need it. I can afford it now."

"I'll be okay. But if things get tight, I'll keep you in mind."

"You do that," she said with a teasing grin that was as natural and radiant as the blazing sun itself.

Church let his eyes wander from Michelle long enough to scan the park, recognizing for the first time the appeal of the laid-back city. It seemed to be a place where a decent lifestyle could be hollowed out. Atlanta was by location and definition a major southern city. But the pace of life was frenetic, as it was in any city its size. This place, though only a few hundred miles away, was entirely different.

Eventually, he broke the spell, "Since you might be supportin' both of us, isn't it about time you to headed back to the store? I stopped by there first, peeked in the window. When I didn't see you, I remembered you liked to come here."

Michelle took a glance at her watch, though time was something else she worried little about these days. She had a devilish thought. "Yeah. I think you're right." She stood suddenly, reaching down to grab his good hand. "Come on. You're coming with me. I wanna see the look on Sandi's face when I introduce you."

Church smiled a thin smile that didn't show complete understanding, but followed her instructions. The knowledge struck him that following her bidding was something he could get used to.

As he stood to join her, Michelle's eyes were suddenly drawn to the face of a man staring directly at her. He was sitting behind the wheel of a dark sedan parked on one of the streets that formed the square of Crawford Park. Her face blanched for a second, until she saw a middle-aged woman climb into the passenger side of the car, pulling the man's attention away. She slapped the driver hard on his shoulder. The car was cranked, and it drove away.

Church's gaze traced hers, then watched with her as the benign vehicle disappeared around a corner. "It's okay, Michelle," he said, squeezing her hand gently, causing her body to release its brief tension.

They walked out of the park, his left arm around her waist, her hand on his shoulder. She playfully tousled what remained of his brown mane, released from its ponytail and splayed across his collar from beneath the cap.

"One thing, though," she said, leaning back to look, "we may have to do something about that hair."

If you would like to know more of the story behind what led to Michelle and Church being reunited, and the adventure that introduced them to each other the previous year, read:

By Proxy: A Final Good Deed

CPSIA information can be obtained at www.ICGtesting.com
Printed in the USA
LVOW051418170612

286487LV00001B/5/P

9 780578 104638